THE THIRD PERSEPHONE
BOOK OF SHORT STORIES

Persephone Book N° 150
Published by Persephone Books Ltd 2024

All the stories still in copyright are reprinted by kind
permission of the author or the author's estate.

Front endpaper – 'Greenfinch', a block-printed furnishing
fabric designed by Lotte Frömel-Fochler (1884-1972) for
the Wiener Werkstatte in 1911 and exported to the USA,
© MAK: Museum of Applied Arts, Vienna.

Back endpaper – late 1980s/early 1990s cotton print designed
by Furphy Simpson and exported to the USA. When they graduated
from the Royal College of Art in 1976 Val Furphy and Ian Simpson
formed a design partnership which is still flourishing nearly
fifty years later, © Furphy Simpson.

Typeset in ITC Baskerville by
MLJ Typesetting & Design, Wolverhampton

Printed and bound in Germany by
GGP Media GmbH, Poessneck

978 191 0263402

Persephone Books Ltd
8 Edgar Buildings
Bath BA1 2EE
01225 425050

www.persephonebooks.co.uk

THE THIRD PERSEPHONE
BOOK OF SHORT STORIES

PERSEPHONE BOOKS
BATH

CONTENTS

@@@@@@

THE THIRD PERSEPHONE
BOOK OF SHORT STORIES

TURNED
Charlotte Perkins Gilman
(1911)

In her soft-carpeted, thick-curtained, richly furnished chamber, Mrs Marroner lay sobbing on the wide, soft bed.

She sobbed bitterly, chokingly, despairingly; her shoulders heaved and shook convulsively; her hands were tight-clenched. She had forgotten her elaborate dress, the more elaborate bedcover; forgotten her dignity, her self-control, her pride. In her mind was an overwhelming, unbelievable horror, an immeasurable loss, a turbulent, struggling mass of emotion.

In her reserved, superior, Boston-bred life, she had never dreamed that it would be possible for her to feel so many things at once, and with such trampling intensity.

She tried to cool her feelings into thoughts; to stiffen them into words; to control herself – and could not. It brought vaguely to her mind an awful moment in the breakers at York Beach, one summer in girlhood when she had been swimming under water and could not find the top.

* * *

In her uncarpeted, thin-curtained, poorly furnished chamber on the top floor, Gerta Petersen lay sobbing on the narrow, hard bed.

She was of larger frame than her mistress, grandly built and strong; but all her proud young womanhood was prostrate now, convulsed with agony, dissolved in tears. She did not try to control herself. She wept for two.

* * *

If Mrs Marroner suffered more from the wreck and ruin of a longer love – perhaps a deeper one; if her tastes were finer, her ideals loftier; if she bore the pangs of bitter jealousy and outraged pride, Gerta had personal shame to meet, a hopeless future, and a looming present which filled her with unreasoning terror.

She had come like a meek young goddess into that perfectly ordered house, strong, beautiful, full of goodwill and eager obedience, but ignorant and childish – a girl of eighteen.

Mr Marroner had frankly admired her, and so had his wife. They discussed her visible perfections and as visible limitations with that perfect confidence which they had so long enjoyed. Mrs Marroner was not a jealous woman. She had never been jealous in her life – till now.

Gerta had stayed and learned their ways. They had both been fond of her. Even the cook was fond of her. She was what is called 'willing', was unusually teachable and plastic; and Mrs Marroner, with her early habits of giving instruction, tried to educate her somewhat.

'I never saw anyone so docile,' Mrs Marroner had often commented. 'It is perfection in a servant, but almost a defect in character. She is so helpless and confiding.'

She was precisely that: a tall, rosy-cheeked baby; rich womanhood without, helpless infancy within. Her braided wealth of dead-gold hair, her grave blue eyes, her mighty shoulders and long, firmly moulded limbs seemed those of a primal earth spirit; but she was only an ignorant child, with a child's weakness.

When Mr Marroner had to go abroad for his firm, unwillingly, hating to leave his wife, he had told her he felt quite safe to leave her in Gerta's hands – she would take care of her.

'Be good to your mistress, Gerta,' he told the girl that last morning at breakfast. 'I leave her to you to take care of, I shall be back in a month at latest.'

Then he turned, smiling, to his wife. 'And you must take care of Gerta, too,' he said. 'I expect you'll have her ready for college when I get back.'

This was seven months ago. Business had delayed him from week to week, from month to month. He wrote to his wife, long, loving, frequent letters, deeply regretting the delay, explaining how necessary, how profitable it was, congratulating her on the wide resources she had, her well-filled, well-balanced mind, her many interests.

'If I should be eliminated from your scheme of things, by any of those "acts of God" mentioned on the tickets, I do not feel that you would be an utter wreck,' he said. 'That is very comforting to me. Your life is so rich and wide that no one loss, even a great one, would wholly cripple you. But nothing of

the sort is likely to happen, and I shall be home again in three weeks – if this thing gets settled. And you will be looking so lovely, with that eager light in your eyes and the changing flush I know so well – and love so well! My dear wife! We shall have to have a new honeymoon – other moons come every month, why shouldn't the mellifluous kind?'

He often asked after 'little Gerta', sometimes enclosed a picture postcard to her, joked his wife about her laborious efforts to educate 'the child', was so loving and merry and wise –

All this was racing through Mrs Marroner's mind as she lay there with the broad, hemstitched border of fine linen sheeting crushed and twisted in one hand, and the other holding a sodden handkerchief.

She had tried to teach Gerta, and had grown to love the patient, sweet-natured child, in spite of her dullness. At work with her hands, she was clever, if not quick, and could keep small accounts from week to week. But to the woman who held a PhD, who had been on the faculty of a college, it was like baby-tending.

Perhaps having no babies of her own made her love the big child the more, though the years between them were but fifteen.

To the girl she seemed quite old, of course; and her young heart was full of grateful affection for the patient care which made her feel so much at home in this new land.

And then she had noticed a shadow on the girl's bright face. She looked nervous, anxious, worried. When the bell rang, she seemed startled, and would rush hurriedly to the

door. Her peals of frank laughter no longer rose from the area gate as she stood talking with the always admiring tradesmen.

Mrs Marroner had laboured long to teach her more reserve with men, and flattered herself that her words were at last effective. She suspected the girl of homesickness, which was denied. She suspected her of illness, which was denied also. At last she suspected her of something which could not be denied.

For a long time she refused to believe it, waiting. Then she had to believe it, but schooled herself to patience and understanding. 'The poor child,' she said. 'She is here without a mother – she is so foolish and yielding – I must not be too stern with her.' And she tried to win the girl's confidence with wise, kind words.

But Gerta had literally thrown herself at her feet and begged her with streaming tears not to turn her away. She would admit nothing, explain nothing, but frantically promised to work for Mrs Marroner as long as she lived – if only she would keep her.

Revolving the problem carefully in her mind, Mrs Marroner thought she would keep her, at least for the present. She tried to repress her sense of ingratitude in one she had so sincerely tried to help, and the cold, contemptuous anger she had always felt for such weakness.

'The thing to do now,' she said to herself, 'is to see her through this safely. The child's life should not be hurt any more than is unavoidable. I will ask Dr Bleet about it – what a comfort a woman doctor is! I'll stand by the poor, foolish thing till it's over, and then get her back to Sweden somehow with her baby. How they do come where they are not wanted – and don't come where they are wanted!' And Mrs Marroner, sitting alone in the quiet, spacious beauty of the house, almost envied Gerta.

Then came the deluge.

She had sent the girl out for needed air towards dark. The late mail came; she took it in herself. One letter for her – her husband's letter. She knew the postmark, the stamp, the kind of typewriting. She impulsively kissed it in the dim hall. No one would suspect Mrs Marroner of kissing her husband's letters – but she did, often.

She looked over the others. One was for Gerta, and not from Sweden. It looked precisely like her own. This struck her as a little odd, but Mr Marroner had several times sent messages and cards to the girl. She laid the letter on the hall table and took hers to her room.

'My poor child,' it began. What letter of hers had been sad enough to warrant that?

'I am deeply concerned at the news you send.' What news to so concern him had she written? 'You must bear it bravely, little girl. I shall be home soon, and will take care of you, of course. I hope there is not immediate anxiety – you do not say. Here is money, in case you need it. I expect to get home in a month at latest. If you have to go, be sure to leave your address at my office. Cheer up – be brave – I will take care of you.'

The letter was typewritten, which was not unusual. It was unsigned, which was unusual. It enclosed an American bill – fifty dollars. It did not seem in the least like any letter she had ever had from her husband, or any letter she could imagine him writing. But a strange, cold feeling was creeping over her, like a flood rising around a house.

She utterly refused to admit the ideas which began to bob and push about outside her mind, and to force themselves in. Yet under the pressure of these repudiated thoughts she went downstairs and brought up the other letter – the letter to Gerta. She laid them side by side on a smooth dark space on the table; marched to the piano and played, with stern precision, refusing to think, till the girl came back. When she came in, Mrs Marroner rose quietly and came to the table. 'Here is a letter for you,' she said.

The girl stepped forward eagerly, saw the two lying together there, hesitated, and looked at her mistress.

'Take yours, Gerta. Open it, please.'

The girl turned frightened eyes upon her.

'I want you to read it, here,' said Mrs Marroner.

'Oh, ma'am – No! Please don't make me!'

'Why not?'

There seemed to be no reason at hand, and Gerta flushed more deeply and opened her letter. It was long; it was evidently puzzling to her; it began 'My dear wife.' She read it slowly.

'Are you sure it is your letter?' asked Mrs Marroner. 'Is not this one yours? Is not that one – mine?'

She held out the other letter to her.

'It is a mistake,' Mrs Marroner went on, with a hard quietness. She had lost her social bearings somehow, lost her usual keen sense of the proper thing to do. This was not life; this was a nightmare.

'Do you not see? Your letter was put in my envelope and my letter was put in your envelope. Now we understand it.'

But poor Gerta had no antechamber to her mind, no

trained forces to preserve order while agony entered. The thing swept over her, resistless, overwhelming. She cowered before the outraged wrath she expected; and from some hidden cavern that wrath arose and swept over her in pale flame.

'Go and pack your trunk,' said Mrs Marroner. 'You will leave my house tonight. Here is your money.'

She laid down the fifty-dollar bill. She put with it a month's wages. She had no shadow of pity for those anguished eyes, those tears which she heard drop on the floor.

'Go to your room and pack,' said Mrs Marroner. And Gerta, always obedient, went.

Then Mrs Marroner went to hers, and spent a time she never counted, lying on her face on the bed.

But the training of the twenty-eight years which had elapsed before her marriage; the life at college, both as student and teacher; the independent growth which she had made, formed a very different background for grief from that in Gerta's mind.

After a while Mrs Marroner arose. She administered to herself a hot bath, a cold shower, a vigorous rubbing. 'Now I can think,' she said.

First she regretted the sentence of instant banishment. She went upstairs to see if it had been carried out. Poor Gerta! The tempest of her agony had worked itself out at last as in a child, and left her sleeping, the pillow wet, the lips still grieving, a big sob shuddering itself off now and then.

Mrs Marroner stood and watched her, and as she watched she considered the helpless sweetness of the face; the defence-less, unformed character; the docility and habit of obedience which made her so attractive – and so easily a victim. Also she

8

thought of the mighty force which had swept over her; of the great process now working itself out through her; of how pitiful and futile seemed any resistance she might have made.

She softly returned to her own room, made up a little fire, and sat by it, ignoring her feelings now, as she had before ignored her thoughts.

Here were two women and a man. One woman was a wife: loving, trusting, affectionate. One was a servant: loving, trusting, affectionate – a young girl, an exile, a dependant; grateful for any kindness; untrained, uneducated, childish. She ought, of course, to have resisted temptation; but Mrs Marroner was wise enough to know how difficult temptation is to recognise when it comes in the guise of friendship and from a source one does not suspect.

Gerta might have done better in resisting the grocer's clerk; had, indeed, with Mrs Marroner's advice, resisted several. But where respect was due, how could she criticise? Where obedience was due, how could she refuse – with ignorance to hold her blinded – until too late?

As the older, wiser woman forced herself to understand and extenuate the girl's misdeed and foresee her ruined future, a new feeling rose in her heart, strong, clear, and overmastering: a sense of measureless condemnation for the man who had done this thing. He knew. He understood. He could fully foresee and measure the consequences of his act. He appreciated to the full the innocence, the ignorance, the grateful affection, the habitual docility, of which he deliberately took advantage.

Mrs Marroner rose to icy peaks of intellectual apprehension, from which her hours of frantic pain seemed far indeed removed. He had done this thing under the same roof with her – his wife. He had not frankly loved the younger woman, broken with his wife, made a new marriage. That would have been heartbreak pure and simple. This was something else.

That letter, that wretched, cold, carefully guarded, unsigned letter, that bill – far safer than a check – these did not speak of affection. Some men can love two women at one time. This was not love.

Mrs Marroner's sense of pity and outrage for herself, the wife, now spread suddenly into a perception of pity and outrage for the girl. All that splendid, clean young beauty, the hope of a happy life, with marriage and motherhood, honourable independence, even – these were nothing to that man. For his own pleasure he had chosen to rob her of her life's best joys.

He would 'take care of her,' said the letter. How? In what capacity?

And then, sweeping over both her feelings for herself, the wife, and Gerta, his victim, came a new flood, which literally lifted her to her feet. She rose and walked, her head held high. 'This is the sin of man against woman,' she said. 'The offence is against womanhood. Against motherhood. Against – the child.'

She stopped.

The child. His child. That, too, he sacrificed and injured – doomed to degradation.

Mrs Marroner came of stern New England stock. She was not a Calvinist, hardly even a Unitarian; but the iron of Calvinism was in her soul: of that grim faith which held that most people had to be damned 'for the glory of God'.

Generations of ancestors who both preached and practiced

stood behind her; people whose lives had been sternly moulded to their highest moments of religious conviction. In sweeping bursts of feeling, they achieved 'conviction', and afterwards they lived and died according to that conviction.

* * *

When Mr Marroner reached home a few weeks later, following his letters too soon to expect an answer to either, he saw no wife upon the pier, though he had cabled, and found the house closed darkly. He let himself in with his latchkey, and stole softly upstairs, to surprise his wife.

No wife was there.

He rang the bell. No servant answered it.

He turned up light after light, searched the house from top to bottom; it was utterly empty. The kitchen wore a clean, bald, unsympathetic aspect. He left it and slowly mounted the stairs, completely dazed. The whole house was clean, in perfect order, wholly vacant.

One thing he felt perfectly sure of – she knew.

Yet was he sure? He must not assume too much. She might have been ill. She might have died. He started to his feet. No, they would have cabled him. He sat down again.

For any such change, if she had wanted him to know, she would have written. Perhaps she had, and he, returning so suddenly, had missed the letter. The thought was some comfort. It must be so. He turned to the telephone and again hesitated. If she had found out – if she had gone – utterly gone, without a word – should he announce it himself to friends and family?

11

He walked the floor; he searched everywhere for some letter, some word of explanation. Again and again he went to the telephone – and always stopped. He could not bear to ask: 'Do you know where my wife is?'

The harmonious, beautiful rooms reminded him in a dumb, helpless way of her – like the remote smile on the face of the dead. He put out the lights, could not bear the darkness, turned them all on again.

It was a long night –

In the morning he went early to the office. In the accumulated mail was no letter from her. No one seemed to know of anything unusual. A friend asked after his wife – 'Pretty glad to see you, I guess?' He answered evasively.

About eleven a man came to see him: John Hill, her lawyer. Her cousin, too. Mr Marroner had never liked him. He liked him less now, for Mr Hill merely handed him a letter, remarked, 'I was requested to deliver this to you personally,' and departed, looking like a person who is called on to kill something offensive.

'I have gone. I will care for Gerta. Goodbye. Marion.'

That was all. There was no date, no address, no postmark, nothing but that.

In his anxiety and distress, he had fairly forgotten Gerta and all that. Her name aroused in him a sense of rage. She had come between him and his wife. She had taken his wife from him. That was the way he felt.

At first he said nothing, did nothing, lived on alone in his house, taking meals where he chose. When people asked him about his wife, he said she was traveling – for her health. He would not have it in the newspapers. Then, as time passed, as no enlightenment came to him, he resolved not to bear it any longer, and employed detectives. They blamed him for not having put them on the track earlier, but set to work, urged to the utmost secrecy.

What to him had been so blank a wall of mystery seemed not to embarrass them in the least. They made careful enquiries as to her 'past', found where she had studied, where taught, and on what lines; that she had some little money of her own, that her doctor was Josephine L Bleet, MD, and many other bits of information.

As a result of careful and prolonged work, they finally told him that she had resumed teaching under one of her old professors, lived quietly, and apparently kept boarders; giving him town, street, and number, as if it were a matter of no difficulty whatever.

He had returned in early spring. It was autumn before he found her.

A quiet college town in the hills, a broad, shady street, a pleasant house standing in its own lawn, with trees and flowers about it. He had the address in his hand, and the number showed clear on the white gate. He walked up the straight gravel path and rang the bell. An elderly servant opened the door.

'Does Mrs Marroner live here?'

'No, sir.'

'This is number twenty-eight?'

'Yes, sir.'

'Who does live here?'

'Miss Wheeling, sir.'

Ah! Her maiden name. They had told him, but he had forgotten.

He stepped inside. 'I would like to see her,' he said.

He was ushered into a still parlour, cool and sweet with the scent of flowers, the flowers she had always loved best. It almost brought tears to his eyes. All their years of happiness rose in his mind again – the exquisite beginnings; the days of eager longing before she was really his; the deep, still beauty of her love.

Surely she would forgive him – she must forgive him. He would humble himself, he would tell her of his honest remorse – his absolute determination to be a different man.

Through the wide doorway there came in to him two women. One like a tall Madonna, bearing a baby in her arms.

Marion, calm, steady, definitely impersonal, nothing but a clear pallor to hint of inner stress.

Gerta, holding the child as a bulwark, with a new intelligence in her face, and her blue, adoring eyes fixed on her friend – not upon him.

He looked from one to the other dumbly.

And the woman who had been his wife asked quietly:

'What have you to say to us?'

PLUCK
Gertrude Colmore
1913

She came into the ABC tearoom almost timidly, yet with complete self-possession.

The room was nearly filled, chiefly with very young men, and it was not easy to find a seat. She paused at the door, looking to right and left; then her eyes lighted on a free table, and she made her way to it.

She was daintier than most of the women who came to that particular shop; she had what the youth at a neighbouring table called a genteel air. She was dainty, too, in her ways. When her cup of coffee, her boiled egg and roll and butter were brought to her, she ate and drank in a leisurely, somewhat fastidious fashion, opening the egg carefully so that the yolk did not overflow and stain the plate with a yellow stain, as was the fate of so many plates in that close room, where haste or habit or hunger trampled on the graces of life.

The youth at the neighbouring table watched her with admiring and curious eyes. He had finished his meat pie and tea, and had nothing to do but read the racing news or look

about him while he smoked a cigarette. The girl was more attractive even than the tips given by his favourite racing expert, and he looked at her more than at the paper in his hand.

She was a cut above the girls he was used to, so he told himself; more stylish, more of the lady; too modest-looking, he thought, for an actress, yet as cool in her ways as if she were used to being looked at by all the world. Wasn't she perhaps an actress after all? Surely – in the shop window – or was it the papers –? Somewhere – he became more and more sure – somewhere – he had seen the face – certainly – with other faces. In a row of portraits was it? – or a row of photos? – or – or –

Suddenly he knew. Like their cheek to give herself such airs! They had plenty of that. But he knew; he wasn't to be taken in. Of course, of course, that was it; he remembered now. She was a well-known suffragette.

The youth's face had changed; the naive admiration had gone; in its place was a smirk of contempt. The girl, as unconscious of the one as she had been of the other, continued slowly to eat her meal, pausing now and again to make notes in the margin of a book which she had taken from her bag and which lay open on the table beside her plate.

She did not notice that a youth had left a neighbouring table and taken a seat at her own; she was certainly startled when a voice said close to her: 'I know who you are.'

Startled she was for a moment, but her eyes were calm as she returned his gaze: 'Indeed!'

'Yes, and I could –' He looked round the room. 'I know

most of the fellows here, and they're dead set, I can tell you, against you and your lot. You might have a rough time of it if I was to give you away.'

Her look would have been pathetic but for its fearlessness. 'I'm used to rough times.'

'Rough times are for rough women. I wonder you aren't ashamed of yourself.'

'I suppose you are the kind that would wonder.' She looked at him scrutinisingly. 'And yet – you might be amongst our admirers, if you could only manage to understand.'

'Understand? Understand, indeed! 'Tain't my understanding that's wrong.'

'You're quite sure of that?' She half smiled as she spoke.

'It don't take any particular understanding to know what's decent behaviour.'

'Decency is a difficult question.' She was still quite good-humoured. 'You must admit, though, that we have some good qualities – pluck, for instance.'

'Not my idea of pluck – to go –'

'What is your idea?'

'Well, I heard of a plucky thing the other day – a woman, too, it was. There was a child by the canal, Regent's Park way – you know how these little beggars will play close down by the water – fell in, and a woman fished him out.'

'Went in after him, do you mean?'

'Yes, that's what I mean; deep water. There's pluck for you, the real article.'

'Could she swim?'

''Pears she could. She was off with her coat and shoes in

no time, the fellow said who told me, and into the water like a knife. What do you think of that?'

The girl shrugged her shoulders. 'It doesn't take half the pluck to do a thing like that it does to go on a deputation.'

'You mean to tell me – ?'

'Well, she could swim, you see. And besides, a good deal of water isn't a quarter as cruel as a flood of brutal men.'

'All very well to say that, but . . .'

'Say! I know it. You haven't been in a mob of savages; I have.'

'And you haven't been in the water and risked your life to save a child. And to sneer at a woman who'd do a thing like that, well, it's – it's all of a piece –'

'I'm not sneering. I only say it doesn't take half so much courage to do the one as to do the other. And I know what I'm talking about.'

'Oh you do, do you? And pray how do you know what sort of pluck it takes to jump into the water like that woman?'

Again she shrugged her shoulders. 'Because, as it happens, I was the woman.'

'You? You?'

At the sight of his face she laughed.

'You're kidding me,' he said, 'making fun. By Jove –'

'Oh no. You ask your friend. I had a purple coat and skirt on and a green felt hat and a white blouse; and in pulling me out – for I had been in some time and was rather done – my arm got hurt.' She turned back her sleeve and showed a bandage. 'You ask your friend.'

'That's right, I remember,' he said. 'And you did that – you?'

'Yes, I, and I tell you it wasn't half as bad to do as many of the things I've done. Now I must go. Good morning.'

As she rose, he rose too. He could not take off his hat to her since it hung upon a peg close by; but he moved a chair aside for her to pass, and stood with bent head as she made her way between the tables to the door.

MARRIAGE À LA MODE
Katherine Mansfield
1921

On his way to the station William remembered with a fresh pang of disappointment that he was taking nothing down to the kiddies. Poor little chaps! It was hard lines on them. Their first words always were as they ran to greet him, 'What have you got for me, Daddy?' and he had nothing. He would have to buy them some sweets at the station. But that was what he had done for the past four Saturdays; their faces had fallen last time when they saw the same old boxes produced again.

And Paddy had said, 'I had red ribbing on mine *bee*-fore!'

And Johnny had said, 'It's always pink on mine. I hate pink.'

But what was William to do? The affair wasn't so easily set-tled. In the old days, of course, he would have taken a taxi off to a decent toyshop and chosen them something in five minutes. But nowadays they had Russian toys, French toys, Serbian toys – toys from God knows where. It was over a year since Isabel had scrapped the old donkeys and engines and so on because they were so 'dreadfully sentimental' and 'so appallingly bad for the babies' sense of form'.

'It's so important,' the new Isabel had explained, 'that they should like the right things from the very beginning. It saves so much time later on. Really, if the poor pets have to spend their infant years staring at these horrors, one can imagine them growing up and asking to be taken to the Royal Academy.'

And she spoke as though a visit to the Royal Academy was certain immediate death to anyone . . .

'Well, I don't know,' said William slowly. 'When I was their age I used to go to bed hugging an old towel with a knot in it.'

The new Isabel looked at him, her eyes narrowed, her lips apart.

'*Dear* William! I'm sure you did!' She laughed in the new way.

Sweets it would have to be, however, thought William gloomily, fishing in his pocket for change for the taxi-man. And he saw the kiddies handing the boxes round – they were awfully generous little chaps – while Isabel's precious friends didn't hesitate to help themselves . . .

What about fruit? William hovered before a stall just inside the station. What about a melon each? Would they have to share that, too? Or a pineapple, for Pad, and a melon for Johnny? Isabel's friends could hardly go sneaking up to the nursery at the children's mealtimes. All the same, as he bought the melon William had a horrible vision of one of Isabel's young poets lapping up a slice, for some reason, behind the nursery door.

With his two very awkward parcels he strode off to his train. The platform was crowded, the train was in. Doors banged open and shut. There came such a loud hissing from the engine that people looked dazed as they scurried to and fro.

William made straight for a first-class smoker, stowed away his suitcase and parcels, and taking a huge wad of papers out of his inner pocket, he flung down in the corner and began to read.

'Our client moreover is positive . . . We are inclined to reconsider . . . in the event of –' Ah, that was better. William pressed back his flattened hair and stretched his legs across the carriage floor. The familiar dull gnawing in his breast quietened down. 'With regard to our decision –' He took out a blue pencil and scored a paragraph slowly.

Two men came in, stepped across him, and made for the farther corner. A young fellow swung his golf clubs into the rack and sat down opposite. The train gave a gentle lurch, they were off. William glanced up and saw the hot, bright station slipping away. A red-faced girl raced along by the carriages, there was something strained and almost desperate in the way she waved and called. 'Hysterical!' thought William dully. Then a greasy, black-faced workman at the end of the platform grinned at the passing train. And William thought, 'A filthy life!' and went back to his papers.

When he looked up again there were fields, and beasts standing for shelter under the dark trees. A wide river, with naked children splashing in the shallows, glided into sight and was gone again. The sky shone pale, and one bird drifted high like a dark fleck in a jewel.

'We have examined our client's correspondence files . . .' The last sentence he had read echoed in his mind. 'We have examined . . .' William hung on to that sentence, but it was no good; it snapped in the middle, and the fields, the sky, the sailing bird, the water, all said, 'Isabel'. The same thing happened every Saturday afternoon. When he was on his way to meet Isabel there began those countless imaginary meetings. She was at the station, standing just a little apart from everybody else; she was sitting in the open taxi outside; she was at the garden gate; walking across the parched grass; at the door, or just inside the hall.

And her clear, light voice said, 'It's William,' or 'Hillo, William!' or 'So William has come!' He touched her cool hand, her cool cheek.

The exquisite freshness of Isabel! When he had been a little boy, it was his delight to run into the garden after a shower of rain and shake the rose bush over him. Isabel was that rose bush, petal-soft, sparkling and cool. And he was still that little boy. But there was no running into the garden now, no laughing and shaking. The dull, persistent gnawing in his breast started again. He drew up his legs, tossed the papers aside, and shut his eyes.

'What is it, Isabel? What is it?' he said tenderly. They were in their bedroom in the new house. Isabel sat on a painted stool before the dressing table that was strewn with little black and green boxes.

'What is what, William?' And she bent forward, and her fine light hair fell over her cheeks.

'Ah, you know!' He stood in the middle of the room and he felt a stranger. At that Isabel wheeled round quickly and faced him.

'Oh, William!' she cried imploringly, and she held up the hairbrush: 'Please! Please don't be so dreadfully stuffy

and – tragic. You're always saying or looking or hinting that I've changed. Just because I've got to know really congenial people, and go about more, and am frightfully keen on – on everything, you behave as though I'd –' Isabel tossed back her hair and laughed – 'killed our love or something. It's so awfully absurd' – she bit her lip – 'and it's so maddening, William. Even this new house and the servants you grudge me.'

'Isabel!'

'Yes, yes, it's true in a way,' said Isabel quickly. 'You think they are another bad sign. Oh, I know you do. I feel it,' she said softly, 'every time you come up the stairs. But we couldn't have gone on living in that other poky little hole, William. Be practical, at least! Why, there wasn't enough room for the babies even.'

No, it was true. Every morning when he came back from chambers it was to find the babies with Isabel in the back drawing room. They were having rides on the leopard skin thrown over the sofa back, or they were playing shops with Isabel's desk for a counter, or Pad was sitting on the hearthrug rowing away for dear life with a little brass fire shovel, while Johnny shot at pirates with the tongs. Every evening they each had a pickaback up the narrow stairs to their fat old Nanny.

Yes, he supposed it was a poky little house. A little white house with blue curtains and a window box of petunias. William met their friends at the door with 'Seen our petunias? Pretty terrific for London, don't you think?'

But the imbecile thing, the absolutely extraordinary thing, was that he hadn't the slightest idea that Isabel wasn't as happy

as he. God, what blindness! He hadn't the remotest notion in those days that she really hated that inconvenient little house, that she thought the fat Nanny was ruining the babies, that she was desperately lonely, pining for new people and new music and pictures and so on. If they hadn't gone to that studio party at Moira Morrison's – if Moira Morrison hadn't said as they were leaving, 'I'm going to rescue your wife, selfish man. She's like an exquisite little Titania' – if Isabel hadn't gone with Moira to Paris – if – if . . .

The train stopped at another station. Bettingford. Good heavens! They'd be there in ten minutes. William stuffed the papers back into his pockets; the young man opposite had long since disappeared. Now the other two got out. The late afternoon sun shone on women in cotton frocks and little sunburnt, barefoot children. It blazed on a silky yellow flower with coarse leaves which sprawled over a bank of rock. The air ruffling through the window smelled of the sea. Had Isabel the same crowd with her this weekend, wondered William?

And he remembered the holidays they used to have, the four of them, with a little farm girl, Rose, to look after the babies. Isabel wore a jersey and her hair in a plait; she looked about fourteen. Lord! how his nose used to peel! And the amount they ate, and the amount they slept in that immense feather bed with their feet locked together . . . William couldn't help a grim smile as he thought of Isabel's horror if she knew the full extent of his sentimentality.

* * *

'Hillo, William!' She was at the station after all, standing just as he had imagined, apart from the others, and – William's heart leapt – she was alone.

'Hallo, Isabel!' William stared. He thought she looked so beautiful that he had to say something. 'You look very cool.'

'Do I?' said Isabel. 'I don't feel very cool. Come along, your horrid old train is late. The taxi's outside.' She put her hand lightly on his arm as they passed the ticket collector. 'We've all come to meet you,' she said. 'But we've left Bobby Kane at the sweet shop, to be called for.'

'Oh!' said William. It was all he could say for the moment.

There in the glare waited the taxi, with Bill Hunt and Dennis Green sprawling on one side, their hats tilted over their faces, while on the other, Moira Morrison, in a bonnet like a huge strawberry, jumped up and down.

'No ice! No ice! No ice!' she shouted gaily.

And Dennis chimed in from under his hat, '*Only* to be had from the fishmonger's.' And Bill Hunt, emerging, added, 'With *whole* fish in it.'

'Oh, what a bore!' wailed Isabel. And she explained to William how they had been chasing round the town for ice while she waited for him. 'Simply everything is running down the steep cliffs into the sea, beginning with the butter.'

'We shall have to anoint ourselves with butter,' said Dennis. 'May thy head, William, lack not ointment.'

'Look here,' said William, 'how are we going to sit? I'd better get up by the driver.'

'No, Bobby Kane's by the driver,' said Isabel. 'You're to sit between Moira and me.' The taxi started. 'What have you got in those mysterious parcels?'

'De-cap-it-ated heads!' said Bill Hunt, shuddering beneath his hat.

'Oh, fruit!' Isabel sounded very pleased. 'Wise William! A melon and a pineapple. How too nice!'

'No, wait a bit,' said William, smiling. But he really was anxious. 'I brought them down for the kiddies.'

'Oh, my dear!' Isabel laughed, and slipped her hand through his arm. 'They'd be rolling in agonies if they were to eat them. No' – she patted his hand – 'you must bring them something next time. I refuse to part with my pineapple.'

'Cruel Isabel! Do let me smell it!' said Moira. She flung her arms across William appealingly. 'Oh!' The strawberry bonnet fell forward: she sounded quite faint.

'A Lady in Love with a Pineapple,' said Dennis, as the taxi drew up before a little shop with a striped blind. Out came Bobby Kane, his arms full of little packets.

'I do hope they'll be good. I've chosen them because of the colours. There are some round things which really look too divine. And just look at this nougat,' he cried ecstatically, 'just look at it! It's a perfect little ballet.'

But at that moment the shopman appeared. 'Oh, I forgot. They're none of them paid for,' said Bobby, looking frightened. Isabel gave the shopman a note, and Bobby was radiant again. 'Hallo, William! I'm sitting by the driver.' And bareheaded, all in white, with his sleeves rolled up to the shoulders, he leapt into his place. 'Avanti!' he cried . . .

After tea the others went off to bathe, while William stayed

and made his peace with the kiddies. But Johnny and Paddy were asleep, the rose-red glow had paled, bats were flying, and still the bathers had not returned. As William wandered down-stairs, the maid crossed the hall carrying a lamp. He followed her into the sitting room. It was a long room, coloured yellow. On the wall opposite William someone had painted a young man, over life-size, with very wobbly legs, offering a wide-eyed daisy to a young woman who had one very short arm and one very long, thin one. Over the chairs and sofa there hung strips of black material, covered with big splashes like broken eggs, and everywhere one looked there seemed to be an ashtray full of cigarette ends. William sat down in one of the armchairs. Nowadays, when one felt with one hand down the sides, it wasn't to come upon a sheep with three legs or a cow that had lost one horn, or a very fat dove out of the Noah's Ark. One fished up yet another little paper-covered book of smudged-looking poems . . . He thought of the wad of papers in his pocket, but he was too hungry and tired to read. The door was open; sounds came from the kitchen. The servants were talking as if they were alone in the house. Suddenly there came a loud screech of laughter and an equally loud 'Sh!' They had remembered him. William got up and went through the French windows into the garden, and as he stood there in the shadow he heard the bathers coming up the sandy road; their voices rang through the quiet.

'I think it's up to Moira to use her little arts and wiles.' A tragic moan from Moira.

'We ought to have a gramophone for the weekends that played "The Maid of the Mountains".'

'Oh no! Oh no!' cried Isabel's voice. 'That's not fair to William. Be nice to him, my children! He's only staying until tomorrow evening.'

'Leave him to me,' cried Bobby Kane. 'I'm awfully good at looking after people.'

The gate swung open and shut. William moved on the terrace; they had seen him. 'Hallo, William!' And Bobby Kane, flapping his towel, began to leap and pirouette on the parched lawn. 'Pity you didn't come, William. The water was divine. And we all went to a little pub afterwards and had sloe gin.'

The others had reached the house. 'I say, Isabel,' called Bobby, 'would you like me to wear my Nijinsky dress tonight?'

'No,' said Isabel, 'nobody's going to dress. We're all starving. William's starving, too. Come along, *mes amis*, let's begin with sardines.'

'I've found the sardines,' said Moira, and she ran into the hall, holding a box high in the air.

'A Lady with a Box of Sardines,' said Dennis gravely.

'Well, William, and how's London?' asked Bill Hunt, drawing the cork out of a bottle of whisky.

'Oh, London's not much changed,' answered William.

'Good old London,' said Bobby, very hearty, spearing a sardine.

But a moment later William was forgotten. Moira Morrison began wondering what colour one's legs really were under water.

'Mine are the palest, palest mushroom colour.'

Bill and Dennis ate enormously. And Isabel filled glasses, and changed plates, and found matches, smiling blissfully. At one moment, she said, 'I do wish, Bill, you'd paint it.'

'Paint what?' said Bill loudly, stuffing his mouth with bread.

'Us,' said Isabel, 'round the table. It would be so fascinating in twenty years' time.'

Bill screwed up his eyes and chewed. 'Light's wrong,' he said rudely, 'far too much yellow'; and went on eating. And that seemed to charm Isabel, too.

But after supper they were all so tired they could do nothing but yawn until it was late enough to go to bed . . .

It was not until William was waiting for his taxi the next afternoon that he found himself alone with Isabel. When he brought his suitcase down into the hall, Isabel left the others and went over to him. She stooped down and picked up the suitcase. 'What a weight!' she said, and she gave a little awkward laugh. 'Let me carry it! To the gate.'

'No, why should you?' said William. 'Of course, not. Give it to me.'

'Oh, please, do let me,' said Isabel. 'I want to, really.' They walked together silently. William felt there was nothing to say now.

'There,' said Isabel triumphantly, setting the suitcase down, and she looked anxiously along the sandy road. 'I hardly seem to have seen you this time,' she said breathlessly. 'It's so short, isn't it? I feel you've only just come. Next time –' The taxi came into sight. 'I hope they look after you properly in London. I'm so sorry the babies have been out all day, but Miss Neil had arranged it. They'll hate missing you. Poor William, going back to London.' The taxi turned. 'Goodbye!' She gave him a little hurried kiss; she was gone.

Fields, trees, hedges streamed by. They shook through the

empty, blind-looking little town, ground up the steep pull to the station.

The train was in. William made straight for a first-class smoker, flung back into the corner, but this time he let the papers alone. He folded his arms against the dull, persistent gnawing, and began in his mind to write a letter to Isabel.

* * *

The post was late as usual. They sat outside the house in long chairs under coloured parasols. Only Bobby Kane lay on the turf at Isabel's feet. It was dull, stifling; the day drooped like a flag.

'Do you think there will be Mondays in Heaven?' asked Bobby childishly. And Dennis murmured, 'Heaven will be one long Monday.'

But Isabel couldn't help wondering what had happened to the salmon they had for supper last night. She had meant to have fish mayonnaise for lunch and now . . .

Moira was asleep. Sleeping was her latest discovery. 'It's *so* wonderful. One simply shuts one's eyes, that's all. It's *so* delicious.'

When the old ruddy postman came beating along the sandy road on his tricycle one felt the handlebars ought to have been oars.

Bill Hunt put down his book. 'Letters,' he said complacently, and they all waited. But, heartless postman – O malignant world! There was only one, a fat one for Isabel. Not even a paper.

'And mine's only from William,' said Isabel mournfully.

'From William – already?'

'He's sending you back your marriage lines as a gentle reminder.'

'Does everybody have marriage lines? I thought they were only for servants.'

'Pages and pages! Look at her! A Lady reading a Letter,' said Dennis.

My darling, precious Isabel. Pages and pages there were. As Isabel read on her feeling of astonishment changed to a stifled feeling. What on earth had induced William . . . ? How extraordinary it was . . . What could have made him . . . ? She felt confused, more and more excited, even frightened. It was just like William. Was it? It was absurd, of course, it must be absurd, ridiculous. 'Ha, ha, ha! Oh dear!' What was she to do? Isabel flung back in her chair and laughed till she couldn't stop laughing.

'Do, do tell us,' said the others. 'You must tell us.'

'I'm longing to,' gurgled Isabel. She sat up, gathered the letter, and waved it at them. 'Gather round,' she said. 'Listen, it's too marvellous. A love letter!'

'A love letter! But how divine!'

Darling, precious Isabel. But she had hardly begun before their laughter interrupted her.

'Go on, Isabel, it's perfect.'

'It's the most marvellous find.'

'Oh, do go on, Isabel!'

God forbid, my darling, that I should be a drag on your happiness.

'Oh! oh! oh!'

'Sh! sh! sh!'

And Isabel went on. When she reached the end they were hysterical: Bobby rolled on the turf and almost sobbed.

'You must let me have it just as it is, entire, for my new book,' said Dennis firmly. 'I shall give it a whole chapter.'

'Oh, Isabel,' moaned Moira, 'that wonderful bit about holding you in his arms!'

'I always thought those letters in divorce cases were made up. But they pale before this.'

'Let me hold it. Let me read it, mine own self,' said Bobby Kane.

But, to their surprise, Isabel crushed the letter in her hand. She was laughing no longer. She glanced quickly at them all; she looked exhausted. 'No, not just now. Not just now,' she stammered.

And before they could recover she had run into the house, through the hall, up the stairs into her bedroom. Down she sat on the side of the bed. 'How vile, odious, abominable, vulgar,' muttered Isabel. She pressed her eyes with her knuckles and rocked to and fro. And again she saw them, but not four, more like forty, laughing, sneering, jeering, stretching out their hands while she read them William's letter. Oh, what a loathsome thing to have done. How could she have done it! *God forbid, my darling, that I should be a drag on your happiness.* William! Isabel pressed her face into the pillow. But she felt that even the grave bedroom knew her for what she was, shallow, tinkling, vain . . .

Presently from the garden below there came voices. 'Isabel, we're all going for a bathe. Do come!'

'Come, thou wife of William!'

'Call her once before you go, call once yet!'

Isabel sat up. Now was the moment, now she must decide. Would she go with them, or stay here and write to William. Which, which should it be? 'I must make up my mind.' Oh, but how could there be any question? Of course she would stay here and write.

'Titania!' piped Moira.

'Isa-bel?'

No, it was too difficult. 'I'll – I'll go with them, and write to William later. Some other time. Later. Not now. But I shall *certainly* write,' thought Isabel hurriedly.

And, laughing, in the new way, she ran down the stairs.

THE CHEAP HOLIDAY
Evelyn Sharp
1923

The little aunt sat and dreamed, while Cousin Paul and his wife gave the family a picturesque account of the wonderful holiday they had spent in Germany. 'Most enjoyable time I ever had,' boomed Cousin Paul. 'Hotels excellent, if you know your way about; cooking perfect –'

'And all dirt cheap!' supplemented Cousin Mary, who regarded herself as existing primarily for the purpose of supplementing Cousin Paul. 'A five-course dinner, wine, coffee and liqueurs – for 4½d. Just fancy!'

The family, in unison, fancied. Gratified at the effect already made, Cousin Paul proceeded to embroider. 'For about a half-penny you could travel to all the places worth visiting in the Umgebung – I should say, the neighbourhood,' he explained; and the family, applauding, noted with clannish pride that Cousin Paul had returned home a linguist.

'Yes,' chimed Cousin Mary, 'and we travelled right from the south of Germany to Hamburg – or was it Dresden, Paul? – for *eight pence*. Only think!'

The family only thought. Cousin Paul appeared to be making calculations. 'No, my dear,' he corrected; 'that was on the way out. Coming back, the mark had slumped again, and owing to my forethought in not taking return tickets it cost us only five-point-three pence.' He turned to the silent aunt, anxious that no one should be excluded from the approving chorus. 'How's that for a holiday, Aunt Joanna?' he roared at her jovially.

The little aunt jumped. She had been in the family – though not of it – for upwards of sixty years, but she had never quite got used to being roared at. 'It sounds to me very mathematical, dear,' she said, with her conciliatory smile. 'I never could do sums, so perhaps it is a good thing my travelling days are over.'

But Cousin Paul, who had never asked questions for the dull purpose of getting them answered, had already forgotten her, and was embarking on a florid description of the purchases he had made.

'I didn't want the things; but your Cousin Mary – well you know what women are!' said Cousin Paul, though, whatever might be said of those to whom this remark was addressed, this was certainly not one of the things that Paul knew.

'Well, dear, everything was so *cheap*,' simpered Cousin Mary, who had listened so long to Paul's definition of women that it had now begun to fit her nicely. 'You couldn't expect any true woman to resist a fur coat – oh, but a *ravishing* fur coat, girls! – that was going for a few shillings. It would have been simply *wicked*, wouldn't it, Aunt Joanna?' Fortunately, Aunt Joanna was not really expected to unravel this ethical problem.

The little old aunt never knitted; and it is possible that Satan, in his search for idle hands, saw Aunt Joanna's folded in her lap, and was consequently responsible for the excursion her spirit took in the next few minutes. But it may have been equally ascribable to a passage in the letter that lay in the underpocket of her grey alpaca gown.

'We have had nothing but a little weak cabbage soup for days,' wrote Freda, the professor's wife. 'Everything is now sold except poor Mamachen's fur coat, which we were trying to keep because of her rheumatism: for alas! We can no more buy fuel or warm underclothing . . .'

Suddenly Aunt Joanna was looking in at the neat Berlin apartment where she had spent such happy holidays in the past. But the great carved sideboard was gone; so was the stuffed sofa on which the favoured visitor was invited to sit. The round polished table and solid oak chairs were no longer to be seen, nor the black clock, nor the handsome crimson carpet. A gaunt old lady sat on a stool in the corner of the room, and moaned as if in great pain. At the window, a man with despair in his eyes, his frame bent and shrunken, stood looking hopelessly out. As Freda stole from the room with the fur coat over her arm, Aunt Joanna saw that even the wedding ring was gone from her thin finger.

Up from the street below, in a voice strangely like Cousin Mary's, floated the gay remark of the passing tourist: 'After that enormous lunch I simply can't *face* tea yet awhile. Let's go and buy that diamond ring instead!'

'Don't you believe it,' Cousin Paul was saying, as Aunt Joanna's spirit wandered back again into the family circle.

'There's plenty of everything in Germany. Haven't I seen it with my own eyes?'

'Shops filled with luxuries,' chorused his wife. 'Furniture, clothes, jewels – well, they must come from *somewhere*, mustn't they?'

'I am an observant man,' resumed Cousin Paul, whose knowledge of women was only equalled by his knowledge of himself; 'and you may take my word for it, there's no more distress in Germany – than there is in this country!'

'God help the poor souls!' was the quite amazing remark that came from the spot in the family circle where Aunt Joanna appeared to be sitting. It was, however, so incredible a remark that those who heard it at once attributed it to their excited imagination.

'And to think,' was Cousin Mary's parting observation when the visitors took leave, 'that we very nearly went to Belgium, where the mark, or whatever it is hasn't slumped at all! Wouldn't that have been *tragic?*'

No doubt it was a sense of awful tragedy happily averted that made the little old aunt relapse suddenly into hysterical laughter. The family charitably attributed it to her customary eccentricity.

DECISION
E M Delafield
1928

@@@@@@

'If I do this – it will change the whole course of my life,' thought Elaine.

She was trying to be detached, clear-headed, and calmly resolute. But it was foreign to her temperament to be any of these things, even at the best of times – and for purposes of detachment, clear-headedness and calm resolution, the climax of an illicit love affair may be looked upon as the worst of times.

She had met Louis five times, and on each of these occasions, he had made love to her.

Progressive love, Elaine candidly characterised it to herself.

She had succumbed almost instantly to his admiration, his audacity, his undoubted charm.

He was everything that Charlie was not, and Elaine, after being married for ten years to Charlie, found that this, in itself, was stimulating and attractive.

Elaine, in common with the vast majority of her sex, considered that one thing, and one alone, constituted unfaithfulness in a wife. She had listened to Louis's impassioned declarations, she had told him the story of her life, she had received his kisses, and returned them – but she had not been unfaithful to her husband.

Yet.

The honesty that is so often the penalty of intelligence, compelled her to add this qualifying monosyllable.

For she was at least as violently in love with Louis as he was with her, and it was her nature to proceed to extremes in all matters of the emotions, but never to do so whole-heartedly and without misgivings. It was either her supreme misfortune, or else her one redeeming quality – she was never quite sure which – that she had a conscience.

It was now at war, hysterically and inopportunely, with her inclination.

'Charlie trusts me.'

'So does Louis. He thinks I love him enough –'

'I can't deceive Charlie –'

'I can't let Louis down.'

'It's not too late, even now –'

'It's too late. I've promised Louis –'

So she had. She had promised to let Louis join her for a week in Brussels, where she was going under pretext of sketching with a Painting Club.

Louis had advanced arguments that, if not new, had at least been moving.

'It's not as if I wanted to break up old Charlie's home – neither you nor I, darling, could bear to hurt him . . . But you've got a right to some life of your own, and don't you think you owe me something, after all . . . Elaine, my sweetest, perhaps?

You've made me care for you as I didn't think I had it in me to care for any woman . . .'

A part of Elaine's consciousness was aware that Louis had undoubtedly been made to plumb the depths of his own powers of caring on the other, previous occasions – but all the same, it was this part of his pleading that finally induced her to speak the words of yielding.

Perhaps she did owe something to Louis after allowing him to make love to her as he *had* made love.

To lead a man on, and then to turn round and put on the airs of virtue . . . On the other hand, to be married to a man who, if dull, was kind and faithful, and then to turn round and . . .

'I shall go mad,' reflected Elaine.

She stood in the dining room of her nice and respectable suburban home, her suitcase packed and labelled, her passport in her handbag, and her new and becoming little orange travelling hat on her head.

She gazed at herself in the glass that intersected the many fumed-oak convolutions of the sideboard, and idiotically wondered whether she would look quite different when she came back, *afterwards.*

But it was not – was just not – too late.

Even now, she could decide not to go. She could tell Charlie that the whole thing had fallen through at the last minute. He was not a person who required many explanations.

And that would end it – for always.

Louis was not the man to give any woman a second chance of fooling him. She would have to live the rest of her life without Louis – and without the thrills, the excitement, the secret glow, that the thought of Louis had engendered.

There would be nothing left. Except the inner knowledge, that must belong to herself alone, that she had had the courage of renunciation.

'I've never done a decent thing in my life,' Elaine abruptly told herself, and this inaccurate generalisation, curiously enough, seemed to make it suddenly easier to be brave.

'It's now or never – only I must not give myself time to think –' She went to the writing table, and with shaking hands snatched at paper and pencil.

'Louis' she wrote, 'I can't do it. Forgive me – but of course you won't. We had better not see one another again.'

Tears blinded her.

But it was done.

The piercing ring of the telephone bell made her start violently.

'Hullo!'

'Elaine, what's happened? I've been nearly mad – waiting at Victoria. You know you've missed the boat-train?'

'*What?* Oh my good Heavens, this clock is nearly an hour slow and I'd forgotten it – Fool!'

'You can still do it, if you get into a taxi this minute – I can reserve places on the second half of the train. You've got just twenty minutes – *Race –*'

'Right!' Her voice was clear and excited again as she slammed down the receiver and, almost in the same moment, tore open the door and dashed into the hall, on the chance of finding a taxi on the rank at the end of the street.

BROTHER W
Malachi Whitaker
1929

A man of about sixty sat in a crowded railway carriage thinking so deeply that he might have been alone. Though the night was wet and the air raw, perspiration formed in the thin hair at his temples, and made a frustrated effort to run down his cheeks. He wore a bowler hat, a high, dirtyish-white collar, under which was an imitation shirt-front of purple paper made up by himself, and a new black overcoat, too large for him.

Owing to some malformation, he could never quite shut his right eye, the under lid of which, bright red and shining, seemed to be pinned down on to his cheek. His eyes were large, a pale greenish-grey. He had a grey moustache. As he sat, his hands, coming out of their long sleeves, clasped loosely on his knees, his expression was one of extreme misery.

The carriage of the local train was badly lighted. It had a low, yellowish-white roof, smeared and dirty. The seats were of horsehair, smooth, slippery, and cold. On the uneven floor were several small pools, made by the rain from umbrellas, which trickled for a time like springs. Sleet, falling sideways

on the steamed windows, ran a straight, heavy course to the window-bottoms; in one case entering the carriage and running down the horsehair at every jolt. Workmen smoked and jested. Two or three young girls, laughing and breathless from their last-minute jump on to the train, compared notes interminably. 'I thought we were never going to catch it' – 'I've torn my stocking, what a nuisance' – 'Look at Hilda, hasn't she got a red face?' – 'You look at your own!' – 'Didn't we have to run for it?'

All the time the elderly man, William Aykroyd, stared in front of him, blinking rapidly, as he always did, to keep his right eye clear. He did not want to go home, only habit was driving him back. He was a bachelor. His brother James, also a bachelor, with whom he had always lived, had died just a week ago. He began to think about his brother – 'young' James – three years his junior. Their father had died fifty, their mother thirty, years ago. They had lived, the two of them, together for almost thirty years, and for twenty of them, he, William, had not spoken to his brother James.

He remembered the trivial quarrel which had started his long silence. It had seemed such a big thing at the time. James had slyly borrowed his new suit, and gone out in it without permission, and William could not forgive him. William did not say a word when the culprit returned, he merely ignored him, did not listen to his explanations, and refused to speak to him. For twenty years he had kept this up. At first James, round-faced, merry-eyed, improvident James, had taken it as a huge joke, teasing him, taking his arm and walking with him to the train, calling him 'Brother W', pretending it was more formal than 'William', and in other ways trying to break down the ridiculous barrier which pride had raised between them.

William refused to respond. Both he and his brother worked as compositors for a jobbing printer. They had worked together, but after a year or two James made a change, so that he should not be continually near his silent brother. At that time, if William were compelled to send word about work to James, he would always do it through a third person. He would call up a boy and say, 'Go, tell James Aykroyd that William Aykroyd wants him to do so-and-so.' Early on, James would send exaggerated messages back, to which William pretended not to listen.

The brothers took their lunches and ate them in front of the rusty iron stove at the bottom end of the room. During the lunch hour the gas engine which ran the clanking machinery stopped. The smell of ink and lye pervaded the room. Sometimes they were alone, as the other men and the machine-feeders went home on fine days, and for an hour there would be no sound but the chink of a cinder as it fell out of the stove, or the rustle of the paper in which their food was wrapped. Neither of them went out for fresh air. They would read old newspapers, or James would borrow a 'blood' from one of the boys. If they did not read they would look at the stove or out of the grimy windows.

James could never get used to the silence. He kept forgetting, and saying something excitedly to his brother: 'Tip's coming to the Hippodrome next week!' or, 'What do you think of City's chances for the Cup, now?' after a win at football. William's mouth would tighten, he would look away, and after a minute James would get up with a crestfallen look, and he would take a turn around the room.

James was always trying to break the silence. Both brothers frequented the one music hall of the town. James, hiding his round face behind his coat collar, would stand near to his brother in the queue, and as they entered would endeavour to sit beside him. When they were both laughing at some joke, James would turn and say, 'Wasn't that a good one?' but he had never caught his brother off guard. As soon as there was an interval, William would rise and change his seat, even choosing a worse place.

At home, their life became strange, almost unbelievable. There were only two bedrooms in the house. The boys had grown up together, and had always slept in the same bed. After the death of their mother, neither of them showed any desire to move, to have a separate room. They continued sleeping together, even after the quarrel, in the same rickety iron bed they had always slept in. When they got up the first thing they did was to throw back the bedclothes. Before leaving for work they would turn the mattress and make the bed, ready for night.

Each made his own breakfast. Each had a gas ring and a small pan. They made tea and boiled an egg or fried a little bacon separately. They cut from separate loaves of home-made bread. On Wednesday evening of one week James would come home, light a fire, set the oven on, and bake a sufficient quantity of bread to last the two of them a week. The next Wednesday would be William's turn. Their mother had taught them to bake; they would never have dreamed of buying their

bread. All other food they bought separately, each getting what he needed.

James began to lose his spirits after a year or two of silence on his brother's part. Sometimes he would say humbly, 'The bread's very nice this week, William,' hoping for some reply, but none ever came.

The train was drawing near the station. One of the young girls rubbed the dirty window with the back of her glove, but instead of looking out merely showed the soiled glove to her companions with a look of exasperation. A workman knocked his pipe against the iron-rimmed sole of his boot. William Aykroyd stood up and took from the rack an old leather bag to which the smell of stale bread clung. He sat forward on the seat, holding his bag with both hands, looking as if he were almost anxious to be out of the train and away to some warm, comfortable home in which he would be enveloped with loving care.

Ten minutes later he opened the door of his house. His new coat glistened with melting snow and raindrops. He felt in his pocket for matches, lit the gas, and pulled down the paper blind. It was Wednesday, time for the bread to be baked. He lit the fire with waiting coal and chips, and drew out the oven damper. Running some water, he put the pan on the gas ring, but forgot to light it. He had intended to make some tea. Lately he had often forgotten. There seemed to be no use making tea when James was not there to irritate him. James was extravagant, he had saved very little money, and would often bring good things home for his tea; a piece of fish or meat to fry, and some vanillas, of which he was very fond, for what he

called a 'finisher-off'. William, more frugal, contented himself with a sausage, a small meat pie, or another egg.

As soon as the fire began to make itself felt, William washed his hands and set the baking bowl to warm in front of the blaze. He emptied a packet of flour into the bowl, and rubbed lard and salt into it. He lit the gas ring under the neglected pan of water, and took from a shelf a small packet of yeast. When the dough was kneaded and rising he sat on a low stool in front of the fire, so near that steam arose from his damp trouser legs. The house was silent, except for the drone made by a strong flame driven under the oven damper.

After he had sat for a few minutes he got up and opened a cupboard door, taking from the top shelf a large jug full of silver coins, all the money that his brother James had saved during his fifty-six years of life. There would be no more than thirty pounds, William knew. He had counted it before. He had decided, coming home in the train, to use the money to buy a tombstone for his brother.

Even as he so resolved he could not believe that his brother was dead. James had been brought home a fortnight ago, unconscious, and had lain in bed for a week. William had gone out immediately to fetch a doctor, and a woman, a neighbour, who knew something about nursing, to look after his brother. Just before the end – on the Tuesday night – the neighbour, Mrs Pigott, came running downstairs shouting nervously, 'He's conscious, Mr Aykroyd!'

William remembered how he had gone up the stairs into the cold bedroom, with its inadequate gas flare, and seen James lying helpless in bed, moving his stiff lips, saying 'William' with

great difficulty, over and over again. And William had stood looking at him, with water – perhaps tears – running out of his never-shut eye, struggling to answer, 'I am here, James,' but some demon had pressed a hand over his mouth. It was no use; after not speaking to his brother for twenty years he could not do it now. Then James's voice had become silent, the flickering light had faded from his eyes; he was dead.

As he cut up the dough and put it into the blackened loaf-tins, William thought about the funeral, about himself and the thin young parson riding in the solitary cab, about the three wreaths of flowers, one from himself, one from the neighbours, and one from James's workmates. He thought about the new grave that he had bought because the family grave would hold no more, and of the extra money he had given to have it bricked. He had paid for everything, not knowing that James had saved thirty pounds. Now there should be a splendid tombstone for him.

Just as he had never wished to sleep in the other bedroom after his mother had died, now he did not wish to sleep upstairs at all. He had brought bedding down and made a bed on the old couch, and it pleased him. He shut off the upper part of the house, pretending it was not there. He liked to go to bed in the firelight, in a strange room, so that he would not feel so lonely or miss James so greatly. He felt that he would like to call out, 'James, are you there?' but even yet, he could not do it.

The bread was baked at last, its warm smell filled the little living room. It was late enough to go to bed. William took off his clothes, tearing the paper front as he did so. This was an idea of his own, to save washing. He had a fresh one every day,

as he could get the paper for nothing. He remembered how James used to laugh at these different-coloured fronts, which were sometimes blue, sometimes green, or as today, purple. He used to laugh at the purple ones. Just before he got into bed, William opened his leather bag and was astonished to find that his lunch was still there. He must have forgotten to eat it. He thought it would do for the next day. He shut his eyes, but his mind stayed awake, thinking of James.

The next day, at lunchtime, he rolled up his apron and put on his long black coat. It was fine, but very cold. He had noticed a sign, near the cemetery, 'Roland Tonks, Monumental Mason'. He thought he would go to see Roland Tonks, whose name pleased him.

The shop which he entered was filled with fancy stones and marbles. There was also a yard, in which a man was working, but this held only small crosses and stone slabs, some with unfinished inscriptions on them. As he waited for Mr Tonks, who presently came in exhaling an odour of mutton and onions, William read through a glass window the bald, sad names – Agnes Wetherall, John George White, Roger Suddards – which advertised to casual passers-by that still another body was gone to crumble in the forgetting earth.

Mr Tonks seemed to have the idea that William was married, and that it was his wife who had died; and was continually suggesting, with his head on one side, that he thought something with a nice female figure – 'an angel, perhaps?' would do for 'her'.

In the corner of the room stood a granite obelisk, eight or nine feet high. William kept looking at it. It seemed remote, a thing apart from the rolls and scrolls. It reminded him of his twenty years' silence to James. All the time that Mr Tonks talked to him he looked at the great stone.

'How much will this one be?' he asked at length, putting out his hand and touching the cold, glittering granite.

'That's something rather better. That is, indeed, a monument,' answered Mr Tonks; 'but perhaps it's a little dear, a little more than you might like to give. It's a hundred pounds.'

Many days after this, William came again to look at the obelisk. He had not yet made a decision and Mr Tonks was getting disheartened. People often came to his shop in great grief, and if he could not help them to decide, sometimes they said they would 'leave it till later', and when they had given it a little more thought, left it for ever.

He was surprised when William came one Saturday to order the granite monument.

'You see,' explained his customer slowly, 'there's two brothers. I'd like you to write, "In memory of James Aykroyd", then he pulled a small notebook from his pocket, and gave the dates of his brother's birth and death.

'After that, put, "Also of his brother William, born –"' When he had given the date, he hung back, perplexed.

'You'll have to wait,' he said; 'I can't give you the date of William's death.'

'If you send me a note, it'll do,' said Mr Tonks comfortingly. He was at his desk, writing out a receipt, and casting covert, happy looks at the wad of notes William had brought.

William's face was drawn and thin. His pale eyes, the right one seeming to bulge out over its reddened lid, looked as if they had been sleepless for a long time. His movements were uncertain, and he listened to the voice of the other man with strained attention.

'I'll send you a note when I get home,' he said; 'that is, when I've had time to look it up. Have you got it written down, "Also of his brother William?"'

'Yes,' said Mr Tonks. 'And we'll see that only the very best work is put into it. You wouldn't like a verse, perhaps?' he suggested.

'No,' answered William. 'Good day.'

'You're forgetting your receipt, Mr Aykroyd,' called Mr Tonks, trying to speak sadly, and not succeeding.

Early the following week, Mr Tonks received a note, written simply on a soiled envelope. It was delivered by hand, and read, 'Brother W. Died –' Here followed a date, written clearly.

'Why,' said Mr Tonks, examining in perplexity first the note and then the calendar hanging near his head, 'that's today.'

HIS LIFE BEFORE HIM
Madeline Linford
1931

When the cat died, the family decided that the next household pet should be a dog. They all agreed that they were a little tired of cats, with their sleek concealment of nasty traits – stealing, for instance, under a mien of proud aloofness and disdain. A dog would be friendly and companionable, fetching Father's slippers for him, going for walks with Norman. Mother said she did not want the kind of dog that leaves hairs all over furniture, and Father repeated many times that a dog, if the household decided to adopt one, must be treated like a dog and kept in his place, not spoiled by pamperings or with titbits at all times of the day. Auntie mentioned Pekes and those dear little fluffy dogs with tails curled over their backs – she couldn't remember their name for the moment – but Norman was rudely assertive that he, for one, wouldn't be seen out with an insect, and Father said he refused to accept, or pay the licence for, any dog that hadn't a bit of spunk about it, and that a lapdog was, of all animals, the most contemptible.

In the end they bought a Sealyham puppy, two months old. Cook's young man owned the mother, the father was a fairly successful winner at second-rate shows, and the young man offered to sell one of the litter for a sum which he described as a gift and Father as extortion. When the negotiations were brought to an end, which both parties accepted without enthusiasm, Norman bought a shilling manual on Sealyham terriers and a threepenny pamphlet on 'The Dog in Sickness and Health'. He talked authoritatively about 'points' and the symptoms of distemper and told Mother the kind of dog biscuits that should be included in the grocer's list.

'Two months old!' said Auntie. 'Shan't we all seem very big and old to him?'

And so they did.

The puppy was thrust into the drawing room by Cook, who had small time to spare for dogs with her young man waiting in the kitchen. Father had just returned from the office and Norman from the Technical School, and to both of them time seemed to be gnawing very slowly through the hour that must pass before dinner was due.

'Here is the first general news bulletin,' said the wireless. 'Copyright reserved.'

The puppy shambled cautiously into the room, still rather unsteady on his short legs, his apprehensive dark eyes bright with uneasiness. He gazed at each of those four huge strangers and his formless, eager love hung poised in uncertainty as to which of them would give it the sign for release. The unfamiliar smell of the carpet stretched an eternity between him and the kennel where he had lived with the warm and friendly

odours of his mother and sisters. He wagged his stump of a tail in a timid flutter of ingratiation.

Then Auntie swooped down to the floor and grabbed his fat, white body in her arms. 'Oh the beautiful, beautiful boy! Was he shy, then? Poor little chappie!'

That was better. He flicked up his tongue to reach Auntie's chin in a passion of gratitude. Here was someone who would put milk in his dish and crumble his biscuits, who would be forgiving to little faults of behaviour. He pressed his ice-button nose against her neck and fell instantly into a sleep that wiped out the big room and the unknown people and swept him back to the haven of his mother's placid side and the little grunts and whinnies of his sisters.

'Now then,' said Father, who hated sentimentality and women's gush, 'stand him on his feet and let's have a look at him.'

Auntie jerked him awake and back to the carpet again. 'Those white hairs,' said Mother. 'They'll be all over the place. You've got two on your sleeve already. Wouldn't it have been better to have chosen a black dog? It will be a terrible business trying to keep him clean.'

Norman snapped his fingers at the puppy, and the bright, dark eyes, which had wistfully followed the withdrawal of Auntie, turned hopefully toward this new suggestion of goodwill.

'He looks all right to me, but, of course, you can't tell at that age. His head's miles too big now.'

'He ought to be all right,' said Father, 'considering the price I paid for him. You can get a mongrel from the Dogs Home for five shillings. Good enough dogs, too, they are.'

'He's a little lamb,' cried Auntie, 'a little white baby lamb.'

'He seems quiet enough, anyway,' Mother said. 'I can't bear dogs which are always barking or digging holes in the flowerbeds.'

'Oh, he'll learn what is expected of him,' said Father. 'A firm hand and no nonsense is the way to train a dog. Once give in to them and they're the masters, not you. He'll have to understand from the beginning that he has to do what he is told or else get punished.'

The puppy, still in the centre of the vast wastes of carpet, looked from one to the other as their voices caught his attention. He had had a long, an infinitely long, day, tumbling with his sisters, chewing the maternal tail, and hurrying in eager rushes to greet the young man when he came with plates of food. Now he was tired and a little empty ache troubled his stomach. It was surely time that someone assembled round him once more the happy bits and smells and warmnesses that made up his existence.

'There's the gong,' said Mother. 'Take him to the kitchen, Norman, and tell Cook to keep an eye on him. If her young man hasn't gone by now, it's quite time he had.'

'Come on young fellow. We'll have to find a name for him, by the way.'

'Yes, and to teach him to answer to it, and follow properly – that's the first thing,' said Father.

Auntie's longing gaze yearned after the puppy as Norman picked him up and walked to the door.

'Two months old!' she said, with a little moan in her voice. 'He's got his whole life before him.'

SOMEONE AT A DISTANCE
Phyllis Bentley
1932

@@@@@@

'In ordinary life,' observes M Estaunié in one of his subtle
psychological novels, 'we come and go, we talk, we haven't the
slightest evil intention; and because we turn to the right rather
than to the left, speak one word instead of another, someone at
a distance is injured, someone of whom we did not dream, of
whose very existence indeed we are probably ignorant.'

When one begins to consider, one is surprised to find how
many cases one knows where that has been the truth. Old Mr
Trumpington, for instance, knew Richard Marden only vaguely,
by sight, and did not in the least wish him ill; while of the existence of Philippa, George Steevens, and the fair fluffy little girl
in Yorkshire he was completely ignorant. Young Smithers was
even less to blame, for he did not even know Richard Marden.
And yet –

Philippa Marden heard a taxi come round the corner of
Cardigan Place. She drew her dark brows together in a look
of pain; no doubt that was her husband, returning from his
fortnight's business trip abroad. O God, why had she ever

married him? There were too many answers to that question, unfortunately, and none of them the right one; at the time of their meeting at a seaside resort she had been flattered that he, an experienced man of the world, ten years older than herself (which made her feel young), should pay her attention; he was rich; she was tired of living at home amid a large family and working for her bread in a narrow world which seemed to have neither appreciation of her sombre beauty nor scope for her social gifts; life in a London suburb sounded rather attractive to her provincial ear; Richard Marden's cool, competent manners pleased her; he was handsome, too, in a way, with his rather prominent grey-blue eyes and well-groomed greying hair, his height and his 'well-preserved' slender figure.

She had used all these reasons to persuade herself to marry him; had done so, and seemed likely to regret it all her life. Not that he ill-used her, starved her, kept her short of any money, neglected her, or in short gave her any excuse for a display of temper; he was apparently a most correct and affectionate husband; it was just that Philippa felt nipped by his cool, implacable egoism as by an east wind. All her warm and generous impulses were dying, had to die that she might stay alive. Were they at the play or at a concert, did they discuss an idea or a book, his sneering criticism always took the bloom from Philippa's enjoyment, froze her enthusiasm for what was beautiful and good.

Perhaps he detested enthusiasm only when it was directed upon objects other than himself, however; for Philippa had seen him moved furiously enough when his self-love was wounded; he had come home once, for instance, raging about an office-boy who had ruffled him by some piece of unintentional rudeness so slight that Philippa could scarce forbear to smile at it. The boy, however, had lost his place, for Marden never forgot or forgave an injury, however small. Philippa had already had personal experience of this; her husband still, for instance, six months after their marriage, sometimes jested, with an icy irony which chilled her to the bone, about a trifling delay of hers upon their honeymoon which had caused them to miss an unimportant train. Yes, all the generous warmth of her heart, all the fires of nobility which had surely once flamed in it, were sinking, chilling, dying, beneath her husband's freezing glance. It must be so, or she could not have acted as she had towards George Steevens.

Steevens was the new junior partner in her husband's firm. He was very tall and very fair, but not handsome or heroic, at any rate at first sight; a rather vague young man, with rather rough manners and a rather bad North Country accent – when he spoke at all, which was not often. He was not married, though he was understood to be engaged to some girl or other at home away in the north – Philippa visualised her, from the stray hints he let drop, as a fair fluffy little thing with a giggle – so he lived in lodgings which Marden had found for him not far away in Burton Street.

Naturally he came to the Mardens' a good deal, but he was not a great asset in ordinary society; he sprawled about as though the chairs were too small for him, blushed when spoken to by a woman, and treasured some very antiquated provincial notions about manners.

He had two great qualities, however, which appeared elsewhere; he was a fine engineer, and a fine tennis player. Philippa had first seen him in this latter capacity; Marden had taken her to see his junior partner play; and as she watched the magnificent display of strength and skill presented by Steevens's fine young body she felt her heart slowly warm again. Afterwards, when Steevens was presented to her, Philippa had been a little disconcerted at first by his crude bashfulness; but soon that was only an added attraction to her, for it made her feel more strongly than ever that she was the one woman in the world for him. She with her social tact and cleverness – even Richard admitted that she had that; indeed she sometimes suspected it was the reason he had married her – her quick understanding, her gift for easy expression; Steevens with his solid ability and his driving power: what a pair they would have made! What a career she could have made for him! Ah! If only she had met him before she married Marden!

If she had met him before she married Marden, Philippa reminded herself, the situation would still have been hopeless, for there would still have been that fair fluffy giggling child whom Steevens had promised to marry. She probably adored him. If Philippa had met George Steevens before her marriage to Marden had chilled her heart, she would have played fair by that fluffy giggling child, she would have scorned to rob another woman of her love. But Philippa had married Marden, and her heart was chilled, and rob another woman of her love was precisely what she had set out to do and done. It was not difficult; there were plenty of opportunities; Marden had positively asked her to be kind to George Steevens; the lad, he said, was farouche, difficult, capable of flaring up and rushing away if his susceptibilities were injured, and goodness knew

where his susceptibilities lay; let Philippa soothe him and play him and keep him attached to her husband – his abilities were great, and the partnership was a splendid opening for him; it would be a kindness to the young man himself.

Not that Marden meant, of course, that Philippa should by the very slightest step depart from the path of her wifely duty. No! Philippa did not accuse him of that; such baseness was not in his character; she recognised with a shudder that he trusted her – his pride was too great for him to do anything else. Well! She had betrayed his trust; she had talked to George Steevens, and taught him to talk to her – that they were both strangers to London and to the suburb was a help. She loved George Steevens, and taught him to love her. She was beautiful, and she knew it, and she could not help feeling that, despite everything, she was the one woman in the world for him; she was older than he was, more experienced, more articulate, she knew what she wanted; and so they had passed from the few minutes' conversation which Marden approved to appointments, letters, secret meetings in park or street. And then Marden had been called abroad for a fortnight.

It was because Philippa had touched the heights and depths of love in that fortnight that she had given Steevens up. She loved, and her heart grew warm and generous again; she remembered that poor child in Yorkshire, who would be left weeping and desolate, robbed of her love; she remembered her broken faith to her husband; she remembered her own noble youthful dreams; she remembered that Steevens was younger than herself; she saw ghastly visions of his ruin if her husband should ever discover the intrigue between them.

Well, he should never discover it; Steevens should not be
ruined, the little Yorkshire girl should not be desolate; Steevens
was young and would soon forget Philippa; they would give
each other up. Or rather, since with this pair the initiative had
always had to come from Philippa, she would give him up. In
his grubby, uninteresting little sitting room which had become
so dear to her she made this plain to him; their only honourable course was to give each other up.

Perhaps in her secret heart she may have hoped that he
would be stubborn and refuse to do her bidding; but he had
always allowed himself to be persuaded by her, and he did not
assert himself now. They bade each other a tragic farewell and
parted.

That was last night. It seemed remote, distant across centuries of pain, but it was last night only; today was the day of
Marden's return. And now Marden was approaching in a taxi,
had drawn up to the door, was on the threshold; had crossed
it and taken Philippa with cool correctness in his arms. Well,
he must never know, never, never know, thought Philippa as
she asked if he had had a pleasant journey, took off his coat,
fussed affectionately over him, and, though it was rather late,
rang for tea; he should never know; she, with her social gifts,
her tact and cleverness, would keep the secret from him always.

Just then old Mr Trumpington and young Smithers came
out of their office building together. Young Smithers, who was
a decent sort of fellow, stepped aside with a kindly smile to let
his venerable colleague pass. 'Poor old chap!' he thought to
himself, noticing the old solicitor's snow-white hair and beard,
his faded blue eyes peering with a kind of pathetic perplexity

out of his gentle, thin, almost waxen old face, his bowed shoulders and tottering gait, the way he leaned heavily on his neat umbrella. 'Poor old chap! He isn't the man he was. He's getting feebler. The hot weather's trying him.' He thought of Mr Trumpington's long and honourable career and spotless reputation, and felt a wish to say something to show the respectful compassion which he entertained for the old man.

'You still walk to the office and back every day, sir?' he murmured, in an admiring tone.

'Oh, yes!' threw out Mr Trumpington with a negligent air. (Young Smithers saw, however, that he was pleased.) 'Yes. I have always done so.'

He quickened his step as if to show how lightly he regarded the practice of walking, how easy it was to him; and he stumbled a little by the gate.

'Mind the step, sir!' called young Smithers behind him.

'Thank you! Thank you!' replied Mr Trumpington. He slightly touched his hat to show his gratitude for the warning, but his tone was rather testy; and he did not turn round, but tottered rapidly away.

Indeed, he had felt a sharp pang at the sound of Smithers's kind young voice. Was he, then, getting so old that he had to be warned to mind steps? Was he getting so old that he looked as though he needed help on the streets? Was he, Harry Trumpington, the gay, the dashing, the brilliant Harry Trumpington, really getting old? Surely not, he told himself staunchly; he felt as young as ever; his mind was still perfectly clear – except perhaps round the middle of the day, but what of that? As young Smithers had said, he still walked to and from the office every day, and that was quite a long way, almost a mile – or say three-quarters. Or perhaps, after all, half a mile was nearer the mark, he reflected honestly. But even so, that was two miles a day. Not many men of eighty could walk their two miles a day, six days a week. He threw up his head and stepped out more briskly. But no, it was only five days a week, after all; on Saturday he did not come to the office in the afternoon. That was one mile on Saturday, then, and two miles on five other days; how much was that, now?

Suddenly he felt confused and puzzled; he was not quite sure; it seemed such a complicated sum.

'Ah, young Smithers was right, was right,' he thought: 'I am getting old; I can't multiply two by five and add one now; I am turning into an old, doddering man; I stumble over steps; I have to go to sleep for an hour or two every afternoon, or else I get confused and muddle the beginnings and endings of my words; I am set in my habits; if my chair isn't in its usual place by the hearth, or if a meal is late, I feel quite upset, my heart beats fast and irregularly; as for this walking to and from the office that I'm so proud of, even that I do mechanically, just because it's a fixed habit. I always walk the same way; down Burton Street and along the square to the office, along the square and up Burton Street when I'm going home. I timed it and found it was a minute quicker than going by Cardigan Place – how many years ago? It was when we first took that house, I suppose; how many years ago was that? Twenty? Oh, more than that, many more than that; it was before Edith died; it must have been thirty years ago. Thirty years! And ever since then I've always walked along the square and Burton Street. Ah, yes! Young Smithers

was right; I'm an old man. Can it really be so many years since Edith died?'

As he tottered along the side of the square, old Mr Trumpington now thought about his wife. At first he thought of her as she had been in her last sad years, and then he went back to that sweet and lovely time when they were in the spring of life together; she was young and rich and pretty, with such spirit! Ah, what a bright, winning, lively creature she had been! And he was young and poor, with all his way to make; but he was clever, and tenacious, and daring, and bold, and sure to do well, so everybody said; he was not a doddering old man who stumbled over steps then, he was not set in his habits then. He recalled some of his old triumphs, and chuckled, and threw back his head; his blood flowed more freely through his chilled old veins, he laughed to himself again and gave another knowing shake of his head.

So young Smithers thought he was a stumbling old dodderer, did he? Set in his habits, was he?

He'd show them! He'd show them! After all, a man was as old as he felt; and he felt very little older than the dashing Harry Trumpington who had cut out Smithers's father with Edith, carried her off under his very nose; Edith's father had preferred Smithers, but Harry Trumpington had dashed boldly in and won her. He'd show them that Harry Trumpington was not an old fossil yet; no, not by a long way, not by a very long way indeed. Striking the ferrule of his umbrella triumphantly upon the pavement, old Mr Trumpington, a smile upon his face, turned firmly and decidedly to the right, and, breaking the habit of thirty years, went homeward up Cardigan Place.

Tea was over; Philippa was talking volubly, with intent to conceal.

'You're not looking very well,' said Marden. 'I shan't have to leave you alone again.'

Was it mere fancy, or did his tone really sound ironical? Had he heard anything? Could he possibly have made a guess? Oh, he must never know, he must never guess, thought Philippa, wildly; and she redoubled her efforts to amuse him, to distract his mind, to convince him that nothing particular had happened in his absence, that she was glad to see him home again. Fortunately, she was clever at that sort of thing.

But presently Marden said: 'Have you seen anything of young Steevens while I've been away?'

How was she to answer that? After a sickening pause, which she felt her husband could hardly but notice, she decided to go as near the truth as possible. 'Yes,' she said, quietly. 'I've seen him several times. He's a queer boy.'

'We might perhaps ask that girl of his here for a week or two,' suggested Marden. 'What do you think?'

'Oh, Richard!' cried Philippa involuntarily. Controlling herself, she added at once: 'Need we? She's sure to be very crude.'

'As you wish,' said her husband indifferently.

Philippa breathed again. He had noticed nothing, then; the danger was over; she was safe. Now to turn the conversation to some distant topic, turn it naturally, with ease. His travel experiences were exhausted; she glanced about in search of a subject.

'Why!' she exclaimed, thinking she has found what she

sought. 'Here's that nice old man with the beautiful white beard coming down the Place.'

'What, old Trumpington?' said Marden curiously. He rose and strolled to the window.

'I don't know his name,' said Philippa. Delighted to have distracted his attention from the Steevens topic, she followed him, and, putting her arm about his shoulders, slightly leaned on him.

'Yes, it's old Trumpington all right,' said Marden. 'What is he doing here at this time, I wonder?' he went on. He looked at his watch. 'Yes,' he said in a puzzled tone, 'he must be going home.'

'And he usually goes up Burton Street, doesn't he?' said Philippa, eagerly pursuing this safe topic.

She felt her husband's hand on her arm, his fingers digging into her flesh; and saw his face, furious and distorted, close to hers. Panic seized upon her, a sense of disaster filled her heart.

'How do you know he usually goes by Burton Street?' demanded Marden.

His voice was terrible. 'How do I know?' repeated Philippa stupidly.

'Yes, you, a stranger,' urged her husband. 'How do you know? You who don't even know his name?'

Ah, God, of course it was from Steevens's rooms . . .

'Everyone knows,' stammered Philippa. She turned pale, 'I've heard it said –'

'You're lying,' began Marden, coldly.

Old Mr Trumpington turned out of Cardigan Place into the main road. He knew Richard Marden only vaguely, by sight,

69

and did not in the least wish him ill; while of the existence of Philippa, George Steevens and the fair fluffy girl in Yorkshire he was completely ignorant. Young Smithers was even less to blame, for he did not even know Richard Marden. And yet –

THE MATERNAL INSTINCT
Winifred Holtby
1934

'But, of course, he's lovely, Cynthia,' Fanny said. Cynthia looked across her son's drowsy head at her old school friend and smiled.

Perhaps it was the smile that infuriated Fanny; but Cynthia had not meant to be superior. She was only thinking of the fire-lit nursery and the shadows darkening the green garden beyond the windows; of Robin's sweet confident weight upon her knee, and her husband's income, and the security, the comfort, the steadying sense of responsibility, and of life fulfilling itself.

And here was Fanny, come after ten years, to witness her apotheosis. Dear, odd Fanny, who had always admired her so absurdly. In the days when Cynthia too was poor and irresponsible they used to go about together, to cinemas and galleries, and parties in draughty studios, whenever Cynthia had a free night from the Art School, and Fanny actually had no political meeting which she felt she ought to attend. And now here they were together again, and Cynthia was grown up and a wife and mother, while Fanny was still the same rootless, excitable, immature young woman. All women, Cynthia decided, really were children until they had children of their own.

So she looked across at Fanny and she smiled.

'Anthony must have done pretty well,' Fanny remarked clumsily.

'Oh, yes. I suppose he has. Though, of course, what with taxes and things, it doesn't come to much. And there's his old father to keep. He's always a marvellously good son.' Four thousand a year was really not such a tremendous lot. Not with supertax.

Cynthia was rightly proud of her husband. When he had been demobilised his sole assets were a small gratuity, two decorations, a scar across his face, a dependent invalid father, a young wife, and a knowledge of flying. From these he had made all this. His courage and enterprise gave Cynthia a poor opinion of those ex-soldiers who were always complaining that they had never found a proper job since the war – like that young man who was to have married Fanny. Anthony had never found a job; he had invented one.

'You went to South America, didn't you?' Fanny asked.

'Yes,' said Cynthia, bored. She had told the story so often. 'After the war Anthony hadn't a bean, but he took an old plane out to Buenos Aires as agent for the manufacturers and flew it all over the continent, booking orders. He used to visit little tinpot states, and put the wind up them saying how many planes their rivals had bought, and how awkward it would be for them if they started bombing. They fell for it like anything. It was fun at first, but a bit boring afterwards, and we were awfully glad to come home and settle down. Weren't we, my blessing?' She buried her face in the baby's lovely neck, that smelled of buns and talcum powder, and warm flannel.

'Do you mean military aircraft?' asked Fanny harshly.

'Any old craft we could sell. Fanny, as nurse is out, will you help me to bath him? Every woman ought to know about babies, says I.'

'I suppose you know about this Chaco business?'

'This what?'

'This fighting between Bolivia and Paraguay.'

'Not I. I don't read the papers. I've got something better to do, haven't I, my precious? I leave all that to Tony – except a glance at the gossip paragraphs. Really, when you have a child –'

'This ought to interest you.' Fanny had flushed bright red and was licking her dry lips. How funny unmarried women were, Cynthia thought. Was she trying to change the conversation because she was shy at seeing Robin undressed? Full of inhibitions, probably, poor thing.

'Bolivia and Paraguay – I expect you know them – have been fighting intermittently in the Chaco district for about four years now. There's no real reason why they should go on. They accepted arbitration once. They're both wildly in debt. But they go on buying armaments. The other day in parliament someone asked the President of the Board of Trade about our own exports, and it seems that we've sent out in the past twelve months over five million cartridges to Paraguay, and over a hundred machine guns, some tanks, and ammunition of all sorts to Bolivia. It's paying somebody to keep them at it.'

'I dare say. Do you mind passing me that basket? Now, look at him, Fanny!'

'Cynthia, the statement didn't mention aeroplanes, but then it only went back a year. They have got aeroplanes.'

'Now for the hot water. Just a second, Fanny. Somebody ought to invent a self-filling bath for babies. I think babies are really shamefully neglected by inventors.'

As Fanny made no gesture to help, Cynthia thrust Robin into her arms and fetched the water herself.

'Last August,' persisted Fanny, 'the Paraguayan Minister in Paris protested that Bolivian planes were bombarding not just forts in Chaco but Mennonite colonies. Villages, you know, with defenceless civilians – old people and babies.'

'Really?' Cynthia was inspecting a tiny rough patch behind Robin's ear.

'Do you remember that air raid during the war, Cynthia? When we saw the house just after the roof had fallen in on three children and that wretched mother, who'd just run down the path to bring the dog in, had to be held back by the neighbours because she struggled to go in to them, while the walls were still crumbling in?'

'Don't be so ghoulish. It's horrid to gloat over horrors in front of Robin.'

'I suppose that these women in Chaco love their children. And the Minister said that hospitals had been raided too, five times. Cynthia, how can you bear it? Those aeroplanes may be the very ones your husband induced them to buy by rousing suspicion against their neighbours. Those people are only peasants . . . They wouldn't want to organise air raids unless someone taught them to do it . . . How can you bear it for your lovely Robin to be nursed on blood? That's what it is. All this' – she waved her hand around the nursery with a wild gesture – 'paid for by that.'

'Well, really, Fanny. I do think you might try to control yourself a little. What morbid, disgusting nonsense. "Nursed on blood" indeed! If you knew these villages you'd see they were only savages. Anthony's one of the few people who really have done well for the world. He's encouraged trade and given employment and done pioneer service. Robin will grow up to be very proud of him.'

But Cynthia did not lose her temper. She made allowances. Some frustrated spinsters were really not fit, she knew, for civilised society. She must find Fanny a nice husband. She drew the bath nearer towards her and took Robin from Fanny's arms and sat for a moment, her son upon her knee, wrapped in the comforting consciousness of love and virtue, a serene and noble figure of maternal dignity.

HOME ATMOSPHERE
Sally Benson
1938

Mildred Kirk came briskly into the living room. She wore a knit sweater-suit of a hard, bright blue which neither sagged nor pulled, but gave her admirable figure the wooden perfection of a model in a store window. She was smiling and as she smiled she blinked her eyes rapidly in an alert, interested way. Walking to the fireplace, she stooped down and picked up a half-smoked cigarette from the tiles and put it in a large bronze standing ash receiver.

At this movement, her husband, who had been reading the paper, looked up guiltily. 'Oh,' he said.

She turned toward him, still smiling. 'You just forgot,' she told him. 'Didn't you?'

'Must have,' he agreed. 'Thinking of something else, I guess.'

He laid his paper across his knees and sat with an expectant look on his face, as though he were waiting for something.

She sat down neatly and stared for a moment at the fireplace. A fire was laid in what seemed at first glance to be an expert manner – even lengths of shiny, dark cherry for kindling and on top of them three birch logs with curling, silvery bark, but there was no paper and no ash. Not a sign of ash.

'It's just that I think there is no reason why an open fireplace must be used as a catchall,' she said. She looked around the room and her eyes softened somewhat. 'I love this room,' she went on, 'It really looks like home. Don't you think it looks like home, Willard?'

His eyes wandered slowly to the polished maple gate-legged table, the couch facing the fireplace with the long refectory table at its back, on which stood a lamp with a blue Chinese base, bronze bookends representing ships in full sail, a set of four ashtrays with the matchbox that went with them, and a Lalique glass bowl filled with artificial fruit; they rested on the aggressively bright chintz at the windows, the shades with cord fringe, the large, expensive radio, the four Windsor chairs and the two upholstered ones; on the long dull-gold frame of the mirror hung by a blue cord over the fireplace, and the ornaments on the mantelpiece – two brass candlesticks holding tall, dark-blue candles, a small mahogany clock, and a green glass vase of bunched bayberry.

Mildred Kirk moved impatiently in her chair. 'Well?' she said, 'I asked you a question.'

He smiled feebly at her. 'Well, Mil, why shouldn't it look like home?' he asked. 'It *is* home, isn't it?'

'When I *think*, when I *think* of the place you and Billy used to live in, it makes me shudder,' she said. 'How you stood being cooped up in two rooms with a little boy, I don't see.'

He frowned slightly. 'Billy's a good kid.'

'Of course he is,' she answered, her voice conciliatory. 'No one could ask for a better little boy, I didn't mean that. I meant

this is much nicer, isn't it? Living in the country and having a real place, a place you can move around in? Billy loves it. You just have to look at him to see he loves it.'

'Where is he, anyway?' Willard Kirk asked.

'Playing down the street with the Simpson boys. At least, that's what Mattie says.' She shook her head humorously. 'Now, you got home before I did. Why didn't you ask her? He is your little boy and I'm the one who asks where he is, the minute I come in the house.'

He picked up his paper again. 'Oh, I knew he was all right. Mattie wouldn't let him go anywhere that wasn't all right.'

'You seem to place a great deal of confidence in Mattie,' she said. 'Not that Mattie doesn't mean well, but you couldn't exactly say she knows much. And with both of us away at work all day – well, sometimes I feel uneasy.'

He threw his paper to the floor. 'Now, look here,' he began. 'Are you going to start that again?'

She looked at him and drew the corners of her mouth down as though she were going to cry. 'Really,' she told him. 'It's impossible to say a word to you without your flying off the handle. You should thank your lucky stars you married a woman who loves your little boy and takes an interest in him. I'd like you to hear what the people in my office say, that's all. *They* think it's wonderful that I was willing to move out here, commute and everything, just so we could have a real *home*. A home needs a firm hand, let me tell you. And it's not so easy when I'm away all day and have to leave everything to a maid.'

He looked at her and decided that she was darned pretty – you had to say that for her.

'And a maid,' she went on, 'that's some sort of Polish woman and doesn't understand one thing about how a child should be brought up.'

'Now, listen,' he said. 'Mattie's all right. Mattie's taken care of Billy since he was born and she's all right.'

'But *how* has she taken care of him? How do you know how she's taken care of him? You're always away all day. You don't know what she does.'

His face cleared and he began to laugh. 'All you've got to do is look at him. Just look at him!'

'I don't deny,' Mildred Kirk said, 'that she feeds him well and looks after his clothes and all that. It's the things she tells him – all about that woman being chopped to pieces with an axe in whatever place she comes from. And about how drunk her father used to get, and her mother's black eyes.'

'Oh, that stuff!' he commented impatiently. 'Why, when I was a kid the best time I ever had was following an old bum who used to work at the livery stable and listening to his yarns. Stuff like that doesn't amount to anything.'

She blinked her eyes rapidly for a moment and then smiled again. It had a curiously professional quality, a sort of calloused sweetness. 'Anyway,' she said, 'some day I hope we can afford a real maid. One that looks nice. Nice and neat. You must admit that no matter what kind of uniform I buy for Mattie, she looks funny. And while she's lovely to you and all that, she isn't always so nice to me, let me tell you. But of course you wouldn't notice that.'

'I never notice how Mattie looks.' He picked up his paper. 'Go on, get it off your chest. Just what are you getting at now?

All this stuff about Mattie not being good with Billy! Go on, get it over with.'

Mildred Kirk wrinkled her forehead and looked down at the floor. With the clear, light blue of her eyes hidden, she seemed prettier and younger. 'Well,' she said, 'Mattie's sulking again.'

'Her arches hurt her. She told me so.'

'Arches nothing! She simply doesn't like to have people in. I merely went to the kitchen to ask her to make sandwiches and leave out glasses when she got through with the dishes and she began to sulk. Here she is alone all day, her time all her own, and I want her to do one simple little thing. Yes, she's all right with you and Billy, but she resents doing one thing for me.'

'Mattie has a lot to do,' Willard Kirk protested mildly. 'And she's no chicken. She always gets that way. Send her out to a movie or something and she'll get over it. She loves the movies.'

'I'll not cater to the whims of a feeble-minded Polish woman,' she said indignantly. 'She's going to show respect for me or I'll know the reason why. Absolutely on her own all day here alone and running things with a high hand! You've spoiled her, that's what! You cater to her far more than you do to me! I have a good notion to tell her if she isn't happy here, she can leave!'

Willard Kirk got up from his chair and walked toward his wife. 'Listen, Mildred,' he said, his voice flat and hard. 'Mattie stays. Mattie isn't ever going to go until she walks out of here of her own free will, and she'll never do that. Why, you don't know. You just don't know, that's all. She practically raised Billy.

Came all the way down from the Bronx every morning before I went to work and stayed until I got home at night. No matter what time let me tell you! I don't care if she does sulk once in a while! So do I! So would you if you were getting old and on your feet all day and sometimes half the night. Good Lord! Can't you *see*?'

He stopped talking abruptly and went over to the window, where he stood looking out on the little suburban street, the sidewalks spotted with small pools from the recent rain, 'Mattie stays,' he repeated without turning around, 'and that's that.'

Mildred Kirk got to her feet. She pulled at her skirt, smoothing it over her firm, pretty hips. 'As you say,' she said. 'I'm just your wife. I'm just trying to make a home for you. And a home where the people in it aren't happy all the time doesn't seem much of a home to me. No one can sulk in this house. No one! And no matter what you say, I'm going to speak to her.'

He turned around and faced her angrily. 'What –' he began.

She looked at him, smiling. 'You don't have to worry,' she said. 'I told you I was just going to *speak* to her.'

In the kitchen, Mattie took the small chopping bowl down from the second shelf and put a few chives and a leaf of tarragon in it. Pretty soon, she thought, she would hear Billy's step on the back porch. She gave a nervous glance at the clock. It was after dark, but he had no streets to cross. Not that she hadn't told him many times, 'Look, darling. Look, like this, see, and then like that. And if no cars coming, then walk slow across.'

She turned over the idea in her mind of walking to the corner to see if she could see if he were coming. But then dinner

@@@@@@@@

would be late, and That Woman's tongue would start up again.

The familiar events of the coming evening took shape in her head – dinner and then, an hour after, Billy's bath. Maybe let him play in the tub a while, she thought, as they were having company. Then bed and a nice talk in the dark. She frowned, thinking deeply of something especially good to tell him tonight, because she had been short with him about being late for school.

She got olive oil and lemon from the icebox and then she began to chop, slowly and deliberately. She heard the swinging door open behind her and knew That Woman stood there. She turned toward her with only slight deference.

Mildred Kirk was still smiling and her voice was clear and pleasant as she spoke, 'I came to ask you a question, Mattie,' she said. 'A question I wanted to ask you before Billy got home.'

Mattie shifted her weight from one foot to the other.

'It's this,' Mildred Kirk went on. 'Aren't you happy with us, Mattie?'

Mattie's expression was stunned and uncomprehending.

'Because we want you to be happy,' Mildred Kirk said. 'We can't have anyone around us who isn't happy here. So I thought maybe you had too much to do. Maybe you thought you had too much to do. Do you, Mattie?'

'My feet sometimes,' the older woman began, her face flushing a dull red.

'Exactly,' Mildred Kirk agreed, nodding brightly. 'So we've reached a decision. We've decided that Billy is quite big enough to bathe and undress himself. Quite big enough! And to put himself to bed. That will relieve you of that duty and you won't feel yourself so rushed when you are asked to make a few sandwiches for our friends.'

Mattie swallowed painfully. 'Mrs Kirk?'

She looked at the clear blue eyes and the alert smile of the young woman and could go no farther.

'So that's settled now, isn't it, Mattie?' Mildred Kirk asked. 'And any time you feel you have too much to do, simply come to me and we'll see if we can't relieve you in some way. Do you understand, Mattie?'

She stood there smiling another moment and then she turned and the swinging door closed behind her.

Mattie stared at the door and a murderous rage filled her heart. Sharp, hot pokers of fury pierced her brain and for quite a while she was not aware of anything but this fury. Then through it she heard the thump of Billy's bicycle as he wheeled it against the side of the house, and she turned back to the table and mechanically took hold of the chopping bowl. But her knees were weak and she pulled the kitchen stool toward her and sat down. The evening loomed starkly ahead of her. No bath, no talking in the dark, no stories. That Woman had taken the last moment of the day from her, the only moment now when Billy was still her baby. That Woman could do anything. Mr Kirk had married her, hadn't he? She had got him.

As Billy's sturdy little shoes clumped up the back steps she had to put her head down in her hands a moment, trembling with fear, before she had courage to turn and face him.

'A fine hour to come home,' she scolded. 'A fine time.'

LE SPECTATEUR
Irène Némirovsky
1939

They had eaten well. The creaminess of the quenelles brought
out the truffles' deep, dark flavour: not too overpowering, but
blending in with the tender flesh of the fish and the delicate,
white sauce, rather as the deep notes of the cello had mingled
with the sound of the piano in the delightful concerto he had
heard yesterday. If one used one's imagination and experience
it was possible, thought Hugo Grayer, to extract the maximum
pleasure from life, and innocent enjoyment. After the exquisite and complex taste of the quenelles, the Châteaubriand
steak with potatoes had an austere simplicity reminiscent of
classical design. They had drunk a small amount of wine –
Hugo had a delicate liver – but it was a 1924 Château Ausone.
What a bit of luck it had been to discover such a rare wine in
an apparently simple restaurant on one of the Parisian quays.
With a smile Magda said, in English, 'You are a marvel, Hugo
dear!'

She took his arm. He was short and very thin, and looked
as if he had been created by a particularly refined artist using

only a limited palette of colours: grey for his suit, hair and eyes, a touch of pale ochre for his face and gloves, a few spots of white on his stiff collar and forehead, and a gleam of gold in his mouth. His companion, taller than him, solidly built and rosy-cheeked, was wearing a little hat, fashionably and jauntily perched on top of her silvery curls like a bird on a branch. She walked by his side with long, confident strides that rang out on the old cobblestones.

It was an August day in Paris, on the Quai d'Orléans by the Seine. Hugo kept congratulating himself that this year he had postponed his departure to Deauville: the weather was fine and Magda quite entertaining. He did not like dining with pretty girls; at his age it was better to keep his pleasures separate. For a lunch like this what he needed was a hardboiled, cynical old American such as Magda, who appreciated her food and had good taste in wine. She admired him, but that left him indifferent: he had always been admired for his taste, his wealth, his splendid collection of porcelain, his knowledge of ancient Greek writers, his generosity and his intelligence. He did not need other people's admiration, yet Magda amused him. It was better, and more unusual, to be amused than admired . . . better and more unusual to be amused than loved.

'Egoist.'

A weeping young woman had called him that once. The sensual memory of her tears still touched his heart pleasurably: she had been so young and so beautiful. He had been young then, too. Egoist . . . He might have replied that in this world of mad, brutal men and their stupid victims, the only harmless people were egoists like him. They did not hurt anyone. All the misery suffered by human beings, thought Hugo, is unleashed by those who love others more than themselves and want that love to be acknowledged. Whereas he just wanted to lead a peaceful, quiet life. There was no great secret about it. One had to think of life as an interesting theatrical production, every detail of which deserved praise, and then it all acquired great beauty. He showed Magda a dank little street between two old houses, where a girl was standing by a gate clutching a crusty loaf of bread to her chest. Hugo looked at her kindly: a few basic elements – an anaemic child, a pale golden loaf, some ancient stones – had by chance come together to form a graceful, touching picture that pleased Hugo Grayer.

'I've had my share of sadness, like everyone else,' he said to Magda. 'Old Fontenelle used to insist that no sorrow, however wretched, could survive an hour's reading. But for me it isn't books or works of art that console me, it's the contemplation of our imperfect world.'

'Fontenelle must have led a peaceful existence like yours,' said Magda laughing.

Her laugh was the only thing about her that Hugo did not like; she laughed like a neighing horse.

'It's not that peaceful,' he replied.

He did not know why, but he felt both proud and annoyed when it was implied that he was happier than other people. He was like a pedigree dog pulling on its lead, trying, for a change, to get at the food of lesser breeds.

'I've had my ups and downs,' he said, thinking of his mother's death. They had often quarrelled: she was a horrible woman. But her last moments and the deathbed reconciliation had been brief; there were no tears or shouting, and due to their measured, almost aesthetic observance of convention, all had been forgiven. And he thought about his divorce twenty years ago, and about De Beers, which had just dropped a hundred points. Well, a man like himself had worries on a spiritual plane that the mass of humanity could not possibly grasp. He had suffered, truly suffered, because of certain books, unsuccessful trips, silly women, dreams and gloomy premonitions. A night spent in an ugly hotel room overwhelmed him with sadness. Some gaudy wallpaper, in an inn where a cold had kept him in bed for a week, had been at the root of a chronic melancholy, a tendency to migraine, and gloomy speculation about the future. And now this remark of Magda's had irritated him: she was too down-to-earth to be able to understand him.

But Magda had stopped at the spot on the quay where the Seine gently curves round to the right. Hugo thought how ugly and sharp the usual expression, 'the river's elbow', was, evoking the image of an old beggar woman lifting her arm to ward off a blow. In fact it was a graceful and exquisitely elegant movement. The Seine twined itself round Paris like a woman putting her arms round her lover – a very young woman, affectionate and blushing, Hugo said to himself, as he watched the water glitter. How he loved its flow, its pale colour . . .

Nearby there was a quiet little square.

'It's all so beautiful!' murmured Hugo. 'Europe has the charm of those who are going to die,' he said, stroking the river's grey stone parapet as he went on walking. 'That's what makes it so seductive. For several years I've felt particularly

drawn to these threatened cities: Paris, London, Rome. Every time I leave I have tears in my eyes, as though I'm saying good-bye to a terminally ill friend. It was the same in Salzburg before the Anschluss . . . God, it was so moving, listening to Mozart's music on those cold summer nights and thinking of Hitler a few miles away, tormented by insomnia and greed. One was witnessing the end of a civilisation. One was watching a country shudder and die while singing, just as one might feel the beating heart of a wounded nightingale in one's hand. Poor, charming Austria . . . And then all this,' he said, pointing at Notre Dame, 'destroyed in air raids, ruined and in ashes, how horrible! And yet . . .'

He felt a little out of breath. He could not keep up with Magda, who was walking too fast for him, but vanity would not allow him to admit it. (Magda was, in fact, older than him but considerably more robust.)

'Women are indestructible,' he thought.

He suggested sitting on a bench in the square; the weather was too nice to be shut up in a car.

'So do you believe in this war?' she asked, as she looked at herself in her little handbag mirror and rearranged her curls, which resembled the carved chunks of solid silver decorating a Victorian soup tureen. A young street urchin, fascinated by so much glamour, stopped in front of her and stared. She smiled.

'So do you believe in this war?' she repeated.

'My dear friend,' said Hugo emphatically, 'do you believe in the bullet that comes out of a loaded revolver when the trigger is pulled?'

They contemplated Notre Dame with compassion.

'The fate of those old stones affects me more than that of human beings, Magda.'

The little boy was still standing in front of them. Hugo Grayer took some small change out of his pocket.

'Here you are, child, go and buy yourself some barley sugar.'

Surprised, the child looked down, hesitated, then took the money and walked away.

'After all, it took centuries to build an irreplaceable cathedral and it takes only a few seconds to create a man, similar to all other men, for they are interchangeable, alas, with their vulgar passions and pleasures and crass stupidity.'

'Yes,' said Magda, 'at mealtimes during the Spanish war, when I thought about the El Grecos that might be destroyed, I couldn't eat a thing. I could truthfully hear a voice repeating in my ear, "the El Grecos, the El Grecos you'll never see again!"'

'There were certain scenes from the Spanish war in the cinema that could match the El Grecos,' Hugo sighed.

Magda gazed at the sky, trying to look as if she was thinking about the war in Spain. Actually she was wondering if her stockbroker had managed to sell her Mexican Eagle shares in time. Dear Hugo was so detached from worldly concerns, unsurprisingly since he possessed one of the largest fortunes in Uruguay. And she thought about the two big rooms on the first floor of her home in New York, briefly considering the best combination of colours: purple and pink, perhaps? That could be fun, with her Italianate mirrors painted with birds and flowers . . . Hugo smiled in the sunlight. Even though it was the height of summer, the light wasn't too bright, but soft and gentle. He would go to the Louvre and look at *L'Homme au verre de vin,* one of his favourite paintings, before going home to dress for dinner; he had been invited to dine outside Paris by a Brazilian woman friend who lived in Versailles. Yes, it was strange to watch old Europe sinking like this, like a ship taking on water from all sides, plunging into those terrible depths where God's voice ceaselessly resounds. In a few weeks or months would the ancient towers of Notre Dame be blown up by bombs, hurling their martyred stones to the heavens? And all those beautiful old houses . . . What a pity! He felt compassion, as well as a suitable indignation, and the comfortable peace of mind one experiences when watching a play. There is a lot of blood, and a lot of tears, but they are flowing a long way away from you and will never affect you. He himself was a neutral, 'a citizen of no man's land' was how he smilingly described himself. There was a handful of people on earth (Magda was one) who, by virtue of their birth, ancestors, family ties, and a quirk of fate, had so many different racial strains within them that no country could lay claim to them. Hugo's father was Scandinavian, his mother Italian. He had been born in the United States, but had become a national of the small South American republic where he owned some property.

Young men and women strolled slowly along with their arms round each other's waists. How would they all feel, if one day . . . ? What curious conflicts of emotion and duty they would have! And their poor bodies, made for pleasure! No, the human body was certainly not created for pleasure, thought Hugo; he put his hand over his eyes, for the sun suddenly shone brightly between two dark clouds that had come from nowhere: man had been created to endure hunger, cold and exhaustion and his heart was made to be filled with primitive, violent passions – fear, hope and hatred.

Benevolently he watched the passers-by. They didn't understand the resources within them, or that the human species could endure almost anything. Hugo Grayer was deeply convinced of this. The way things were at the moment, it took courage to come to Europe every year as he did. He might find himself trapped, an innocent man, among these nations going up in flames, just like some poor rat in a burning house. So what, he would leave in good time. With some difficulty he wrenched his thoughts back to Magda, who was asking his advice about the house she had recently bought in New Jersey. Then they got up and walked back to the Boulevard Saint-Germain, where the car was waiting for them. Then they went to Versailles for dinner, and Hugo went back to his hotel. He was still asleep the next morning when the citizens of France were reading the announcement printed in capital letters on the front page of their newspapers: '22 AUGUST 1939. THE OFFICIAL GERMAN NEWS AGENCY STATES: THE GOVERNMENT OF THE REICH AND THE SOVIET GOVERNMENT HAVE DECIDED TO AGREE A PACT OF NON-AGGRESSION.'

There were those who thought: 'Things will sort themselves out again.'

Others thought: 'There's nothing to be done this time, we'll have to leave.'

It was like hearing a knock on the door in the night, warning you that your sleep is over, that you must set off again, and for a moment your heart seems to stop beating. Women looked at their husbands, or at sons old enough to fight, and prayed, 'Not that! Have pity! Lord, take thou this cup from me.'

That same morning a thousand candles were lit in churches 'for peace'. In the street people stopped at newspaper stands, and strangers talked to each other; their faces looked calm but very solemn. Hugo had lived in Europe long enough to be able to interpret warning signs like this. He asked for his bill. He was sad to be leaving but of course there was nothing he could do here. He handed out generous tips.

'Monsieur is going?' asked the chambermaid. 'It's because of what's happening, isn't it? Everyone wants to go back to their own country. It's only natural in a way.'

Where would Hugo go? Well, first to America, where he had heard there was to be a sale of antique ivory: he was beginning to get bored with porcelain. After that, he'd see. It was very disappointing to think that he wouldn't see Cannes this year.

'Of course I'd love to stay,' he said, 'but there'll be air raids . . .'

When he looked at all the strong, handsome men who might be going to their deaths, he felt a sort of ironic affection for himself, for his fragile bones, his narrow spine and his long pale hands that had never in their life done any ordinary, rough work; they had never touched an axe or a weapon, but they knew how to stroke old books, look after flowers, or gently rub boiled linseed oil into some valuable piece of Elizabethan furniture.

However, the weather was so beautiful that he decided to put off his departure until the next day, and still he lingered. War was declared on a radiant September day. That day, on the Alexandre III Bridge, Hugo came across a middle-class family going for a walk: father, mother and a son still young, but almost old enough to join up. The father looked at his watch and said:

'We've been at war for twenty minutes.'

'It's remarkable how resigned these Europeans are,' Hugo Grayer thought. Some pigeons flew away with happy squawks.

Hugo would leave the next day. He sighed. He was starting to think that Paris would not be bombed . . . not straight-away . . . but there was the potential inconvenience, petrol rationing, the best restaurants being closed . . . Yet how interest-ing it would have been to see the start of this war! What would everyone feel? How shaken they would be! What would come out of this terrible crisis? Heroism? A longing for pleasure? Hatred? And how would it manifest itself? Would men become better? More intelligent? Or worse? It was fascinating, all this, fascinating! Behind each human face lay a mystery that, until now, had only been seen in works of art. Yet, above all, he felt a kind of detached pity, like that of a god who, from the empy-rean heights, watches the futile activities of mankind. Those poor people! Poor mad people! Never mind – the human body was made for suffering and death. And maybe these monoto-nous, grey lives would be livened up by enthusiasm, by passion, by new experiences. Like all fortunate, intelligent men, Hugo was inclined to be pessimistic about his own prospects but opti-mistic on others' behalf. It was nevertheless quite clear that he could do nothing to help them and it would be madness to stay.

He left France at the same time as Magda. Their ship was neutral, of course. It sailed serenely across a blue sea. It

was moving further away from Europe. Soon they would not think about it any more. It would be like the stage after you have left the theatre, like a blood-soaked Shakespearean tragedy when the curtain comes down and the footlights are turned out. The horror was unreal but the memory of it still held a certain beauty. Sometimes, on a fine evening, in the bar or on deck, people competed with one another to recall these historic moments:

'When I knew it was about to start, I wanted to see how the French were taking it: I went to Fouquet's.'

'Well, I went all round Paris, I was seeing history in the making. I stopped in all the cafés in Montparnasse. It was so moving! And, because it was dark, there were people kissing each other in every corner.'

But by the second evening Europe was already forgotten.

In his cabin Hugo was undressing. On a tray next to his bed there was a bowl of fruit, some iced tea and a book. He wanted desperately to go to sleep. He was one of those men who would continue to enjoy some of their childhood pleasures until the day they die: deep sleep, the subtle taste of little cream cakes dusted with icing sugar, the best fruit. He greatly missed his French servant, whom he had been forced to leave in Paris in the first hours of the war. The poor devil had been called up. They had almost cried as they parted.

'He stole so much from me that in the end he became as attached to me as a peasant does to the ox that provides him with a living by ploughing his fields. Poor Marcel . . . I'd send him some sweetmeats, but he'll be dead before they reach him. His health was bad and, after eight years' service with me, he was very spoilt. It's funny to think of him having wartime adventures,' he thought to himself, as he carefully chose a peach.

He usually fell asleep like that, half undressed, one hand on his book, the other luxuriantly squeezing a piece of fresh fruit, as if it were a woman's breast. He would then wake up fifteen or twenty minutes later, put on his pyjamas, cut an orange or a grapefruit in half, drink a few mouthfuls of the delicious iced juice sprinkled with a little sugar, put down his book and sleep until morning. But tonight a prolonged ear-splitting blast of sound disturbed his sleep. He listened to it incredulously at first, thinking that he was dreaming about Paris and was imagining he was one of those wretched Parisians who were probably just then listening to the sirens in their beds. But he was Hugo Grayer, a neutral, on a neutral ship on a sea that belonged to no one! The call of the sirens reached Hugo's ears from the depths of the sea and the pinnacle of the heavens, like an echo of those ringing out in a sorrowing Europe: it was a harsh, inhuman voice, quivering with anguish and concern, calling out to all mortals, 'Watch out! Be careful! I can do nothing for you except warn you!'

He leapt out of bed and began to dress. Were they being shipwrecked? Impossible, the sea was so calm . . . Was it a fire, a submarine attack? Doors banged. People ran along the corridors. He put on trousers, socks and a pullover. He had never felt so alert before and yet he was very calm.

However, he could not get his jacket on: he could not find the sleeve. But so what! It was warm and 'is not the body more than clothing?' This thought stunned him for a moment. From what buried memories did those ancient words come?

In shirtsleeves, his lifebelt correctly fastened, but his soul uncertain and angry (it wasn't fair, he was a neutral. He wasn't mixed up in their arguments, why had they disturbed him?), Hugo Grayer went up on deck. He was not afraid. Perhaps a very intelligent, well brought-up man can't experience panic-stricken, primitive, animal terror? He was furious. It seemed to him that there must be someone to call to account, someone who had not done what he should, the captain of the ship perhaps, or the company that owned it? He had an acute sense of how ridiculous his situation was. It was vulgar, hateful, to be walking about in shirtsleeves, wearing a lifebelt, on the deck of a torpedoed ship.

For now he knew. He had heard other passengers talking as they ran: they were being pursued by submarines. 'A mistake they won't make again,' Hugo Grayer had said at the bar the previous night, forgetting that human nature is fallible and man's memory short.

He felt reduced to the level of savages. It was as if, tattooed and with a ring in his nose, he had suddenly been forced to dance. He was a civilised man! He had nothing to do with their war! There were moments when he thought he was still dreaming. Yes, this all had the incoherence, the brutal speed and unreality of a nightmare, right down to the colours that one sees only in dreams: the purple ink of the shadows, the livid brightness of torches, the blinding light of reflections in the swirling water. Split into small groups, the passengers were waiting at the embarkation points where the lifeboats were to be lowered from the upper deck. In the darkness Hugo could see diamonds twinkling on bare hands. That's where his people were; he went to join them. The women had put their fur coats on over their nightdresses and were wearing their jewels safely next to their skin, believing this to be more secure than leaving them in a case that might be dropped as they jumped into the sea.

Mechanically Hugo adjusted his lifebelt and looked at the black water. The first boats were just being lowered when there was a blast of gunfire. A smell of explosives wafted past Hugo's astonished nostrils; it was a smell he had never come across before but something in him recognised it; it was a coarse, violent smell that aroused a muffled excitement rather than terror. A shudder ran right through him, from his narrow feet to his pale hands, and it seemed to him that death was touching him, blowing in his mouth and grabbing him by the hair. Nearby there were screams of pain and fear. There was a second, then a third burst of gunfire.

An invisible hand was shuffling, shaking up and mixing all these hitherto separate groups of people, as if they were ingredients in a cocktail shaker. First- and third-class passengers, women in mink coats, young German-Jewish children on their way to an Uruguayan orphanage with an American charity: they were all running together now, bumping into each other as they rushed towards the boats that were slowly being lowered into the sea. A shell whistled past Hugo. It did not hit him, but someone nearby who pulled him down as he fell.

At that very moment the moon rose with a horribly theatrical brilliance, just like a spotlight lighting up a stage set. Hugo saw a woman who had been cut in half. Her head with its dark hair, her ears with their silver earrings, and her torso, were intact, but her legs had been blown off. There were cries of 'torpedo!' and everyone crowded onto the starboard side, away from the expected point of impact. The crowd was now behaving as one, quivering like an animal about to be whipped. Hugo got up and ran further off. The first torpedo had missed them. The second arrived. It seemed strange still to be alive. The second went through the bow of the ship.

There were very few boats left that were of any use: some of the lifeboats had been smashed and several sailors killed by the shelling. Hugo realised that he would not get a place on one; there were too many women and children on board. He jumped into the sea. He didn't know how to swim. Buoyed up by his lifebelt, he made futile and exhausting efforts to get away from the ship. The waves played with him, tossing him from one to the other with ironic condescension.

A lifeboat went past, but no one saw him. At last he was noticed by some sailors on a raft. They had picked up some women and children floating in the sea, and now Hugo. They wanted to get away from the torpedoed ship but the wind was blowing them back: they were still close, horribly close . . . They did not have time to worry about the survivors lying at their feet. Hugo had injured his hip jumping into the water. He was lying amongst people as drenched as him, as frozen as him, and as dazed as him, none of whom could give him any help. There were two little girls beside him. They must have been part of the group of orphans travelling to Uruguay; their wet hair hung limply over their pale faces. He could give them nothing. He tried to talk to them, to reassure them. They did not reply, they did not understand. Like him, they were awaiting death, for although the ship was still afloat it must soon capsize and the raft would go down with it, sucked in by the backwash.

Hours passed, as slow and confusing as a night of fever. He was shivering with cold. The wind that had seemed so soft was in fact bitterly cold. It would soon be daylight.

He asked one of the sailors:

'Are there many dead?'

He did not know. A woman sitting near Hugo, probably one of the chambermaids, as she addressed him formally, answered:

'Monsieur cannot imagine how many bodies I've seen.'

The ship was still afloat. Fascinated, he watched the black hull that, like a careless fish, would soon dive below the water, taking them with it. Was Hugo afraid of death? He had always thought not – but it's one thing to see death at the end of a long road, a natural end to a long and happy life, quite another to think that this very night, this very morning, these very moments, might be his last. And what a death! In the dawning light he looked at the water.

It was terrifying. It was being churned up by the wind, bringing to the surface a sort of scum that could not be seen in broad daylight or from the top deck of a ship; foam, seaweed, and the thousands of bits of rubbish floating there since the previous day, or since time began, creating a greenish sludge that Hugo contemplated with horror. Where was the fresh sea of a September morning on a French beach? Was this what it concealed in its depths? The waves rose and fell all around him, and he was surrounded by steam, shadows and ghosts.

Occasionally he became confused again. What was he doing here? Hugo Grayer, a victim of the war, how ridiculous! With every wave, he thought, 'This time, it's the end!', but the raft was solid. It was not sinking, yet it was not making any progress.

'If I could row, it would help,' Hugo thought.

But where would he find the strength to pick up oars? His hip was so painful . . . He felt as if he had been lying there for weeks, or even months, although in moments of lucidity he realised that it was barely daylight, that the torpedo had struck in the middle of the night, that he had been suffering like this for only a few hours – the period of time that had once separated lunch from dinner, or a concert, or one pleasure from another. Five or six hours at most! How short that was! How long! How long it is when every second trickles by in beads of anguished sweat! How cold he was! Suddenly his stomach heaved and he vomited. He wanted to turn his head away out of a sense of decency, but found his neck was too stiff to move; he remained lying down, vomiting over himself like an animal.

'Monsieur is ill,' the woman next to him said compassionately. The awful retching had relieved him for a moment and he was able to reply, 'No, it's nothing.'

He suddenly remembered that once – a century ago, or was it yesterday? – he had said to someone – Magda? Someone else? – that he would have been curious to know what sort of emotions would be aroused by extreme danger. Now he knew. He also knew that everything was not immediately lost, that shame, pity and human solidarity stayed alive in people's hearts. It gave him some comfort to know that he had answered with a measure of dignity. He wanted to do better. Painfully, he breathed:

'Thank you.'

'You're very cold, monsieur . . .'

She was no longer speaking so formally. She took Hugo's pale, inert hands in hers and held them; she squeezed them, gently rubbing each one as she lifted it . . .

There was no end to the suffering his poor body could endure. His hip was being stabbed cruelly and relentlessly, as if a wicked and intelligent lobster was digging at him with its pincers. Seasickness added to his appalling feeling of cold and abandonment. The day was passing. He dozed; cried out. No one could help him. They looked at him with pity; that was all they could offer him. To hell with their pity! He too had watched with compassion as French soldiers went off to fight. Enough, he'd had enough! It was time for these horrible waves to stop! It was time for some warmth! Time to stop seeing those little girls' faces in front of him, as pale and lifeless as dead fish! How tolerable misfortunes appear when they only affect other people! How strong the human body seems when it's another man's flesh that bleeds! How easy it is to look death in the face when it's another man's turn! Well, now it was his turn. This was no longer about a Chinese child, a Spanish woman, a Central European Jew, or those poor charming Frenchmen, but about him, Hugo Grayer. It was about his body being tossed about in the spume of the waves, his vomiting; it was about his frozen, lonely, wretched, shivering self! How often, before going to bed, had he casually crumpled the newspaper he had been reading, in which there were stories about air raids, torpedoes or fires, oh, so many of them that one wearied of pity? So tomorrow, decent, untroubled people would briefly consider the picture of a calm, smooth sea with its floating wreckage, and would not lose an hour's sleep over it or pause over their breakfast. His body would be bloated by the water, eaten by sea creatures, whilst in a cinema in New York or Buenos Aires the screen would show 'The first neutral ship torpedoed in this war!' Then it would be old news, of interest to nobody. People would be thinking about other things, their ailments and their little troubles. Boys would grab hold of girls' waists in the dark; children would suck their sweets.

It was appalling, unfair! The whole lot of them were behaving like chickens that allow their mothers and sisters to have their throats cut while they carry on clucking and pecking at their food. They did not understand that it was this passivity, this silent acquiescence, that would, when the time came, also deliver them up to a strong, merciless hand. Hugo thought suddenly that he had always proclaimed his hatred of violence and how it was one's duty to be opposed to evil. Hadn't he said that? Perhaps he had not had time to say it, but one thing was certain: he had always thought it, professed it, believed it! And now here he was in this terrible situation, while others . . . others, in their turn, would maintain their fastidious scruples, parade their well-meaning neutrality, and enjoy a delightful peace of mind.

Meanwhile the hours dragged on . . .

GOOD BEDS — MEN ONLY
Elizabeth Myers
1940

Here is the lodging house standing awry in the rain. Above the open door swings an enamel sign: 'Good Beds – Men Only'.

Two vagabonds stand outside in the gusts, arguing; a tall thick man of forty or so, and a woman with her back to thirty but holding bold beauty yet: Chris and Sue.

These homeless partners have been so long abroad on the roads together that they have forgotten how they ever met. Sometimes the red birds in their desperate hearts are singing in unison but often Chris and Sue are engaged in a blazing row.

They dictate to one another: they come to blows. It is a rough house all the time. Why don't they separate then?

Well, why don't *you* and your husband separate? You wrangle the live-long day, but you share the same candle at night! And that is just the answer too – the candle that is shared at night.

So Chris and Sue stand quarrelling in the creaking wind.

'See what it says: "Men Only",' bawls Chris. 'I can't walk no more either: I got sore heel. You'll have to go on to some place else, Sue.'

'Why must I?' demanded Sue, truculently.

'Cause it's Men Only 'ere,' shouts Chris, getting ready to hit her. 'Can't you read nothin', you? It says "Good Beds – Men Only"! Give us that shillin'. It says Beds a Shillin'. Come on. I'm done for.'

'What about me?' Sue asks, near to her temper.

'You? Oh – you walk on to hell! But see that you meet me outside 'ere sharp eight in the morning. You'll have to help me get some breakfast, so you better doll up. *Where's that shillin'?* Blast you for a mean contrary bitch!'

Sue dashes down a shilling into his outstretched hand. It is all the money they have. Chris, without any enquiry as to how Sue will fare, without so much as a 'Goodnight' or a 'Kiss my foot', straightaway limps into the lodging house. Sue mounts the steps and peers in after him. She moistens her lip, prepares to run, then calls in a name that makes even Chris turn and tingle.

Sue wanders off into the rain. She will have to walk about the whole night, for she has no money for a bed, and the coppers are only too smart at givin' you the bum's rush if you settle down in some damn doorway!

She pulls up the collar of her disastrous coat, thinking about Chris with rage and disgust.

You've had your bellyful of this sort of life! It's time to give over and go – where? *Some*where. Get a home, a room. Clean yourself up and get a job! Once, why once you was a waitress.

@◎@◎@◎@◎

A waitress is Somebody. She got civic rights. But you, Sue, you got no claims on lawful protection. Just the opposite! They'd run you in as soon as look at you, 'cause you got no 'ome, see! That's the Law. People are put in prison for havin' no 'ome. So you'll get one, somehow. Turn respectable. Wear hat again.

She thinks of the future with deep despondency. No, you can't stand no more.

Why is Chris such a bastard to travel round with? They *could* be 'appy. But, no – the 'igh 'anded 'ound – he wants it all his own road. Like all men.

'Good Beds – Men Only'! That was just the way things went. Whatever was good was for Men Only! They always got it soft; there was always some poor bitch of a woman pathetically ready to be a mug for 'em.

She wants to cry out in her impatience and despair. She wants to get away from Chris who is crushing her life. She wants something new and strange to happen. She wishes to destroy for ever the incomprehensible and relentless continuity of all men. Good Beds – bloody Men Only!

She viciously kicks something out of her path, then stoops and picks it up. She examines her find under a gas lamp; it is a wallet crammed with banknotes – at least one hundred pounds, at least that. She walks on, bursting with laughter.

Here's the escape you wanted! Who said you never had luck? So you need never go back to Chris now, my beauty! You're free. Go where you want, you! Buy hat! Buy hundreds of hats!

She flattens her face against the window of a travel agency. You can go to America and start somethin' over there. Or you can go to Turkey and blinkin' China if you can stand that war racket and birds' nest soup!

You can open a shop. You can open the whole world. Best of all you're shot of Chris. No more goin' hungry so that he can get a bellyful. No more trampin' the town on windy nights while he sleeps on Good Beds – Men Only.

She continues gleefully on.

When Chris flops out of that lodging house in the morning *you* won't be there. You'll be Gone. Sure-o. Mug for no man!

He'll soon understand what he's lost. He'll call and call and you'll never come. You can put over a fast one as well. Take too much for granted – some blokes. Look after himself in future. How pitiful he'll be. What a hell of a mess he'll make of things. Who'll give him a wash? The dirty boozy monkey – he'd never wash if you didn't scrub him sometimes. Who'll mend his clothes and get him food? Blubber like a child without his victuals.

She suddenly brings up against a lamp-post. No. No. You can't leave him. You can't. But – why? What's a-matter, donkey? You – you don't *love* the so-and-so, do you, Sue? *Do you?*

You poor fool: it's got you all right. You'll never go to America. 'Cause you can't do without Chris. You been partners too long to walk out on him casual.

With a sharp intake of breath, Sue sees his troubled blue eyes – his dark questing face. She thinks of his hugeness, the haven of his strength that, a minute ago, was a horror to her.

Now she is in a long narrow street edged on the one side by steep, crazily-leaning warehouses, and on the other by a low brick wall below which the railway-lines stream steadily away into the country. A train bolts into a tunnel with a protesting shriek. She would like to yell with it. She, too, is doused in a tunnel – the tunnel that is Chris and all their dark tottering life together.

Tears drop out of her eyes: tears of chagrin as she perceives how she is fettered.

Why don't you take Chris with you, then? No need for all this parting. Money would make a new man of him. You daresay! He'd be a different man, dressed proper and with his worries halved. It was the life they led made him such a swipe to get on with.

Still he wouldn't thank you. It'd be tonight's tale of the shillin' all over again. He's taken money off you, with no conscience, all the time, all the time. He'd get this lot off you, an' all. That was his sort. He wouldn't change. Did the leopard?

Yes – but – he'd look lovely dressed like a toff. Then other women 'ud want him. And he'd soon give *you* the go-by if a change came in his fortune.

Get wise to yourself, darling. While Chris is derelict he'll stick to you all right, all right. But if he got wealth he wouldn't want *you*. For a handful of notes you can buy a young girl – lovely, vivacious, a-shine. That's life.

Oh gor, Sue, ain't you just perfect. You been belly-aching all night 'cause you can't live *with* Chris,: now you're belly-aching 'cause, you can't live *without* him. Oh, gor! Oh, gor! You peach! You poor mug! Life's bloody hell with him, but without him – what would you do – where would you go? It would be strange for you not to get a beating, and strange, too, without those rough hungry kisses.

Well, Chris ain't the only fellow in the world, is he? Don't forget, this money would put you among the swells. Swells take their sex with saccharine. Feather beds, soft lights, sweet music! But you couldn't do with that. You'd burst out laughing in the middle! Those people wouldn't have the same feeling for life as you. Eh – Sue? Besides, you ain't concerned with sex. Sex ain't love. Life would be a damn sight easier if it was.

So you'll never be able to leave Chris. Well – the hell! Who's talkin' about leaving, anyway? What's brought all this on? What *could* part Chris and you? Why – the money you've found; whichever way you used it, you'd lose Chris.

You got a fortune there, honey! Yes – but a fortune looks like it's going to ruin you! That's funny, ain't it! So what, Sue? So what?

See here – it'll never be 'Good Beds' for you, but I think you got strength, if it ain't in your arm. You got the courage to pay cheerfully for what you want. You're going to give up this fortune you just found, you're going to forego ease 'n' comfort, as your price to keep Chris. Well – get on with it! What you waiting for now?

Sue opens the wallet and looks for the owner's name; then she spends the rest of the night tramping to his distant address. She forces the wallet through the letter box, and by eight o'clock of the new day she is lounging against the lodging house, smoking half a cigarette she has picked up from the pavement, waiting for her 'purchase' to flounder out and probably knock her down by way of a loving greeting.

THE SUMMER HOLIDAY
Diana Gardner
1941

What insensate heat! Margot dug her elbow into a cool place in the duvet and turned the page of her novel. She had bought it on the day of publication in a bookshop in the rue de Rivoli, eager to possess it, but now she found it almost boring. Presently she laid it face down on the fold of the sheet and turned onto her back. The corners of the room, peacock blue because of the venetian blinds, seemed to her to pulsate with the heat. She shut her eyes and propped her legs on the bedrail. From the café below came the murmur of men's voices. Apparently it mattered little to the black-moustached proprietor of the hotel that the Germans had once more broken loose on France. 'They are so far off. Our army is good,' he had said. He had spent the last three evenings peeling his vine.

It did not seem to matter to Graham either, she reflected, hearing his voice suddenly below. Although to be quite fair to him he had never professed interest in the war. It was run by businessmen and fanatics, he had always said. Hitler, Chamberlain: one a crank, the other a fool! His pointed face peculiarly sallow, Graham would shrug his shoulders – a habit which he had learnt in France and which suited him. She stretched her arms above her head. What a miracle he had got that job in Paris, and with an American firm. It made them safe. They even had an American passport, because of his mother. It did not matter if the Germans did come.

The voices below grew clearer. She could distinguish Graham's: he was telling a doubtful story slowly. She waited for the climax. In the road a laden cart scrunched by. Soon the sun would slant away from the hotel and her room would freshen. Before dinner she would have a delicious cold sponge-down – and how well they fed you in France! Even after nine months of war. She did not wish ever to return to England. Over here Graham had six weeks' holiday: an English firm would have allowed him no more than three.

She smiled at the thought of how he enjoyed his fishing – bless him! The slow-flowing river, banked by eucalyptus trees, was his playground. He looked good in his white linen shorts and navy blue shirt; tanned like a Frenchman – like a native. She was his English wife – fair-skinned, blue-eyed. They were a nice couple, she felt. She dressed well, for they had no children and could therefore afford to. Oh, why on earth had there to be this ridiculous war, she thought savagely, opening wide her eyes.

As she bathed she said to herself: Hitler-Chamberlain. What a couple to get the world so mixed up. Graham was right in his detached, lazy way. Once a Frenchman with very little English, in a railway carriage, had asked him his politics. 'CO, I suppose,' Graham had replied. 'Commanding officer!

A militarist?' asked the puzzled Frenchman. 'No, a conchie,' had been Graham's answer, with an amused smile. There was a good deal of sense in those politics, she chuckled, as she squeezed the sponge out on the nape of her neck. It meant that he and she could holiday in the sun while her sister worried her life out in London, a grass widow with a husband at the front.

She put on her silk dressing gown and, winding up the venetian blinds, looked out onto the narrow street. The house across the way was now getting the sun, and below, the panama hats of two elderly Frenchmen nodded authoritatively over a bottle of red wine.

'What if the Boches do break through?' asked one querulously. Old and simple, she thought. They'll never get so far.

But over dinner – and the bifsteak was particularly good – she asked Graham what would happen if the Germans did come.

He drank his wine slowly.

'They'll never manage it, my sweet,' he smiled, showing his strong teeth. 'Most of what Hitler says is – bunk.'

But that evening a little crowd gathered round the radio and the waiters left their jobs to come and listen against the bar. The announcer read the news with an anxious ring in his voice. Paris was threatened. 'What! Already?' said Graham, 'Pretty quick work.' Thank God for an American passport, thought Margot. Tension rose in the bittersweet-smelling café. 'I think I'll go outside for a few minutes,' said Margot.

She went into the cool street. It was filled with the perfume of flowers opening after the heat of the day. At that moment a car tore by containing two staff officers. It was followed closely by a motorcyclist going at full speed. The set expression of their faces sent a chill through her.

What if Paris should fall?

She went back to Graham. He was playing cards with three men.

'You look pale, my sweet,' he said – his accent was faintly American. 'Anything the matter?'

Her heart was heavy and disturbed. 'No – I don't think so.'

They went to bed late. Although it was almost too hot to sleep Graham was soon off. Margot lay worried, staring at the pale furniture. At about three in the morning a tremendous bustle started in the road outside – the sound of lorries and cars passing almost incessantly. At daybreak she could discern the laden traffic going west.

The exodus of refugees had begun.

Next day Margot was on edge. The noise of the traffic went on all the morning. The proprietor was likely to burst into tears at any moment: France was upset, in a plight. Was the Boche to come again? Brokenly he described his grandmother's experiences in the last occupation. When he began the tale for the third time since breakfast Graham went outside.

Margot followed him. They made their way through the groups of cars and people which had begun to collect and, in the scorching sunlight, went down to the river. Graham looked carefully for the tide.

'Can't do anything before seven this evening,' he said gaily.

Margot sounded out of control: 'Graham!'

He looked up quickly.

'What's the matter with you?' She relaxed a little.

@@@@@@@@

'Oh, you know,' she waved her arm in the direction of the village – the roar of the traffic could be heard plainly. 'All that business.'

'Well, it needn't affect us,' he said gently, 'we're neutrals. You ought to thank your lucky stars you're safe.'

'I know – but –' She was not convinced. She tore up a blade of grass and began to split it. 'It is pretty momentous though, isn't it?'

'What is?'

'Well – all of it.' Why didn't Graham see? She felt they were beginning not to understand each other.

'Oh, forget it,' he said irritably, 'I'm going fishing.'

'Graham!' Her eyes were wide open.

'Well, what about it?' He waited. But she could not answer. She knew he was being quite consistent: he had never taken sides about the war. She had always known it and had never expected anything else.

'Well, what of it?' He persisted, with dark, accusing eyes.

'Oh, I don't know.'

She went limp.

'Very well then,' he said and looked at the river, 'I'm off to find a place for tonight. There's a better reach higher up.'

He walked away quietly, his brown legs swinging through the uncut grass on the river bank, his shoulders swaying comfortably.

Margot watched him for about half a mile. Once or twice she nearly called after him, but stopped – and he did not look back. Her mind now worked quickly.

When all she could see of him was his bobbing dark head above the grass on the bank she turned and hurried back to the village. The hotel was now crowded with people eager to get something to eat. As she pushed by to reach the stairs she heard a man and a woman speaking English. They were standing just inside the café door, stuffing rolls and coffee down their mouths.

She went straight up to them.

'How are you getting away?'

The man answered quickly. 'By car to Bordeaux, if we're lucky. We hear there's a steamer there.'

'Will you take me with you?' she asked calmly. 'I have nearly fifteen pounds in French money, and I can find a British passport.'

The man and woman looked at one another. He raised his eyebrows, and she answered with a quick nod.

'Our car is only a two-seater,' said the man. 'But we can manage, I think. The point is – we're going now. You'll have to buck up.'

She gave them a rapid smile.

'All right.'

She ran upstairs to her room, took out a small suitcase from the bottom of the cupboard and packed it with a few essential things. Very carefully she wrote a short note for Graham and propped it against his photograph on the dressing table. He regarded her from an angle, his pipe between his teeth, and his sports shirt open at the neck. A faintly cynical turn to the mouth struck her for the first time.

Above the noise of the traffic in the road outside she heard an impatient klaxon.

She took the suitcase and a warm coat and went quickly downstairs, past the hot and hungry travellers, into the road.

◎◎◎◎◎◎◎

The proprietor was doing his best to serve them all. When he saw Margot he called out, 'They say they are not more than thirty miles down the road. What will become of us?'

She had no time to answer even if she had wished, for the driver of the two-seater was signalling to her to hurry.

She pushed her way past a small cart piled high with a family's belongings and two bewildered children, and climbed onto the back of the car. In the heat and confusion she could not hear what the driver said to her. She just nodded. 'Hang on – that's all,' he repeated. 'We're going to make it as fast as this crowd'll let us.' She nodded again, but she had begun to feel numbed – as if it were happening to someone else.

The car started off, past the pony carts and wheelbarrows, the delivery vans and overcrowded saloons. Several had feather mattresses on their roofs, and on one a split windscreen told its own story of machine-gun bullets.

They overtook a good deal of the traffic without difficulty and soon had turned off down a short hill under some trees. It was cooler there and Margot's head began to clear.

'You all right?' called the driver.

'Yes, thanks,' she answered, clutching the back of the hood. At the bottom of the hill flowed the sun-dappled river. On the opposite bank stood a white village, surrounded by eucalyptus trees.

Somewhere upstream Graham was looking for a place to fish.

THE HANDBAG
Dorothy Whipple
1941

Mrs West had been alone for the weekend, but there was nothing new in that. William was often away. He didn't tell her
where he was going and she would not ask. He merely said
he wouldn't be at home on Tuesday, or Wednesday, or at the
weekend, or whenever it was.

But Mrs West generally managed to find out where he had
gone by going through the papers in his desk. He meant to
keep the desk locked, but he often forgot and his wife took
every advantage of that.

William had plenty of opportunity of getting away. He was
a Councillor; probably he would shortly be an Alderman, the
youngest Alderman, and probably, too, the Leader of his Party.
He was very anxious to secure these honours and his wife knew
he was being careful to keep in with everybody.

As a Councillor and a member of the Health, Education, Gas
and other committees, William attended many Conferences.
His wife used to go with him and she enjoyed them very much.
They were always held at such pleasant places, at Brighton,

Harrogate, Bournemouth for instance, and they stayed at the best hotels. The Corporation paid William's first-class expenses and he used to manage to make those do for both of them.

That was all over now. William first took to making excuses for not taking her, then he went without her without making excuses, and now he did not even tell her when or where he was going. The higher William rose in public life, the further he pushed her into the background.

She had discovered lately that he was making her out to be an invalid. People stopped her in the street to ask with sympathy how she was.

'Such a pity you weren't well enough to come to the Ball the other night,' someone would say, and Mrs West was obliged to smile and accept her imaginary illness because she would not let it be known that William had never told her about the Ball.

Dinners, luncheons, receptions, prize distributions, William went to them all without her. She knew nothing of them until she saw an account of them in the paper, with Councillor William West prominently mentioned, or until such time as she found the desk unlocked and went through the discarded invitations. All of them were inscribed for Councillor and Mrs West, yet he never told her of them and she was too proud to charge him with them.

She didn't know precisely why he behaved in this way. She thought there must be several reasons. William had always been a vain man, but the older he got the vainer he became. He was forty-eight – she was the same age, but looked older – he was handsome in a dark, increasingly florid way and

he fancied himself considerably on a platform. He liked to show off, but not before his wife. He felt she judged him. She cramped his style, she knew when he was not telling the truth. He felt freer without her.

Mrs West also surmised that William was ashamed of her. She was plain, she had no taste in dress. She had done her own housework and economised for years, though they had maids and were prosperous now. There were no frills about her, she admitted, but she had made William very comfortable and had borne with his exacting, uncertain, often foolish behaviour for more than twenty years. She surmised, shrewdly, that William valued his comfortable home, his good food, but no longer wished to be seen about with the one who secured these things for him. He was ashamed of her. She wasn't smart enough for him.

If she had been Mrs Wintersley, now, it would have been different, thought Mrs West, sitting alone over the weekend. Mrs Wintersley was a youngish widow who had lately entered public affairs and taken her place on the Council. Mrs Wintersley was smart, there was no doubt about that. She had made quite a commotion on the Council and was in enormous demand at public functions: Prize Distributions, Women's Luncheon Clubs, the openings of schools, bazaars and so on.

Mrs West had seen Mrs Wintersley many a time, though Mrs Wintersley did not know who she was. Mrs Wintersley would probably have been astonished, thought Mrs West, to discover that the plain little woman sitting at the next table at the Rosebowl Tea Rooms the other day was the wife of the resplendent William West.

Mrs Wintersley had heard Mrs West's voice, because Mrs West often answered the telephone when Mrs Wintersley rang William up. Mrs Wintersley was always ringing William up. Mrs West supposed it was all right; they were both on the Council.

At the Rosebowl Tea Rooms, Mrs West had enjoyed her obscurity and had taken the opportunity of observing Mrs Wintersley very closely. She didn't like her, she decided. She was very well dressed and very well made-up, but she had a hard mouth and restless eyes, eyes always seeking for an audience. A person, Mrs West concluded, who could not live without limelight. She was afraid William was also like that.

Mrs Wintersley, when Mrs West had seen her before, had generally been in black, but on this particular afternoon she wore becoming blue-green tweeds. Everything about her toilet was carefully chosen as usual and Mrs West noticed that even her handbag exactly matched her suit. It was made of the same blue-green tweed and as it lay on the table while Mrs Wintersley had tea, Mrs West observed it, as she observed everything else about Mrs Wintersley.

Going through William's desk in his absence over the weekend, Mrs West had come upon an invitation for Tuesday evening to the Speech Day at the Girls' Grammar School. The Address and the Prizes, the pasteboard announced, would be given by Councillor Mrs Wintersley and the invitation was inscribed as usual: 'Councillor and Mrs West. Platform.'

At the beginning of William's public career, Mrs West had often been asked to give prizes and she had managed, she thought, rather well. At any rate, William used to congratulate her in those days, when they were both new to the platform together. But of course, Mrs West thought diffidently, William had left her far behind long ago.

The invitation was for Tuesday and it was Tuesday now. On the previous day William had returned from wherever it was he had been; Mrs West had not been able to find out where this was, since there was no reference to any conference in his desk.

William was now seated at the breakfast table, buried behind the paper. Mrs West had finished breakfast and was just about to leave the table when the maid brought in the morning post. William lowered the paper long enough to see that there was nothing for him before disappearing behind it again. For Mrs West, however, there was a parcel. She wondered what it could be. She rarely received parcels unless she sent for something from the London shops. Holding the parcel on her knee, out of the way of the breakfast things, she undid the wrappings.

Within them lay, of all unexpected things, a green tweed bag.

Mrs West stared uncomprehendingly. A green tweed bag?

Then, glancing towards William and observing that he was still buried behind the paper and had seen nothing, Mrs West bundled the bag back into its wrappings and took it swiftly out of the room. She hurried upstairs, stumbling in her haste, and gained her bedroom. Locking the door, she tumbled the bag from its wrappings again. There was a letter with it. With shaking fingers she drew the sheet of notepaper from the envelope. It was headed: The Troutfishers Inn, Patondale, and was addressed to Mrs West, 3 The Mount, Lynchester.

Dear Madam, We have pleasure in returning to you a handbag found in room number sixteen after you had left this morning. . . .

Mrs West went slowly to her bed and sat down upon it. The bag was Mrs Wintersley's. She would have known it anywhere. But why had it been sent to her? Why addressed to Mrs West, at 3 The Mount?

It took Mrs West several minutes to grasp the truth. William and Mrs Wintersley had spent the weekend at the Troutfishers Inn together. A flush of anger, humiliation and hurt rose in Mrs West's faded cheek. She knew William was foolish, vain, unkind, but she had never thought, she told herself, that he would do this kind of thing. Never.

She sat on the bed, her head low.

What a fool he was! He was endangering the very thing he cared most about – his public career. Aldermen were not allowed moral lapses; at least they must never be found out. But William, fool that he was, had registered at the inn in his own name. He had done that, she knew, because of his fixed idea that everybody knew him everywhere. He would think it useless to attempt to hide his importance under an assumed name. But he would suppose, and rightly, that no one knew his wife. No one did know her. He had seen to that. It would therefore be quite safe, he would think, for Mrs Wintersley to pose as Mrs West. But she had left this bag behind – there was nothing in it but a handkerchief and a lipstick with no incriminating mark of ownership on either – and they had sent it to the address William had given in the book.

Mrs West sat on the bed, the bag beside her, turning things over in her mind.

'William,' she said at lunch. 'I think I shall go to the Speech Day at the Girls' Grammar School tonight.'

William looked up.

'I haven't accepted for you,' he said.

'That's all right,' said Mrs West equably. 'I rang up the Headmistress this morning to say I should be there.'

William frowned.

'Why should you go?' he said. 'It will be very boring.'

'All the same,' she said calmly. 'I think I shall go.'

And at eight o'clock she was there, in a moleskin coat and a straw hat with a blue rose in it, waiting in an anteroom with the rest of the 'platform' for the arrival of Mrs Wintersley. William looked put out. Mrs West knew it was because she was there, but she didn't mind. She felt quite easy and comfortable; it was someone else's turn to be humiliated now, she told herself.

Mrs Wintersley arrived, beautifully dressed in black with a tiny hat, a floating veil and a bunch of lilies of the valley pinned under her chin. She was effusively greeted by everybody, including William. Mrs West stood apart, but when the Headmistress, in her Oxford hood, reading out the names of the guests and their places on the platform came to the name of Mrs West, that lady saw Mrs Wintersley turn sharply in astonishment. Mrs West felt her prolonged stare of amused surprise, but she herself continued to smile imperturbably from under her straw hat. Let Mrs Wintersley smile while she could, she thought.

Mrs West found that she had been given a place of honour next to Mrs Wintersley, with William beside her. Nothing could have been more convenient to her purpose.

'Shall we go?' said the Headmistress.

As they filed out, Mrs Wintersley fell back to speak to William West.

'I left my bag behind at the inn,' she said in an undertone.

'Good Lord,' he exclaimed. 'How did that happen? I thought women never moved without their bags.'

'It wasn't the one I ordinarily use. It was the one that matches my tweed suit. There was nothing in it.'

'That's better,' said William. 'Well, I'll write and ask them to return it to the office.'

Mrs Wintersley's face cleared. She advanced, amidst a burst of handclapping, to her place on the platform.

Mrs West followed her. It was quite pleasant, she thought, to be at one of these affairs again. She liked the rows of young faces below her, the palms beside her, the flowers, the long table covered with a ceremonial cloth and piled with suitable literature, silver cups, shields and medals.

Behind the front row of the platform there were other rows containing people of less importance, minor councillors, school mistresses, and so on.

The Press took flashlight photographs of Mrs Wintersley with Mrs West small beside her and William towering beyond. The platform then sat down and the school sang its opening song.

The Headmistress came behind William and asked him, in the absence of the Mayor, to propose the vote of thanks to

Mrs Wintersley later. William nodded importantly, exchanged a glance with Mrs Wintersley and began to make notes on a small card concealed in the palm of his hand.

After the song, the Headmistress announced that she would read her report.

While she read, Mrs Wintersley sat gracefully, conning her notes or smiling at the girls. Mrs West rather grimly regarded her. She did not hear a word of the report. It was over before she realised it and she had to hasten to join in the applause.

There was another song. Mrs Wintersley received a few whispered instructions from the Headmistress. The address, Mrs West had long ago noted on her programme, was to be given next, before the distribution of the prizes.

The song ended; the school sat down again. The Headmistress rose to announce that she had the greatest pleasure in asking Mrs Wintersley to give her address. A few words in eulogy of Mrs Wintersley and the admirable work she was doing in the city followed and amid great applause Mrs Wintersley rose.

She stood there, waiting for the clapping to die down and Mrs West looking up at her, saw the confident smile and the sparkle in her eyes. Mrs Wintersley was collecting her audience; she was enjoying herself.

At a sign from the Headmistress, the applause ceased. There was silence, a hush of expectancy. Mrs Wintersley, with a slight cough, laid one finely gloved hand on the table and in her ringing voice began:

'Ladies and gentlemen. Girls.'

She inhaled a long breath.

'I am very glad . . .' she said.

As if she were tired of holding it, Mrs West brought from under her voluminous moleskin sleeve a wholly unsuitable green tweed bag and laid it on the table beside the prizes.

'I am very honoured,' Mrs Wintersley was saying, 'to have been asked to come here tonight . . .'

Distracted by the movement on the table under her eyes, Mrs Wintersley, frowning in annoyance, glanced down. She came to a dead stop. Her voice dying on the listening air, Mrs Wintersley stared in as much horror at the green tweed bag as Macbeth at the apparition of the dagger.

With an audible gasp, she put out a shaking hand towards it. The platform, the school, craned in amazement to see what it was that had so affected her. The Headmistress stood with a petrified stare. William West half-rose to his feet, watching the approach of Mrs Wintersley's hand towards the green tweed bag. But on the very point of touching it, Mrs Wintersley suddenly snatched back her hand as if something had burnt it. With a hoarse exclamation, she turned on Mrs West. But the sight of that lady smiling imperturbably from under her straw hat seemed to complete Mrs Wintersley's strange collapse. She whipped round, turning her back on the school, presenting a convulsed face to the platform.

'I . . . I . . .' she stammered. 'I can't go on . . . Something . . . I'm not well. I'm . . . Let me pass, please.'

Plunging through the chairs, the occupants of which got hurriedly up to make way for her, tripping clumsily over the red drugget laid down in her honour, Mrs Wintersley rushed headlong from the platform. In the staring silence, her smart hat awry, her veil flying, her high heels rattling loudly over the

wooden floor, Mrs Wintersley fled down the length of the hall, followed, to the astonishment of all, by Councillor William West.

As they made their amazing exit through the door at the end of the hall, uproar broke out. Five hundred girls, their parents and the occupants of the platform burst into excited comment. The Headmistress, stern, drawn to her full height, struck on her bell. But silence did not follow. Confusion continued to reign. The Headmistress advanced to the front of the platform and with lips compressed struck the bell again and again and again. She struck until the tongues were still and all eyes upon her. Then calmly and coldly she spoke:

'Mrs Wintersley is evidently indisposed,' she said. 'But she will be adequately taken care of and our programme must go on. There will be no address. We shall proceed at once to the distribution of the prizes. Er . . .' The Headmistress faltered in her turn. She looked uncertainly behind and around her. Who could give the prizes now? Who was there important enough? She stood there, at a loss. Mrs West leaned forward from her place, smiling helpfully. 'Shall I give the prizes?' she said.

PEOPLE DON'T WANT US
Janet Lewis
1943

Kathryn Douglass watched the children go down the road
to meet the yellow school bus, saw them climb on board,
and so depart from her jurisdiction for the next six or seven
hours. It was a lovely morning, March in California. There
were new blossoms here and there in the thick new green
of the yellow jasmine. Across the road the apricot orchard
was on the verge of blossoming, all the twigs ruddy with new
sap and swollen with the shapes of buds still sheathed in
their deep red. In a day or two it would all seem white and
snow-laden.

Mrs Douglass traversed her grassy lawn, paused at the
door long enough to break a long spray from the yellow jasmine, and returned to her disordered living room. The floor
was woolly with lint; the dust was so thick on the piano that it
could be pushed up in rolls with a finger; newspaper littered
the floor, the chairs, the sofa. Standing there, with the long
yellow-blossomed spray drooping from her hand, Mrs Douglass
surveyed confusion, and the depression which she felt was not

all due to the lack of house cleaning. Related to it, yes, but not caused by it.

For a week now she had been saving up the dust for Mrs Larsen, who was to have come this morning and gathered it all up, and presented Mrs Douglass with rooms so clean that she could ignore the thought of dust again until the following Thursday. But this morning at eight o'clock Mrs Larsen had phoned that she was ill with the flu. Mrs Douglass was trying to finish a story, and she had counted heavily upon having this day to herself, at least until the hour when the children returned from school. But Mr Douglass was bringing strangers home to dinner, and it was for once imperative that the dust be removed at least from the living room. But if she began upon the living room the rest of the house would demand similar attention, and there was a company dinner to be prepared besides. The story would be shot. It added up rather badly, so badly in fact that Mrs Douglass had hunted up a long-unused telephone number and had phoned Anna. Would Anna come, for friendship, and clean house for her? She did not like to ask her to come so far. Since they had moved from the old place, she had seen Anna only on special occasions, such as the day before Christmas, or the day before Thanksgiving, and sometimes on a Sunday afternoon at the height of the strawberry season. The small faraway voice with the foreign accent had replied that Anna would be happy to come. She would come right away.

Mrs Douglass picked up the funny sheet from the floor where Billy had been enjoying it, picked up the main news section from her husband's chair, and began to restore the paper to something like its former coherence. She spread it out on the table, laying the spray of yellow jasmine temporarily beside it, and took a quick look at the headlines. As usual, that spring, they were bad. This was that spring when it became more and more apparent each day that the men at Bataan and on Corregidor were expendable, that they were being abandoned, that no help was going to be sent to them in spite of the hopes held out from day to day. There were also the usual items about the approaching evacuation of the Japanese from the West coast. Harriet's boy was in the Philippines, somewhere. A lot of the boys from Salinas had been sent there, and he was with them. Harriet was no older than she was, but had married earlier, and her first child had been a boy. So that now he was at Bataan. Billy, through an accident of time, was going to escape this war. But it was only an accident. It might just as well have been Billy who was out there.

She folded the paper. She had an impulse to hide it, before it should reach Anna's eyes, and she looked about for a place in which to put it where it might be less conspicuous. But in the end she laid it on the table, just as she usually did. After all, Anna Yoshida could read English. She was not like her old mother, who still could neither read nor speak the new language. And whether she could read the papers or not, she knew perfectly well that she had become an enemy in their midst, willy-nilly, on that Sunday morning last December.

Mrs Douglass had gone with Billy and Marion before Christmas with gifts for all the Yoshidas, as usual, except that among Christmas preparations greatly reduced by the excitement of being at war and the making of blackout curtains, the gifts for the Yoshidas were nicer than usual, for a purpose, in order to say, 'You have not become barbarians for us overnight.' The winter rains had, as usual, surrounded the small unpainted house with a quarter acre of black adobe mud. Beyond the mud the rows of celery plants stretched orderly and green, but the big field in which the strawberries used to grow had been let go to weed. The Yoshidas were not at home. The place was as deserted as if the temporary absence were symbolical of the long absence to come. Everyone knew then that 'something would have to be done about the Japanese.'

They left the presents by the front door, hoping that the rain would not whip under the porch and spoil the pretty wrappings; they scraped the gumbo from their shoes as best they could before climbing back into the car, and drove, rather sadly, away.

A short distance down the road they passed the old place, and the children, who could not remember it very well, looked at it curiously, while their mother noted further changes, consisting mostly of the absence of familiar trees or shrubs. The removal of the rose hedge across the front of the lawn made the place look neater, it was true. The bushes had been breaking down the old wire fence with their weight. But how sweet they had been in early April, the two scented pink ones, the two scentless and thornless, and the one deep damask red! They had all been so happy at the old place that Kathryn Douglass sometimes wondered why they had left it. Then she had to remind herself that it was too close to the bay, that the children woke with bronchial coughs from the low-lying winter fogs, and that the fields round about had been deep in mud and water during the winter months, like the Yoshidas' front yard. Of course the new place on the higher ground was much pleasanter, but she still regretted her old neighbours. She regretted the Yoshidas.

It was not that she was exactly intimate with the Yoshidas. Far from it. But there had been built up through the years a tenuous bond, even an affection, it seemed to Kathryn Douglass, made of experiences shared – weather and work, fear, loss, happiness, and the children. Perhaps she was fond of the Yoshidas only because they had been a part of the children's earliest years. At any rate, she never drove down the road past the old place without a pang of homesickness and regret; and now that she stood looking down at the morning paper, blackened with so much disaster and hate, she felt a great desire to protect Anna Yoshida from the actions of her race, from the weight of the times which had so little to do with Anna, or with Kathryn Douglass, or with the children playing on the grass at the old place.

It had all begun, as she remembered, the day that the cat had left home with the four new kittens. She had not left to stay, but, as Marion had said, had only taken them down the road to see the paper goldfish. It would have been a most natural thing to do, for in the yard beside the newly erected frame house down the road two poles had been set up, and from a rope stretched between the poles floated, or leaped, or subsided, according to the wind, five magnificent paper kites, in the form of carp. The wind entered at their round open mouths and puffed them out to splendid dimensions. The longest must have been six feet, the smallest at least four.

The sun glistened upon the gold crosshatching of their scales, vermilion, orange, blue, black, green, and on the round circles of their eyes.

It was May, the fifth of May, and the air was balmy, the wind not too erratic. The locust trees at the Dutchman's house had been in bloom, and their fragrance had swept the fields. Marion had followed the cat, and her mother had followed Marion. Marion wanted a fish kite. Marion was three? Or was she four years old? Her mother had to pause and calculate.

They had known that the Dutchman had leased his acres to some Japanese on a five-year lease, and they had watched the frame house being put up, unpainted, very simple, a child's plan of a house, but they had not yet spoken with any of the new arrivals. To please Marion, Mrs Douglass had gone in search of the owner of the kites. They had found Anna on her knees in the strawberry field.

A small figure in blue trousers bound close about her ankles, wearing an old-fashioned cotton sun bonnet with a ruffle at the back to cover her neck, Anna rose from her work and came to meet them. With one hand she pushed back her bonnet and wiped the sweat from her face. She had need to push back the bonnet to look up at the tall woman who was interrupting her. In her other hand she held the box into which she had been packing berries. The hand was brown and very small.

Mrs Douglass inquired about the kites. Anna shook her head. She explained. The kites belonged to her son, a first son in the Yoshida family. No, it was not his birthday, but this was Boy Day, and on Boy Day the boy's friends and well-wishers give him fish kites. These fish are the carp who do not like to live in muddy water, but who are always trying to swim upstream. They are given to a boy on Boy Day in order to teach him to be like the carp, to seek pure water and a pure life and to swim upstream. They are not given to girls.

Marion took in the fact that fish kites were not for girls and looked disappointed. Anna was sorry but firm. She offered strawberries to Marion, and Marion was consoled. Of Mrs Douglass she inquired:

'Do you have a boy?'

Mrs Douglass shook her head, feeling meanwhile the pride in this small brown woman before her that she did indeed have a boy, and a first son. Anna said, very kindly and yet a little shyly:

'When you have a boy, we will bring you kites on Boy Day.'

It was a promise, and when it was made Mrs Douglass had no way of knowing that it would ever be fulfilled. And yet when, after the lapse of years, Billy had been some eight months in this world, the Yoshidas appeared on the fifth of May, the promise was kept, and two kites, one black and gold, one gold and vermilion, flew over the Douglasses' grass plot. In the meantime, what had the Douglasses actually come to know of the Yoshidas? Very little, perhaps. What mattered was the way they felt about the Yoshidas.

The next winter Anna came one day a week and helped Mrs Douglass with the laundry and the house cleaning. It had been a piece of luck for Mrs Douglass, for the old place was so far from the end of the bus line that none of the charwomen from the town would consider coming there. And Anna took up so little space around the house. She was quiet and conscientious and cheerful. Kathryn Douglass was distinctly grateful to her. Then, as the winter approached spring, Anna excused herself. She now had to help in the fields. From the distance, as she drove down the road, Kathryn Douglass saw her figure, bent low to the ground, weeding, planting, cultivating, in the last cold foggy mornings of February, in the wet days of March. 'The mud never sticks to the Japanesers' feet,' was the saying down the road. When other people said the adobe was too wet to work, the Yoshidas kept right on with their plans.

Anna's father died in March. There were days of solemnity, according to the Buddhist rites. It was then that Mrs Douglass learned that Anna's husband, in marrying her, had consented to assume her family's name, because there was no son in Anna's family, and the name would have perished. That explained why the old Mrs Yoshida was really Anna's mother, not her mother-in-law.

The first time that Mrs Douglass saw old Mrs Yoshida she almost felt within her hands again the soft, paper-bound copy of a Japanese fairy tale which she had cherished when she was Marion's age, a story about an old woman who lost her rice dumpling and went through strange adventures in her attempt to recover it. The face of old Mrs Yoshida, brown and soft and encircled with wrinkles, was for all the world like the face of the old woman in the illustrations. Perhaps it was for that Mrs Douglass felt so fond of the old Mrs Yoshida. At any rate, without a word of any language in common between them, they got along beautifully.

Mrs Douglass had the dimmest of ideas about the Buddhist faith. She had read, once upon a time, a little book in French called *Les Paroles du Boudhha*, and had reflected that in the main the Buddha had sounded very Christian. She had a natural Western aversion to the idea of nirvana, and that was doubtless important to the doctrine, but the teaching of pity and kindliness was Christian enough. She had an idea that Buddhists were distinct from Shintoists, and she preferred Buddhists. But even in her state of occidental ignorance she could not overlook nor misunderstand the deep religious feeling of the Yoshida family at the time of their loss.

Old Mrs Yoshida worked in the fields too. The little boy played at the end of the furrows by the raised edge of the big ditch or dabbled in the wooden irrigating troughs. They were all in the fields the greater part of the day, and the house was silent and deserted.

Then, toward the end of May, Mrs Douglass heard that Anna had been taken with 'very bad pains' as she was working in the berry patch, and, although the doctor was sent for and came as soon as she could, the baby came faster, several months too early, a girl. The doctor wrapped up the little creature, so imperfectly equipped for life outside her mother's body, and took her to the hospital, where the infant was tucked into an incubator and given a mixture of oxygen and carbon dioxide.

The baby lived. When she was returned to Anna, she weighed less than three pounds, but she was healthy. They named her May, for the month in which she was born, and in order that she might have an American name when she should be ready for school. At home they called her Michiko.

Kathryn Douglass had never seen any human being so small or so exquisite. Anna came in from the fields – she had hardly been away from her work for more than three days – and unwrapped the bundle lying on the double bed.

'The hands,' said Kathryn Douglass, 'they're unbelievable!' And they were, the palm the size of a five-cent piece, the fingers with the perfection of the stamens of a flower.

She brought down later some garments which had been too small for Marion ever to wear, when she was a baby, glad that they were still fresh and untubbed and new-looking, and Anna laid them aside for the baby to grow into. Marion came too, to observe, silent and round-eyed.

They were all glad that the baby throve. Month by month she gained, making up the handicap of her early birth, until the time came when she was introduced to food other than that with which Anna's brown breast had supplied her. Kathryn Douglass was surprised and flattered when Anna came to her, asking advice about infant diet. She brought out the government pamphlet by which Marion's existence had been ruled, and underlined paragraphs for Anna, and read them to her, and then gave her the booklet; and Anna, abandoning the advice of old Mrs Yoshida, followed the instructions with conscience. Michiko was fed according to the advice of the Children's Bureau, the best American advice. When she was three years old it was hard to remember, or even imagine, how minute she once had been, how fragile, with what precarious hold on life. Brown-skinned and red-lipped, and round of face, she ran about the farmyard and the wide acres in cast off overalls of her brother Isamu. Kathryn Douglass was perhaps to be pardoned for feeling a possessive interest in her. And in the Yoshida family.

@@@@@@@@

Through the years she had come to know the interior of the Yoshida house, the big kitchen upon which all the other rooms, the bedrooms, opened, for there was no living room. In a glass vase in the centre of the kitchen table there was always a collection of chopsticks; it was like the glass tumbler full of spoons on an American farmhouse table. She knew the wood stove and the kerosene lamps, the Japanese calendars which were the only adornment of the room, the muddy shoes removed and left by the back door, the summer kitchen, windowless and cool, with big stone crocks; and, in the yard, the small bathhouse, the packing shed at the edge of the fields. She always entered the house with hesitancy, in fear of intrusion, and was always greeted with the greatest deference. It was always like entering into someplace foreign, and yet it was familiar, being so bare, so reduced to the first elements of housekeeping.

Gifts from the Yoshida fields entered the Douglass kitchen, the freshest lettuce, the biggest and greenest bunches of celery, boxes of strawberries or raspberries, and salad greens for which there were no English names and for which Mrs Douglass never could learn the Japanese. Perhaps it was a feathery green thing like carrot tops in appearance, tasting faintly like oxalis, more delicate than chicory; perhaps some other unfamiliar leaf, but always good. Sometimes Mrs Douglass bought bean curd and soy sauce from Anna, but always under protest, for the Yoshidas did not like to sell her things; they liked to make presents. That was of course very Japanese. But Kathryn Douglass liked to make presents too, and it kept up a pleasant social intercourse, full of small surprises, and

– there was no denying it – brightened the days not a little. The Douglass family remembered for a long time a Christmas gift of raspberry wine, red as no grape wine ever was, pellucid and rich and smelling like berry patches in the summer sun.

There was also to be remembered the rainy autumn when Mrs Douglass had been ill. She had been sick for a week, or longer, and the household was in confusion, when Anna appeared on the doorstep, indignant and wronged.

'You should tell me,' she said to Mr Douglass, 'because when Mrs Douglass is sick I will come and work and not charge you anything.'

He had been glad enough to have her there, but when it came time to pay her, and he was unable to force any money into her hand, he was indignant, and scolded his wife. He did not like to be beholden to people who worked so hard, who existed on such a narrow financial margin as the Yoshidas. He could afford to pay and Anna could not afford to work for nothing, he argued, but his argument had no effect upon Anna.

'Just the same,' he said, 'you shouldn't let her do it.'

'*You* talk to her,' said his wife.

Looking back upon it, Kathryn Douglass hardly knew how the affection had sprung up, and did not try to over-estimate it. The bond was tenuous, but it was there, and it held, even after the Douglasses had left the old place and moved some eight miles inland for the dryer climate. At holiday time the Yoshidas' old car drew up at the new place, or Kathryn Douglass would come home from shopping late some evening to find the porch piled with vegetables enough for a whole neighbourhood. Marion accumulated charming and semi-useless Japanese

belongings, and time of its own weight endowed small events with great meaning. Marion was practically grown up, Billy was going to school, and Kathryn Douglass no longer had a baby about the house. Sometimes she thought wistfully of Marion's earliest, staggering promenades; little and curly-headed, with such fat short legs that her mother sometimes thought she must be knock-kneed, a two-year-old Marion had a way of escaping from her mother's distinct recollection. Yet when the small image did return, coloured and clear, to Kathryn Douglass's eye, often as not the child would be standing at the edge of the Yoshidas' lettuce patch, or leaning, to watch with Isamu, the water running in the wooden irrigating troughs. So that to remember her daughter as a child was often the same thing as to remember Anna, Michiko, or Isamu.

And now the Yoshidas were to be exiled, along with all the other coastal-dwelling Japanese. Kathryn Douglass had no doubts about the wisdom of the measure. She had no theories about understanding the Japanese mind. She had never possessed any. Part of the charm of the Yoshidas was that she never 'understood' them. She was only fond of them. Yet she did not distrust them personally. She felt that it would be wise to remove all the Japanese from the coast, as much to safeguard the loyal Japanese from the consequences of the treachery of the disloyal as to protect the coast from the acts of traitors. She did not doubt that there were traitors; neither did she doubt that there were very many loyal Japanese. But she had no theories about how to separate the loyal from the disloyal. There seemed no way to X-ray a mind and find out what went on within it.

She did not know just what the Yoshidas thought about the war. Her one interview with Anna since Pearl Harbour had been shortly after Christmas. The Japanese had foreseen that they were to be moved. Anna had asked to be given recommendations for housework. She would not be working in the fields any more. The fields would not be replanted this year.

The Yoshida car stopped beyond the gate. Kathryn Douglass, still standing with her hands upon the morning's summary of tragedy, heard a small commotion of farewells, and then Anna came into the yard with her arms full of packages. She came into the living room, bent over her bundles, smiling and bowing, a small brown woman, bundled into an old brown coat, so that she looked like a wren with her feathers rounded out against the cold. Her hair was sleek and black; her eyes were bright. There was still, on her lower lip, as when Kathryn Douglass had first seen her, a kind of little blister, or scar, like a small grain of rice. She put her bundles down on the table. The paper disappeared from view.

'Anna,' said Kathryn Douglass with belated compunction, 'I forgot that you were working out this winter. Did I break into one of your regular days?'

'That's all right, Mrs Douglass,' said Anna. 'I told the lady I couldn't come today. I make it up to her some other time, maybe Sunday, when she has a party.

'I wouldn't have wanted you to do that,' said Mrs Douglass, wondering guiltily if the other lady were feeling as disconcerted as she herself had felt a short time earlier.

'That's all right, Mrs Douglass,' said Anna. 'Don't you worry about that. I told you so long time ago that when you need me I come.' She continued, shyly, 'I brought some things. You want to see them now?'

'Of course. What kind of things?'

Anna giggled. 'Oh, not much. Just some funny things for the children.'

The wrappings began to fall to right and left. Two boxes emerged, of satiny balsa wood. Anna slid back the cover of one and began to lift out little packages wrapped in crumpled tissue paper. A tree, with a gnarled black trunk and brilliant green pine needles, very small. A jointed rod with little pulleys. A black lacquered platform. A black lacquered gate or bit of fence. A little man, frozen in a pose of utmost effort, leaning back and pulling on an invisible rope. A stuffed fish. A rope. Pinwheels of gold and black. Anna smiled at the mystification in the other woman's face. She began to fit the various small things together. She was very intent. She had forgotten just how everything should be, and stood, with the fantastic little pinwheels in her hand, meditating, then seemed to remember, laid them aside, and began with the man and the gate.

The plan began to emerge, and after a few minutes there it was, a scene, mounted on the lacquer platform, of a very proud Japanese father hauling on a rope from which floated, beyond the tip of the tiny lacquered pole, a fish kite, black and gold. The pinwheels stood out from the tip of the pole; the pine tree was part of the background, and the little gate braced the pole. The father, dressed in black and purple, with his forehead blue where the hair had been shaved, and the long hair done up on the top of his head, looked as if he had come straight from an old print. He was tradition personified. The whole scene was altogether charming and exquisite. Anna stood back and admired it.

'There,' she said. 'For Boy Day. For Billy.'

Kathryn Douglass admired it too. She felt something curiously like a lump in her throat as she tried to make the proper remarks of appreciation. No other offering could have brought back so suddenly into the dolorous morning the wide fields in May and the first kites which she had ever been privileged to own. Two mothers of sons, they stood in the dishevelled room and admired the little man in all his pride and firmness.

'The other box?' inquired Mrs Douglass.

'Oh, that one? Not so pretty. For Boy Day, too, but you could give it to the girl.' Anna took out a bear and a triumphant fat little boy with flying black locks. These figures, set upon another black lacquered platform, with another little twisted tree, and some other bits of scene setting, became the tableau of an infant hero who had wrestled with a bear and overthrown him. The bear lay at his feet with his paws in the air. It was very amusing. Mrs Douglass knew that Marion would adore it.

'But, Anna,' she said, 'these were given to Isamu. Don't you think you ought to keep them?'

Anna shook her head sadly. 'No place.'

'Then let me keep them for you until you all come back again. We will enjoy them just as much.'

'No,' said Anna. 'Maybe we never come back, not here. Who knows? You take them. I like you to have them.'

She gathered up a last package, wrapped in newspaper. She said sadly, 'Onions, lettuce. You can use?'

@@@@@@@

'Of course,' said Mrs Douglass quickly. 'Awfully glad to have them. Oh, it *is* too bad that you all have to go away. We are going to miss you.'

Anna looked down sadly at the package of onions and lettuce.

'Yes, we miss you too,' she said. 'I guess it better, though. People don't want us here. We make them feel bad. So we better go.' Then she became very practical. 'You go now, Mrs Douglass, you go work. I take care everything. Don't you worry. I go work.'

In the security of the back bedroom where she kept her typewriter Mrs Douglass sat and looked at the last pages of her story. She was not in the least interested in it. Perfunctorily, she typed out a few sentences, then sat back and stared at the page.

The little man with the fish kite had looked wonderfully elegant on the piano, and the quintessence of all that was Japanese. How long would she have the courage to leave it there, after today? she wondered. Not that she didn't like it herself, or that her husband would object, or even that she was afraid of being called pro-Japanese by the neighbours, but that Harriet might come in, or some other person who, like Harriet, had felt already the bitterness of the war to its full extent. Thinking of Harriet, she could not admire herself for her own tolerance. Her husband was just a year or so too old for the Army, her boy many years safely too young; she was going to be out of it as far as most personal loss was involved. And yet Harriet was her own cousin, and Harriet's boy – well, he could never have been as close to Billy as she had been to Harriet, but still, it was mostly for that boy that she woke each morning with such a sense of desolation. There was still a chance that he might come through, of course, but how slim a chance she did not like to think.

She reread the sentences she had written and found them very dull. She tried to recast the thought in sprightlier language and the effort made her feel slightly nauseated – drained, empty, and ill. The whole business of writing stories in such times seemed so useless. Yet people did need something to read besides the newspapers, something not too far above their daily lives. Even Harriet. She would do anything for Harriet, even write nonsense. Then her cousin's drawn face crowded between her and the typewritten page.

'It is silly, Katy, to try to underestimate the danger. I might just as well begin facing it now as later. If we get him back, God knows that will be wonderful . . . if he doesn't have to suffer too much before we get him back. You don't think the Japanese love us any more than they do the Chinese? I think they hate us worse – they've been saving it up for so long. And you know what you told me about your friend, that girl who came in from Shanghai on the *President Hoover*? Remember?'

Kathryn Douglass remembered; she had told it all to Harriet. That was before there had seemed to be any danger of Harriet's having to be concerned with such terrors herself. She wished that Harriet would not remember. But Harriet insisted.

'Remember, you told me how she came out to see you, after the boat docked? She was so brave, so self-contained, so calm about having been through a bombing – several bombings – you thought she was a miracle. You gave her the best lunch you could cook – fresh strawberry shortcake, and all that, and she was so gracious to the people you had invited to meet her. I know – they were people she had asked to see – you weren't putting her on exhibition. And you sat and marvelled at her all through luncheon. Remember? And then that awful gastritis, that had her all but screaming, and she thought it was cholera, because she'd been working with the coolies before she left?'

'Of course I remember, Hattie, but don't let's talk about it now.

'Why not?' said Harriet. 'It tells me something I have to know. Corregidor isn't going to hold out forever. She was a nurse, but still she was too sick to tell you what to do for her. So you phoned the doctor. And you gave her that salt-and-sugar enema. And she began to vomit. And when it was all over and you had her tucked in bed, she began to talk. And that was just like the vomiting and the enema all over again, except that she poured it out of her memory, all the horror, the mutilations she had seen, the Chinese babies gathered up from the streets, some alive, and some not.'

'Don't, Hattie, for the love of goodness, don't remember.'

'But I have to,' said Harriet. 'For an hour she lay there and told you all those things that you told me, all those things that she had either seen herself or heard from Chinese or from other missionary nurses – and not just for Shanghai but for all China. They all knew it, those people, knew what was happening to China and what was going to happen to us, and we didn't really listen to them; not as we should have. So now I have to remember, because I don't want to go on in a daydream through the rest of this war.'

Kathryn Douglass laid her arms across her typewriter and bowed her head on them and felt almost as sick as her friend had felt. And in all her misery, suddenly she was seeing a dark evening on the road to the old place, figures gathered on the muddy ground before the Yoshidas' house, figures surrounding Anna, who stood with Isamu clasped to her breast, a small Isamu, three years old, and through the dim air she could see Anna's face, and the anguish with which she held the little boy so close to her.

'The horse kicked him,' said Anna, whispering, 'kicked his head.'

All the other figures about Anna were helpless with anxiety, and the air itself was filled with their concern, their tenderness, their pity. Well, Isamu had not died. The white scar was under his thick, soft black hair. It was all right. At least, that was all right.

With a sigh she lifted her head from her arms, straightened the pages of the manuscript which lay beside the machine, and slowly got back to work. After all, Anna had given her this morning for a purpose, and besides, there was a deadline to meet. It meant something to the Douglass finances.

About twelve-thirty she pulled the last sheet from the typewriter, clipped the story together, put the cover on the machine, and went in search of Anna. She found her on her knees, putting a lustre on the living room floor with a piece of lambskin cut from a long-discarded bedroom slipper. The room was immaculate. There were flowers on the mantel, more sprays of her yellow jasmine, and the brass andirons shone like gold; the greenery through the windows was as fresh as after rain

because the windows had been polished. The little man still balanced his weight against the pull of the fish kite on the piano. The room had never been more charming. Leaning against the doorjamb, because her knees seemed to be shaking, Kathryn Douglass considered that it would not matter that evening whether the hostess were entertaining or not. The room itself would be sufficient hospitality.

Anna looked up at her, smiling.

'I getting along fine,' she said. 'You have good morning?'

'Awful morning,' said Mrs Douglass, realising that her head ached and that she felt totally exhausted.

Anna's face looked suddenly disconsolate.

'But I finished the story,' Mrs Douglass hastened to explain. 'I can copy the rest of it this afternoon and mail it in the morning. It's all right. I just feel tired.'

'Oh,' said Anna. 'I get you quick some lunch. I proud you finish the story. I make you quick some tea.'

They went into the kitchen together. As she brought out eggs and butter, laid places for two on the kitchen table, Mrs Douglass felt that she was indeed very tired. She had returned to Anna after a vague but terrifying experience, and she felt a great desire to protect Anna from that experience. She must be careful about what she said to Anna. She sat down at the table, resting her head on her hands while Anna scrambled the eggs and made the tea. When Anna slipped into the chair across from her she could not help taking comfort from the sight of her soft brown face. Very proud, very unassuming was Anna Yoshida. It sounded like an impossible combination, but there it was. Very remote, to a foreign way of life, and yet affectionate, near, familiar. Of what age was Anna? Mrs Douglass wondered. With a skin like that, so easily wrinkled and so often exposed to the elements, it was hard to decipher the years. And the other clues to a woman's age, the way she wore her hair, or liked to dress, were entirely missing. Anna's hair was brushed back smoothly from her round forehead and pinned in a knot at the back of her neck. Her clothes were any garments which would keep her warm.

'Where were you born, Anna?' asked Kathryn Douglass.

'In Japan,' said Anna.

'But when did you come to this country?'

'Oh, long ago. I was a little girl.'

'But you did not grow up like the Nisei.'

'No, I grow up old style.'

The onions were very crisp and delicate, the tea fragrant and hot. As she sipped the tea her eyes met those of Anna above the cup, and Anna's eyes were reassuring. Mrs Douglass began to feel less tired. Either it was the effect of the tea, or of something harder to describe.

'How is Michiko?' she asked.

'Oh, she's fat,' said Anna, laughing.

They talked about the children, Isamu, Marion, Billy. 'I never finished to pay the doctor yet,' said Anna. 'I always want to. But the celery this year – everybody have such good crops, we have almost to give it away.'

'The doctor? For what?' said Mrs Douglass.

'Why, for Michiko.'

'Michiko? After all these years?'

'Yes – that very bad, after all these years. I still want to.'

@/@@/@@/@@/@

Kathryn Douglass nibbled at an onion, smaller than a pencil, crisp as snow, and thought of all the sweet crisp celery, all the big green heads of lettuce, all the fragrant berries the Yoshidas had coaxed from the Dutchman's fields since she had first known them. She thought also of how little they had asked in return, or had received, besides the privilege of living unmolested on those wide acres in sight of the mountains and in sight of the bay. She wondered if they had ever bought any new clothes. But Isamu and Michiko could go to school, walking along the dike by the big ditch across lots to the schoolhouse. It was a nice school. Kathryn Douglass knew most of the children there. They were the Manchesters, the Kellys, the Cardozas, the Combatalades, the Ferrantis, the Perraults, the Mocks, the Yoshidas. It sounded like an international settlement, but it wasn't. It was only a nice country school. On the other hand, it was heaven.

'Michiko fat,' she said dreamily. 'Imagine. Do you remember when all the things I brought her were always too big for her? Anna, did you get your licence for the car again?'

'Yes'm,' said Anna. 'We had lot of trouble with it, but I do what you say. I send white slip to Tadashi and he sign it. So it all right.'

Tadashi was Anna's nephew. He was a Nisei, and the car was in his name.

'Where is Tadashi?' asked Kathryn Douglass, off her guard.

'He in the Army,' said Anna.

So here it was again, the war. They had almost lost it. For a while two women, fond of each other, interested in each other's children, they had almost put it out of existence. But there it was again. And again she felt very tired. She said wearily:

153

'That was a nice lunch, Anna. Now I'd better go copy that story.'

'You tell me,' said Anna, 'what you want for supper, I get things ready. I fix vegetables and set table. So you lie down and rest little bit before those people come.'

'You spoil me, Anna,' said Mrs Douglass.

'I don't p'raps have much other chance to spoil you ever again may be,' said Anna.

They had been so careful. They had hardly mentioned Anna's going away. But that was foolish.

'Anna,' said Mrs Douglass, and felt her throat tighten in spite of herself, 'you must write to me, you know, and tell me what you need, and what I can get for you. I will always be so glad to do anything I can. You will remember that, won't you?'

'Yes'm,' said Anna. 'I write. I promise.'

Kathryn Douglass could see the tears in the eyes of Anna Yoshida, very bright tears in the corners of very bright, almond-shaped eyes. She blinked hard. There were tears in her own eyes.

'You go work now,' said Anna Yoshida. 'Let me get busy. This kitchen, it so dirty, Mrs Douglass, I ashamed for you.'

IT'S THE REACTION
Mollie Panter-Downes
1943

Miss Catherine Birch trotted through the lobby of the ministry where she was employed, automatically waved her pass at the doorman, and joined the hurrying throng of men and women pouring down the London street towards the bus stops and tube stations. Their haste was contagious. She began to scurry along as though a vitally important evening lay before her. Most of the other female employees of the ministry were girls with hatless manes of long, glossy hair hanging round their shoulders or setted up in red or blue snoods. The evening was warm, and they raced along bare-legged in their flimsy sandals, their bright, cheap coats hanging open. In contrast, Miss Birch seemed to be wearing a great many clothes. Her tailored suit, felt hat, Liberty-silk scarf, stockings, gloves, chubby rolled umbrella, briefcase, and sensible morocco-grained leather bag gave her something of the appearance of a schoolmistress bringing up the rear of a double column of dryads.

In the tube, the ministry faces thinned out and merged with greater London. Miss Birch stood in the packed train with her near-morocco purse pressed against the bosom of a stout matron in slacks, while her hatbrim brushed the cheek of a young American soldier who was despairingly studying the map of stations over their heads. Her mind went on fretting over that morning's row in the department. She didn't really know how it had happened. She had felt tired and out of sorts, someone's stupid inaccuracy had inflamed her, and the next thing she knew, she was having it out with Mr Danvers. After the row was over, her hands shook and her voice was weak and quavery. She went to the women's washroom before lunch, wishing that she could lock herself in and have a good howl. Nan Cruddock, from the department, was there, powdering her nose and drawing a modish square mouth over the Victorian bow with which nature had afflicted her. 'Know what I think, Birch?' Nan had said kindly as she leaned towards the mirror, while alongside her Miss Birch dabbed her cheeks with a leaf torn from a little book of papier poudre. 'Know what? It's about time you had some leave. Ask Danvers for some, go off down to the country and find a cow to look at, and for God's sake relax. If you don't, you're for the ministry heebie-jeebies – in plain English, darling, a breakdown. Heavens, I must fly!' And she had rushed off to lunch with the usual mob of people. She was a good-hearted creature, though, in spite of her flightiness, and there might even be some common sense in what she said, Miss Birch had reflected later over her solitary sandwich in the canteen. Maybe things had been working up to the morning's flare-up for quite a while.

The train filled and emptied, the American boy got out, and Miss Birch leaned against other bosoms before she got

to her own station. It was ten minutes' walk from there to Richelieu House, the block of flats where she lived. Three or four of the neighbourhood shops were still open; this district resembled a village, flowing on in its muddled eighteenth-century way round the twentieth-century blocks of steel and concrete which had grown up in it. Miss Birch called in at the little tobacconist-newsagent on the corner by the public house and bought some cigarettes. The woman behind the counter said, 'I've got your Player's this evening, but only loose – no packets. Will that do?' Miss Birch said that it would. Tucking the chubby umbrella under one arm and digging down for change, she had a sudden sociable impulse to start up a little conversation, to say something which would keep her standing there in the shop, sniffing the smell of frying that was coming out of the back room. She said in a friendly voice, 'My goodness, how your plant has grown! It's really a beauty now,' nodding towards a potted cactus which stood on a table next to a sleeping ginger cat. The woman glanced at it and said, 'Yes, it's doing well, isn't it?' Miss Birch picked up her handful of cigarettes and went out. The impulse hadn't come to anything after all. If it had been Nan Cruddock, now, she knew perfectly well that with half a dozen words Nan would have leaned over the counter and dragged that woman into her life. With a roll of those round blue eyes, she would have built up something warm and friendly in no time. It was years now that Miss Birch had been calling in for her cigarettes and never getting much beyond a 'good evening'. Never, that is, except when the Blitz was on and everything was different.

Miss Birch went on thinking about the Blitz as she walked to her own block and went up in the lift with a Mr Masters, who lived on the same floor.

'Evening,' he said pleasantly. 'Having a lovely bit of weather, aren't we?'

'Lovely,' said Miss Birch.

Mr Masters let himself into his flat which was close to the lift, and Miss Birch walked on down the passage, fumbling for her key. Behind the little black doors she could hear people talking on the telephone, playing their radios, running their bath water. No doubt all the other tenants on Floor K could hear, if they chose to listen, her footsteps ringing out now down the passageway. When she left, early in the morning, milk bottles stood outside the doors with newspapers folded on top of them. The neat, sealed bottles were like footprints discovered on the floor of an ancient cliff city, a sign that life existed somewhere in this echoing honeycomb. Except for the laughter behind the black doors and the occasional chance encounters in the lift, Miss Birch might have fancied herself alone in Richelieu House.

She opened her door, and, crossing to the window, jerked up the blind which she had prudently lowered before leaving so that the afternoon sun would not take the colour out of the blue divan cover and matching armchair. With all those pretty Chinese cushions, a guest would never have suspected that the divan was Miss Birch's bed until, seating himself, his knees flew up and hit him on the chin. There was a small gate-leg table at which she had her meals, sitting upright on a blue chair. Black-framed Medici prints, reproductions of old Italian masters, hung in an even row on the distempered cream wall above the bookcase. In the opposite wall were doors leading to a box of a bathroom and a cupboard of a kitchenette.

Miss Birch remained for a few minutes at the window, still grasping umbrella and briefcase, absently watching the barrage balloons lolling over London. They fitted in with her train of thought. She could remember when they didn't look like absurd silver jumbos browsing in space but when she had thought of them as guardians and felt consoled because they were there. By leaning to the right and twitching the net curtain aside, she could see down into the street where, five minutes or so earlier, she had been buying her cigarettes. Seen from above, the jagged space where a bomb had fallen just behind the public house was more noticeable than it was from the road, now that they had cleared the debris away. A land mine had come down, too, not far away. After that awful night, the woman at the tobacconist's had taken Miss Birch into the back parlour to show her the broken windows and the rubble dust lying thick over everything. 'It's a wonder the whole place didn't come down, and that's a fact,' she had said, fetching a packet of cigarettes up from under the counter and shoving them over to Miss Birch.

'Here you are, dear. Pop 'em in your bag. They're short, but if we don't get our smokes to quiet our nerves we'll all go barmy, more than likely.'

Miss Birch left the window and began taking off her outdoor things, noting that the evening looked settled enough to warrant leaving the chubby umbrella at home tomorrow. She hung her suit carefully on a hanger and changed into an old print summer dress which she kept for wearing at home. After that she usually laid the table for supper. When it was over, she would wash up, perhaps glance over the report she had brought home with her, mend a pair of stockings, and go to bed early with a book. It was her usual way of spending a nice quiet evening, but this evening, for some reason, she didn't feel like setting it in motion right away. Her head ached badly, probably the result of this morning's row. She went into the bathroom and took a couple of aspirins. Then she came back and sat down in the armchair by the window.

The details of the office upset flitted through her mind again, but only for a moment. Footsteps sounded outside in the corridor, a door banged, and several people seemed to be laughing and talking together. Miss Birch heard a woman's voice saying emphatically, 'But if we didn't phone we'll never get a table.' The pint milk bottle at Flat 6, just across the passage, must have had a party, which was now proceeding out en masse to find some dinner. At one time the occupants of Flat 6 had meant rather more than a milk bottle in Miss Birch's life. They were a Mr and Mrs Chalmers, and night after night in the blitz they had unrolled their mattresses alongside Miss Birch's mattress in the corridor on Floor K. Miss Birch, over a shared thermos of tea, had learned that Mrs Chalmers had married when she was eighteen and that Mr Chalmers was allergic to cats. She came to know by heart such small, intimate details as the colour of their pyjamas, the smell of Mrs Chalmers' face cream. And early in the morning, just before the all-clear sounded jubilantly over battered London, Mr Chalmers would begin to snore.

Those nights, terrible as they had been, certainly had had their compensations. It seemed to Miss Birch, looking back, that the inhabitants of Floor K had been one jolly family, recognising each other with especial friendliness among all the other prone tenants of Richelieu House. There had been little Mary Rycroft from Flat 2, a pretty child who looked as though she oughtn't to be out alone in a rainstorm, let alone a blitz. There had been Mr Masters, strolling down the row of mattresses to ask Miss Birch's help with a tough word in the *Times* crossword puzzle or to have a little chat about books. One evening he had noticed that she was reading *Nicholas Nickleby*, and the next evening he had ambled along to say that he had taken her advice and was starting on his tenth reading of *Pickwick Papers* that very night. 'You're right, Miss Birch,' he had said. 'There's nothing like the old fellows for keeping one's mind off the fellows up there,' and he had nodded towards the racket overhead. 'Pickwick seems to make 'em unimportant, somehow.' They had got really close, like old friends in those talks in the stuffy corridor, listening subconsciously for the warning scream, the sudden hole in the air, the slow glacier of bricks and mortar slipping into the street below. Now he was only a man who took off his hat politely in the lift and said 'Evening' before fumbling for his key, going in, and shutting his front door.

Little by little, as normality came back and the passages of Richelieu House were no longer filled with flitting figures carrying torches and pillows, the sense of being neighbours had worn off. Mrs Chalmers, if she and Miss Birch met in the lift, said, 'Do you know, I've been meaning and meaning to ring you,' and at the back of her worried baby eyes and plucked eyebrows, Miss Birch could see the thought forming that one of these days they must really ask the old girl over, fill her up with gin, do something about it. After a while, even that thought disappeared. Mrs Chalmers simply said 'Hello' and smiled vaguely, as though Miss Birch were someone she had once met at a party.

Sitting in the blue armchair, the headache nagging at her, Miss Birch wondered if it wasn't partly her own fault. Maybe there was something she could have said or done, some magic password which would have kept that wonderful new friendliness going. If she hadn't frightened them off, Mary Rycroft or Mr Masters might have been dropping in for a chat this evening. She pictured Mr Masters saying in his breezy way 'This is something like!' as she brought out the beer that she would make a point of keeping in the refrigerator for him. While he drank it, leaning back against the Chinese cushions and flicking his cigarette ash, manlike, over her blue rug, she would tell him about this morning's dust-up with Danvers. Telling it to him, getting his calm, man's point of view, would be a relief far greater than the good howl she had promised herself all day. He would say, 'Don't worry, my dear girl, it's nothing,' and sure enough it would be nothing. Then he would get up, glass in hand, and wander over to the bookcase. 'I might have known that you'd be the woman to read William Blake,' he would say cosily.

With sudden determination, Miss Birch stood up. She peeped in the mirror, patted a few stray wisps of hair into place, and gave a nervous twitch to the neck of her dress. Then, looking in her bag to make sure that her key was there, she opened the door of her apartment, closed it behind her, and began walking rapidly down the passage towards the lift. Mr Masters's electric bell had a different note from hers, she noticed. It sounded loud and startled, and Mr Masters also looked startled when he answered it. 'Why – come in!' he said after the faintest possible pause. Her picture of him had been correct, insofar as he was holding a bottle of beer and an opener in his free hand. He was in his shirtsleeves, and when she walked past him into a frowsier version of her own room, she noticed that his tie was lying on the table with the evening paper, some gramophone records, and a bowl of ice cubes. He made a lunge towards it, and she said, 'Oh, please don't bother to get smartened up for me! It's quite warm this evening, isn't it?'

'Feels to me as though we're going to get a bit of thunder,' he said. 'Sit down, won't you? I was just . . .' and he made an embarrassed gesture with the beer bottle and the opener.

'Do go on,' said Miss Birch. 'I do hope you don't mind my dropping in informally like this. As a matter of fact, I haven't a thing to read, and I wondered if you'd very kindly lend me a book.'

It sounded prim to her own ears, like something she might have written on a memo form in the office. Mr Masters stopped looking nonplussed and, setting down the beer, gestured to the row of untidy bookshelves against the wall corresponding to the one where Miss Birch's Medici prints hung. 'Help yourself,' he said. 'I don't know that you'll find anything much there, but you're welcome.'

She came forward and made a pretence of looking at the titles. Smiling up at him, she said, 'You know, I always think of you as a bookish sort of person. Remember our talks about Dickens and Thackeray and Trollope in the old blitz days?'

The information that she had thought about him at all brought Mr Masters' surprised expression back again. 'Oh, those,' he said uneasily. 'Well, thank God that time's a long way back now. Seems like a nightmare, doesn't it? I don't believe we'll ever get 'em coming over like that again, either.'

'Oh, I hope not,' said Miss Birch.

With lightning, cruel clarity she knew that the visit wasn't going to come off. Nan would have been sitting down within two minutes in the one armchair in the place, crossing her legs above the knee, sharing Mr Masters' beer, smoking his cigarettes, roaring with laughter at jokes that wouldn't be bookish quips about Trollope and Thackeray. Miss Birch, peering blindly along the shelves, was tongue-tied. She pulled out a volume without even bothering to look at its title and straightened up. 'Might I borrow this?' she asked. There didn't seem to be much more to say. Mr Masters became heartier and obviously a good deal relieved as he accompanied her to the door. 'Any time you want to borrow another, just pop along,' he said.

Miss Birch's room seemed very still in the evening sunlight as she let herself in. She walked over to the window and stood looking out again at the silver blimps floating aimlessly against the sky. London looked beautiful in this clear light, calm and radiant, as though its sirens would never sound again this side of the grave. Listening to that implacable silence, Miss Birch felt the delayed tears stinging at the back of her throat and nose. 'It's the reaction,' she said aloud, as though she were defending herself to someone. 'You can't go through month after month of that and not get a reaction sometime.' She dropped Mr Masters' book into the chair and became suddenly busy, laying the checked cloth on the gate-leg table and putting the milk for her cup of Ovaltine on to boil. It was going to be another nice quiet evening after all, she thought hopelessly.

TELL IT TO A STRANGER
Elizabeth Berridge
1944

The war had been on nearly three years when Mrs Hatfield, on one of her periodic visits home, found a young reserve policeman whistling on her front doorstep and leaning against the splintered door. He had news for her: the house had been ransacked. After a moment's coldness in her stomach, Mrs Hatfield raised her eyebrows.

'Perhaps you would allow me to come in and see for myself,' she said.

The young policeman knocked the door open and stood aside for her. He wondered how long she would take to dissolve into an understandable hysteria. But she went through the whole house, noting silver ornaments missing, seeing the drawers pulled out, photograph albums and old accounts lying with West Indian shells over the floor. Upstairs her linen savagely mauled, cashmere shawls gone, the one good fur cape. Cut glass bottles, beautiful wineglasses that responded finely to a flick of the thumbnail – this seemed the full extent of the haul. In her bedroom she stood in silence a long while. She saw that although her carpet was ripped across one corner it could be repaired. This was not a total loss – but by the evening it would be, when she told the story to her fellow guests at Belvedere. The policeman was saying: 'Helped himself to the whisky all right. Sergeant finished off the rest,' he grinned amicably. 'Must've worked in a raid,' he said, and again grinned, this time in admiration. 'Some nerve.'

Really, thought Mrs Hatfield through her preoccupation, if he wasn't a policeman I do believe he would become a criminal. She said curtly: 'I suppose you would like a list of the things missing?'

'Well, you don't have to do it at once, ma'am.' He was a little put out by her lack of emotion. 'But I'll have to ask you to step round to the station with me to have your fingerprints taken . . .' That touched her, pricked the present into her calm, and he felt obscurely pleased. It always got them that way. A look of horror, of flinching, came into her eyes. Again, the thought of the evening comforted her – how would they take it, she wondered.

'That's quite all right,' she said, and without another look at the furniture, now stripped of its shrouds, she went out into the streets with him.

That evening on the train she felt even more exhilarated than when she had seen the dogfight in the sky. How they had listened as she described the tiny metal flashes high over the town, how they had sighed when the smoke poured out, like lifeblood into the clear sky.

Mrs Hatfield had moved out to Belvedere just before the bombing started, when it was a not very successful guest house,

despite the palms in the coffee room and the planned garden. But when the guests at the promenade hotels saw the sun pick out the bitter spikes of barbed wire set in concertina rolls along the beach, and heard the cry of rising gulls as shells whistled deadly out at sea, every room at Belvedere was taken, and an annexe planned.

Sitting back in the blue-lighted train, Mrs Hatfield thought back over those two years. There was no doubt about it, she was a happier woman, more alive than she had ever been. It's a dreadful thing to say, she told herself, but this war's been a blessing to some. Hastily she brushed away all thought of the shadier blessings, and fixed firmly on the unemployed. You're happy when you're working, she thought. As the train stopped, the jerk shattered her conclusion: Jack had hated working. Although in the colonies you never did much anyway. I never could please him, she thought with sudden pain. She pleased the others, her friends now. Mr McAdam, Miss Blackett, Doreen, and Mrs Kent. She almost loved Mrs Kent, for indirectly all her happiness hinged on her. For if she had not kept on with Belvedere – Mrs Hatfield almost shuddered.

'I've been ransacked, my dears, everything –' slowly the train slid on its way, like a cowed animal, unobtrusive as possible. Then from the outer darkness the rise and fall of a distant siren swept across the country, starting from the coast, and as in a relay race, handing on the warning to towns nearer the capital.

For a moment Mrs Hatfield felt panic, the country lay so dark either side of the track and there was no stopping. The clank and swing of wheels over points drowsed her into a numb sense of security. This could go on forever, this invisible rushing through dark fields, wooden stations, hidden towns – it was all so effortless and smooth. She lifted her feet and looked at them; they were not walking, yet she was being carried incredible distances.

Almost imperceptibly another sound wove itself into the darkness, a gentle hum-humming, fast gaining on them. The train attempted to go even faster, but at this the humming increased until the whole countryside lay petrified under the heavy throb-throb-throb. Deliberately, delicately, the air rushed down, and somewhere to the right earth fountained up like oil from a gusher. Again, nearer the track this time, and clods of rich meadow grass and clay fell heavily onto the roof of the train, plastering windows and doors. A third and fourth followed swiftly, the full effect dulled by the soggy earth. Then came machine-gun fire, sharp and tearing as sudden rain on corrugated iron.

'This is war,' thought Mrs Hatfield, and her heart lifted and throbbed in time with the great steel heart in the sky. But her feet were cold and numb and hung heavily on to the floor. She heard the guard go by, calling in a low voice, as if fearful of being overheard, 'All blinds down. Screen all lights. Jerry overhead.' He repeated this with flat authority as he ducked along the corridor. How stupid, thought Mrs Hatfield; she almost laughed, a dry bad-tasting tremor of her tongue. Who else could it be? Doggedly the train went on. Passengers, white-lipped, told each other it was impossible to hit a moving object in the dark. Besides, the Hun flashboards weren't fitted with proper sights, everyone knew that.

In her compartment Mrs Hatfield sat erect. For a moment she felt almost petulant; this was too much to tell. She could not allow this episode to crowd out the other. I have been ransacked, she told herself firmly. My beautiful wineglasses, Jack's last present to me. But she was listening to the sudden quietness, the suspense throughout the whole train, spreading from carriage to carriage. The hum-humming was growing less. It was lost in the nightwind.

Immediately the corridors were filled with strung voices, some jaunty with relief, others low and shaken. The train had stopped. 'Good heavens,' said Mrs Hatfield aloud. 'This must be my station.' She called from the doorway to make quite sure, and then got out of the train. It drew away silently, some of its windows broken by bullets which were now souvenirs. She watched it go, her ears still blocked with the noise of the thrumming sky.

Shaking a little, she went over the humped bridge and along the road. Overhead the wires sang between her and the faint moon, cold as the rime on the hedges.

'I'll be better when I get home,' she thought, and it warmed her to speak of Mrs Kent, of Belvedere, as home. They were waiting for her, she knew it, waiting for her to walk in between the palms and bring them news of the world at war. News without the slickness and positivity of the radio, the newspapers, which contained, as they felt, an oblique reproach.

She had something to tell this time. Here was some real news, directly touching her, and through her, every person at Belvedere. The war had at last affected them personally; they were no longer grouped outside it, they shared in the general lawlessness. Lack of respect for property. What are we coming to? Police finishing off the whisky, wouldn't be surprised if, and so it would grow, filling more than an evening, filling the days, recreating their lives, and more important, affirming their belief in the past.

As Mrs Hatfield hurried down the lanes she felt exultant, almost like an envoy back from untold perils. She looked ahead and thought: I must have come the wrong way. For there was a glow in the sky. A haystack, she thought again. Then she stopped thinking and hurried on, for somehow she knew it was not a haystack burning, and she never came the wrong way.

She ran into the drive of Belvedere, and said stupidly, 'But there's nothing there.' It was the wooden annexe burning, the flames driving back the ambulance men and village firemen.

'You can't go any nearer, ma'am,' said one of them, struggling with a hose.

'Where are they?' asked Mrs Hatfield. She was white and the bones showed through the flesh of her cheeks. The man shook his head and motioned to the heaps of bricks and blazing rafters. 'Better ask the ambulance people,' he said, and wrenched the hose round.

'They can't drop bombs on Belvedere,' cried Mrs Hatfield, with tears suddenly released and streaming down her face. She started to shout, to drown the flames with noise, 'Doreen! Mrs Kent! I've got some news – some news –' One of the ambulance men came over from a group of silent people.

'Now then, now then,' he said, 'we're doing our best. Got one or two out, but they can't do much until the fire dies down.'

Mrs Hatfield ran to the stretchers she saw on the ground. A maid, one of the newer arrivals, a porter. 'Chance in a million,' she heard one of the onlookers say.

'I've been ransacked,' said Mrs Hatfield to herself, gently, conversationally, 'ransacked.' She looked round at the people staring at the fire. They would not care. She ran up to a pile of rubble – maybe it was the lounge – and started to tear away the bricks and glass. As the hole grew deeper a childhood tale flashed through her mind. The Emperor has ass's ears, the poor little barber who had to shout his secret into the earth, and the song of the corn repeating it. The Emperor has ass's ears.

The firemen watched her incredulously.

'There's pluck for you,' said one. 'Poor old girl, friend of hers, I suppose.'

He went over to her. It was singeing hot even here. He seized her beneath the armpits.

'You can't!' he shouted as the flames found fresh ground.

Mrs Hatfield looked up at him.

'My lovely wineglasses,' she said.

THE TWO MRS REEDS
Margaret Bonham
1944

Lucy's quick moving, her air of confidence, sat oddly on a new patient; when she came through the swing door of the ward, on the rebound of Sister's advance, the six women in maternity looked at her with a touch of curiosity. Her manner towards the dragon Sister might almost have been called matey. If they had not already graduated from labour to convalescence the women would have found encouragement in this brisk and competent attitude; as it was, they sensed in her a kind of liaison joining staff and patient. Suspended still between the world and the ward, Lucy was part of neither and of both.

Lucy herself was aware of this division more than they. Her labour had not begun; not yet by circumstance made passive in bed, she refuted the passive role of a walking patient, using her medical knowledge, her familiarity with hospital routine, as a lever to ease herself halfway on to the staff. This was her second child; she knew her way. At the birth of her first two years ago she had made herself remembered less by the difficulties of her confinement than by her passionate clinical interest in its stages. Her questions were not of the kind to be fobbed off with 'Never mind, dear'; she knew too much; she would be answered. Now this familiarity, this gulf of knowledge, separated her from the ward. Talking to the women while she unpacked into her locker, Lucy sensed the total difference of attitude, which was in part emphasised by Sister's remark as with a plate of green and red pills she flashed past the almost exclusively literary content of Lucy's suitcase: 'Mrs Furneaux, dear, are you here for a baby or a reading course?' Not only this, but Lucy seemed to treat her pregnancy with irreverence; showing unnatural bravado in the face of nature, she ran up the ward in Sister's absence, climbed on windowsills to adjust the ventilation, and got on her bed with a sort of vault. The women were amused, but a little shocked. It was to them no less eccentric that Lucy should take pleasure in the surroundings, the atmosphere and the smell of hospital, in their eyes a kind of prison from which God speed their release. When Lucy, saying she was cheesed off with smocks, had gone to change into a dressing gown the thought circulated unspoken, she'll tell a different story when she starts; but they only half believed it.

Once in her dark wool gown severely corded round what she hoped would soon be her waist, Lucy felt herself entirely an initiate; her clothes from the world were laid aside. Now she was at last severed from reality, from responsibility quite cut off, bound for a period into the rule and routine of women, as if in a clinical convent. By teatime she was on terms with everyone; with the nurses, who found her as knowledgeable as an extra nurse; with the patients, whom she amused by her excessive activity. She became no longer part of neither world, but an intimate of both.

By morning the ward had come round to the view that she would have her baby with the same competence. There was no surprise when she breezed into the kitchen at half past eleven saying her contractions had begun; the word pains was omitted from Lucy's vocabulary, she said it had the wrong psychological effect. With unabated energy she came back to the ward and brushed her hair, tied it from her face with a black ribbon, went off to the labour room as unconcernedly as to the bath. The women were deeply interested in the progress of Lucy's confinement, exacting bulletins from the nurses. At noon Nurse Field told them Lucy was arguing with Sister that she was having second stage contractions, a theory which was ridiculed by Sister but subsequently proved to be accurate. At half past twelve Lucy had eaten her way through roast mutton, turnips and rice pudding, at one she had told Nurse Howe that it was not painful and all a question of psychology, and at one-fifty, refusing an anaesthetic, she had produced a daughter and argued with Sister about sitting up to look at it. If it had not been for their acquaintance with Lucy; and for the fact that no sounds had indeed issued from within the labour room except an occasional buzz of hilarity, the women would have been incredulous; but they could not in any case dispute the panache of her return to the ward, delayed till teatime by the arrival of visitors at two. By that time one might almost have expected Lucy to walk back; even her bed, propelled by Sister and Nurse Field, seemed to move at speed unlike the beds of other patients. Lucy was still amiably arguing. Re-established

177

in the corner farthest from the door, provided with a large tea, she began to tell everyone about how she had enjoyed herself. After that she leaned on her elbow and wrote letters very fast. Sister went off duty and the social temperature rose.

Between seven and eight was the visiting hour for husbands; here again circumstance and conditioning separated Lucy from the others. Their men were all in the Forces, some on leave, some abroad; Louis was a farmer. That in itself was barely eccentric; but the man was not only agricultural but French, and not only that but he and Lucy behaved with a facetious disregard of all the conventions of affection; for the hour of his visit they laughed, argued, insulted each other happily in French and English. The other husbands who were on leave almost knelt by their wives' beds. When Louis departed, telling the nurse his baby was a fright, Lucy felt she had become in the eyes of the ward finally inhuman. The affection they felt for her was the affection one gives to a pet monkey. But encircled in knowledge, unbroken by emotion, her relationship with the staff remained normal; she was the best patient.

When the visitors left an air of anti-climax, of boredom, settled on the ward. Books seemed unreadable; babies and bedpans precluded an early retiring for the night. Disinclined to read and now fettered with the realisation that for nine days she was condemned to inactivity as surely as if she were in chains, Lucy watched through the long windows the light dissolving to dusk over the distant harbour. Approaching night was one of the less pleasing moments in hospital; with the drawn curtains, the lights, the conscription of staying in bed and the routine of sleep came a sense almost of claustrophobia. Before

the babies were brought in a new patient arrived; but since she went straight to the labour room the only stir she caused in the ward came indirectly from Lucy, who, when Nurse Field told them Mrs Reed was getting on nicely, said vaguely, 'I used to be called Reed too.'

'Before you were married?' said Mrs Skilling from the opposite corner.

'My first husband,' said Lucy, dropping another minor bomb; seeing that everyone wondered and no one cared to ask when and where he had been killed, she added, 'I divorced him.'

The other patients looked at her as though she had said, 'I ate him.' Mrs Skilling, recovering neatly, called from her corner, 'Was he a bad lot, dear?'

'He was six jugs of a pig,' said Lucy. Sitting up in bed in a white silk jacket buttoned to the neck, with her black hair tied like a child's and the grey tulips Louis had brought on the locker beside her, she had an air of such expensive innocence that it was difficult to believe either in the birth of her baby eight hours before or in a Past containing a criminal and discarded husband. (All the women concluded Mr Reed had been a monster, had probably and at the least beaten his wife; casual unpleasantness was meant to be suffered, not brought into court.) Fearing lest Lucy had feelings after all – though this hardly now seemed possible – they would not enquire further. Lucy in fact would have been quite happy to tell them about the maddening Thomas Reed, and indeed had opened her mouth to say she hadn't been able to stand being called bohemian every time he opened his, but the babies postponed her confidence. All the women wanted to see Lucy's daughter; and though Lucy and Louis had agreed that to anyone with an objective view it must be clear how like a little ape she was, they all said, 'Bless her, she's lovely.' With this extrovert vision Lucy was aware that almost all the babies, ugly though they might be, were better-looking than hers. She was not dismayed; her first child, Guy, even more simian at birth, had quickly grown into beauty; this baby with the same heritage would change after the same fashion. Nevertheless at present it *was* a fright. Lucy said so; no one believed in her conviction.

About three o'clock in the morning they brought in Mrs Reed; the wheels of her bed squeaked, effectively waking the ward. She came in like any patient except Lucy, quiet in the faint light from the passage, flattened; the line of her body hardly raised shadows in the counterpane. Lucy, irrational in her disturbed sleep, took an instant dislike to her. Through one prejudiced eye she watched Mrs Reed trolleyed into place next to her own bed, hovered over; left in the mystic silence of someone who has gone through it with the wrong psychological approach; her nose is too sharp, she said to herself, and turned over, and slept.

In the morning (not the false dawn of tea and washing, temperatures and babies and bedpans from a quarter to five till six, but that moment when you woke again to the full sun and finding yourself in the middle of the ward with a chair on your feet and the day staff sweeping where your bed had been) Lucy's attitude to Mrs Reed became one of a fainter and more reasoned antipathy. It was difficult to dislike people whole-heartedly till you had heard them speak. Mrs Reed, though she recovered quickly from being flattened and soon had knees and feet under the counterpane like everyone else, seemed disinclined to open her mouth. Lucy and the other patients proffered the amiable trivialities; 'Yes,' said Mrs Reed, or 'No.'; but that was all. Whatever Lucy's moral views might be, her social code was strict; if for no other reason than that life should be as pleasant as possible she believed in the duty of man towards man, that one should shut doors behind one, give up one's seat in the bus, eat silently, and bear one's part in the conversation with as much ease and animation as one could command. People who did none of these things, Lucy considered, were socially about as useful as bedbugs. Giving her the benefit of her condition, Lucy shut up till Mrs Reed should see fit to make a move; it was now up to her.

In any case, when one talked, one talked to the whole ward; conversations with the next bed had a way of becoming immediately general. When the subject was not confinements it was children, homes or knitting; though she was seldom unwilling to talk, it was not long before Lucy would have enjoyed a change to books or politics; but here there was no common ground. She was not much interested in other people's children; she liked the wrong kind of house and she did not knit. Nevertheless she discussed bed-wetting, three-piece suites and cardigan patterns as if all were familiarities in the Furneaux household; in the intervals she read something heavy, and wished she could be allowed to smoke.

The following afternoon (Mrs Reed being apparently in excellent health but still tacit) Lucy was sitting up in bed vaguely thinking about her. Spring sunlight flooded the ward through the high windows, lay in pools on the polished amber wood of the floor; Louis's grey tulips stood curling open on the centre table with white narcissi on either side. Sister was off duty and the nurses laughed in the kitchen. While Lucy's senses were enjoying the sun and the ward, and her hands were occupied in cutting cord dressings from a roll of lint, her mind was busy putting Mrs Reed into a catalogue of types. Mrs Reed's nose was not as sharp as Lucy had first thought, but her hair was lank and looped into a knot and she had an emotional look in her eye when her baby was brought in, which Lucy mistrusted. She wore a mauve bedjacket knitted in a shell pattern. Always cleaning the house, Lucy said to herself, lace tablecloths, probably goes to chapel, doesn't smoke, drink or paint the face; doesn't lose her temper with children; has little weeping scenes in corners hidden away where someone will find her; no, let me not be malicious as well as an intellectual snob, cross that out, but I fear she's a prig all the same. Pleased with her classification, Lucy finished the cord dressings and lay back enjoying the sun, the ward, the absence of household cares, and everything else except the wireless. As soon as Sister went off duty someone asked one of the nurses to switch it on. Lucy and Sister were united in a dislike of jazz; as soon as Sister came in she switched it off. For this Lucy felt a positive affection towards her; which in Lucy was a good deal; and everyone else liked her less, which was very little indeed. Now condemned till five o'clock to hear jungle noises or worse, Lucy sighed and abandoned the thought of reading the *New Statesman*; instead she reached for her dressing case, combed her hair, tried out a new candy-pink lipstick and voiced again her need for a cigarette.

'There's gasping I am for one too,' said Mrs Reed, as suddenly as if someone had at last wound her up.

Lucy's social code deserted her; she looked for a moment almost stunned. The fact that Mrs Reed had in one sentence clicked out of the catalogue was not the only surprise. 'You're Welsh,' said Lucy accusingly.

'Machynlleth,' said Mrs Reed, sounding like a block in the cistern.

Her grounds for dislike thus doubly cut away from under her feet (for unlike most of the English she loved the Welsh), Lucy had to reconsider Mrs Reed in the light of her nationality and her vices. The picture was quite altered. She was for once glad of the wireless which enfolded them in intimacy; the rising, singing notes of Mrs Reed's accent were a kind of substitute for the music she would have liked to hear. They talked of Wales.

'My first husband was called Reed, too,' said Lucy much later.

'There's coincidence, now,' said Mrs Reed; 'a lucky name it's been for me. Glad I am of the day I met mine, indeed. Was he nice to you?'

'Horrible he was,' said Lucy, who had been trying out a Welsh accent under Mrs Reed's tuition. 'So I divorced him,' she added in her normal voice.

'I would do it myself if it was like that,' said Mrs Reed; 'wasting time it is to stay together when you don't get on.'

'Wouldn't you get cheesed off if your husband kept telling you how to run the house?'

'I would indeed.'

'Not I must say that my housekeeping is very polished,'

said Lucy. 'I expect I don't feel about it the way I should; but that's no reason to keep telling me I ought to live in a caravan. Rudeness I can't stand, can you? Anyway there wasn't anything we did agree about, except parting.'

'Very young you were when you married him, isn't it?'

'Nineteen.'

'What can you expect, now? Twenty-eight I was. Old enough to know my own mind, and no better husband than Tom could I hope for.'

'Tom?'

'Thomas his name is; what was yours?'

'Daniel,' said Lucy rather wildly; a sudden irrational and absurd conviction held her. Impossible as it seemed, it was the sort of thing that would happen in any events involving Thomas; and, malice apart, this was their part of the country; it was not unnatural that Thomas should have returned here after they parted in London. Lucy began to stack the pile of dressings, scissors on top, saying with the same uninflected interest, 'What does he look like?'

'Here he is, see,' said Mrs Reed, diving into her locker and throwing across to Lucy a photo of Thomas that almost turned her up. He was wearing a uniform, and saying to the photographer, Man, look at the *dust* on your camera. Lucy murmured something; what it was she never knew. Years of social training came to the rescue, and with a feeling she was going to see the funny side of it any moment she said, 'What a magnificent piece. Mine was fair.'

'Very dark Tom is. There's a joke it would have been,' said Mrs Reed, laughing, 'if they were the same.'

Lucy gave what the women novelists call a mirthless smile, saying, 'Where's he stationed?' All unselfish thoughts of Mrs Reed's married happiness were discarded; she prayed for Burma.

'Bristol,' said Mrs Reed. 'Coming on leave any day he'll be, and mad to see the baby.'

'Tea, Mrs Furneaux, dear,' said Nurse Howe, slapping the bedtable across Lucy's knees and stopping to look at her. 'Feeling all right?'

'I've got indigestion,' said Lucy quickly. Her mind more than occupied with Thomas, she took four piece of bread and butter and a slice of cake off the tray and ate her way through them while all the awful and embarrassing potentialities of the situation revealed themselves, one after the other, in turn. On and off she giggled. She thought of Thomas's face when he was confronted with both his wives side by side, in adjoining beds. Lucy would have given a lot to see that; but it was finally off the menu; she had gone too far with her maligning of Thomas and now she was committed to a Past with a fair man called Daniel. She began to feel like someone in an early film, tied to the rails before the oncoming express. Whatever happened, whether Thomas could through some agency be warned beforehand, or whether Lucy could contrive to be asleep with the sheet over her face, there she had to stay in bed. Mrs Reed must in any case remain innocent of the fact that she had wedded Lucy's leavings. The awful part was that there was simply no privacy to be had; impossible with Mrs Reed three yards away, to confide in one of the nurses and get her to snap up Thomas at the entrance doors. Lucy hoped Thomas would have the grace to send his wife a telegram; this she doubted, knowing him; but in any case he could only come within certain hours, and for those periods, Lucy decided she would have to sleep. Boring it would certainly be, odd it would surely look to everyone else since she had never yet slept during the day, but there it was; it just showed, if any confirmation were needed, that she should never have married Thomas.

The second Mrs Reed must have done some licking into shape when she took over; for Thomas did send a telegram. It arrived the next morning, and throughout the next day Lucy watched Mrs Reed grow perceptibly younger, less lank and sharp, emerging as an almost pleasing creature. When Lucy had married Thomas, then a clerk in her father's firm, it had taken her no more than three weeks to see through his alluringly dashing manner to their total lack of tastes in common. They had been brought up in different worlds; they had no bonds. Now with the experience of eight years behind her, Lucy begun to understand that circumstance and not Thomas had been the trouble; it was in Thomas to be a good husband of a kind, and it seemed he had found the right wife. The second Mrs Reed would like the things he liked, keep his house immaculate, give him all the lace mats and sustaining meals and potted ferns that Lucy had wanted to throw at his head. All Thomas wanted, for his part, was a nice, safe, affectionate, bourgeois existence; Lucy, with her books, her Salvador Dali on the bedroom wall, her communist friends who wore red ties or (even worse) no ties and her desires for mushrooms cooked in vermouth at two in the morning, had brought him to the edge of the bohemian abyss. Having thought this out,

Lucy felt a little more amiable towards Thomas; but not much; she could not forgive the caravan.

The day passed in its pattern. At intervals Lucy said she felt tired; cursing Thomas, she lay down in the afternoon and pretended to sleep, so that no one should think it odd if she slept again from seven till eight. It was not Louis' night for a visit; there was a late bus only three times a week. Before seven o'clock and the moment the after-supper routine was over Lucy dived under the bedclothes, again cursing Thomas, and composed herself for an hour at least of stale air and ennui.

Few women could have resisted listening, and Lucy was not one of them; her ears under the sheet were agog for Thomas's arrival. When his footsteps clipped across the floor she began to wonder if a discreet look would be possible; but her decision that it would had no time to be translated into action before someone landed her an indiscreet, sudden and hearty slap on the behind.

Lucy was so surprised she sat up. She could not have glared with more malevolence at Louis if he had been the as yet absent Thomas himself. 'Chérie,' said Louis mildly, 'I am a surprise. Bernard had to drive in for something official so I came with him.' Voluble with her fright and thanking heaven for the French language, Lucy went for him ferociously with one eye on the door; name of a this and that, said everything was now upset; was there then no telephone between the house and the hospital? Let that pass, said Lucy at top speed, in such a crisis there was only one thing to be done; listen, species of turnip, she said, and poured out the crisis in a torrent, with the directions for coping. 'Then you can come back and say Bernard is not yet ready; dis ça en anglaise; tu comprends, cochon?'

'Entendu,' said Louis; enjoying himself vastly, saluting her in false farewell, he took himself off to cope.

'There's late Tom is, the devil,' said Mrs Reed quite cheerfully; calm and flowering, she sat up in a pink jacket and looked at the door.

There's lucky for you he's the same unpunctual so-and-so, Lucy said to herself. Having her baby had been nothing to this; she felt even more like someone in a film, untied from the rails almost under the train's wheels; but she trusted Louis.

Thus, when Thomas came through the swinging doors into the passage he found himself accosted not by a nurse but by some kind of foreigner in very English tweeds. Thomas gave him a nod and thought to proceed; but no. 'You will come and see your baby, please?' said Louis in as official a voice as his costume allowed. It was not official enough; can't speak English properly, poor cheese, was Thomas's only reaction. 'Well, no, thanks,' he said. 'I'd rather see my wife first.'

'First one looks at the babies,' said Louis, 'then one sees the wives. In here.'

'No, really, old man, my wife's waiting. Thanks all the same.'

'Please.'

'Oh, *hell.*'

'A quarter past seven, now,' said Mrs Reed to Lucy. 'Give it to him I will when he shows his face. Is it your husband makes you laugh, cariad?'

'Like a drain,' said Lucy. As clearly as if she were there she saw Thomas and Louis in the nursery, surrounded by eight babies in little baskets, having it out. The process was short; in two or three minutes Thomas, rather red, came into the

ward and made his way to his wife's bed; his boots slapped
self-consciously on the floor. Lucy was now enjoying herself;
the situation, she felt, was taking on the qualities of a bedroom
farce. Over Mrs Reed's head she caught Thomas's eye. Mrs
Reed looked at Thomas, Thomas looked at Lucy, and Lucy
made a face. Thomas went redder. Honour thus appeased,
Lucy lay back and waited for Louis to return and say his piece.

Thomas's leave was only forty-eight hours, as Lucy had
discovered with some relief from his wife; nevertheless it was
astonishing how many times he managed to ease himself into
the ward during the next day. Authority was blind to husbands
on leave. Lucy could see that Mrs Reed was waiting for a chance
to introduce her to Thomas, and with matching determination
gave her no opening. It seemed to Lucy that she spent most
of her time feigning sleep; being conscientious about her act-
ing, she had to go on sleeping for half a day after Thomas's
departure. Thomas may have imagined, but it was as well that
he did not hear, the things Lucy said about him under the
bedclothes; and for all the reading she was getting through she
felt she might with greater profit have filled her suitcase with
an oxygen apparatus.

Once Thomas was safely out of the way Lucy's friendship
with Mrs Reed increased. Thomas and a feeling for Wales
encompassed all they had in common; yet by some trick of
temperament they got on together. Lucy had a natural trick
of discretion; before long she almost believed in Daniel. With
touches of embroidery she built up a creation of his character and appearance which became her private pride. On her
eighth day (which everyone thought was her ninth, Lucy by

constant repetition having effectively confused them) she got up for a bath; thereafter, at last unconfined, she seemed to merge herself back on the staff. Mrs Reed was out of bed a day later, but somehow remained a patient.

On her twelfth day, since Lucy's mother was there to look after the house, they let her go home. Louis came over with a car to fetch her, waiting in the passage till Lucy's protracted parting with the ward should come to an end. Most of the women by now were new patients; terrified of Sister, who was swabbing, they were shocked at Lucy's facetious air. Lucy, half of the world in her imminent departure, leaned against the end of someone's bed; 'I always thought it was steel wool,' she said, 'but I see it's cotton.' Hitching her still simian baby on one elbow, wearing now though not without constriction her black trousers and a grey jacket, she went out of the ward in the alarmed silence that greeted this reference to Sister's heavy competent hand. Arm-in-arm she and Louis went down the stairs, through the cold hall and out into the sun.

'Cochon,' said Lucy, 'do you know what I've done?'

'What have you done?'

'I've asked Thomas's wife to come and stay.'

'Lucy, sometimes I ask myself, will you ever learn?'

'No,' said Lucy, 'I never will, will I? Quel enfant, hein? C'est ta faute, ça.'

'Écoute, toi . . .'

Holding the baby and launching into argument again, Lucy got in the car beside Louis and they slid off down the winding drive, out into the country and towards home.

THE COLD

Sylvia Townsend Warner

1945

The Cold came into the household by Mrs Ryder. At first she said she had picked it up at the Mothers' Union meeting; later – it was the kind of cold that gets worse with time – she attributed it to getting chilled through waiting in the village shop while that horrible Beryl Legg took over half an hour to decide whether she would spend her points on salmon or Spam. Never a thought for her child, of course, who by now should be getting prunes and cereals. Whoever the father might be, one would have expected the girl to show some maternal feeling – but no!

The next person to get The Cold was old Mr Ryder, the Rector's father, and he immediately gave it to old Mrs Ryder. They did not have it so badly, but at their age and after all they had gone through in London before they could make up their minds to evacuate themselves to their son's country parish, one had to put them to bed with trays, just to be on the safe side. Dry and skinny, they lay in the spare room twin beds like two recumbent effigies on tombs, and chattered to each other in faded high-pitched voices. Segregated from the normal family life, they had re-established that rather tiresome specialness which sometimes made it difficult to realise that they were really dear Gerald's parents. It is very nice to be cultivated, of course, but somehow in wartime it does jar to labour upstairs with a heavy supper tray and hear, beyond the door, two animated voices discussing Savonarola; and then to hear the voices silenced, like mice when one throws a shoe in their direction, as one knocked on the door and called out brightly, 'Supper, darlings!' and to know, as clearly as if one had seen it, that old Mrs Ryder was stubbing out one of her cigarettes. That jarred, too, especially as she smoked such very heavy ones.

From the old Ryders The Cold descended to the third and fourth generation, to Geraldine and her two boys. Thence it leaped upon the Rector. 'Leaped' was indeed the word. He had set out for the funeral looking the picture of health, he returned haggard and shivering, and so terribly depressed that she had said to herself: 'Influenza!' But it was only The Cold – The Cold in its direst form.

'No!' exclaimed Mrs Allingham, indefatigable secretary of the Women's Institute. 'Not the Rector?'

'If you had been in church on Sunday you wouldn't need to ask.'

For the indefatigable secretary was a matter for regret on Sundays, when she was more often seen taking her terriers over the Common than herself to Saint Botolph and All Angels. Such a pity! – for in every other way she was an excellent influence.

Recovering herself rather too easily, for it showed that such recoveries were nothing to the rebuked one, Mrs Allingham went on: 'All seven of you! For I can see you've got it too. You poor things! My dear, what do you do about handkerchiefs, now that the laundry only collects once a fortnight? Can I lend you some?'

'Stella washes them.'

'Your marvellous Stella! What would you do without her? I hope she is still standing up.'

'I can't imagine Stella failing us,' said Mrs Ryder with satisfaction.

In the sixth autumn of the war Mrs Ryder was a little tired. She was feeling her age. Her last tailor-made was definitely not quite a success and, say what you will, people do judge one by appearances: she could not help noticing that strangers were not as respectful as they might be; though no doubt the unhelpfulness of Utility corsets played its part in the decline of manners. In the parish, too, there was much to grieve the Rector and the Rector's wife. The old, simple, natural order of things was upset by all these changes, the grocer's son actually a Captain, as much a Captain (and indeed senior in captaincy) as dear Geraldine's Neville, the butcher's wife in Persian lamb, the resolutions at the Parish Council only to be described as Communist, and the girls, her own Girls' Club girls, behaving so shockingly that she often wondered what the mothers of these poor American soldiers would think if they only knew what their sons were exposed to. But she had Stella. And having Stella she had all things.

No one could pick holes in Stella. There were no holes to pick. Stella was physically perfect, not deaf, nor halt, nor imbecile. Stella did not wear glasses and did wear a cap and apron.

Stella was functionally perfect, she did not dawdle, she did not waste, she did not gossip, she was clean, punctual, reliable, she was always cheerful and willing, she scrubbed her own back kitchen and mended the choir surplices; and though of course her wages were perfectly adequate, no one could say that the Ryders bribed her to stay with them. Stella stayed through devotion, she could have got twice as much elsewhere. Finally, Stella was a good girl. In a time when manners and morality had gone down alike before expediency, when householders snatched at trousered and cigarette-smoking evacuees if the evacuee would 'help with light domestic duties', when even the houses that ought to set an example employed girls with illegitimate babies and glossed over the capitulation with pretexts of being compassionate and broad-minded, Mrs Ryder continued to boast the ownership of a virgin, a strong womanly virgin who wore skirts, fastened-up unwaved hair in a sensible knob, and said, 'Yes, ma'am.'

Naturally, one took care of such a treasure. Stella's cold was given quite as much consideration as any other family cold and dosed out of the same bottle. In the worst of the epidemic Mrs Ryder said that if Stella did not feel better by midday she really must be sent to bed. For several evenings Mrs Ryder and Geraldine washed up the supper dishes so that Stella might sit quietly by the stove with the surplices instead of shivering in the back-kitchen; and when Stella's cough persisted after the other coughs had died away Geraldine went in specially by bus to look for blackcurrant lozenges and came back with some wonderful pastilles flavoured with horehound.

But it was a long time before Stella's cough could be distinguished from the other coughs by outlasting them. The Cold was such a treacherous type of cold. When you thought you'd got rid of it, it came back. Like beggars, said old Mrs Ryder (for they were downstairs again, one could not keep them in bed indefinitely). Like dandelions, said her son. Geraldine said that she believed it was nutritional. Of course one ought not to complain, the food was marvellous really, more marvellous than ever if one thought about poor old Europe; but still, it wasn't the same, was it? She had met Mrs Allingham, and Mrs Allingham had enquired, of course, about The Cold, and had said that in 1918 everyone had just the same kind of cold, it was quite remarkable. What did the Grand-grands say? Did they have colds in 1918? 'We had much better rum, and more of it,' said old Mrs Ryder. She looked at her husband very affectionately; he stroked his beard and looked back at her, and so they both avoided seeing Mrs Ryder catch her breath like one who holds back a justified reproach because experience has shown that reproaches are in vain. The Rector, even more imperceptive, remarked that it was very kind of his parents to make poor Stella a nightcap, he hoped it would do her good. He had seen rum do a lot of good when he was a chaplain in Flanders. Stella was a good girl, a very good girl. They would be badly off without her.

For some reason Mrs Ryder and her daughter now began discussing how tomorrow they really must polish the stair-rods and the bathroom taps. They would make time for it somehow if Mrs Ryder did the altar vases before breakfast and Stella took the boys with her when she went to the farm for milk. If the boys wore their rubber boots, the slush wouldn't do them any harm.

John was five, Michael was three. You couldn't really call them spoilt, they were just wartime, lacking the influence of a father about the house. But not spoilt. Besides, Geraldine liked boys to behave as boys; it would be too awful if they grew up like Neville's ghastly young brother who would sit for hours stroking the cat and turning off the wireless whenever it became worth listening to. A dressing room had been made over as their playroom, but it was bleak up there, and naturally they preferred the kitchen. If anyone spoilt them it was Stella, who didn't seem able to say no to them. And if they were rather fretful just now, it wasn't to be wondered at, it was The Cold.

The doctor's sister, a rather uncongenial character with independent means, used to refer to Mrs Ryder and her daughter as Bright and Breezy. They had a great deal in common, she said, but Geraldine had more of it, and was Breezy. Geraldine now had more of The Cold. Her sneezes were louder, her breathing more impeded, her nose redder, and her handkerchiefs more saturated. Throughout The Cold Mrs Ryder had kept on her feet: as a daughter-in-law, mother, grandmother, and wife to a Rector, she could not do otherwise; but Geraldine had not merely kept on her feet, she stamped and trampled. She scorned precautions, she went everywhere and kissed everybody, just as usual. She did not believe, not she! in cosseting a cold. What are colds? Everyone has them, they are part of English life. Foreigners have things with spots, the English have colds. She made having a cold seem part of the national tradition, like playing cricket and Standing Alone.

@@@@@@@

And so, when they had all got rid of The Cold and even Stella only coughed at night, Geraldine seemed to be breaking the Union Jack at the masthead when she woke the echoes of the kitchen with a violent sneeze, and asserted:

'I'm beginning another cold. And what's more, I can tell it's going to be a snorter. So watch out, one and all!'

'I do hope not, Miss Geraldine,' answered Stella.

It was rather touching the way Stella still called her Miss Geraldine – as if to Stella the passage of time were nothing, a tide that flowed past the kitchen threshold but never wetted her feet.

'No jolly hope!'

Geraldine went out. Presently she could be heard telling her mother about the new cold. Mrs Ryder sounded unenthusiastic; she said she only hoped it would not last so long this time, as otherwise it would spoil Christmas. Stella went on rubbing stale bread through a sieve for the wartime Christmas pudding. It needed a lot of breadcrumbs; in fact, you might as well call it bread-pudding and be done with it; but Mrs Ryder said the children must be brought up to love Christmas. They stood on either side of the table, rolling bread-pills and throwing them at each other.

The recipe for the wartime Christmas pudding which needed a lot of breadcrumbs also called for grated carrot. When she had finished the breadcrumbs, and put them on a high shelf where she hoped the children might not get at them, Stella went into the back-kitchen and began to clean carrots over the sink. If you rub stale bread through a fine sieve for any length of time, you are apt to develop a pain between the shoulders. She had such a pain; and the change of climate from the kitchen which was hot, to the back-kitchen which was cold, made her more conscious of it. When she had cleaned the carrots she went back to the kitchen. The two little boys were still there and Mrs Ryder had been added.

'Oh, Stella, I came in to say that I thought we would have onion soup tonight, as well as the fish cakes. Mrs Hartley thinks she has another cold coming on.'

'Yes, ma'am. I wish to . . .'

Mrs Ryder swept on. 'And, Stella, of course I know how busy you are, but all the same I think it would be better *not* to leave the babies alone in here. When I came in I found John playing with the flat irons. Of course they were cold, but they might have been hot. Perhaps a little more thoughtfulness . . . With such young children one cannot be too thoughtful.'

'Very well, ma'am. But I wish to leave, ma'am.'

'Beddy-bies, beddy-bies!' exclaimed Mrs Ryder. 'Come now, John, come, Michael! Kiss dear Stella goodnight, and off with you to your little beds. Now a nice kiss . . .'

'Don't want to,' said the child.

Mrs Ryder seized a child under either arm, waved them in the direction of Stella's face, and conveyed them out of the room, shutting the door on them with a firm sweet, 'God Bless you, my babies!' Then, flushed with exertion, with difficulty withstanding the impulse to go with them, she turned back, hoping that her ears had deceived her and knowing too well that they hadn't.

'I wish to leave, ma'am.'

'Stella! What do you mean?'

'I wish to leave, ma'am.'

There she stood, grating carrots as if the children's Christmas were nothing to her.

'But, Stella . . . I trusted you. After all these years! Why, we all look on you as a friend. What has happened to you?'

Could it be, could it be? Stella was short and the kitchen table was high and anything may be happening behind an apron. In a convulsion of the imagination Mrs Ryder rehearsed herself saying that one should not penalise a poor girl for a solitary slip, that kindness, a good home, the example of a Christian home life which means so much, etc, etc. A harlot hope raised its head, and at the same moment she heard Stella say quite idiotically:

'I think I'm catching another cold.'

'Good heavens, girl, is that a reason for going? I've never heard such nonsense.'

'It's nothing but one cold after another – cold, cold, cold, work, work, work! It's not a fit place for me. Both my aunties were chesty, and if I stay here I shall go the same way, I know it. What's more, I'm going tomorrow. I don't mind about my money, I'm going tomorrow. I want to get away while I've still got the strength to.'

'In wartime,' said Mrs Ryder, in her sternest Mothers' Union manner, the manner only unfurled for urgent things like War Savings Rallies and Blood Transfusion Drives, 'in wartime, when our boys are shedding their blood without a moment's hesitation . . . and you are positively running away from a simple cold in the head. I cannot believe it.'

Without a spark of incredulity she banged the door behind her.

There was the Rectory hall. There were the coats and the children's rubber boots and the umbrellas, and the brass letter-tray, and the copper gong, and the stair-rods ascending. There was Gerald writing in his study, and Geraldine gargling in the bathroom, and in the sitting room the two old Ryders chattering like lovebirds. Here was her home, her dear (except for the old Ryders), her dear, dear home, where everything spoke of love and loving labour: the happy, busy home that was – Mrs Allingham's own words – a beacon to the parish.

She must be! Mrs Ryder thanked God that self-respect had stood like an angel between her and a fatal false step. 'Stella has gone. Poor Stella! . . . I could not keep her.' A few such words, and a grave grieved silence, nothing that was not true, strictly true; and the Sewing Circle might draw its own conclusions. Cooking, sweeping, scrubbing, doing everything that for so long Stella had done, she could still hold up her head.

But now . . .

Not Stella? Not your marvellous Stella?

The words seemed to dart at her from every side, stabbing through the unsuccessful tailor-made into her ageing flesh. Tomorrow the Sewing Circle met at the Rectory. Only self-respect withheld her from running back into the kitchen to throw herself on Stella's mercy, to beg, on her knees, even, to beg and implore that Stella would change her mind, would stay, would at any rate stay to see them over Christmas. Self-respect was rage and fury. Presently they died down. But she

remained in the hall, knowing that any appeal to Stella would be in vain.

Tomorrow the Sewing Circle met. They met at three in the afternoon. Stella would be out of the house before then.

TEA AT THE RECTORY

Dorothy Whipple

1945

It was Christmas Eve and, at four o'clock in the afternoon, almost dark. The Miss Whartons, at their gate, hesitated which way to go to the Rectory, whether by the field path or the road. Their grand-nephew Richard waited for them to make up their minds, which always took time.

He sighed and was ashamed of himself. In the desert, in Italy, in Normandy, he had thought of his great-aunts with much affection. Since his parents had been killed and his home destroyed in the Blitz, his thoughts had no one to turn to but his aunts. All the time he was in hospital he had longed to get home to them, remembering their kindness, their endearing oddity. Why then, now that he was with them, was he so often exasperated, and not only with them but with all of life, with everything, big and little? Why did going to tea at the Rectory seem the last straw, seem so unbearable? He told himself it must be because he wasn't well yet, but he really felt that things would never be right again. Never. How could they be in this war-shattered world?

He waited, looking at his aunts. In the last wild light from the winter sky, or any light at all for that matter, they were an odd-looking pair only to be met with, surely, in the English countryside. Two maiden ladies in tweeds and felt hats, unfashionable, indefatigable in spite of their seventy-odd years, voluble, argumentative, and much given to erratic and frequently startling gestures. They were pointing vigorously with their stout sticks, now to the field, now to the road, and now for some unexplained reason to the whole sweep of the sky, arguing meanwhile.

Richard, listening – he tried nowadays to listen closely to keep his mind from his dark thoughts – wondered why so many people of his aunts' class and generation had such difficulty with their r's. Had it been a fashion in their youth, was it a pose, or was it a real speech defect? There was nothing else posey about the Miss Whartons, but to roll an r was beyond either.

'My dear,' one would say to the other, 'I'm afwaid I shall have to wepwimand Wose.' Rose was the small maid, frequently in trouble, at Rambler Cottage. The aunts were now taking Wichard to tea with the dear Wector. 'If only they would make up their minds which way to go!' he thought, standing there with his fists doubled on his hips, tall, thin – far too thin – and still, after the interminable years of war, only twenty-six.

The argument came to a sudden end. The sisters had decided upon the field path. They never went this way after nightfall, they explained, because of the darkness under the elms, but since Richard was with them, it would be all right. Everything seemed all right to the Miss Whartons when Richard was with them.

He helped them over the high stile; first Aunt Emmy, then Aunt Jemmy. Their baptismal names, Emmeline and Jemima, had very early in life been thus shortened. They hurried down the field path now, brandishing their sticks so wildly that Richard often flinched as if about to be hit. Once he would have called out 'Hi!' in laughing protest, but now he said nothing.

Volubly, the Miss Whartons conjectured who would be at the Rectory for tea. Mrs Ware, Mrs Burton, Miss Pike were sure to be there, because they always were. They hoped Pamela Lane was home for Christmas; if so, she would also be there and she was such a dear girl, they assured Richard.

'But if Miss Pike awwives with a bag today,' cried Miss Emmy, raising her stick in a threatening manner, 'you can expect twouble. Because I shall tell her what I think of her and her kettle-holders. There's no social gathewing of any kind in this village any longer but Miss Pike is there to thwust her kettle-holders upon the guests. Well, I've had enough, and today I shall tell her so.'

'You have my full permission, dear,' said Miss Jemmy.

Hurrying over the rough path, they chattered on, but they were not so inconsequent and unobservant as Richard thought and hoped. Their chatter was partly designed to cover his silence, to enable him to be silent. The hearts of the two old ladies yearned over the war-torn boy. They wanted desperately to heal and help him, but feared they did not know how. They feared too that they had annoyed him by that foolish argument at the gate. At least, it appeared foolish in retrospect, because the Rectory was only a quarter of a mile away and what could it matter which way they went?

The Miss Whartons almost always came to this conclusion about their arguments, and would make the warmest amends and apologies to each other, each laughingly protesting that the other was right, or even if she wasn't, it didn't matter.

'It does matter, my dear,' one would say, and the other would say, 'No, of course it doesn't.' And they would both laugh heartily. Outsiders were frequently bewildered by this rapid change of front, but the sisters understood each other very well.

They felt, however, that Richard, since he had come home from the war, found them exasperating. They wanted to reform their ways, but they kept forgetting, and behaved as they had behaved for the last seventy years. They were remorseful now and hoped there would be a nice tea at the Rectory, that Miss Pike would not be too tiresome, that Pamela would be there, that the Rector would be able to do something for Richard. They didn't know what, but something. That somebody would do something, since they couldn't. If only they had a piano. It was a dreadful thing to be without a piano for Richard, who was so musical. But there was no room at Rambler Cottage that a piano could have been got into; they were all far too small. Everybody had been so kind, putting their pianos at Richard's disposal, but he wouldn't go and play on any of them. Poor boy – how long would it be before he was healed of the terrible years of war?

Richard strode beside his aunts. 'Why am I going to this place?' he asked himself. 'Why do I drag about like this? I'm crushed. Crushed. Ye gods, what am I doing – going to tea at the Rectory!' He felt, like one about to be given an anaesthetic, a fear of what he might say. He felt he might break out with all his savage, bitter thoughts this afternoon. He felt that

the very mildness of the company might provoke an outburst that would hurt his aunts and do what he hated most: draw attention to himself and his suffering.

The bare branches of the elms reached up into the night sky. The little church lay at the foot of the grassy hill. Above it shone a single star. The star of Bethlehem, perhaps. How often he had thought, abroad, of Christmas in England. In the heat of the desert, tormented by dust and flies, he had kept himself sane by thinking of the Pastorale he would write for Christmas when he was home once more. But now that Christmas was here, and he was here, he couldn't do it. He never would do it, he told himself.

They went through the wicket gate, through the churchyard where the old stones leaned peacefully under the yews. In the Rectory drive, Richard halted. He wanted to say, 'I'm not coming in. You shouldn't expect it of me. Damn it all, what do I want with tea at the Rectory?' But when his Aunt Jemmy said, 'Come along, dear,' he went forward obediently.

Miss Jemmy rapped with the brass knocker on the white Georgian door. The ladies stood with their muzzles lifted like two dogs waiting to be let in, Richard as if he would bolt at any minute. An ancient maid, far too old ever to have been called up, admitted them to the panelled hall. The Miss Whartons surrendered their sticks as if entering a museum – and a museum this place probably was, reflected Richard, following his aunts up three shallow steps to the drawing room.

When the door was opened, such a rush of heat and noise was let out that he fell back. The room seemed to be full of women and shrieking birds. It was a second or two before he realised that the birds were on the wallpaper and quite silent. It must be the women who were shrieking. Certainly they seemed to be rising at him from all sides, taking him by the hand, saying how d'you do, lovely for you to be home for Christmas, it is so nice, are you better, I'm so glad, you're not quite well yet are you, sit here, nearer the fire, have some tea, sugar, muffin, or sandwich.

He answered at random and, sitting down at last, found himself almost at floor level on a plush chair without sides. Queer what a chair can do to you. This one gave him an inferiority complex. It also embarrassed him. When he stretched out his legs, he appeared to be lying at full length; so he drew them up and let his knees poke above his head, since that was the only alternative. His cup shuddered on its fluted saucer, betraying the trembling of his hands. He was annoyed; this wretched tea party had set his hands off again just when he had thought they were cured.

He bit into his muffin. It was cold and damp like a piece of felt left out all night. He put it down and looked round the lofty room. A period piece. Victorian, with the life of the prime mover of that age portrayed in huge engravings round the walls. The Coronation of Victoria, the Marriage of the Queen, the Christening of the Prince of Wales, the Marriage of the Prince of Wales, august, very tidy assemblies such as we shall not see again. Under them stood a full-sized grand piano. He dared bet, he told himself, that no one ever touched it.

He took up his muffin again, since he had to. If he didn't dispose of it, it would hold everything up. With this piece of muffin, he could prolong tea indefinitely. He thought of doing it, in revenge for having come. But he took another bite and looked round at the company.

Among the collection of felt hats, bobbing in animated conversation, his host's bald head was conspicuous and his hostess's snow-white hair. Also the scarlet cap of a girl at the other side of the room. Not a bad-looking girl either, though he felt no interest in her. He supposed he must have been introduced, but hadn't noticed it.

He located his aunts. Miss Emmy was at some distance. Beside her was a middle-aged woman at whose feet, leaning trustfully like a dog, was a large American-cloth bag, stuffed to capacity. In every pause of the conversation, Miss Pike laid a hand tentatively on this bag, but under Miss Emmy's threatening eye she withdrew it.

In the circle of chairs, Miss Jemmy was next but one to her nephew. Mrs Ware was between them. Richard, having disposed of his muffin and refused all else, now became aware that she was telling him how much money she had made for the Red Cross from the sale of her raffia baskets.

He murmured in congratulation. 'This room,' he thought, 'is frightfully hot,' and wrenched at his collar. Miss Jemmy glanced at him with anxiety. 'That is one of my wastepaper baskets,' said Mrs Ware, indicating a sort of Leaning Tower of Pisa in straw beside the mantelpiece. It was ornamented, though that is not the word, by the usual female figure in a crinoline and poke bonnet. The bonnet hid the face, which was convenient because Mrs Ware was not good at faces. 'I sometimes put a row of delphiniums instead of hollyhocks,' said Mrs Ware, 'and I sometimes put my lady the other way round.'

'Really?' said Richard, looking wild.

'Of course, I don't only make wastepaper baskets. I make shopping and garden baskets. In fact, every conceivable kind of basket, and I do so enjoy it. It is my way of expressing myself, you know. The Rector and dear Mrs Kenworthy have always been so encouraging. They have one of my baskets in every room, and since there are twenty-four rooms in the Rectory – a William and Mary house, you know – you will understand that they have been very good customers of mine. Of course, you know,' said Mrs Ware confidentially, 'I made them one for nothing. One for the Rector's study. I left the lady out on that one – just put extra flahs. I thought it was more suitable.'

'Wichard!' cried Miss Jemmy, making everybody jump. 'Piano! Play something while you have the chance, dear boy. Play. Play.'

'Please do,' invited the hostess, rising at once to open the piano. 'I'm afraid no one has played on this piano for quite some time. But we keep it tuned, you know. Mr Wharton, do give us the pleasure of some music.'

Richard, looking hunted, went to the piano. He wasn't fond of performing in public, but anything would be better than sitting on that chair, by that furnace of a fire, at the mercy of Mrs Ware and her raffia baskets. He sat down and touched the keys. The piano was all right. What of the audience? The faces, all turned towards him from the circle round the fire, irritated him. 'I wish I liked the human race,' he thought, his hands tentatively on the keys. 'I wish I liked its silly face. Bah!' he thought, crashing out a few of Henry Cowell's cluster chords. The felt hats jumped perceptibly. 'Yes, that makes them sit up,' he thought. But he hadn't made up his mind what to play, so he let them off for a few minutes, playing quietly.

One by one the hats turned inwards to the circle. They didn't know what he was playing. Something modern, they supposed. They tried to look as if they were listening, but they couldn't keep it up. Sitting silent, talk was collecting inside them. Talk is like love; the more it is suppressed, the more it must come out. It gathers force from hindrance. From nods and becks and an occasional whisper, they began to lean one towards the other and a hum arose.

Richard, hesitating, without ceasing to play, between Ornstein and Sorabji, crashed into more Henry Cowell. But they were beyond surprise. They were well away now, he noted, and had given up all pretence of listening.

Except the girl, Pamela Lane. She was directly opposite Richard at the piano and could watch him. 'These young men,' she thought. He wasn't much older than she was, but what he had gone through! He looked savage and bitter, and he played as if he meant to get his own back – possibly on the world. She saw him glance sideways at the company and burst into fresh discords. 'Why must they talk when he's playing?' she wondered. It was so rude. If they couldn't understand, at least they could keep quiet.

The music, though unheeded, was nevertheless having an effect on the company. The louder Richard played, the louder they talked. Pamela sat up straight on her chair, her lips parted in alarm. Richard looked across at her and smiled. He saw that she was in on the game. He burst into Rubinstein's octave study, and almost burst into laughter.

The talkers jerked like marionettes. The Rector so far forgot himself as to get up and shovel a lot of coal on the fire. The room and its occupants seemed bewitched. Richard wondered what on earth all the talk could be about. Fragments reached him 'That girl of Swinton's.' 'What again?' 'Dear Mrs Burton, are you sure of your facts?' 'Those wretched goats – completely eaten the hedge –' 'They say, though of course I don't know –' And the tones of his Aunt Emmy, alas, as strident as anybody's. He looked at her. She had a hand on Miss Pike's bag. 'No, Miss Pike,' she was saying. 'No kettle-holders. I won't buy any of your kettle-holders and no one else wants to. You make a nuisance of yourself at every social gathewing, Miss Pike. Now do be sensible and give it up. Or make something else. Move with the times. Kettle-holders have gone out. All kettles have heat-pwoof handles nowadays.'

But Miss Pike, struggling indignantly, freed her bag and, in spite of Miss Emmy, brought out a bundle of velveteen squares. These she passed round the circle. But the company took no more notice of Miss Pike's kettle-holders than of Richard's music. Absently, talking hard, they passed the bundle on. Until, when it reached Miss Emmy, it remained on her knee, whether from malice or preoccupation Richard did not know. He caught Pamela's eye and laughed outright. Their young faces lit with laughter, they rocked in their places. Everything seemed deliberately funny. She was so glad he could laugh, and he thought she was lovely. That swinging hair, those dark eyes – were they blue? – and that lovely laughing mouth! Why hadn't he noticed when he came in that he was in the presence of a most beautiful girl?

And now an end to all this tomfoolery. 'This is what I wanted to play,' he told her mutely across the piano, beginning the Pastorale. 'This is what I wanted to write as soon as I came home. It's for Christmas. It was like this,' he thought, playing. The winter silence, the Mother and Child, the trustfulness of the animals, the star and the following men. It's old and always new. Simple and still a mystery, holy, homely. 'It was like this,' he thought, playing, listening both to himself and to what was beyond. 'It's like this,' he said to the girl, using no words, feeling his way on the keys. 'Listen. I only half hear it yet, but do you? Can you hear? It's like this,' he played. His face was happy. He looked at her and smiled.

He played as far as he heard. More would come. More would come, now that some strange terrible obstruction in his spirit had gone. His hands fell from the keys. He looked at the company. Everybody was quiet. The faces were all turned towards him, smiling. He smiled too, and getting up from the piano, he went over to Pamela and sat down beside her.

'It needed somebody of his own age,' thought Miss Emmy gratefully.

'Miss Pike,' she cried, startling that aggrieved lady. 'Give me some of your kettle-holders. I'll buy some after all. I'll stuff them and they'll do for the shoes. Now that is a good idea, Miss Pike. Stuff the things and sell them as shoe-polishers. They'll go like hot cakes.'

'I believe they would,' said Miss Pike, beaming happily. 'I'll take your excellent advice, Miss Emmy. You see,' she said confidentially, moving closer, 'I had only my old dining room curtains that I could use for the NSPCC and I simply didn't know what I could make from them but kettle-holders.'

'And your windows are huge. No wonder you made so many,' said Miss Emmy, now all sympathy. 'Well, I think you'll find shoe-polishers –'

'It feels like Christmas, doesn't it?' said Richard, lighting Pamela's cigarette with a steady hand. 'My first at home for five years.'

'I hope it will be a happy one,' she said.

'It is,' he said, smiling at her.

TEA WITH MR ROCHESTER
Frances Towers
1946

School was an unpleasing Victorian building, the colour of carbolic disinfectant, with a pseudo tower perched on top of it, a shrubbery of laurels and rhododendrons, and asphalt tennis courts. Prissy knew she would hate it.

That first afternoon they had tea in Miss Pinsett's study, because Aunt Athene had brought Prissy, and she was not the kind of person to be sent away without tea. Nor was she the kind of person to pay Miss Pinsett the deference that Prissy felt was due to a headmistress. She put her elbows on the table and held her cup between both hands, not bothering at all to be gracious or to say anything clever. Her hair was done in two unfashionable gold shells over her ears and a veil floated from her absurd little hat. Miss Pinsett, in her grey coat and skirt and white frilled shirt, looked very neat, like a prim zinnia near an untidy rose. Their voices were different, too. Aunt Athene talked in a rose's voice, a yellow tea-rose's, and Miss Pinsett in a zinnia's, crisp and clipped.

Presently Aunt Athene put down her cup and wagged her left forefinger at Miss Pinsett.

'Not too many mathematics, Miss Pinsett, but as much music as possible. I think music is the most important thing in life.'

'But, shurly . . .' began Miss Pinsett.

'Yes, yes!' said Aunt Athene, 'when all else fails, there is still music. What consolation has algebra ever been to a broken heart?'

The diamond in her ring welled up with light that flashed like a star and fell as she moved her hand to adjust the little hat. There was a faint pink smudge on the teacup where her lips had touched it – Prissy hoped Miss Pinsett wouldn't notice – but the rock cakes and the fish paste sandwiches had been left undisturbed. Prissy was too miserable to eat, and Aunt Athene never did, anyway.

'Goodbye, *chérie.* You had better run away to the other girls now, while I talk to Miss Pinsett.'

'Shurly, shurly, Priscilla is not going to cry.'

Aunt Athene made a funny little face that said as plain as plain to Prissy, but not to Miss Pinsett – 'Isn't she an old idiot?'

'Cry?' said Aunt Athene, raising her gold eyebrows. 'Prissy has Spanish blood. She is as proud as Lucifer, and as detached as . . . as a fish. Believe me, Miss Pinsett, I shouldn't care to look into the notebook marked "Private" that she sums us all up in. No doubt you'll figure in it, too. Oh! you'll have a chiel amang you taking notes.' She laughed her four glassy notes – so pretty, so heartless.

Aunt Athene had her own cruel way of being kind. She had saved the situation by making one quite thankful to see the back of her. How did she know about the notebook?

Miss Pinsett rang the bell and handed Prissy over to the school matron. It was the last she was to see for a long time of the study with its Axminster carpet and Medici prints and rows of encyclopaedias.

Aunt Athene's gardenia scent seemed to follow her out into the hall.

'Was that lady your mother, dear?' asked Matron.

'My mother is dead. It was one of my aunts.'

'Aren't you a lucky girl to have an auntie with such luffly hair! Pure gyold!' bubbled Matron, wiping her mouth. Gush, thought Prissy. It made her feel as stiff as a poker . . . quite hard and cold.

Prissy discovered that one was too tired at school even to dream. No sooner was one's head on the pillow, no sooner, it seemed, had the gargling and hairbrushing ceased and the cubicle curtains been rattled back, than the rising-bell clanged rudely and noisily in the corridors. One's spine ached where it had bridged the sag in the middle of the mattress. A sharp peppermint smell of toothpaste in the dormitory mingled with the smell of burnt toast coming up from below.

But the worst thing was that there wasn't a moment of the day to play ball by oneself. She had 'played ball' ever since she was nine years old. She could not 'make up' without her ball. She needed solitude and secrecy and the rhythm of the ball's being bounced on a mossy path to spin out of herself an imaginary world and people it with characters as real as any of flesh and blood.

It was so safe (much safer than hours spent with pencil and paper, which might have led to inquiries); because no

one could guess what was happening. If one came in looking rather pale and mad, with smudges under one's eyes, they
might say one was a queer little fish and had been overdoing
it out there alone in the garden, they might give one hot milk
and send one to bed; but they couldn't know. Not even Aunt
Athene, with her piercing look, could ever catch a glimpse of
that other world.

All the same, said Prissy to herself, thinking of the holidays,
one must watch out for Aunt Athene. It was queer about that
notebook. Not that she would ever look at anything marked
'Private'. Oh, no! She was much too fastidious a person.

The notebook was a comparatively recent affair. It was a
kind of a diary, really, and was concerned only with the real
world. Somehow, Prissy knew that the things one just 'thought'
and the things one 'made up' came from different parts of
oneself. One thought with one's mind, but 'making up' came
from so deep inside that one couldn't tell where.

'Thinking', confided to one's diary and not to be seen by
any honest mortal eye, gave one a delicious feeling of superior-
ity. One was not so impotent as the grown-ups imagined. When
one was sent out of the room on some improvised errand
because of Mr Pargeter's saying – 'Little pitchers have long
ears,' it was satisfactory to remember the entry – 'Mr P is brown
and squirmy. He is very like an earwig. If he was trod on, there
would be a dark, oily smear and a bitter smell.'

There were poems in the diary, too. Prissy wished there
were some way of finding out whether they were real poems.
Aunt Elena, perhaps; but was her opinion worth having? Her
favourite reading was a mouldy old book called *Urn Burial*,

that she read in bed; and she liked creepy, rustling things like tortoises and cacti. She had a dark, haggard face that made one think of an old graveyard, but her eyes were so dark and deep that when one talked to her, one talked *into* her eyes, the way one drops a pebble into a pool to watch for the ripples.

The mistresses and the girls were too ordinary for words, too dull to put into the diary. Only Miss Hornblower was a little different because she took the Shakespeare class, and one got the feeling now and again that she was keeping back something too precious to tell. 'You little owls, with your dull, stupid eyes!' she cried out once, her nose twitching with exasperation. She looked as if she were going to cry, and suddenly one saw that it was dreadful for her. She had really been in that wood near Athens, and now she had crashed into the classroom, and it was common and awful, and they were all common and awful, too.

Perhaps Miss Hornblower felt about Shakespeare as one felt about *Jane Eyre*, which one had extracted surreptitiously from the VIth Form library and read in secret under the flap of the desk.

What agony when the tea-bell clanged rudely and woke one up out of that dream! Gone were the vases of purple spar, the pale Parian mantelpiece. The master of Thornfield Hall had vanished, like the Devil through a trapdoor. But, stumbling down the corridor, one still saw the flash of his dark eyes, heard the deep sardonic tones of his voice. Eating the thick hunks of bread and plum jam, one thought with anguish of the seed cake Miss Temple took out of her drawer.

Towards the half-term a personality disengaged itself from the indeterminate background of moon-faces and pigtails to the extent of being half-confided in. Bunty Adams served as a very inadequate substitute for the ball game. The host of imaginary characters had retreated too far into the depths of Prissy's being to be recalled. Besides, they were not to be shared. One would as soon have said one's prayers aloud. Bunty was not even quite on the diary plane, but she was a receptive little thing and proved a rapt audience for the real-life dramas staged by Prissy, in which Aunt Elena and Aunt Athene played their parts, rather touched-up, rather two-pence-coloured, as befitted creatures translated into the sphere of Art.

And then there was Mr Considine. But Prissy did not speak of him, because gradually he had come to assume all the characteristics of Mr Rochester, and Mr Rochester belonged to that part of Prissy's experience which was too poignant to be shared. Her voice would go all trembly if she tried to tell Bunty about Thornfield Hall. 'Jane, I've got a blow; I've got a blow, Jane!' Was ever a woman so honoured? He was so strong, so fascinating. And rather wicked, she supposed. For what was that queer business about Adele? Prissy felt rather wicked, too, as if she had a guilty secret to hide. Aunt Athene's eyes were so piercing, and she was so particular about what one read.

But she tried out a poem on Bunty, one day, in the dusk of the shrubbery, with the red electric trains clanking up to London beyond the iron railing. She read it in a thin, strangled, unnatural voice.

I looked out of my window this morning
And saw the hawthorns in bloom.
When the golden day was just dawning,
Their scent came into my room.
They were white as the tents of the Arabs
And humming with little brown bees,
With dark little bees like scarabs,
And my heart flew out to the trees.
It is lulled in those bowers so airy
By the incense-and-pepper smell
That will make of my heart a fairy,
Of my breast but a hollow shell.

'Oh, Prissy! I think it's super. If you hadn't told me, I could easily have thought it was Shelley or someone. I could, really.'

'Oh, no – not *Shelley*!' said Prissy, modestly. 'Of course I had to find a rhyme for 'Arabs', and there is only one. You don't think it sounds dragged in?' she inquired, anxiously.

'Definitely not. I think it's maharvellous.'

Oh, if only Bunty were a person of authority!

It was queer seeing Aunt Elena again, after all the things one had been saying about her; like meeting a person who had figured the night before in a vivid dream. She was waiting on the platform, in her old toque with the crushed wallflowers. Her kiss was like the peck of a hen; so perfunctory that it bereft one of affection.

But Aunt Athene at the front door, looking more like a rose than ever, drew one down into a secret garden of spices.

When one returned to No. 7 Queen Anne Terrace, it was

like opening some old, adorable book and stepping between its covers. The wrought-iron gate had come from Spain. One looked through it into a paved courtyard, and there was the house, that looked so powdery one felt one could brush off the cedar-red bloom with one's fingers. The porch with its fluted columns, the shell under the fanlight, the blue front door and the tip-tilted windows were the frontispiece. Aunt Athene had come from inside the story to greet one.

You know those golden almonds of light that holy people have behind them in old pictures? Aunt Athene seemed to have one, too, like a person walking in beauty. Not that her light came from God. Oh, no! Her other world was certainly not Heaven.

'How funny everything looks! I'd forgotten it was like this,' said Prissy, looking about her. Everything was more beautiful even than she had remembered. After the drabness of school, the drawing room simply took one's breath away. It was pale, and patternless except for the startled silver deer on the curtains, and colours showed up in it as though spotlit. The celadon bowls, the bowls of peach-blow and *sang-de-boeuf*, shone with a lustre that seemed to shed tinted pools of reflected light, and their delicate curves against the cream walls made one want to stroke them. The tea kettle was bubbling over a blue flame and there was a faint smell of methylated spirit and freesias, and a breath from Aunt Elena's greenhouse as of earth freshly watered.

The aunts asked innumerable questions, most of which were easy enough to answer. But now and again an oblique one came sideways from Aunt Athene.

'And is there any *talking* after lights out?'

One had always remembered two cryptic remarks let fall by some grown-up. 'There never was such a person for consuming her own smoke as Elena', and 'Athene has such a beautiful mind.'

Aunt Athene had beautiful hair and a beautiful voice and beautiful laughter. Wasn't that enough? Must she also have a beautiful mind, to set her above other people and make her so fastidious that she wouldn't ever let one go to a cinema or read a book with love in it?

So, when she said in a casual kind of voice – 'Is there any talking after lights out?' one knew what she meant. She meant – 'Are there any *horrid* girls, who try to tell you things you shouldn't know?'

If she only knew how terrified one was of finding out about things one shouldn't know.

But one couldn't believe that reading *Jane Eyre* was wrong. And if it were, if at fourteen one had no right to have discovered so much about love, well, it couldn't be helped. It was the most thrilling, glorious, and beautiful thing in the world. It was like stained glass windows and sunsets and nightingales singing in the dark.

'Not much talking; we're too tired,' murmured Prissy, looking into her empty cup.

And suddenly she thought – 'if she asks me what I've been reading, I shall get scarlet. And, please God, don't let them mention him – not just now, when I'm so tired.'

* * *

The holidays were haunted by Mr Considine. There was always the delicious fear that one might meet him face to face. In a way, one wanted to more than anything in the world, but when there was a prospect of such a meeting, one was seized with panic.

Prissy had always known that he was a very special kind of person. When he came to tea in the old days, she used to have hers in the schoolroom. She remembered that his soft black hat on the hall table looked sootier and richer than other people's, his stick more unusual, his voice coming through the closed door sounded deeper and softer. And afterwards, when he had gone and one was permitted to return to grown-up society, it seemed as if something of his personality still lingered in the drawing room, like the smell of incense in a Catholic church when the Mass is over – a faint tobacco and carnation scent. And the room looked different – kind of hushed and golden. More flowers than usual, the yellow fluted teacups, and a walnut cake. But perhaps it was Aunt Athene herself who seemed the most changed. The pupils of her eyes were so large they almost covered the iris, and she kept moving restlessly about and humming a tune as if she had just come in from a concert. Then she usually went to the piano and played the Brahms *Rhapsody* over and over again, as if she were continuing a conversation in her own mind.

One night during these holidays there was a dinner party for some of the Cathedral clergy and their wives, Mr Pargeter and Mr Considine.

'I should think Prissy might come in for dessert,' said Aunt Elena, stalking in and stealing a salted almond from one of the silver shells.

Aunt Athene was laying the table herself, instructing Prissy in the art for when she should be grown up.

Her arrangement looked sumptuous but careless like a banquet in a picture in the National Gallery; as if subtle and exquisite ladies with high, bald brows and bosoms of snow were to pose on the Hepplewhite chairs. The polished mahogany was a dark pool in which floated the reflections of pink, pointed cyclamens spilling out of a Venetian goblet, and iridescent bubbles of glass.

'A bit medieval, isn't it?' said Aunt Elena. She gave her little sniff, and there was a gleam in her dark eyes. That sudden gleam was what one loved her for, that goblin light in the graveyard. It was queer, the way she often echoed some vague, scarce-formulated thought in one's mind, making one feel that deep in her heart was the fire that would always warm one.

'Dinner with the Borgias,' she said. 'Alexis, and Simon P, perhaps. But what about the clergymen?'

'I think it's lovely,' said Prissy tremulously. 'But may I have my dessert in bed, please?'

For she could not, no, it was out of the question that she should be called upon to face the ordeal of adult quizzical eyes, his eyes, upon her awkwardness, her shivering, skinned-rabbit nakedness, thrust in upon their vinous warmth, their conviviality, their terrible grown-up patronage, in her skimpy tussore and black ribbed stockings, her sharp little elbows sticking out like pins and her arms all gooseflesh.

'Of course you can,' said Aunt Elena, hurriedly undoing the mischief she had done, while Aunt Athene's eyes travelled over her in a *distraite* fashion. 'Yes,' she said, 'yes. It wouldn't be very amusing for Prissy.' *Amusing*, thought Prissy, was hardly the word. It would be more thrilling, more frightful and perilous, than she could bear. Her dream world would be in mortal danger. She trembled to think what she might have to suffer if Aunt Athene were to catch a glimpse of it. Contempt, perhaps; or heartless tinkling laughter. She could imagine that Aunt Athene might even go to the lengths of telling him. 'You must know, Alexis, that Prissy has a crush on you.' The agony of it would kill her.

She had a few other narrow escapes, glimpses of his tall figure at the end of vistas, crossing a street, going into a shop. And then, towards the end of the holidays, the worst happened.

Aunt Athene announced that she was taking Prissy to have tea with Mr Considine.

'But I don't want to go,' said Prissy, off her guard.

'You don't want to go? And why not, may I ask? When a most distinguished scholar has been so kind as to invite a little schoolgirl to tea, she should feel greatly honoured.'

Greatly honoured! But he hadn't asked her, of course. He scarcely knew she existed. Aunt Athene was taking her along as she might have taken a Pekinese or a sunshade. It was too much. She felt too young, too tender, for such an overwhelming experience. To meet one's hero in the flesh was terrible enough, but to meet him in the presence of Aunt Athene was an ordeal beyond one's powers of endurance. Those cool green eyes which missed nothing and dwelt with a faint disdain on schoolgirl blushes and gaucheries! Oh, God! make something happen to prevent it. Aunt Elena . . . if only Aunt Elena could be substituted for that other one. But at the appointed hour, Aunt Athene set off in her lilac dress, her legs looking like glass through the thin silk of her stockings, with Prissy walking, cold with apprehension, beside her.

An elderly maid opened the door, and Aunt Athene stepped into the hall, her delicate scent floating in with her like some invisible attendant spirit.

Prissy felt very strange indeed. She felt as if the foundations of the visible world were shifting under her feet, as if the walls of reality were dissolving and those of the other world sliding into their place.

The pale April sunlight spilled into the hall and touched an old print in a maple frame, and winked in the topaz and agate knobs of a bundle of sticks in a copper jar. A bust of bronze stood in a niche, gazing out coldly into space. Prissy was so strung-up that she saw everything with unnatural distinctness, as if these inanimate things were possessed of a magical potency, endowed as in a fairy tale with a strange life and consciousness of their own. But what was Aunt Athene doing here, in this perilous place? If one met her in a dream, she was no more than a sprite, a quintessence of aunt, who was gone with just one look out of her green eyes, or a tinkle of laughter, or a keyword that woke one up, thinking – 'That was most frightening and important.' For in dreams one sees only those physical attributes of a person which have served to express for one his essential being. But here, on the threshold of the imaginary world, she was too terribly her whole self, taking off her cape and adjusting the hairpins in the gold conches over her ears with those turned-back thumbs and double-jointed fingers that made her hands so speaking and theatrical. Her heels on the parquet floor went clickety-click, with the sharp little taps of a pony on a hard road. Her eyes were dark today, the pupils so dilated that there were only thin rings of green round them.

Aunt Athene followed the maid up the stairs and into a room on the first floor. A tall figure rose from the chair by the fire to greet her. Prissy hovered in the background. She had time to see, before Aunt Athene called attention to her presence, that this was not the drawing room of snow and fire that had so captivated Jane, but a sombre book-lined room with chairs of red-and-gold leather. Then, as if she were crossing a vast stage into a pool of limelight, she came forward, stepping from Persian rug to rug, to take the hand held out to her. But he was still talking to Aunt Athene and shook hands with Prissy without looking at her. His hand was so cold, it gave one a fresh feeling, as of gathering snowdrops in a frosty wood. She stole a look at the face turned away from her. He wasn't so dark or so stern as she had remembered, and his eyes were blue, as blue as a sailor's. Prissy felt a little cheated; as one does, for instance, when someone in a book goes out at a door on the right, whereas in one's mind the door has been all the time on the left.

They were too much interested in their conversation to be aware of her for a long time. She sat on a slippery sofa with elegant golden feet, and drank in everything.

It was a very interesting conversation. Prissy tried to remember every word of it to record in her diary. She was very proud that a relation of hers could evoke the sudden delighted laughter that made Mr Considine wrinkle up his eyes. She was proud of Aunt Athene's beauty, her wit, her tea rose quality.

When tea came in, it would be terrible. They would have to draw her into their orbit. Perhaps she would make a noise gulping her tea.

The maid came in and set down a tray on a table in the corner. For some time they took no notice of it, but left the tea to get stewed in the silver teapot.

Mr Considine was talking of the bazaars of Ispahan, and some old tiles he had bought. The one he cherished most, he said, had a design of a prince in a turban of pale petunia riding on a piebald horse, and the glaze on it was of the texture of flower petals.

At last they came to the tea table, leaving their bazaars and roses. The prince in the turban of pale petunia rode away on his piebald horse through the gates of the secret world.

Aunt Athene poured out the tea in that special way of hers that made everything she touched seem fragile and priceless.

'The Dean's wife has cups that are blue inside, and that always makes the tea seem a queer colour and tasteless,' she said, irrelevantly. 'And, do you know, she has redecorated their bedroom a *newly-married* pink – so trying! With blue curtains, that sentimental blue! I didn't know what to say. One feels so sorry for the Dean, who after all quotes Sir Thomas Browne in his sermons.'

'Poor fellow, poor fellow! *He* can hardly with any delight raise up the ghost of a rose,' said Mr Considine. 'But, then, what should a Dean be doing in the bed of Cleopatra?'

'Hush!' said Aunt Athene, laughing. 'Are the pink sugar biscuits for Prissy? Look, Prissy, isn't that nice? Mr Considine's housekeeper knows what little girls like.'

Oh, damn and blast her!

'I would rather have a cucumber sandwich,' said Prissy, primly.

They went on with their gay, incomprehensible conversation as if she were not there. It was quite safe to steal glances at Mr Considine, recalling the moments when he had played with Jane as a cat with a mouse, the delirious moments when he had broken short a sentence with a betraying word, all the moments of agony and bliss one had shared with the little governess. And that most wonderful moment of all, when he had at last declared his love and gathered her into his arms, and one had nearly fainted with delight.

But suddenly Mr Considine took her by surprise. The blue eyes looked straight into her own, and he said, with an amused smile – 'Prissy has been weighing me all this time in her invisible scales. And what, Prissy, if I may ask so personal a question, is your private opinion of me?'

Prissy gave a little gasp. It was a supreme moment. Something must be said, something original, extraordinary . . . Jane would have known. Oh, for words . . . words telling, arresting enough.

They came, quicker than thought, from she knew not where, in her clear, piping treble.

'I *think*, Mr Considine,' she said, brightly and confidingly out of the innocence of her heart, 'that you are more knave than fool.'

There was a moment of silence so appalling that all the nerves in Prissy's body seemed to tingle agonisingly, and then she felt suddenly sick and very cold, as if a great clammy frog were squatting in her entrails.

A deeply shocked sound came from Aunt Athene.

'I am *ashamed* of you,' she said, in a hissing whisper. 'Don't laugh at her, Alexis, please. If there is anything on earth one abominates, it is a pert, precocious child. I can only apologise for having brought her.'

Out of the abyss of her desolation, Prissy saw with amazement that Mr Considine was convulsed with silent laughter. He was in a paroxysm of mirth that seemed to come from deep inside him, and was betrayed only by the quivering of his mouth and the twitching of his nostrils. Time stood still while he laughed and laughed, and Aunt Athene sat there looking as if a serpent had stung her.

'I don't know when I've had such a dusting,' he said, at last, drying his eyes. 'What have I done, Prissy, what have I done . . . ?'

But the pain in Prissy's throat prevented speech. The other world had crashed about her ears. She was smirched and degraded. She had humiliated Aunt Athene, and though Mr Considine had laughed, he must, in his heart, think her a cheap and common girl. He and Aunt Athene had beautiful minds . . . Oh! you could tell they had, with their talk of music and Cleopatra and the ghost of a rose. So beautiful.

Aunt Athene turned sideways in her chair, as if she could no longer bear the sight of Prissy, and Mr Considine began to talk hurriedly. They took no more notice of her. She was cast into outer darkness, she was with the lost and the damned. Presently Aunt Athene rose to go, gathering up her gloves, and looking in the little glass in her handbag at her cool disdainful face.

'Wait a moment,' said Mr Considine. 'There is something in the next room I'd like to show Prissy.'

Aunt Athene, with a faint shrug of her shoulders, sat down again.

'Come, Prissy,' said Mr Considine, smiling down at her.

It was terribly kind; but it would only make matters worse, thought Prissy, wretchedly.

Mr Considine shut the door of his study, and led her to a cabinet, on the shelves of which, neatly arranged and labelled, was a collection of strange and interesting objects.

'Look, Prissy, at this pink shell. If you hold it to your ear, you can hear the voice of the sea.'

He took out the great cold shell and put it into her hands. It had lovely curves, and ribbed lips, and on the delicate rose-colour were freckles of brown. The tears poured down Prissy's cheeks as she held it obediently to her ear.

'You know,' said Mr Considine, 'I wouldn't show this collection to your aunt. She wouldn't care about it. But to me, shells are such . . . *enchanted* things. This one is for you, because you are . . . rather a fairy kind of person.'

'Me!' said Prissy, with quivering lips. She could hardly believe her ears.

'I was so awful . . . I don't know why I said it.'

She began to cry now as if her heart would break.

'My dear child, I think it is the most delightful thing that has ever been said to me,' said Mr Considine. He put an arm about her, stooped, and kissed her cheek.

Oh, holy smoke! Oh, God!

The real world and the secret world clashed soundlessly

together, like two meteors colliding in space. They fused and became one.

In a daze, she followed Aunt Athene down the stairs and out into the street. Her feet seemed scarcely to touch the earth. Aunt Athene walked on in silence, still in her punishing mood. But she couldn't reach Prissy in her secret world. She had only pity now for Aunt Athene and all other women; the shut-out, the unblessed. For was she not Jane's counterpart, her equal?

.

THE EXILES
Mollie Panter-Downes
1947

At last, they made up their minds to it. They would go. It was a plunge at their time of life, as Arthur Stanbury said, but having decided to be bold, they set about it thoroughly and quickly. For months past, while they were still deliberating, they had had their names on the waiting list for a passage, and the final shove that pushed them over the brink of a decision was the fact that they had now been given a boat and a sailing date. They were, in black-and-white, Colonel and Mrs Arthur Stanbury, first-class passengers from England to Durban on a certain day. In no time at all, they had let their flat, tidied up their loose ends of business, and broken the news to their friends.

It was a wrench parting with the flat, on the fifth floor of a gloomy mansion block in Westminster, where the hall porter was an old soldier who had been in Arthur Stanbury's regiment and where their names had stood so long on the notice board in the entrance that the painted letters had begun to fade. Though the corridors were daunting to timorous visitors, the fifth floor was sunny and had, from some of its windows, a pleasant view of the river and the Houses of Parliament. Big Ben reminded the Stanburys a dozen times a day how central they were, how delightfully at the heart of London – near Arthur's club, near the National Gallery (they were fond of pictures), and no distance at all from Whitehall, where the Colonel often bumped into an old crony heading for the War Office.

But now their home was theirs no longer. The new tenants had already dropped in two or three times to ask apologetically if they might take measurements of this and that – a fella, a pleasant young fella (as the Colonel described him later, with obvious loathing), and his painted-up pretty little wife.

'Going to South Africa, I understand?' said the juvenile, a harassed-looking civil servant of forty, as he crawled over the drawing room floor with a tape measure. 'Ah, how I envy you, sir! By Jove, Bunty,' he said to the wife, 'I think it will just take it.' Take it? Take what, the Colonel wondered gloomily. He could imagine the kind of furniture these two would bring, the mess they would make of Violet's room. The little wife smiled at him brightly as she stood there with her pencil and notebook. 'Think of that sunshine!' she cried. She bent down to her husband, and they murmured together of plugs for a radio and the colour of a certain sofa, which, said the wife, she 'saw there' – and she pointed her pencil straight at the heart of Arthur Stanbury's row of beloved first-edition Surtees. The Colonel could stand it no longer. He fled. And soon after that the men arrived to pull the Stanburys more completely, as it were, apart – to crate up the Surtees, the silver cups the Colonel had won at polo, the fine rugs, and the bits of his mother's things from the old home in Somerset, all of which later were to follow on, like faithful dogs tracking after the master and mistress, to the new house in the strange land.

The two Stanburys had varied slightly, their friends might have noticed, in the reasons they gave for the step they were taking. To his acquaintance at the club, Colonel Stanbury said that his wife, with her weak throat, could not possibly face another winter in England like the last. She was delicate, and their flat had been, all those coalless months, an Arctic hut, a polar waste, where you could almost see the icy breath settling on the silver cups and the crackling chintzes. When he spoke of the sunshine, the warm African sunshine, a sort of tremor would shake the grizzled heads and the copies of *The Times*. A sort of groaning sigh would travel around the circle of leather armchairs as their occupants looked out at Pall Mall in the rain, at the gap of the bombed building opposite, and at the shabby young women hurrying along the pavements with their bare, splashed legs nakedly twinkling under their mackintoshes. Violet could do some shopping in Durban, the Colonel would say – fit herself out from top to toe with thin clothes for the hot weather. And again the tremor would seem to shake the copies of *The Times*, as though the elderly men whose veined, brown hands grasped them, around whose clear blue eyes harsh Indian light and Egyptian noons and the long hours of watching on duck-shooting mornings had engraved innumerable little sharp lines and furrows – as though these men, the Colonel's friends and contemporaries, felt mournfully in their bones that the Gulf Stream of the good days was turned away from England's shores forever.

Violet Stanbury made no particular mention of her weak throat when she spoke to people of their departure. Arthur, she said, felt that Things were so bad that they must get out while there was still time. Arthur felt Things very keenly, she would say. As she spoke, Things seemed to assume the shape of a dragon that was now firmly couched in its lair beneath the hitherto benign towers of Westminster. This dragon, she implied, was out to devour the Stanburys and their kind, to gobble their modest, honourable incomes, to push them to the wall and bar every path with the lashings of its hideously powerful tail. In time, Arthur felt, the monster of Things would get the whole country down, and he did not want to be there to see the sorry business. Already he was sufficiently upset by it all, Mrs Stanbury said with a sigh. Maybe he was too old to adapt himself to the changes – or they were too old, as she loyally, not entirely truthfully, put it, for she was a gentle soul.

But Arthur had stalked around London, contemptuous and bitterly complaining, carrying his grumbles from the circle of leather armchairs facing Pall Mall to his wine merchant, from his bootmaker to Todhunter, the spectacled old man in Jermyn Street who had cut his hair for years and who could be trusted to say a few disgruntled words about Things before he had fairly tucked the towel around Colonel Stanbury's neck. There were no standards of craftsmanship today, the two of them would decide as Todhunter's scissors snipped away in the tiny old-fashioned shop while the people in the street passed and repassed behind the big green bottles of lotion and the shaving brushes that were displayed in the window. Look at this brush, now, Todhunter would say, fetching one to show the Colonel. Trash, at the price they were asking! In the old days, he wouldn't have had it in the place. And the dishonesty of everybody, not only artistically but actually. There was no honesty left in the people, there were no manners, there was nothing but this new, slipshod idea of working the shortest possible hours for the largest possible wage. Different in his young day, grunted old Todhunter, brushing the Colonel's erect back as he got up to go.

And, sure enough, bus conductors seemed to snap at Arthur Stanbury as soon as his cold blue eyes lighted upon them; he had only to put down a pair of pigskin gloves for a second on the seat of a railway carriage and they disappeared. His days were embittered with little insults, little pilferings, so that it really got almost to the point where he hated everybody and trusted nobody. It was then that Violet Stanbury began telling people that Durban seemed such an opportunity, with their nephew in South Africa, married and settled there for years, and only too anxious to make arrangements and pave the way for them.

'Having Walter and Eileen there will make all the difference,' she said on one occasion. 'And when we get settled in – Walter thinks there will be a chance of a house later on – and can have all our dear old things around us, it will really seem like home. I shall garden – I have always missed gardening, here in London – and Arthur will be able to ride again. We shall get so much more for our money, as Arthur says. And the climate is apparently quite ideal.'

With such soothing reflections, such cosily optimistic word pictures, she contrived to rattle along through the days that led the Stanburys to their departure. They said their goodbyes, some painful. Chapman, the old hall porter, was almost touchingly upset at their going.

'When they drive a gentleman like the Colonel out of 'is own country, it's a sad business, and that's a fact,' he said frequently.

Chapman also believed in Things that were bad and would get worse and be the finish of them all. His one eye glared mournfully, the points of his smartly waxed, faded moustache stuck out as though they intended to testify to the merits of spit-and-polish right up to the end. He brought his married daughter and her little girl from Stepney to say goodbye to the Stanburys. Mrs Stanbury had always taken a friendly interest in the family. The little girl, Ivy, was sucking an orange as she stood staring around at the packing cases in the hall.

'Do you know, Ivy,' said Mrs Stanbury, 'Colonel Stanbury and I are going to live in the country where oranges come from.'

Ivy said nothing.

'Fancy that!' prompted her mother helpfully.

'Wouldn't you like to come, too, and be able to run out and pick an orange straight from the tree whenever you wanted one?' asked Mrs Stanbury.

'Naow,' said Ivy.

The child was unattractive, Violet Stanbury could not help thinking. But Arthur pursued the point with a strange ponderous playfulness.

'Oh, come!' he said. 'Wouldn't you like to go on a big boat, Ivy, and wake up one morning to find blue skies, sunshine, and no more dirty old London? How about that, eh?'

'Naow,' said Ivy.

Apologetic, Chapman shepherded his women to the door and dismissed the parade.

The worst farewells, strangely enough, were to places rather than to people. The Stanburys were getting on in years, after all, and it was quite possible that they would never see these curiously living bits of stone and mortar again, these streets and spires that suddenly had personalities more intense than those of their dearest friends. One day toward the end, they paid their last visit to the National Gallery, and afterward, without asking each other where they were going, found themselves trudging off arm in arm, as though instinctively, to the Abbey. It was a beautiful afternoon, and the great, blackened building looked like some strong old ship, sailing on its green lawns, removed from and alien to the little red buses and the tiny Londoners swirling about it. Inside, the shadows were full of whispers from the feet of the people who strolled along the aisles. The Stanburys, too, strolled and stopped and moved on again, under the marble stares of the dead statesmen and soldiers. The place, in this golden light, seemed to whisper with more than the echo of shuffling feet, with something far away, infinitely old, and yet so personal that Arthur Stanbury felt like answering, 'Yes?' He stood there, poker-straight and motionless, staring up at the soaring roof until his wife touched him on the arm and murmured that they must go.

On the way home, he said to her suddenly, 'Oh, by the way, Vi, I ordered *The Times* and one or two of the weeklies today.'

'Ordered *The Times*?' Mrs Stanbury repeated rather blankly.

'To be mailed to us, I mean, every day.'

'But won't there be good South African papers, dear?' she asked.

'No doubt,' he said. 'But one might as well keep in touch.'

'Of course,' she said.

'I dropped in at Todhunter's, too. He'll go on sending my special lotion, as usual.'

'I do hope it won't get broken on the way,' Mrs Stanbury said.

'No reason why it should if he packs it up carefully,' the Colonel said shortly.

That night, lying in bed, Violet Stanbury found herself listening to Big Ben's strokes with unusual attention. She was so used to them that they never kept her awake normally, but tonight, perhaps because she was overtired with packing and arranging, she seemed to lie waiting for every quarter hour. The familiar voice boomed out, heavy and imperturbable, as though it spoke for something that would outlast the Stanburys, outlast Things, outlast the lot of them. From the rigidity of Arthur's shoulder, just touching hers in the bed, she knew that he was also awake. All the same, she asked in a hushed murmur, 'Are you awake, dear?'

'Yes,' came his deep voice.

'Can't you sleep, either? How provoking! I suppose we're too strung up by everything.'

He gave a great sigh. They went on lying awake, stretched side by side, listening to the big clock measuring out, piece by piece, the time that was still left.

But at last there was no time left at all. They were in the taxi, driving to the station, having been shut in by Chapman with a final salute and a 'Good luck, Colonel!' His kind, ratty little face, genuinely moved, faded from their sight. Mrs Stanbury made a gallant attempt to laugh. She said waveringly to Arthur, 'Well, it's begun!' After that, they sat in silence, looking out at the heartlessly bright streets, the crowds hurrying along, so strangely indifferent, so preoccupied with their own business. The taxi was held up by a policeman who raised his arm to let a party of women, perhaps as many as twenty, cross the road. Violet Stanbury watched them with a curious intentness as they plunged across the taxi's path, clutching each other's arms, uttering loud screams of laughter and mock fright. They were mostly stout and middle-aged, and looked like charwomen, out together on some spree. Their hair was arranged in cast-iron waves and frizzy curls, as though newly released from the pins, and their jolly red faces shone as they shouted at the policeman.

'Ta-ta!' they yelled. 'Be good now!'

Grinning, he turned and waved the Stanburys' taxi on. The Cockney voices, still yelling 'Ta-ta!' as the driver grindingly shifted gears, seemed like the voice of London itself ironically speeding the travellers on their way. Quite suddenly, for the first time, Mrs Stanbury began to cry. The tears streamed down her face while she fumbled quietly for her handkerchief. She did not want Arthur to see such a ridiculous display, and she glanced at him furtively as she rummaged in her bag. The Colonel looked as though he were noticing nothing. He was sitting in his corner, bolt upright, arms folded, looking out at the street along which they were driving. His face was expressionless, but suddenly Mrs Stanbury noticed his forehead was wet, as though it were a very hot day. She stopped trying to find her handkerchief and took his hand.

And thus silently united, Colonel and Mrs Arthur Stanbury came at last to the place of their departure.

MISS HESKETH GOES HOME
Margaret Lane
1950

Miss Hesketh made an effort, held out her ticket to be clipped, and hurried on to the platform. Another woman would have set down her burdens at the barrier and have proffered the ticket without strain, but Miss Hesketh walked with the rapid staggering gait of one who has too much to carry and not a moment to lose.

She was overburdened, certainly. Her attaché-case was all but concealed under a cluster of bulging paper carriers and her other arm was dragged down as taut as a plummet line by a parcel. It was Friday, the day she did special shopping in the lunch hour, visiting Farringdon Market for fish and vegetables and a City grocer who had served her for thirty years and who gave her modest perquisites. She did this instead of shopping at home on Saturdays, the weekends being so deeply committed that not one drop of further use could be wrung out of them. All the domestic arrears of the week had to be made up, Mother's blanket bath performed and her room turned out, as well as the serious cooking which furnished the larder for a week.

Miss Hesketh made her way through the standing crowd to a seat beyond the bookstall. There was one place unoccupied, and after an anxious glance about her she sat down in it. She did this only because her fingers could bear the pain of her parcels no longer. She would have preferred to stand, and did not feel safe in a station except in an attitude of extreme readiness. She sat very upright now, not relaxing, rubbing her long bony fingers gently through their string gloves, staring with wide-open, slightly bulging eyes at nothing in particular.

In an hour and twenty minutes she would be home. She would be pushing open the iron gate with her knee, walking up the little path of liver-coloured tiles which lay like a weal across every front garden in the terrace, letting herself in quietly and calling out, 'It's only me, Mother,' before going through to the kitchen and putting on the kettle. After that she would go upstairs to the front bedroom where her mother sat all day long among her paraphernalia, and in the moment of entering, with an accuracy born of many years' experience, gauge the emotional temperature. This varied to some degree, but was generally low. Mrs Hesketh was eighty and very helpless, and had nothing to do all day but brood on death. Usually she greeted her daughter with resentment, with the hatred of the prisoner for the free, and a well-rehearsed recital of the day's discomforts. The first task, always, was to rally her. This was not easy, for every subject carried its own taboo. Anything interesting about the office was received, not on its own merits, but as stressing the contrast between the happy lives of everyone else and the misery of Mrs Hesketh. On the other hand, a comforting account of someone else's misfortunes was likely to

be no more successful, since the trials of other people were as nothing compared with Mrs Hesketh's trials. 'They don't know they're born,' she would say bitterly, dismissing bereavements, accidents and sudden death as makeshifts and imitations, impudent pretensions to experience. Even death, on which she brooded with such personal resentment, as though on a fate reserved for her alone, became nothing when it overtook another person. 'Those that can die are lucky,' she would say, when Miss Hesketh tried, with the story of someone else's loss or some accident in the newspaper, to make her feel that even her own life had its compensations.

What cheering topic could she take home tonight? Miss Hesketh kneaded her sore fingers and stared in front of her, her long body rigid, her feet and ankles supporting a barricade of parcels. How long could she preserve her reassuring front, how long conceal the appalling news of which she now felt certain? She had had scares before, of course, and they had come to nothing; but this time it was definite. She was fifty-five, and looked older; there was no other woman in the office over thirty, and Mr Oppenheim had treated her lately with a consideration so exquisite that it could only be guilty. And now at last, without looking at her, he had introduced a strange Miss Goodenough into her room, and had asked Miss Hesketh to explain the filing system.

A spasm of despair went through her, exposing her mind on all sides to the impossible future. Without her job, without that fountain from which they fed, what was to become of them? This was the other side of the medal so resolutely clasped against life's disappointments. The secret of happiness, she always said, is to be needed. If you are indispensable to somebody, if the needs of others leave you no time to think about yourself, that is true happiness. To be useless, uncalled for, that is the only death. She was so moved by this aspect of her mother's condition that she could not bear to think of it.

Miss Hesketh herself had been, in a way, so fortunate. She had for years been so necessary to her mother and to Mr Oppenheim that no amount of fatigue could altogether discourage her. Mr Oppenheim buzzed for her as soon as he arrived in the morning; she stayed late night after night because nobody else, as he said, knew all the details; and as soon as she opened the front door her mother's voice would come reproachfully down the stairs, a voice weighted with all the hours of the day and an unappeasable need of her.

Other unmarried women of her age were haunted by loneliness, but she was never lonely. More, she was never alone. Her mother's nights were not so good as her days, and it was years since Miss Hesketh had slept in her own bedroom. The old woman's sighs, the creakings of discomfort, the dense smell of old age in a closed room were so much a part of Miss Hesketh's experience of darkness that she had forgotten that they were not a natural part of it.

She shook her head, as though in startled reply to some dangerous question, and looked at her watch. The train was due; she must gather her parcels together and stand up. The impossible had got to be faced, a solution found. The journey must be made, the door opened, a cheerful greeting prepared, the kettle put on and supper cooked as though nothing had happened. She told herself this, but still she did not move. She even relaxed a little, and her lips parted. She was experiencing temptation.

* * *

This temptation of Miss Hesketh's, the only really enticing and powerful one that she had ever encountered, had first presented itself to her two years ago, in the guise of a dream. She would be asleep in her mother's room, in the camp bed squeezed between the chest of drawers and the washstand, asleep in the thick darkness of heavy curtains and the mysterious stale smell of bedclothes and medicines, when she would find herself suddenly walking along a country road which had an early morning feeling of innocence and emptiness. The road was not always the same, but this was not important; sooner or later, at some turning, a gateway, across a stream, she would come upon the house.

This house was quite unlike the one Miss Hesketh lived in. She had never, so far as she knew, seen it when awake; it belonged to a world that was different from hers altogether. Yet it knew her, and was familiar, and had a face of such beautiful certainty and welcome that she never came to this point in her dream without a shock of pleasure. However she came upon it, in summer or winter, by open air or through stifling confused passages and corridors, there it was, always serenely waiting against its massive trees, beautiful, elegant, mysterious, and empty.

It was perhaps because it was empty that Miss Hesketh was not afraid of it, for it stood alone before its wooded background, and was approached across a lawn ennobled with cedars, beautiful and intimidating. But the windows had an innocent blankness about them, there were no curtains; the doors stood open and the rooms were full of echoes. Nobody lived there at all.

That was the beauty of the place: she was alone in it. She could wander peacefully from room to room, soothed by the space and light and urbane proportions, could go up the shallow stairs smelling of sun-warmed cedar and lean across the deep windowsills of upstairs rooms, where tentative furry stems of ivy were encroaching. She would lean far out to taste the lovely air. The peace was continuous, it flowed through and about the house like a calm tide, and Miss Hesketh was carried in its arms like a floating bird.

The happiness that possessed her in this house was so intense, so buoyant, that she really seemed to float; she was not conscious of her feet in walking, nor of her body at all. The element that she moved in was as much solitude as air. She was always completely and unavoidably alone.

This dream, never quite the same but always constant in the quality of its pleasure, at first came rarely, and it was something to be remembered with surprise. Why, good gracious, I had that dream again! The feeling of peace would return at odd moments of the day. And then it began to come more often, and at times when she was neither fully asleep nor wholly awake, in that last early morning hour before her mother's creaking and grunting became too insistent to be ignored; or at the office, towards the stale and peevish end of the day, when her feet were cold and her head hot, and the room stuffy.

Then she would have the most curious and complete illusion that she was walking across a dewy lawn in the half-light, and not in her bed or at her desk at all; and she would suddenly know where she was, and a sense of delicious happiness would invade her, as definite as a flavour in the mouth. The difficulty was to bring oneself back to the airless bedroom or stuffy office, and not just lie or sit in a trance of pleasure, lips parted, pale eyes staring, and gone, quite gone. It was not the sort of thing you could allow to grow on you.

Yet it did grow. It began to insinuate itself at the oddest moments, when she was darting across a street, or standing patiently in the solid mass of bodies on the moving escalator. It even seemed as though it chose the most difficult and disagreeable moment, when she had most need of herself. Let the crowd be particularly thick, the work on her desk particularly confused, or her mother's voice particularly rasping, with that edgy note in it at which the heart sank, and the dream would be there, at her elbow. She only had to shut her eyes, let it invade her like an anaesthetic, and the world would recede to a distant roar and finally to silence. It was sometimes so clear and insistent that in spite of her refusal the two worlds, for minutes at a time, would exist for her side by side, and it would take an exhausting effort to make the unreal vanish.

She had reached the point, now, where she indulged herself whenever she dared, whenever she judged it safe, and the rest of the time kept a strict watch against temptation. It was not safe now. Friday afternoon, Waterloo in the rush hour, the last few minutes before her train came in, were, of all others, the time and place where she must not succumb. The train was always crowded; it was rare to get a seat; usually she travelled in the corridor, or in the middle of the carriage, grasping the edge of the rack with one hand and harbouring her parcels with her feet. Tonight, of all nights it was necessary to be clear, to keep her mind settled on what she had to do when she got home. Impossible though it might be, it had got to be faced. Her job was finally sinking under her, and when it had irrevocably gone, what was to become of them? The whole weight of her mother's helplessness, of the house, and of their shared life in it, was on her shoulders. She was essential; she had the incredible luck, as she had often assured herself, to be vitally necessary, so that her life had that rarest of luxuries, a meaning. As a result, of course, it was without escape. Every hole had been stopped.

It had been a mistake, Miss Hesketh told herself sharply, to sit down. People were standing close to her, the platform was crowded, the noises of the station were all around her, she was conscious of the cold air she breathed, with its December undercurrent of vinegar and fog, and yet – here was the new and alarming thing – she was quite clearly conscious as well of another sound, the summer murmur of a stream under a bridge. Miss Hesketh knew that bridge and stream; she had leaned often on the parapet and studied the water's evidence of the seasons; in winter a dark rapid flow straining the pale stalks of watercress, in summer the water sprinkled with leaves and stars. It was from this bridge that one had the most satisfying view of the house.

She gave herself a little shake and bent for her parcels. She would stand up, go to the edge of the platform, shoulder her

way to a good position, brace herself for the hellish assault on the train. It was coming in now, she could hear the slow rumble and the steaming sigh; the crowd was already surging all one way. She bent, and felt for her bags, but failed to grasp them. She groped a little, uncertainly, then slowly straightened herself with a puzzled look and sat still. Her mouth fell open and her gloved hands moved gently on one another. She seemed to be staring at the train.

* * *

It was extraordinary, Miss Hesketh thought, that she had never noticed this before, but the windows were definitely flickering, as though with firelight. It was winter, after all, and getting dark. Had someone been lighting fires in the downstairs rooms?

She crossed the grass, and was aware of its frosty stiffness under her feet. The evenings were drawing in. She went up the shallow steps to the terrace, beautiful and bare with its parapet of flaking stone, and saw that what she had suspected was indeed true: the downstairs windows were dancing with the lovely animation of good fires burning in darkened rooms. She went in, her feet scarcely touching the ground, and found that the house was warm. The firelight was everywhere, leaping in the big grate and sending tongues of light over the fluted columns and the panelled walls. There was a smell of cedarwood, as though something old and delicious had been opened in a well-warmed room; as though candles were burning somewhere among fir branches; as though there were preparations for a festivity.

* * *

Doors slammed and whistles blew, and Miss Hesketh paused at the turn of the stairs, vaguely troubled. There was something unclear about the situation; it was confused; she knew how important it was to keep her wits about her, and she stood with her fingers resting on the handrail, waiting until this odd sensation should pass. It did at last. The disturbing noises faded, the smoke, the shrieks, the echoes died away. She went on peacefully upstairs, this time with a strong and swelling sense of certainty. The wavering light was everywhere, the warmth, the delicious smell, the blessed emptiness. Above all, it was the feeling of sanctuary that delighted her. Her dreamlike progress from room to room was like quietly stirring in a loved embrace.

* * *

This went on for a long time, it might have been hours or days; and sometimes Miss Hesketh was aware of being alone no longer, but this made little difference to her happiness. There were voices occasionally, too, at a great distance, and they were concerned with her and seemed to hope for an answer; but it was all too dim and confused for her to be bothered with it. There were even faces at times, and there were some that recurred: a man's face, strange but not unkind, and the disciplined face of a young woman, framed and enhanced by some white and veil-like structure. But they made no demands on her, she was not necessary to them. She ignored them after a time.

Once or twice, breaking the even flow of her peaceful existence, there were dreams of a particularly unlikely sort. One
was, absurdly enough, that she was being bathed, like a child,
by someone else; and another was a passing illusion that she
was lying in bed in a huge room with many beds and unnatu-
rally high windows. The room was quiet and clean and did not
frighten her, but she could not account for it. More than once
she thought she was sitting with many others at a long and
beautifully scrubbed table in a room full of sunshine and the
smell of polish. Plates of bread and butter were being passed
from hand to hand, in a peculiar silence. For some reason this
distressed her. Also, she kept looking at the bright fire burning
in the room, and the strong hinged fireguard fastened across
it with a padlock. She had the uneasy feeling one has when
something is wrong, one cannot quite say what.

These unaccountable moments, however, were too rare to
break the spell of her exquisite solitude, or cause her more
than a momentary doubt. She would shake them off, to find
herself gazing from the upper windows at the rain-drenched
cedars, or sitting on the terrace in the summer evening, listening to the stream. Somewhere, she knew, there was something
that worried her, but she could never remember it. She felt
light as thistledown, yet at the same time remote, becalmed;
as though she had been carried by the tide to an immense
distance, and was no longer in any danger of recall.

SEASIDE INCIDENT
Margaret Stanley-Wrench
1951

As she walked, Lydia was unpleasantly conscious of the chilly wind dappling her bare arms with gooseflesh, and hugged the thin shawl closer. The muslin dress rippled round her legs, making a fresh, frilling noise, like leaves in high summer. On the right, a sparkling sea pounced on the sand in brittle, kitten-ish dashes; sunburnt fishermen were busy tarring their boats; handsome, powerful men, with blue eyes, who looked up and winked at the elegant young woman walking there alone.

Lydia made up her mind to walk to the end of the new esplanade. How wonderful it was to be living in an age of progress. Why, two or three years ago this very place had been nothing but a cluster of fishing huts, and now it was a busy watering place, only half a day's journey from London in a fast chaise!

It had been kind of Tom to send her here after her illness; few men would trouble about a sick woman, one who was grow-ing older too. It was so easy to find a fresh young girl, easy to discard one past her first bloom. Yes, Tom was kind, there were few such as he . . . yet life without him was freer and happier. But how otherwise could a woman exist, without money, talents or assets other than an elegant shape, and a small hand and foot?

A young man was leaning over the sea wall ahead; he seemed to be scribbling something, a letter, or the verses which boys of sensibility ground out to a pattern. The breeze ruffled his hair, bright as horse chestnuts shaken from their doeskin shells. Tom's was thin and greying now.

Lydia found herself staring at the stranger, admiring his broad shoulders and those ruffled curls, which made her long to touch them; they would be thick and warm as a bird's plumage. To her embarrassment, he looked up, meeting her eyes, and for the first time in years she blushed. His glance was sparkling and impertinent; a man had no business with such long, thick eyelashes either.

Annoyed, she turned to stare at the piles of building material on the other side of the road, and, for a moment, did not realise that the new esplanade had petered out into ruts, stones and knops of turf, till her foot turned over on a clod of earth. With a squeal of pain, Lydia fell, and lay, a drift of muslin, her little reticule spilling its contents over the grass.

Now he'd think she'd fallen deliberately. She flushed angrily, but the young man was at her side, his merry eyes now full of concern. He knelt down, feeling her leg, not amorously, but with cool, professional hands.

'I have some medical training, madam,' he explained. 'You are fortunate only to have strained your ankle. I'll wet my handkerchief and bind it; cold water will relieve the contusion.'

Like a stocky pony, he bounded over the low wall, dashed to the sea, was back in a moment, and had bound his wet handkerchief deftly and comfortably round her foot.

'There, is that more comfortable? Take my hand; see if you can stand.'

'Thank you, sir, I am most grateful. I cannot think how I could be so stupid.'

Once more he appraised her with those merry hazel eyes, till, as if she'd gazed too long at the sparkling sea, her senses were dazzled and confused. But he said seriously:

'Do you live far, madam? Can you walk, if I support you? Or shall I fetch a chaise from the town?'

'No, no, I can walk quite well. I am staying only half a mile from here.'

Lydia bit her lip. Did it sound too obvious? But she couldn't bear to lose him yet. And the foot didn't hurt . . . much. She put her hand on his arm and together they walked back.

How quickly, too quickly, in spite of slow steps, they reached her lodgings. But she had never talked with a man so freely. He spoke eagerly, like a boy, of all he'd been doing; told her of spending the spring in the Isle of Wight.

Then he talked of Canterbury, where he and his brother had been staying. The brother was called Tom, too; the name, with its associations, came between them, making her sad for a moment.

Speaking of his sick brother, his voice had trembled, but now it danced with merriment as he described a mad party he'd attended.

Conversation discovered joint friends; this gave their meeting respectability, sanctioned the adventure, silencing her apprehension about what Tom would think if he knew.

Forgetting she had been sick and was thirty, her dark eyes shone, her cheek had been whipped by the wind to a carnation bloom, and tiny, vine-like tendrils of dark hair strayed from the modish turban.

They had reached her lodgings. Lydia turned:

'You will come inside? After your great kindness, you must not leave without refreshment.'

He paused, looking at her like a child whose longed-for treat has come true. Lydia found herself regretting her vanished youth, wishing she were the girl of twenty again, free and unspoiled. Yet her girlhood self would have had nothing to give. That was the bitter thing, in youth one was sealed up, stiff, prudish; with age one could unfold, give graciously, yet then the gift was tarnished, perhaps unwanted . . .

How fortunate that Tom had left her the travelling case of liqueurs. She lifted out one of the small decanters, and two of the fragile, gold-banded glasses.

Her guest strolled round the room, looking at the green African parrot in its cage, picking up a book, unfolding music. His voice was excited and his hand, holding the paper, trembled.

'You like Haydn, too? And you read Spenser! Why, you have marked my favourite passage. I believe that we were destined to meet . . .'

'If only we had been, if only we could be drinking to the future!' she thought, lifting the glass of golden liqueur.

He turned to her, and their eyes met. She felt as if drowned in those dazzling, golden-brown orbs; as if he could see everything, know, understand, and forgive, yet they asked something of her, too. She took a step forward, and, in the moment before the embrace, knew that although this would bring her bitter sorrow, it might bring him some form of salvation.

Poor child, poor child, how he needed kindness and love. She smoothed his thick hair; curling tendrils of it caught on her hand, as his arms clung desperately, and his mouth reached for hers.

When, hours later, Lydia sat alone, her dark, cloudy hair fallen from its Grecian knot, she realised that, for the first and last time, she was in love, and without hope. A girl would have been full of happiness, drowsy with love; a girl would have remembered, and been satisfied with all he had whispered in her ear, his kisses, the joy he had shown in her beauty and love. But Lydia, a woman, knew, too well, that he had taken her gift as a hungry man takes bread or water.

She rose, and moved around the room. Yes, temporary home as it as, her own possessions gave it personality; a Wedgwood vase, shaped like a Grecian urn, framed reproductions of Claude and Poussin, tastefully bound copies of Spenser, Chaucer and Shakespeare. Tom laughed at her, his learned lady, laughed, and bought what books and music she wished, as one might buy bones for a performing dog. The Aeolian harp, too, that hung and made queer, jangling music that fitted well with her mood and longings, it was like her, an instrument to be strummed on by a passing breeze!

Lydia wandered about the room, trying vainly to find some signs of the lover who had gone. Nothing was left, only the two gold-rimmed glasses on the table, and the fast-fading echoes of his voice in her mind. Then she saw a fragment of paper on the floor. In a bold, sensitive handwriting, lines of verse he had scribbled:

When I have fears that I may cease to be
Before my pen has glean'd my teeming brain,
Before high-piled books, in charact'ry,
Hold like rich garners, the full ripened grain;
When I behold, upon the night's starr'd face,
Huge cloudy symbols of a high romance,
And feel that I may never live to trace
Their shadows, with the magic hand of chance;
And when I feel, fair creature of an hour!
That I shall never look upon thee more,
Never have relish in the faery power
Of unreflecting love; then on the shore
Of the wide world I stand alone, and think,
Till love and fame to nothingness do sink.

Underneath, very small, were initials: J K.

Holding the verses close to her, as if they were infinitely precious, Lydia walked to the window. For a moment her tears made the bright sea even brighter, then she could look out steadily and courageously again. He had gone, but in the few hours of their love and friendship Lydia knew she had granted, and been given, in her turn, immortality, and that he had endowed her with more richness than a lifetime of love.

Note by the author upon the publication of this story in John O'London's Weekly on 19th January 1951. The only evidence I have about 'The Lady from Hastings' is in a letter from John Keats to his brother George and his sister-in-law dated October, 1818. Here is the relevant quotation: 'Since I wrote this far I have met with that same Lady again, whom I saw at Hastings and whom I met when we were going to the English Opera. It was in a street which goes from Bedford to Lamb's Conduit Street – I passed her and turned back: she seemed glad of it – glad to see me, and not offended at my passing her before. We walked on towards Islington, where we called on a friend of hers who keeps a Boarding School . . . I pressed to attend her home. She consented, and then again my thoughts were at work what it might lead to, tho' now they had received a sort of genteel hint from the Boarding School.

'Our walk ended in 34 Gloucester Street, Queen Square – not exactly so, for we went upstairs into her sitting room, a very tasty sort of place with books, pictures, a bronze statuette of Buonaparte, Music, Aeolian Harp; a Parrot, a Linnet, a Case of choice Liqueurs, &c, &c. She behaved in the kindest manner – made me take home a Grouse for Tom's dinner. Asked for my address for the purpose of sending more game.

'As I had warmed with her before and kissed her I thought it would be living backwards not to do so again – she had a better taste: she perceived how much a thing of course it was and shrunk from it – not in a prudish way, but in as I say a good taste. She continued to disappoint me in a way which made me feel more pleasure than a simple kiss could do. She said I should please her much more if I would only press her hand and go away. Whether she was in a different disposition when I saw her before – or whether I have in fancy wronged her I cannot tell.'

I based the story on what may have happened at that first meeting in Hastings, and conjectured that this lady may have inspired the sonnet quoted in the story.

A BUS FROM TIVOLI
Kate O'Brien
1957

In the hot weather Marian liked to take, at random, one or
other of the many buses that left the Piazza Termini for the villages called Castelli, in the Alban hills; or sometimes she would
choose to go to Tivoli in the Sabines. Eventually she grew
to like best to go to Hadrian's Villa, and to loaf about in that
extraordinary estate through silent evenings. It was a place of
sweet smells and lovely shades; she did not trouble overmuch
to trace Hadrian's grandiose plans, under the grass; she felt
sufficiently aware of the place and sufficiently aware of Rome
in general to be content to walk about in peace, and to accept
what the map at the gate said, and what the occasional sign-
posts said. What she went to Hadrian's Villa for was profound
silence, and the surprising richness of green and leaf. Rome,
so near, was also far in summer evenings from this sad, grassed-
over place of pride and sorrow.

They locked the entrance gate at seven o'clock; the man in
charge got to know her, and gave her a few minutes grace as she
hurried down under the acacia trees and past the little Greek

Theatre. And when she was turned out she always crossed the lane to the trattoria opposite.

This was a pleasant restaurant. She sat in the garden, under vines that trailed from elm tree to apple tree; fireflies dashed about and late birds fussed and fluttered; strong light from indoors threw shadows about the grass, and also allowed her to read at ease. Cats, Roman and self-confident, sat at her feet, and shared her supper. By Roman standards, food was cheap in this place, and it was good. Trout, omelettes, strawberries, and peaches, and sharp wine of the Castelli. She sat in the silent dark as long as she liked. The bus descending from Tivoli for Rome passed the crossroads – a kilometre away, up the lane, every half-hour until eleven o'clock – and she was never in a hurry. About half-past nine or so she would walk up the lane to catch, say, the ten o'clock bus. One night she fell in, on this walk, with an elderly gardener who mistook her for Spanish – he said her Italian had a Spanish inflection. He knew Spain and had lived in a town of Northern Spain that she knew well. So they found much to talk about, and as he was old and rheumatic, by the time she parted from him at his house near the crossroads, she saw the ten o'clock bus dash past for Rome.

It was no matter; there would be another at ten-thirty. The only disadvantage was that in the evening, as at all hours, the high road from Tivoli to Rome is noisy and dusty, and there is nothing to sit on by the bus stops.

Marian was in her fifties, and a heavy woman, one easily tired and who found life in Rome somewhat a physical ordeal. So, although she disliked the appearance of the little, brand new café on the corner, disliked its shape, its white neon lights and its jukebox noises, she went into it, and to her surprise found a seat and a table vacant, crammed though the small interior was with lively, shouting Romans, crowded about the terrible music in the box.

'Could I have a glass of dry vermouth?' she said, in anxious, bad Italian.

A young man in a spotless white coat beamed, bowed and went to get her a glass of dry vermouth. She looked around her, feeling sad. Always she left Hadrian's Villa and the embowered, quiet trattoria feeling sad. But the high road, the noise, the scooters, and the public lavatory style of this – as of all cheap places of refreshment set up by the Romans – saddened her unreasonably.

Unreasonable indeed, she told herself she was, and looked about and lighted a cigarette. The young man came and placed a glass of vermouth before her. Also he brought olives and potato crisps. He stood and smiled on her. She thanked him, and as he did not move she thought she should pay at once. She opened her purse. He waved the money aside.

'No, no,' he said. 'Merely I wonder where you are going?'

'I'm going to Rome. I missed the ten o'clock bus.'

'You are foreign, lady. But you are not English?'

'I am Irish.'

'Ah! Irish! And why do you go to Rome?'

'Because I'm living there.'

'I see,' he said. 'You are living there. Rome is quite near us, here.'

He was a large and powerfully built young man. Very clean; scrubbed and square, and fresh-skinned; handsome in the

Roman fashion, heavily muscular, with firmly marked features. His eyes were intelligently bright – small and green-grey. He looked to be twenty-four or five.

As he stood and stared upon her, smiling kindly, Marian considered him with amusement.

'He's curiously like me,' she thought, 'He could be my son.'

For she had, as she knew with dislike, a heavy Roman look. In youth she had been normally slender, and beautiful of face; but middle age had taken the beauty away, and left her fleshy and Roman looking – Roman emperors she suggested to herself, when she contemplated her ageing head in the mirror; but Nero or Heliogabalus rather than Marcus Aurelius or Hadrian.

'And this boy is like Nero, I'd say,' she thought. 'Indeed – I'm sorry to think it – but this strong young Roman could easily be my son – in looks.'

This reflection, though amusing, did not please her, because Marian did not at all admire the Roman physical type, and very much disliked her own undeniable relation to it.

She ran her hands through her untidy hair.

'You feel too warm?'

'Yes; it's hot here. But it's always hot in Rome.'

'We have a beautiful bathroom here – with a beautiful shower.'

'Oh yes – we have all those beautiful things in my flat in Rome; your plumbing is very good –'

'Very good here. You must meet my sister. A moment, please!'

The young man bowed.

⊘⊙⊘⊙⊘⊙⊘⊙

Relieved that he had left her, Marian shut her eyes and sipped vermouth.

But within a minute a hand touched her gently. A young, small, pretty girl was sitting beside her.

'My brother says that you are going to Rome. Why are you going to Rome?'

Amazed, Marian answered, 'I live in Rome,'

'But why do you live there?'

'I come often to Tivoli and to Hadrian's Villa.'

'Of course. Many people come to Hadrian's Villa. You love it?'

'I like to walk there.'

'Then why don't you stay here?'

'But – I don't want to. I live in Rome.'

'My brother wants you to stay here. Will you not?'

'Stay here? But how – what do you mean?'

'My brother – he has begged me to ask you. We have every comfort here – bath, all conveniences. We will be good to you. My brother is good. He entreats that you stay with us.'

'But what on earth do you mean?'

'I mean what I say. My brother wants you. Could you not stay with him? He is kind.'

Marian stood up.

'Please, I beg you – let me pay now – I must go –'

The young man came forward and took her two hands.

'Will you not stay? Please, lady – my sister has told you, surely? I entreat you –'

'I am old! I'm an old woman!'

He smiled and touched her shoulder. 'I know. I see that. It doesn't matter. Stay!'

Marian put some lire on the table. He gathered them up and put them into her hand.

'Please, please – stay here a little while –'

'Oh heavens, goodnight! You're a crazy child! Why, you could both be my children!'

She ran down the steps, and in a minute the bus for Rome drew up. As it swept her away they stood and waved to her under their neon lights.

The curious, comic episode slid out of mind. Amused and puzzled by it for a day or so, she did narrate it to some friends, writers, painters, film actors – English and American – with whom she, a writer, associated in Rome.

But she told the ridiculous little story to no Italian acquaintance, because she felt that it would be impolite to do so. Also, she was sure that no Italian would believe her, and would gently dismiss her as another dreaming old lady from the queer, northern lands. Her English, Irish and American friends, however, knew her well enough to know that odd little story was true; they theorised gaily over the eccentric young Roman café-keeper; and one or two of them went so far in affection for her as to say that they saw his point – that definitely they saw his point.

Marian, however, did not see his point; and accepting that any youth who could rush such improbable fences within five minutes was in some unfixable way insane, she still wondered how he was empowered in the same five minutes of his lunatic appeal, to engage his young and sensitive-faced sister as his procuress. Nevertheless, she was a novelist and had been on earth for fifty-five years; she had encountered knottier questions than this accidental one of the café-keeper at the Tivoli bus stop. She let it slide. But she did not go to Hadrian's Villa again; and this was a deprivation.

In August, however, she had staying with her in Rome an English painter, a woman much younger than herself, to whom the Roman scene was new. She decided that she must take this friend to Tivoli and Hadrian's Villa. So they went. As they were late in leaving Tivoli after luncheon they took a taxi to Hadrian's Villa. In the trattoria they ate at leisure and fed the cats, and Marian amused Elizabeth with the story of the young café-keeper at the crossroads.

Politely, affectionately, Elizabeth said that she saw the young man's point. Marian laughed.

'Diana and Robert said that too,' she said. 'But it was a madman's point. He's only a big, fat boy. And all in five minutes! And dragging his little sister into it!'

They stayed a long time in the trattoria garden, aromatic and quiet. And when at last they reached the crossroads they had barely missed the ten-thirty bus to Rome and had twenty-nine minutes to wait for the next, the last one. It was a fiesta night, dusty, and intolerably noisy by the roadside.

'We'll sit in the café,' said Elizabeth. 'What harm if the poor boy sees you again?'

'What harm indeed? He'll have forgotten the whole thing anyway – it's more than two months ago.'

The café had grown smarter with summer expansion, and had tin tables set now in a narrow little terrace, above the shops under the neon lights. One of these tables, in a corner, was vacant, and Marian and Elizabeth went and sat there.

Like a shot from a gun the young café-keeper was with them. His face shone with joy.

'You have come back at last! I knew you would! Dry vermouth – I remember! Or would you not have a brandy?'

Marian asked Elizabeth what she would like to drink – vermouth – dry Italian. He was enchanted. He must tell his sister. He would be with them in a moment. He had wished always for her to come back. She must believe him, excuse him – he would return in a moment.

And in a moment he did return – with his sister, and with bottle and glasses. Radiant, happy, sketchily asking permission, he and his sister sat down and he filled the glasses with Asti Spumante. Marian smiled. She detested the wine.

'Lady – you have come again. I have watched for you. I and my sister. Where do you live in Rome? We have searched and asked – oh, we drink now! You have returned! You will stay here now – please? Yes? You, her friend – you too? You will stay here now, as I desire – in this fine, clean house I have –?'

'It is good and clean; my brother is a good boy – and he desires this lady,' said her sister to Elizabeth.

Elizabeth had no Italian, but she understood what the girl said, and she smiled.

'I have watched, I have waited. I have not for a day forgotten you, Irish lady – is that true?' he turned to his sister.

'It is true. He loves you, signora – signorina? There is no peace. Stay with him a little, please. He is a good boy – he is kind.'

'We have all modern comforts. We will consider you and be careful. Oh, you are near Rome here; you can do as you please! Only stay with us, a little time, lady! I knew I must see you again!'

The young man's strong, clean hands were laid, hard and flat on Marian's. His bright eyes blazed on her.

'Answer him. Speak to him,' said Elizabeth.

Marian knew she must do so. Grotesque as the comedy made her feel, it also quite absurdly honoured her. And ludicrously insane as it might be, it was – take it or leave it – an actuality. This cracked young man was as he was and had taken and held to this impossible and grotesque idea.

'I don't know your name, or your sister's,' she said. 'I am fifty-five years old: I take you to be about twenty-five, your sister not yet, I'd say, twenty-one. It is impossible for me to thank you or be gracious about your insane idea. I have to speak in English – I have no Italian to say what I mean – but in English I will tell you to stop talking nonsense, and that I'll be gone on the bus in a minute.'

Marian stood up. The young man rose with her, holding her two hands.

'Do not go! Oh, do not go – now you have returned! We have here every kindness, every comfort –'

'I am going! Oh please be sane!'

'I am not concerned to be sane! Where are you – in Rome? I will visit you! I will behave well, I have a beautiful summer suit, of light grey – let me come! Where are you?'

'He is good, lady. He will bring you flowers, he will bring you wine. Tell him where to find you in Rome! He is good. He loves you – he talks about you always.'

'I will come. I will visit – in my good new suit. I insist I will

visit. You have returned – and you must tell me who you are –
I have searched –'

'Goodbye, goodbye.'

The last bus from Tivoli came roaring down and Marian
and Elizabeth fought their way on to it.

They dismounted in the Piazza Termini.

'I think you should have let him visit you,' said Elizabeth.
'His good, new suit.'

They found their bus to the Chiesa Nuova.

A FAITHFUL WIFE
Diana Athill
1963

A few nights earlier Helen Blundell had said sleepily to her husband Roger, 'You know something? I don't believe, now, that I could ever *bear* to make love with anyone but you.'

'You'd better not!' he had answered, but he had turned over and pushed his head into the curve between her shoulder and her breast. It had been one of the times when their happiness together had crystallised in their lovemaking and they had both been equally and simultaneously aware of it.

Familiarity is supposed to make this dull, thought Helen before going to sleep. Five years of it . . . and she felt certain that she had gladly exchanged what it had once been for the kind of thing she had experienced a few minutes ago, when Roger had been stroking her back. She had felt, then, perfectly convinced that his skin and hers were enjoying exactly the same sensation, as though her back and his hand were parts of the same being. How lucky I am, she had thought, to be married to my own darling love.

She looked a lucky woman, too: relaxed and pretty, saved by an adequate income from domestic anxieties, and by an easy-going nature from creating them when they did not exist. She was readily pleased and amused, and intelligent enough to keep herself so when no entertainment offered. They had no child as yet, but that was not a sorrow. Roger, a consultant engineer, often had to travel, and they had decided that Helen should be free to share this until she was thirty. Her next birthday would be her thirtieth, and she intended to conceive on it – accustomed as she was to things going well for her, she did not doubt that this would happen, so even the prospect of leaving her twenties behind seemed to her promising rather than alarming. The Blundells' friends sometimes quoted them to each other as proof that a good marriage was a possibility, and the wives would say to each other, 'Darling Helen – I'm very fond of her, of course, but she can be a shade smug.'

Now Helen came into the drawing room of one of these friends, coming to lunch alone because Roger was in Manchester, and 'No!' she exclaimed, stopping abruptly just inside the door. 'It can't be!'

The man standing by the fireplace put down his glass, bumped a table in his haste to cross the room to her, put his arms round her, and kissed her on the mouth. 'Helen!' he said. 'It's incredible, you're exactly the same. You're more beautiful.'

'But how . . . ?' said Helen, clutching his arm, and everyone began to laugh.

'I lost my address book,' the man said – he was an American. 'The one with your married name in it. I couldn't remember it. I thought, this is the worst thing that has ever happened, returning to England after all these years and the one person I can't find is Helen. But then, of course, I realised that Dorothy would know, and I called her, and she said you'd be here today.'

'Isn't it marvellous?' said their hostess. 'I couldn't believe it when I heard his voice. I was going to ring you up, then I thought no, it would be such a lovely surprise.'

'Give me a drink, someone,' said Helen. 'Let me sit down, I'm in a flutter. Ralph, I don't know where to begin . . . How long is it?'

Ralph Kuchinsky had been at Oxford as a Rhodes Scholar, a friend of Dorothy's brother. Helen, who had known Dorothy's family since childhood, had met him at their house on her nineteenth birthday, and he had become one of the three men with whom, at that time, she was more or less in love. She had enjoyed him more than either of the others, but at the same time had been less able to take him seriously because of the excessively romantic approach which made him speak too easily of marriage. To Helen marriage was still something remote, far too serious for them ever to attain together. She was capable of many absurdities but she did not have the kind of mind which fools itself, so that to her it was always evident that she and Ralph were playing. But he came from so far away, he seemed so grown-up and confident compared to many of her friends, he was so frankly passionate – in spite of thinking of him as something of a joke, she had hovered very near the brink of commitment with him. Then Ralph had gone to France for six months, leaving her almost sure that they would become lovers on his return – and while he was out of England she had met Roger.

Heavens! she thought now, reaching for a cigarette to hide the laughter which was about to break out. Does he remember Cavendish Square? They had walked round and round Cavendish Square on the night when she told him that it was no good, she had fallen in love with Roger. Ralph's arm had been round her, she had leaned against him as though she were fainting, they had both wept. 'Oh why, why?' she had sobbed, and had turned it into, 'Why does life make us do these awful things to each other?' But what she had nearly said was, 'Why, why didn't you make me go to bed with you last summer so that I could have had that, too?' Goodness, how sad she had felt that evening, and how she had enjoyed it.

'Tell me everything,' she said now to the stranger on Dorothy's hearthrug. 'Are you still writing plays; are you still living in Iowa; are you married?'

'Oh, my God, do you mean to say that I haven't written to anyone since I got married? Married and two kids – twin sons. I'll inflict photographs on you in a minute. And New York now, and no more plays – I've got bills to pay. You remember I had a favourite uncle, manufactured textiles? Well, I've gone in with him, on the promotion side.'

'Do you enjoy it? Are you happy?'

But Dorothy called them in to lunch before he could answer, and the talk became general.

He looks happy, thought Helen. Dear Ralph, how glad I am.

He was shorter than Roger, squarer, with a smooth yellow-brown skin and dark friendly eyes. He had become a little fatter and had lost the slight English accent he had picked up at Oxford,

but he still wore clothes more English than American in style. He was no less amusing than he used to be – though Roger, who did not like wisecracks, would probably find his humour too slick. But Roger would appreciate him when he talked seriously. Helen had forgotten how well informed Ralph was, on such a wide range of subjects, or perhaps this was something he had developed since she last saw him; listening to him, she felt a proprietorial pride in his easy and accomplished talk. An old flame who had turned into the kind of friend they valued – they must have him to dinner next week, she decided.

But Ralph was still more impetuous than she was. He had hired a car for his stay in England, and when the party broke up he took it for granted that he would be driving her home. 'I must see your home,' he said. 'That's going to be a fascinating part of this trip, seeing what's become of you all,' and the talk veered to comparisons between their early ambitions and their achievements. That the past they called up was shared by Dorothy as well made it a safer possession than it would otherwise have been, so that Helen got into Ralph's car with hardly a thought of that other car: the little green sports car he had once owned, with its gear lever in such an obtrusive position. Bump-bump they had gone on to the grass verges of country lanes, and the engine had ticked in the silence after he had switched off the ignition. 'Let's get out, let me spread the rug on the grass; please, Helen; please, darling.'

'No, Ralph, oh please sweet Ralph, please don't, oh darling we must go back.'

'This is more like it,' he said, when he had manoeuvred out

of Dorothy's mews, his voice suddenly more intimate. 'Now tell me about you – the real things. *You* are happy?'

'Very, very happy. I don't know anyone luckier than I am. And you?'

'I'm glad about you – I really am. If you hadn't been happy it would have killed me.'

'And you are too, surely?'

'Well, I like my business. I didn't expect to, but I do. And the kids are great, and Stella's a very sweet girl.' He spoke curtly.

'So you are happy too.'

'I guess you could say that.'

Oh! thought Helen, and decided not to ask any more just then. If something was wrong – oh dear, poor Ralph . . . and her already cheerful mood gave an almost imperceptible lilt. For the rest of the drive they spoke about the circumstances of their lives in a less personal way.

'Now this is a beautiful room,' he said, as he followed her into her drawing room. 'No one but you could have made this room.'

'Darling Ralph, you always did exaggerate. It's a perfectly ordinary English middle-class drawing room, furnished with cast-off pieces from the in-laws and bargains from the Portobello Road. There's hardly a thing here which I would have chosen if I'd had a free hand.'

'It's got something about it, all the same. Here, let me take your coat.'

Helen turned her shoulders so that he could slip it off from behind, but his hands came to rest on them and he pivoted her gently so that they were face to face, very close. She was flustered by this, but she felt that to pull away sharply would be ungracious, so she smiled at him and said gently, 'What fun that you are in our house at last.'

'Let me kiss you,' he said. 'Let me kiss you just once, for old times' sake.'

'Oh, my dear, what nonsense,' and quickly she pressed her cheek against his, then moved away to the other side of the room. There was a little Victorian armchair at her disposal, and a sofa. She sat down on the sofa.

'You'll find cigarettes in that box,' she said. 'Throw me one.'

Ralph brought the box over, sat down beside her, and put his arm round her shoulders.

'No, no,' she said. 'I want a cigarette.' And then, feeling his arm tighten she thought, Oh, Lord, I suppose I ought to stop this quickly. It seemed absurd to put up a defence against a threat which was not serious – indeed, which did not exist – so she was smiling when she withdrew a little and said, 'Look, Ralph, I meant it when I said I was happy. I do love Roger, and I've turned into a very faithful kind of woman.'

Ralph laughed, and she laughed with him. 'I know,' he said. 'And *I* meant it when I said I was glad for you. I still love you, you see.'

'Good heavens, you haven't changed a bit! You're still a terrible, exaggerating old phoney. Is it just the English climate which does this to you, or do you carry on the same way at home?'

'It's you that does it, but never mind, I'll be good. Look, I'll go sit over here and just gaze at you.'

He went to a chair across the hearthrug and sat leaning forward, his hands dangling between his knees, his dark eyes, half amused and half questioning, fixed on hers.

But why won't he stop this? thought Helen. Can't he understand that I *like* being a happily married woman? And what terrible timing, anyway, barely three hours since we met again and in my own drawing room at that . . . His face was a little flushed and her own eyes were sparkling as they stared back into his. Now, what next? she was wondering.

But after a few seconds Ralph lowered his gaze and said quietly, 'You're dead right. This is a crazy way to go on and I won't do it again, I promise. I'll become a model of discretion right now, on one condition.'

'What's that?'

'That you'll have dinner with me tonight. We can go to a theatre or a movie or something – you dictate. But I'm all tensed up with the thrill of being back here – you don't know what it means to me – and I've got a barren evening ahead of me. This is a big experience for me, and it'll go flat if I have to sit around by myself.'

'Well, I was going to wash my hair . . .'

'*Helen!* That old teenager's excuse – I thought better of you.'

Again they laughed together. So long as it's a joke, thought Helen vaguely.

'All right, I'd love to have dinner with you, thank you very much. And I'm going to wash my hair *now*, so there!'

By the time Ralph came to pick her up, Helen's mood had steadied. She had been startled by her face in the mirror under the turban of towel: that near-smile and that extra glow to her complexion. She remembered the deliberately graceful pose into which she had fallen on the sofa, the way in which she had lowered her eyelashes and turned her head: I was flirting with him, she thought, disgusted with herself. Did I drink too much at lunch? And here I am, putting on scent. But I always wear scent when I go out. No, I don't, I often forget it, and I won't use it now.

To behave as though she wished to attract Ralph when no man's response to her mattered in the least except Roger's – it was as though she had skidded for a moment into being another kind of woman, silly and vulgar. And of course Ralph was not still in love with her. She remembered how he had never been able to resist a situation: if a certain emotion seemed apt to him in a certain situation, then he would pro-duce it. In this situation, where she represented his youth and his freedom and his nostalgic love for Oxford and England, it was apt that he should hint at dissatisfaction with his marriage and so on . . . Oh, it's quite absurd, she told herself. Imagine being in bed with Ralph – it would be obscene.

So she went downstairs thinking that all the same he was a nice person, and that it would be amusing to spend an evening with him. She opened the door to him with a pleasure which felt free of any trace of excitement.

Ralph, too, appeared to have moved on to a calmer level. He began to talk at once about national characteristics, then about American politics, and by the time they were sitting at the restaurant table – there had been no more talk of a theatre – they were at ease as old friends, with no undercurrents.

It was curious that to dine alone with a man other than her husband should restore to a meal eaten in a restaurant so much of the sense of occasion that Helen could remember from her girlhood. If she had come to this place with Roger, meeting friends, she would probably have wondered why they were sitting cramped at a small table, intruded on however gently by other people's talk, eating elaborate food which did not retain the taste of its ingredients, when they could have been enjoying a better dinner in the comfort of their own dining room. But this evening she was stimulated by her surroundings. The subdued buzz and tinkle, the colour of the carnations in the fluted vase, the wine-waiter's ceremonial bearing – she relished them all, and she was conscious of how she looked across the table: a pretty, elegant, animated woman, with a presentable man who was appreciating her company.

After dinner Ralph suggested that they should go on somewhere and dance. Helen was surprised, and felt humbled by her surprise. Because Roger did not enjoy dancing she had relegated her own pleasure in it to the past, but she had not realised until this moment that she had become someone who did not know of a place to suggest.

'What about the Blue Room?' Ralph asked.

'We aren't members – we aren't members of any nightclub. You don't seem to realise, my dear, how middle-aged I've become.'

But Ralph, it appeared, was a member; a friend of his in New York who often visited London had lent him his card. 'Would you like to go there, is it a place you like?' he asked, and Helen had to admit that she did not know.

@@@@@@@@

Dark blue velvet walls on either side of a long passage with a purple carpet; a huge bowl of parma violets with a miniature fountain playing out of its centre on the receptionist's desk; a lady's room lined with quilted midnight-blue satin, smelling of Chanel No. 5 and deodorants. There was a grey poodle tied to a chair in there, whimpering for its mistress, and the attendant was knitting a bed jacket: it might have been only a week ago that Helen had last offered comforting words to such a poodle and dropped half a crown into a glass ashtray for such an attendant. She pushed open the padded door to rejoin Ralph with a delightful sensation that her past had been running parallel with her present all this time; that she only had to go through such a door to be back in it, much younger than she had come to think of herself and as familiar with the pattern of an evening like this as anyone there.

Ralph had authority in a nightclub. He was given the table of his choice without demur, as though the wad of five-pound notes which Helen had glimpsed when he paid the bill for dinner were making a visible bulge in his pocket. Helen rested her arm on the back of the banquette to which they were led – it looked pretty there, so white and graceful against the dark material – and looked round her. 'Who can it be who designs these places?' she asked: all that velvet and satin, all that padding and quilting; the small gilt stars studding the blue walls, and the larger stars in the blue ceiling, shedding dim light on the dance floor. It was hideous, a vulgarly conceived incubator for the purpose of hatching money out of alcohol and sex, but she looked at it with pleasure.

'Good old nightclubs,' she said. 'They never change. It's such fun to be back in one again.'

When they danced she felt light in Ralph's arms, holding herself a little away from him, moving so easily that he did not have to exert any pressure to guide her. She was dancing simply for the pleasure of doing it again. Nothing in the evening, so far, had made it seem necessary to establish this; it was only a slightly comic prudence that was making her convey it to Ralph by the cool touch of her fingers and the way she separated from him when the music stopped. And he followed her lead, making no attempt to hold her closer or to keep his hand on her waist, so that she felt that together they were handling this physical contact discreetly and well. She had half expected him to take advantage of it, and was so pleased with him for not doing so that when they were back at their table, sitting side by side, she moved a little nearer him, her arm just touching his in friendly confidence.

'It's wonderful, doing things with you,' he said. 'You always did have such a talent for enjoyment. That's one of the rubs with Stella and me – she's a worrier, she finds it hard to relax.'

'I expect she's more serious-minded than I am. And you can't judge by tonight, anyway, because this is a treat for me so of course I'm enjoying it. I'm horrid sometimes, in the ordinary way.'

'I bet you never tell Roger that champagne gives him indigestion, just as he's taking his first sip, in front of a lot of people.'

'Oh, Ralph! She doesn't do things like that?'

'She does too. It sounds kind of corny, that nagging wife deal, but I can tell you – oh, what's the use? I won't bore you with all that.'

'But I'm not bored . . .' and soon, her elbow on the table and her cheek on her hand, Helen was gazing gravely into Ralph's face, listening to the story of his marriage. She thought him disloyal to tell it, and she disliked the self-pity with which he spoke, but the intimacy of this talk, the flattery, the wisdom of her own comments, so carefully fair to the unknown Stella, all combined to make the occasion more interesting. The position in which she was now sitting had removed the touch of Ralph's sleeve from her bare arm. In that warm room her skin could not really have become cold, but after a minute or two it felt as though it had. With most of her mind she was listening; with a small part of it she was telling herself that it would be a mistake to lean back again so that their former closeness was restored; and in a moment of absent-mindedness, less than three minutes later, she had leaned back.

The next time they danced Helen was distinctly more conscious of Ralph's awareness of her; the discretion of their dancing was no longer making a distance between them. The lightness of their fingers' touching had become as significant as a close clasp. Helen smiled with lowered eyelids, moving her head as though inadvertently to avoid Ralph's cheek. She could feel what he was up to now, and she was *not* letting him embrace her more closely, whatever sensations she herself might be experiencing.

She had a good head for alcohol. She was drinking more than usual, but she did not get perceptibly drunk. As the evening went on she was sure that it was not the wine which was making the dim lights, the music, the plushiness and gleam of the decor act on her as they were intended to act, so that vulgarity was transmuted into luxury, banality sounded melodious, and the intimacy of that banquette became so warmly real. She was no longer bothering about whether she approved of Ralph's attitudes or agreed with his opinions. More often than not she did, but there were moments when she thought, How odd, or, But that's silly, or, He's very conceited; and although these judgements registered quite clearly, they had no bearing on her mood or on her increasing fondness for him. They meant something, perhaps, in relation to her and Ralph, but they meant nothing in relation to the evening.

'It's so strange, when you think of it,' she said softly at one point. 'Spending all one's life with one person. I wouldn't have it otherwise for anything in the world – I'd die rather than be married to anyone but Roger. But meeting you again, being with someone else I know really well – and we did know each other well, didn't we? I mean, you know things about me that even Roger doesn't know . . . I think it's something people ought to do more often. I feel as though I were having a delicious breath of fresh air.'

She knew as she said it that she was crossing the borderline of discretion, but why not? It was true, after all. And she knew when Ralph put his hand over hers that she ought to draw away, but it felt so good, the warm palm soothing on the back of her hand, friendly rather than amorous, that instead she turned her own palm upwards and closed her fingers lightly over his. What could be a more natural expression of their relationship this evening than this comfortable, unurgent contact? When Ralph's fingers closed down and his face suddenly came nearer hers in the half-darkness so that there was nothing for it but to take her hand away, she felt cheated.

It was late before Ralph said, 'Let's have one more dance before we go,' and this time there was no pretence. In the first moment, before she could establish any distance, he pulled her against him, he pressed his cheek to hers, and Helen felt a sleepy sweetness rising in her. Not to enjoy the sweetness seemed perverse. Just for half a minute, she thought, and relaxed in his arms, smiling at this rediscovery of pure, sensual pleasure. But when she felt the pressure of his desire against her thigh she woke herself up and pulled away from him. 'Sweet Ralph,' she said, meaning to speak lightly, but her voice was huskier than she expected it to be, 'this is no way to behave. We are both beginning to be drunk, and it's time you took me home.'

Back in the cloakroom she took longer than she needed to comb her hair and touch up her face, talking about the weather with the attendant as she did so, trying to sound as though she were talking with her greengrocer or someone at the post office. It was necessary that this old red-haired woman should think what a nice, sober, well-conducted lady she was: someone to whom this evening was no different from any part of her daily life. She decided that when she got into the taxi – Ralph had not used his car because of parking problems – she would lean back in her own corner, calm and natural, and tell Ralph how much she and Roger were looking forward to their holiday.

She did this, too. And Ralph leaned back in *his* corner, which was odd. She had expected him to take up a strategic position in the middle of the seat. She was not sure whether it was uncomfortable or comic to be operating so distinctly on two levels simultaneously: to think approvingly, Good, he is going to keep to his own side, and at the same time to feel forlorn at this lonely way of sitting. The forlorn feeling must be quashed, since she *really did not want* any nonsense, but nevertheless, when Ralph reached out and took her hand it became much more pleasant to be in this taxi with him.

'What a lovely evening you have given me,' she said.

'It's you who made it lovely. I only wish I could believe . . .'

'Believe what?'

'Well, I wish I could believe that you were willing to make it even more lovely.' There was a trace of a question mark at the end of the sentence.

'Ralph dear, you know how I feel about you; you know how happy I am to see you again.' She made her voice specially warm and affectionate to counteract the harshness of what she must say. 'But I've told you how things are with me, and everything I said is perfectly true, it really is. I'm sorry, my dear, but please . . .'

'I know, darling. Don't worry, I'm not going to spoil things.' His voice, too, was warm and loving, his hand was so comforting on hers.

She felt gratitude and tenderness towards him. It *had* been a lovely evening, entertaining, refreshing, spiced by the stimulant of feeling herself desired, and now sweetened by his understanding that he should not push things too far. So when, after she had moved nearer to him and was leaning lightly against him, he suddenly put his arms round her, pulled her to him quite roughly, and began to kiss first her neck, then her averted cheek, and then, after a short struggle, her mouth, she was tumbled into an absurd confusion.

@/@/@/@/@/@/@

The levels multiplied. But he said he wouldn't! One part of her was protesting in naive dismay; another part was taking ironic note of this girlish reaction; another part was thinking calmly, We'll be home soon, nothing much can happen in this cab; and meanwhile her body was willingly dissolving.

It was the dissolving which seemed to be prevailing. When Ralph's tongue forced her lips apart and his hand closed on her left breast, Helen felt for the first time that evening not only awareness of his desire, but the stirring of her own, Oh God, she thought, I'd forgotten! It was so long since she had been embraced by someone new, for the first time. This was not – of course it was not, how could she have forgotten – the relaxed and easy pleasure in which nothing was disturbed if she murmured between kisses, 'Did you remember to collect your watch?' This was as reckless and urgent as it was sweet, and to feel it again was like slaking thirst. He feels fat, he feels soft, she noticed, but how he felt was rapidly coming to be beside the point. He bore forward on to her, thrusting her back so that he was half lying on her, and grabbing one of her hands he began to thrust it down towards his crotch.

She had been playing all evening with his desire, but now, when its awakening answer flared up in her, she was horrified. She had to stop it, she knew. Her shoulder strap had slipped, and when for a moment he left her mouth free in order to kiss her body, she wrenched away from him.

'Stop it, Ralph,' she said hoarsely. 'Stop it at once, we can't do this. If you try to go on I shall hate you.'

'Do you really mean that?' he whispered.

Feeling as though she were pushing aside a heavy weight, Helen sat up and nodded. 'Yes, I do,' she said. 'I'm terribly sorry, Ralph, but I do.'

Slowly, shaking his head as though to clear it, Ralph moved away from her to the other end of the seat. 'It's my fault,' he said in a muffled voice.

'It's all right, but it would be too stupid. Where have we got to?'

He looked out of the taxi at landmarks unfamiliar to him and did not answer, leaning forward with his hands dangling between his knees, continuing to stare out of the window while she straightened her dress and smoothed her hair. There were still about ten minutes of the drive left, she saw. She was feeling slightly sick and she wished that he would say something forgiving.

'I suppose we drank too much,' she said, but his silence continued, seeming to her heavy with pain, frustration and reproof, filling her with guilt. Oh, poor Ralph! What nonsense, she told herself. He isn't a boy. It doesn't really matter to him whether he gets me into bed or not; but she could not banish an atmosphere brewed as much by her own body as by his. She did not doubt that she had done what she had to do – but, Oh how sad, she kept saying to herself, Oh, what a shame.

Supposing that she had not stopped him? He would soon be going away again, Roger would never have known: it would have been just this one evening, just this one situation allowed to run freely to its natural end. For an instant the emptiness of her house flashed through her mind – her wide bed, so soft, on which if she were now to say . . . Roger's bed. Was she mad? 'Give me a cigarette,' she said quickly.

In the last few minutes of the drive they restored, between them, a show of calm, speaking of Ralph's plans for the rest of his visit, but all the time Helen was thinking that the moment was approaching when they would say goodnight. It was so sad that his voice had become polite and cool, so sad that if she were to take his hand again he might misunderstand. She caught herself thinking, I could ask him in, just to restore the friendliness, and was shocked that she had thought it, shocked that she continued to argue, But he would understand, now, that it meant nothing. The only safe thing was to shut her eyes and say nothing. But something would have to happen when the cab pulled up; something either warm or cold. The evening was not done with yet.

When the taxi stopped she thought for a moment, with dismay, that he was simply going to open the door and let her get out, scrambling past his knees, but he got out with her. 'Have you got your key?' he asked, and put his hand on her elbow – that was better – as they crossed the pavement, went up the steps.

What am I going to say? she wondered as she groped in her bag. No, I can't ask him in – how can I after being so definite? – it's out of the question. But if he . . . She did not envisage what Ralph might do. Plead with her? Argue with her? Stick his foot in the door and force his way in? He would not do anything, of course, but as she put her key in the lock she found herself thinking, very clearly, Well, if he does come in – that's that.

She turned towards him, standing in the half-open door, waiting. Ralph took her hand, raised it to his lips, and kissed it. Then, gently, he kissed her again on the mouth. 'Goodbye, darling Helen,' he said. 'Thank you for spending this evening with me. It's been wonderful.' And quite cheerfully he went down the steps and got into the waiting cab.

In her hall Helen sat down on the chair by the telephone, kicked off her shoes, and said aloud, 'Phew! What a relief.' Ralph had understood that she had meant what she said – of course he had. Given the kind of people they both were, he could not have done otherwise. The kind of people they both were? . . . 'Well, if he does come in – that's that.' On her bed. On Roger's bed. Oh God, she thought when she was upstairs, it would have been obscene. Roger was the only man she could bear to have on that bed, or on any bed – and that was true, so how right Ralph had been to understand that she had meant what she said.

Tomorrow Roger would come home, and she could have gone down on her knees then and there in thankfulness for the welcome she would be able to give her darling heart. But when Helen was taking off her dress and the zip stuck half-way down, she felt such a violent irritation that she exclaimed loudly, 'Oh, to hell with the damn thing,' and with a fierce jerk she ripped six inches of zip out of the fabric so that she was never able to wear that dress again.

ANNIVERSARY
Siân James
1980

Joanna had been worried about inviting Fanny to dinner. 'She's such a strange girl. She's not our type, not really. I don't know what you'll think of her.' She was even more anxious than usual that everything should be just right. 'Is it too extravagant, Paul? You see, I think Fanny's quite hard-up. I don't want her to think I'm trying to impress her.'

'It's perfect,' I said.

It was. Cream linen mats on gleaming mahogany. A simple table setting. A small centrepiece of pale pink roses. The french windows open to the June garden.

'Iced vichyssoise. Sole. Chicken marengo.'

'Perfect.'

'The Grants, us and Fanny.'

'Just right.'

Joanna was looking sun-flushed and pretty. She's a large girl, then she was larger; Simon was only six weeks old, her breasts were heavy and deep. She wore a white dress with brown and violet splashes.

'Don't worry,' I said, patting her shoulder. She smiled abstractedly at me.

I try to remember how I felt about Joanna in that time before Fanny. Fond of her, I suppose, as always. It doesn't change. I've never loved her passionately. Even when I asked her to marry me I realised that, but in a way had more faith in the steadier beating of my heart; I'd already had several love affairs, some painful. Joanna was rich, that made her different too. In those days I was poor. Now I'm successful enough to keep her in the manner to which she's accustomed, rich enough to pay the upkeep of this large house her father gave us as a wedding present.

'I'll slip up to say goodnight to Sara and Elizabeth,' Joanna said. Sara was six, then. Elizabeth four.

She was still upstairs when Fanny arrived, a few minutes early.

Joanna had told me that Fanny was our age. 'About thirty,' she had said. She didn't look thirty. She looked like a young girl.

Joanna had met her in the nursing home six weeks before when she was having Simon. Fanny had had a son, too, an illegitimate baby. That's all I'd been told about her. I hadn't been interested in her then.

'I'm Fanny,' she said, holding out her hand, a bony well-shaped hand. Her hair was tawny, her skin brown, her eyes grey.

So this is it, I thought. Love at first sight. Recognition, sharp and immediate. Excitement at the first touch of a cool hand. Desire on a summer night, even before the first drink.

'May I bring him in? Thomas? I've got him in the carrycot.'

'Of course. Let me carry him. Joanna, here's Fanny.'

'Lovely to see you again,' Joanna said.

'Where shall I put the baby?' I asked.

'On the bed in the guest room. Say goodnight to the girls, darling, while you're upstairs. Fanny, do you want to go up to see that Thomas is all right?'

'No, he's fast asleep. Can I give you a hand with anything? What a beautiful house this is. It's lovely to be here.'

I wondered about the almost palpable warmth between Joanna and Fanny as I took the carrycot into the guest room (checking that the window was open, but not too widely): Joanna isn't usually sympathetic towards unconventional people. I peeped in at Thomas and was rather disconcerted to find his dark eyes wide open. I backed away, closing the door carefully, looked in at the girls and hurried downstairs. I remember so well the lightness, almost giddiness, of heart I felt; the humdrum old world was still full of surprises, perhaps glory.

By the time I got down, the Grants, Mabel and Geoffrey and their undergraduate son, Adam, had arrived. We had drinks on the terrace, Adam bombarding Fanny with heavy undergraduate humour, Mabel and Geoffrey listening and looking on, Joanna pretending to listen, but with her mind in the kitchen, Fanny smiling at Adam, but looking at me from time to time, I out of my depth in love, carried along by the swift and terrible current, uncaring whether I should sink or swim.

Dinner was perfect, as I'd predicted, the food and wine superb, Joanna relaxed and happy, Geoffrey, often pompous and foolish, talking very well and amusingly before a new audience, Adam quietly concentrating on the meal.

I don't think Joanna had told me that Fanny was a writer; perhaps I'd forgotten it. Her latest book, *Death Valley*, a macabre science-fiction, had recently collected some rave reviews. Geoffrey had read it and told us it was first-rate. Mabel thought she *might* have read it and spent quite a long time describing a different book altogether, Adam egging her on.

'No dear,' Geoffrey said at last.

That's all I remember of the conversation, a taste of *Death Valley*. But I remember Fanny's smile as we talked about it. I remember the way she ate her strawberries. I remember the four or five freckles on her straight, perfect nose. I remember her eyes, grey and luminous.

'You'll take Fanny home, won't you, Paul?' Joanna asked me when the Grants had gone.

'Of course.'

'But I've got the car.'

'I'll drive you back and walk home, it'll do me good.'

I remember Joanna waving to us and looking pleased.

I drove Fanny home in her white Mini.

'I hope we'll see a lot more of you,' I said, lifting the carrycot from the back seat.

'Of course. We're neighbours, aren't we?'

She let herself into the house and held the door open for me.

'Shall I carry him upstairs for you?'

'Please.'

Her tiny house, half a mile down the hill from ours, was

built by an architect – a friend of mine – as a weekend retreat. It gives the impression of a child's treehouse.

'He sleeps in here.'

The room was white and bare. I thought of Simon's large nursery, its sunny colours, its mobiles and toys and Peter Rabbit friezes.

'Is he all right? Are you going to feed him?'

She didn't answer. Only looked at him swiftly and closed the door.

'And this is my room,' she said.

Oh, the complications of previous affairs, and the Herculean labours involved in ending up in any empty room with a space on the floor, let alone a crystal white room, beautiful as a tear drop, and a sea-green bed.

It was so easy. We stood in front of the mirror together and smiled at how easy, and how beautiful, it was.

That's how it started. Seven years ago this month. Does Joanna know about it? That causes me a great deal of anxiety. I don't know. She never asks me to take Fanny home now, simply knows I will, knows that I often call in to see her on my way home from the station. Well, everyone accepts that we have a great deal in common, Fanny and I.

Certainly, Joanna and Fanny are still firm friends. They meet for morning coffee and go shopping together. They have dinner together even when I'm away. Simon and Thomas are inseparable; the terrible twins. We're close neighbours.

Occasionally it seems that I've got it all: a rich, complaisant wife, a beautiful mistress.

There are other times when things seem insupportable.

A few weeks ago Joanna and I were sitting together after dinner watching the sun sinking behind the beeches. For me it seemed such a consoling moment. I'd had a hectic day, a conference, a site meeting, another conference.

'Happy?' I asked.

A dangerous, foolish question.

Joanna turned her head away, but not before I'd seen the tears come to her eyes. 'We could be any ordinary couple,' she said.

The resigned sadness in her voice moved me. I'm so fond of her. She's good and kind and placid. Why is it that I've never had a moment's excitement in her presence? Yes, she's physically rather cold, but men have worn their hearts out over cold women often enough. I put my hand on hers, hating myself.

I suppose I married Joanna for her money. Though as I've already said more than once, I was certainly fond of her, felt protective and warm towards her, but I don't think I would have married her if she hadn't been rich.

We met at a party, a smart literary party. She was out of her depth and I looked after her; that was innocent enough, even chivalrous. She came from Leeds, she told me, had studied Domestic Economy at Edinburgh, didn't have a job, wasn't sure that she wanted one. An old school friend, a girl I knew slightly and disliked, had brought her to the party, she knew no one else. She was staying in London only until the next day.

She was a little older than I was, tall, raven-haired, easy on the eye, even though her elaborate dress was out of place amongst the little silky shifts of the Sixties. Something about her moved me, perhaps I'd already sniffed her moneyed background even in ten minutes' talk. Whatever it was, I rescued

her from the party, took her to as decent a restaurant as I could afford, then back, by a taxi I remember, to her hotel. I gave her my telephone number and asked her to ring me when she was next in London. I didn't kiss her goodnight. I wanted to. But even more, I wanted her to think me courteous and undemanding. I'd never before wanted to give anyone that impression and wondered if I could have fallen in love.

I walked home in a slightly bemused state. I'd gone to the party to find a girl to sleep with.

Next morning I rang her hotel intending to ask her to have lunch with me, but she had already left.

I'd forgotten about her when she phoned me about a month later. I'd recently got my first job and was working hard.

She invited me to have dinner with her and her parents at their hotel. I tried to get out of it. I was meeting a girl that night and besides the invitation sounded so dull.

'What about tomorrow night?' she asked then, her voice so forlorn that I remembered in a flash how she had looked at the party; the anxious expression, the tight little smile. It was new to me, the concern I felt. I told her I'd see her the next night.

I wore the suit I'd bought for my new job and arrived punctually.

Her parents were much as I'd imagined; her mother quiet and overdressed, her father brash and eager to impress, demanding – and getting – good, plain food, and sending the wine back; and talking about his factory, his men, his overseas commitments, his plans for the future. I enjoyed the unaccustomed luxury of the meal and talked almost as much as he did, about the firm of architects I'd been with for ten days, inventing what I didn't know.

I wondered whether I'd be able to get to see Joanna alone after the meal, wondered whether I wanted to. She was certainly good-looking, but not my type. All the same, I tried to think of a respectable place I could offer to take her to.

We moved into the lounge for coffee. 'Would you like a walk?' I asked her after about half an hour. 'Just as far as the park perhaps?'

She was beautiful when she smiled.

Her mother was afraid of the rain. 'Oh, the rain won't do them any harm,' her father said. 'They won't melt.'

He approved of me, there was no doubt about that.

Joanna went up to her room to fetch her coat and umbrella and when she had gone, he turned to me. 'Well, we knew she'd be getting a young man sometime; all the same it's not easy for us. She's all we've got, you know.'

'We'll be back in ten minutes,' I said, my head reeling with the knowledge that I'd been so readily accepted as their daughter's young man, her future husband if I decided on it. Wouldn't you think, I asked myself, that a man in his position would have a shortlist of suitable applicants for his only daughter's hand? Why me? What had she told them about me?

Before I took her back to the hotel, I kissed her. In spite of the umbrella, her face was cold and wet. I kissed her eyes and her lips. Kissing gave me a proud feeling, like doing well in an examination.

I saw her every night that week and when she went back to Leeds I wrote to her and telephoned as though I was really her young man. I was invited to her home for Christmas. We got engaged on Boxing Day. I was twenty-two, she was two years older.

I shouldn't have married her, I suppose. I should have resisted the appeal in her eyes; it was certainly there. From the beginning I was aware that she wanted me, planned to marry me.

I wasn't sure why, but came to the conclusion that I was simply different in some way from the men she was used to meeting.

'Why did you decide on me?' I ask her sometimes.

She manages to smile and look pained at the same time.

'Didn't you do even a bit of deciding?' she asks me.

'Of course I did.'

It's there even now, the gentle vulnerability which took the place of excitement.

The first year of our marriage was the worst. I wasn't even careful enough to hide my miserable affairs.

After Sara was born, I made a conscious effort to be faithful. Fatherhood steadied me. I found Sara enchanting and used to rush home to see her. Joanna seemed fulfilled and relaxed and I was no longer angry about what I'd let myself drift into. No wonder we had a second baby soon. I'm a devoted father. I used to bath them and tell bedtime stories and get up in the night. Joanna thought I was a reformed character. Not that she had ever complained before; not even when I had stayed in town all night or when I got a phone call in the early hours.

We limped along with no serious mishaps for three or four years.

I'm quite pleased to remember that when Fanny took me into her life, I was on the brink of an affair with a young girl from the typing pool. I try to tell myself how much more disastrous that would have been; a young, self-centred girl snatching at my evenings and keeping me from my family.

Fanny saved me from those complications. Our sexual life is well-regulated and fits into my domestic pattern. I drop in to see her on my way home from the station. 'I called in on Fanny as I came past,' I tell Joanna afterwards. 'She may come up later.'

Nowadays, with Thomas and Simon still up and about, it's more difficult, but even snatched minutes in the locked study are more important to me than anything else in my life.

For I love her obsessively. Every pretty young girl reminds me of her. The nape of someone's neck, someone's round elbow, and I am stung again by the bitterness of loving her. She is so self-contained that my love seems pitiful. She doesn't need my love.

What does she need except herself and her small, dark son, her tiny house and her garden dug out of the side of the hill?

Sometimes I ring her before I leave the office. 'Shall I call in tonight?' I have thought about her all day long.

'By all means. Unless you're busy. Are you entertaining? Are you bringing work home?'

She's so understanding. So cool.

I go in and she pours me a drink. 'But I thought you were going straight home tonight.'

'I didn't say that.'

'That's what I understood. Wasn't that why you rang?'

'I rang hoping you'd ask me to call.'

'I don't want to start making demands on you. You should know that.'

I long for her so fiercely that I would welcome any demands, however unreasonable. If she said, 'Don't go home tonight. Phone Joanna and tell her you're staying with me,' that's what I would do, I know it. But I also know that she would never ask it.

'If I were free, Fanny, would you marry me?'

'No, I don't want marriage. Once was enough.'

'What do you want?'

'Freedom. Time to write. Nice moments. Friends. Thomas.'

'Was Thomas a mistake?'

'Certainly not.'

'You planned to have a child?'

'That's right.'

'Why?'

'Why not? I'm not rich, but I have enough money. I wanted a child.'

'Who is his father?'

'Why do you ask? My ex-husband.'

'But you were divorced from him long before Thomas was conceived.'

'That's right. But we went on seeing each other from time to time. We're not enemies. I told him I wanted a child.'

'And he obliged you?'

'Why do you find it offensive? We were married once, that should make it better rather than worse.'

'Did you hope it might lead to remarriage?'

'No. He is remarried. Very happily. He has four children. That's why I knew he wouldn't want a share of Thomas. It seemed an excellent arrangement. Why are you so jealous, Paul? Aren't you happy with me?'

I can never stop questioning her, however many times I resolve not to do so.

'How long were you married?'

'Three years.'

'How old were you when you got married?'

'Twenty.'

'Was he your first lover?'

'Yes.'

'Was he handsome?'

'Yes. Not as handsome as you, but he was well enough.'

'Was he kind to you?'

'Sometimes.'

'Were you unhappy? When you decided to part?'

'Of course I was unhappy.'

Why can't she lie to me, or refuse to answer? I question her until I'm too tormented to go on.

I draw her to me, trying to make her feel my wretchedness as I kiss and leave her. I realise that we are not alike in anything but in our disloyalty to Joanna, and our amorality: she is not in love.

'How was Fanny?' Joanna asks later.

'Exasperating as ever.'

That's the role we play in public, friends baiting each other, lightly disagreeing on every subject. Perhaps even Joanna believes in it.

Perhaps I shouldn't remain with Joanna feeling as I do

about Fanny. But would it be kinder if I left her? I don't know. I'm very fond of her and of my children.

Although no one else is aware of the fact, it is exactly seven years since Fanny first came to visit us. Once again the Grants, at my suggestion, are coming to dinner; they now live in London, we don't see them as often as we did, and Fanny has also been invited. I wonder if I shall tell her later on that I am celebrating seven years of pleasure and torment. Probably not. This summer I have a premonition that we are at some danger point and am chary of precipitating a crisis.

It is a Saturday. We have lunch in the garden. Simon is in disgrace for putting a snail in Elizabeth's salad. Joanna, Sara and Elizabeth beg me to spank him; I look at him fiercely and they all beg me not to – I wasn't going to anyway – but he, probably a tiny bit scared, blurts out, 'Fanny and Thomas have gone to Manchester.'

'Fanny and Thomas have gone to Manchester have they?' I manage to say. 'Fanny and Thomas have gone to Manchester, so that gives you an excuse, does it, for upsetting your mother in this horrid way. Well, you'll have no strawberries, not one. Go and sit over there till we've finished, then you can help Mrs Leigh clear the table.'

Fanny and Thomas have gone to Manchester. My outrage at this trip I hadn't been told about causes me to deal too severely with poor Simon; I can see that he's near to tears. Elizabeth, a little ashamed of the fuss she's made, picks up the snail, now gently perambulating along the tablecloth, puts it in the nearest flower bed and returns to eat a little of her cold meat.

Afterwards I share out the strawberries – between four

– and we eat them joylessly. 'He deserves a lesson,' Joanna says. 'He and Thomas are getting quite out of control.'

After my coffee, I phone Fanny's number, but she has already left. Why has she gone to Manchester when she'd promised to have dinner with us? I can't bring myself to question Simon who is still looking reproachfully at me.

It isn't that I expect to be consulted about all her movements. She never tells me, for instance, when she has a day in London. Quite often I only learn that she is out for the evening when Joanna asks me to babysit for her. 'She's gone to the theatre,' Joanna says. 'Who is she with? What is she seeing?' 'I didn't ask her, darling, does it matter?'

In the afternoon, Elizabeth goes to a birthday party. It's one of the drawbacks of the Thames Valley affluent society that one or other of the children is invited to a birthday party almost every Saturday afternoon, which means that the other two have to be taken out for a treat. This afternoon Sara and Simon, Joanna and I and several thousand other people visit a stately home and an adventure playground. We're late picking up Elizabeth which embarrasses Joanna, and all the time I'm wondering why Fanny has gone to Manchester without telling me and how I can tolerate a whole Saturday, perhaps a whole weekend, without seeing her.

'Will Thomas be back tomorrow?' I ask Simon later, when he comes in to say goodnight.

'Oh no. He's gone for a long time.'

I can't believe it. 'For a weekend?' I suggest.

'Oh no, for a long time. Perhaps for ever.' That's as much help as I'm going to have from Simon.

Geoffrey and Mabel are late. They blame the Saturday crowds on the road, but I suspect that they've been lingering in a pub.

Mabel has recently had a small operation and gives us many details we'd rather be spared.

Geoffrey asks after Fanny, who usually comes up whenever they visit us. 'She's gone to Manchester,' I say, trying to keep some of the bitterness out of my voice. 'At least, so Simon tells us. We're not informed of her plans.'

'Manchester, eh,' Geoffrey says. 'I wonder if she's seeing Adam.'

'Why ever should she be seeing Adam?' Mabel says sharply. 'In a city of over half a million people, the chances are that she could be seeing someone else.'

I'd completely forgotten that Adam was in Manchester. A hard lump rises into my throat.

'Mabel can't bear to think that Adam is interested in Fanny, can you?'

'I'm very fond of Fanny, you know that; there's absolutely no one I'm fonder of. All the same, I think she's far too old for Adam, I admit it. After all Joanna, she's seven or eight years older than Adam, isn't she?'

'I didn't know there was anything at all between them,' Joanna says. 'I didn't realise they ever saw each other.'

'They see each other,' Geoffrey says.

'They simply lunch together occasionally when he's home,' Mabel says. 'That's all. She amuses him. You know how amusing she can be.'

I have to see to the wine so I'm able to keep out of the

conversation and contemplate just how amusing Fanny can be and how I would like to wring her amusing little neck.

'Adam adores her books. He's got every one of them,' Mabel says. 'He has an intellectual interest in her. Nothing more than that.'

I hadn't seen Adam for quite some time and considered myself lucky on that score. Now I was forced to turn my thoughts to him. Apparently he had been promoted to the post of director's assistant on some weekly television programme. Mabel had actually seen him at work in the studio, and spends some time telling us about it. Geoffrey, realising that we're probably not anxious to spend the entire meal hearing about boom microphones and tracking cameras, keeps trying to cut in, while Joanna says, 'Really,' and 'How interesting,' and I'm free to think my murderous thoughts.

She can't be seeing Adam, she can't be. Why not? He's young, fairly handsome, drives a sports car, has an interesting job. He's a stupid ass, that's why not. A boring and pompous ass, that's why not. She can't be seeing Adam Grant. She would have told me something about it. Would she? Has she ever told me anything about the lunches they've had together? Does she give me any information except if I plague her for it, drag it out of her, word by word?

'Of course, Mabel wants him to marry some pure young girl,' Geoffrey says. 'But are there any these days? He'd have to marry her straight from school or even earlier. I was sitting next to couple of young girls in the Tube one morning last week and you simply wouldn't believe what they were talking about. They looked about sixteen, not much more. You simply wouldn't believe what they were talking about. And not keeping their voices down either. Well, I'm not easily embarrassed, you know me. After six years in the navy, a chap isn't easily embarrassed, but I tell you I was hot under the collar.'

'Do tell us what they were saying, dear,' Mabel says. 'After this amount of lead-in, I think we deserve to hear. Oh, Geoffrey, do you remember that dinner party when I kept talking to Sir Donald about my vulva instead of my Volvo. No wonder we haven't seen him since.'

'No, the reason I approve of Adam seeing Fanny is that she might save him from a disastrous emotional entanglement. I don't want to think that he'll fall in love and rush into marriage before he's had time to enjoy himself. He's safe with Fanny. I don't think a man is mature enough for marriage until he's thirty.'

'Paul was twenty-two when we got married,' Joanna says, giving me a small, sad smile.

'And Geoffrey was twenty-four,' Mabel says brightly. 'But of course he's an exceptional man who matured early. Aren't you darling? Aren't you exceptional?'

'Fanny is modern in the way that you two aren't, thank God,' Geoffrey goes on in his most pontifical manner. 'She's completely independent, self-reliant, coolly self-aware. She enjoys sex in a casual way and is determined not to be swamped by any nonsense like falling in love. It wouldn't surprise me if she'd had her little boy, what's his name? Thomas? By artificial insemination. Do you know what I mean? So that he'd be entirely hers.'

Suddenly I can't bear another word. It isn't what he's saying, most of which is probably true, but the way he's assuming a special knowledge of her, a special intimacy with her. I can't bear it.

'She's not so detached as you think,' I say, all the authority of love and brandy in my voice. 'She got married when she was twenty. Fanny got married when she was twenty' – so much was true – 'she was a beautiful, inexperienced girl tumultuously in love.' I could see her before me, candid of eye and beautiful, as I spoke. 'Her husband was quite a bit older than she was, a professional musician, Anton or some such phoney name, with no shortage of girlfriends. After a time Fanny could take no more and she threatened to divorce him and to her dismay, he did nothing to deter her. The divorce went through. She was heartbroken. She's never got over it.'

Geoffrey and Mabel look at me in stunned silence. Geoffrey is the first to rally.

'I hope you haven't told us too much, old boy,' he says, genuine concern in his voice. 'You haven't been too free with the confidential stuff, have you? Anyway, we'll keep it to ourselves, won't we Mabel? Absolutely. Poor little Fanny. What a brave front she puts on it. Well, well, well. Can you ever know anyone? What secrets are you hiding from us, Mabel? Joanna? Life isn't what it seems, it certainly isn't.'

Mabel is silent and grave, but at the same time probably relieved on Adam's account. As for me, I am completely desolate, certain somehow that what I spoke so rashly and brazenly was the truth. My brain, like a computer, has processed all the bits and pieces of information which I've extracted from Fanny over seven years of close questioning and come up with the answer.

'I must keep some pavlova for Simon,' I hear Joanna say.

◎◎◎◎◎◎◎

'He was so upset about Thomas going away that he behaved rather badly during lunch and Paul wouldn't let him have any strawberries.'

* * *

'I didn't know Fanny had told you about Anton,' Joanna says as we're getting ready for bed that night.

I make a non-committal sound. So I was right. I knew it. Perhaps I'd always known it.

I look at Joanna, willing her to continue. I know she's going to wound me, but I want the worst, the whole truth.

'He's got a concert in Manchester tonight, he's filling in for Maguire at the last moment. That's why she went off so suddenly. He doesn't mind her turning up on his out-of-town appearances as long as she stays away from London.'

I try to say something but fail. My mouth opens and shuts but no words come out.

'He's a bastard,' Joanna continues. 'She knows that. All the same, I don't think she'll ever get over him.'

We regard each other with sadness. I watch her putting cream on her face, wiping it off with a tissue. I catch her eye in the oval mirror over the dressing table.

Suddenly I know something else. Joanna knows and has always known about Fanny and me.

'Why do you let it go on?' I ask her as she comes to bed.

'How could I stop it?'

'I don't mean Fanny and Anton. I mean Fanny and me. Why don't you put a stop to that?'

'She needs you,' Joanna says simply. 'She needs you, Paul. And you see, I need her.'

It all clicks into place, smoothly and horribly. Even the reason for Joanna's father being so ready to accept me all those years ago: I was probably the first man she'd ever liked.

Nothing has changed, I tell myself. Fanny will be back. Tomorrow perhaps. Tomorrow evening I'll be able to wander down to see her after supper.

'How was Fanny?' Joanna will ask afterwards.

'Tired. She sent her love. She's coming up to see you tomorrow.'

Nothing has changed, I tell myself, nothing has changed.

'Goodnight love,' I manage to say. 'Sleep, now. Don't worry any more about anything.'

Oh Fanny. Everything has changed.

MACKEREL
Emma Smith
1984

When Alastair McIntyre was five years old his mother disappeared out of his life. Alastair remembered her being there, and then her not being there. She went off with someone. His father, an electrician who worked for the Council, never referred to the man his mother went off with, nor to the circumstances of her going off, nor indeed ever again, except when it was unavoidable, to Alastair's mother.

Alastair had a far clearer recollection of his father's refusal to let him be taken away by the authorities than he had of his mother's mistily sudden departure. The precise words that were spoken above his head he forgot, but the fierce tone of his father's voice and the feel of his father's hands gripping his shoulders in the presence of strangers he remembered.

'I can raise the boy myself,' Douglas McIntyre had declared on that occasion, very forcibly, again and again. 'Nobody's going to put my son in a home while I'm here to stop it. I'm his father. I can manage.'

Impressed by such resolve, and in view of the fact that

Mr McIntyre was a respectable tradesman with a steady job, and of the further ascertained facts that he was not a drinker, not a philanderer, paid his rent on the nail, eschewed hire-purchase, and that, moreover, his neighbours were willing to help out – in view of all this information, the social services finally decided he should be allowed to have a shot, anyway, at managing.

And for the next four and a half years Douglas McIntyre did somehow contrive to give the boy what was officially considered to be an adequate upbringing. Then, one dark and icy December morning, a milk lorry skidded into a bus queue, and Alastair's father vanished from sight and sound as utterly and with as little warning as his mother had done before.

There being now no one to stop it, and no alternative, Alastair, who had reached the age of nearly ten, was put in a home. Or rather, he was put in a series of short-stay homes that culminated, when a vacancy cropped up at last, in a long-stay establishment. Long-stay, short-stay, they were all the same to Alastair – indistinguishable: merely places in which to pass the time while waiting.

He was waiting for his father; and this in spite of having attended his father's funeral. Still he expected to hear, sooner or later, the knock at the door, the ring at the bell, that would mean his father had come to fetch him away. The expectation lay buried so deep in his heart, and in the furthest recesses of his mind, that he was unaware of what sustained him.

Waiting was more than merely a habit. Those hundreds of afternoons when he sat patiently, mostly silent, in the various kitchens of the various obliging neighbours had always ended with the desired result, until it had grown to seem infallible as a law of nature: waiting produced his father.

As to the kindly women whose kitchens he once occupied, their efforts to make a pet of Alastair had been unavailing. Try as they might, he would attach himself to none of them. His attention was fixed elsewhere.

'Why don't you let me boil you an egg, Alastair love? It's a terribly long time for a child your age to have to wait for his tea.'

'No thank you, Mrs Campbell – Mrs Carter – Mrs Hitchens,' he would reply; his father had taught him to be polite. 'My dad'll be back soon.'

His dad had always been back, without fail, for their tea together; had never been late. A vague uneasy subliminal sense that something must be keeping him now, something not his dad's fault, haunted the son of the man who was dead.

During the years that followed the funeral, the meanwhile years as it were, Alastair McIntyre strove to behave according to his father's instructions on what he ought and what he ought not to do, and also, which was a good deal harder, to guide himself by his father's opinions; or by as much of them as memory could salvage. Such tangible assets as football and bike having been mislaid somewhere along the way, these instructions and opinions were all, in the end, that his father had left him; all he had left of his father. They constituted his essential survival kit.

He used to lie awake in the darkness of strange beds, anxiously checking over and over the bits and pieces of his invisible inheritance, trying to codify them for greater convenience: brush your teeth, brush your hair, brush your shoes on the mat, wash your hands before you eat, tell the truth, shut the door, go to school –

'You have to go to school, Alastair.'

He heard his father's voice, clear as a bell. 'You have to be educated – everyone does. I tell you – and don't you ever forget it! – education is the answer. They canna beat us, Alastair! Show them what you're worth, boy!'

His heart in the darkness thudded faster. Who were They? And what exactly was it that he had never to forget? *Brush your teeth, brush your hair –*

'There's aye a logic – aye an answer! Come on, Alastair – use your brains, lad! Stick to it! Never say die! Think, boy! – think!'

The familiar phrases, exhortations, rang aloud inside his head, confused and confusingly. He heard his father; saw him in snapshot glimpses, mending the radio, shaving, punting the Christmas football clean across an enormous rainy space: heard him, saw him, in a jumble of pictures and echoing captions that, as the months and then the years went by, fuzzed and faded, until little by little survival came to depend for Alastair McIntyre on a single word: education; its four syllables magically summarising everything his missing father stood for. Education was the hand that would lead him out of the wilderness.

By the time he was fifteen Alastair held an unbroken record for school attendance; and this in a neighbourhood where truancy was rampant. He never complained of stomach-ache. He never allowed any illness, invented or real, to keep him from going to school. He went every day the school doors were open, and he stayed all day until they closed. He was uniquely

@@@@@@@

immune, it appeared – at any rate amongst the seventeen boys and girls of St George's Residential Home – to all forms of the epidemic disease of absenteeism.

In other ways as well he was exceptional. He neither drank, nor smoked, nor swore; although, being a singularly silent boy, this last eccentricity was hardly noticeable. Nor had he acquired the usual supplementary benefit of a probation officer, never having smashed so much as a window, or nicked so much as a bag of sweets in his life.

These abstentions were not due to religious fervour, as might have been supposed, his politely disinterested attitude towards God resembling what had formerly been his attitude towards the helpful neighbours. The Almighty, he once observed cryptically and reverting to the long discarded accent of his earlier childhood, in his opinion 'didna have the answer'. It sounded as if he were quoting.

Judged by the standards of his peers, Alastair – religion apart – was extraordinary, and marked out as a consequence for persecution. But he was not persecuted. Perhaps it was his local fame on the football field that saved him; or perhaps it was his talent for climbing. His powers as a climber were legendary in the district: he would shin without hesitation up any tree, any wall or drainpipe; had been known to balance, unsmiling, three storeys high, along the centre ridge of the Home's roof to disentangle a kite from a chimney pot. Or perhaps what preserved him was that he could be relied on, although law-abiding himself, to tell no tales. Whatever the reason, or reasons, Alastair McIntyre was spared the mockery of his fellows.

At St George's, indeed, they were rather proud of their freak; a little wary of him, too. Something about the normally pacific Alastair, a certain fierceness fiercely controlled, the occasional eruption of an inner volcanic fire, warned them off provoking his rage. If hands were ever imprudently laid on him, he could fight, and did so, like a boy possessed by a demon.

Mackerel, they called him. And Mackerel was a funny bugger, said Errol and Barry and Bruce and Marilyn and Steve. But they said it with a sort of affection. To which affection Alastair responded not at all. He was not unfriendly; not sullen, or sulky, in the least. He was always perfectly civil. But his attention continued to be focused elsewhere. In the social services file on Alastair McIntyre he was described as withdrawn. Aloof would have been a better word.

During the summer of his sixteenth year Alastair and the rest of the gang at St George's were taken on a week's camping holiday to the Pembrokeshire coast. Until then their only experience of the seaside had been the Home's annual day trip to Clacton, or sometimes, for the sake of a change of candyfloss and one-armed bandits, to Southend.

This Welsh adventure was the inspiration of a controversial young man, Philip Halliwell, who taught English at Alastair's school, and who had recently, with his wife Linda, moved into the street adjacent to St George's Residential Home. In a state of angry enthusiasm he had swept aside every objection, overridden every obstacle, borrowed camping gear and a battered old minibus from a nearby collapsing Youth Club, squeezed from a reluctant Municipal Council the modest amount of funding required, and driven his load of grinning faces triumphantly off to confront them with what he said was real sea – the mighty crested rollers of the Atlantic Ocean.

It had been an entire success, the TV-less candyfloss-less holiday. St George's junior residents had all returned from Wales as bouncingly healthy and as boastfully pleased with themselves as though returning to civilisation from the conquered peaks of Kangchenjunga; all except for Alastair. On him the Atlantic Ocean had had a different effect.

He had felt an affinity with it at once. The unceasing voices of wind and waves had seemed to him to be speaking a dialect that was very ancient and very mysterious, and full of a wisdom he could almost understand. Afterwards he was quieter, if that were possible, than before. In July of the following year, having completed his State-sponsored education, he left school.

Philip Halliwell, the English teacher, left the same school as Alastair the same day and also for ever. He had been offered a Research Fellowship at a New Zealand university on the strength of his book, *It's a Waste of Time, Sir*. The offer came as a distinct relief to the outraged members of the School Board, who had decided to get rid of him in any case, but who preferred their unsatisfactory teachers to agree to the more dignified course of resigning.

Dignity was hardly to be expected, however, of Philip Halliwell, a most uncomfortable person to have on the staff, and doubly so now that his upsetting views regarding the educational system had got into print and undeniably made a splash. The School Board had intended, before being let off the hook by New Zealand, to dismiss him on the justifiable grounds of his unorthodox teaching methods; or non-teaching methods, according to some.

'His classes are Bedlam,' said the Headmaster.

They were certainly noisy; a noise to which Alastair McIntyre had not contributed. He used to sit, that final year, at the back of Mr Halliwell's crowded classes – the only classes in the whole school which always were crowded – impervious to the surrounding hubbub, hearing it as no more than a dim outside echo of the clamour of gulls and the thunderous crash of waves that he was listening to inside his head.

On the evening of the day Alastair left school he called in at Philip Halliwell's house to ask him where the camping equipment had been borrowed from the year before, so that he might apply to the same source himself. He was going back to Wales on his own. His plan was to hitch-hike. He had cash enough, saved up from his pocket money to buy food with once he arrived. All he needed was a tent and a sleeping bag.

Mrs Halliwell, a pretty fair-haired girl wearing jeans and sandals, opened the door to him. She was holding her baby, Susie, eight months old. Pregnancy had prevented her joining the St George's expedition last summer. A little brown rough-haired mongrel terrier pushed by her legs to sniff at the visitor's ankles.

'Oh, hello, Alastair.' They already had a doorstep acquaintance. He could see a clutter of boxes and baggage in the passage behind her. 'Phil's out, I'm afraid, but he won't be long.'

She took him into the kitchen and handed him a cup of tea and was very chatty and frank. They were off to Pembrokeshire

◎◎◎◎◎◎◎

themselves the following day, as a matter of fact, for a couple of weeks. Phil had to make up his mind about this job in New Zealand, yes or no, definitely. He had accepted the Fellowship, but he had still not actually signed the contract. It was a big decision – to go and live on the other side of the world. Because if they did go, they would go for keeps: they would emigrate.

'Everyone says it's a marvellous country, New Zealand – and of course it's a marvellous job. We're terribly lucky –' But she sounded oddly dubious.

Alastair was welcome, she told him, to borrow the little tent and the cooking stove that Phil had used as a student, years ago. And they had a spare sleeping bag, too. Probably they could even manage to squash him into a corner of their antiquated van, if he could put up with having Trotty dumped on top of him. Did he like dogs? What a pity he should be setting off alone, though, for his holiday – not half as much fun! She presumed that Mr Bolton had given permission – had he? Mr Bolton was the amiable but, in Philip Halliwell's view, the deplorably unenterprising father-in-charge of St George's Residential Home.

'He's not bothered,' said Alastair, shrugging.

Philip returned, and matters were duly arranged. But later, on reflection, Linda began to query the justice of what she had so spontaneously promoted. There were sixteen other boys and girls at St George's. 'It doesn't seem fair for us to be taking only one of them –'

'Fair!' cried Philip, boiling over in a flash. His mood was nowadays unpredictably volatile. 'Fair! Is there anything fair about those kids' lives? I ask you, Lin! Where do you suppose they'll be in a few weeks from now – all of them? On the dole queue! And not just the St George's bunch, either.' Unemployment in the area was high, and rising steadily, 'That's what we educate our kids for today. Educate them!' He pushed his plate away, as though the sight of a baked potato sickened him. 'Old Wetherspoon was perfectly right when he called my classes Bedlam. So they were. I didn't teach those kids a thing. What in Heaven's name was I to teach them? How not to care that they've been born unwanted? – born with *redundant*, Lin – that word – that criminal word – stamped on their foreheads like the mark of Cain?'

'Oh, Phil –' She pressed her own wanted un-redundant baby closer to her breast.

'I'm glad it's over – over for me, at least. I can't stand it any more, Lin. Thank God for New Zealand!' He spoke as though their future had been settled. But then in the next breath he spoke as though it had not been settled.

'I thought the whole point of us belting off to Pembrokeshire was so as to have the chance of making our minds up in peace. Fat lot of peace there'll be with that young Mackerel hung round our necks,' he grumbled.

But Alastair McIntyre had never hung himself around the neck of anyone. When they arrived the following evening at their destination, a steeply sloping field overlooking the bay of Porth Mawr, Alastair crawled from the van, stiff-legged with cramp, thanked the Halliwells as politely as though they had been total strangers to him, grabbed hold of his bundles, and promptly made off uphill. Rather disconcerted, they watched him go. Trotty, his travelling companion, whined, and then barked, and then trotted after him. They called her back.

'What a funny boy,' said Linda. 'And his eyes, Phil – have you noticed? – they're funny – something about them. Do you think he takes drugs?'

'*Him?* – take drugs? Good Heavens, no! – not Alastair.'

He pitched his tent at the very top of the field, as far from the Halliwells' tent as it was possible to be. Since he thus unmistakably signified his wish to be left alone, they left him alone – except, that is, for Trotty – and were thankful to do so. They had their own problem to deal with.

Philip hired a deep-sea rod and went fishing off the rocks of one of the headlands – fishing, in his experience, being the best method for coming to grips with any problem. Linda spent the day on the beach with Susie and a restless Trotty and several scores of other families and their dogs. Alastair spent it climbing cliffs.

He climbed the cliffs up and down and sideways. He wandered miles along the cliff path and over the gorse- and heather-covered headlands. He watched, unseen, Philip Halliwell fishing, and Linda playing with her baby. He said nothing to anyone, not even when he bought a pork pie and a bottle of lemonade in the shop in the car park for his dinner, and a packet of fish-and-chips off the mobile canteen for his tea.

He was done with people. The voices he heard were the voices he had been hearing for the last year: those age-old indifferent voices of water surging and sucking in and out of caves; the voices of seabirds wheeling, drifting on the wind;

and the voice of the wind, the confidential tireless wordless voice of the wind in his ears, whispering, fluttering, as it endlessly fluttered and whispered in the dry grasses at his feet. Voices, all, that asserted nothing, denied nothing, promised nothing.

At the end of the day he sat in front of his tiny borrowed orange tent and watched the sun sink in a clear sky towards the sea's horizon. Soon it would be dark, and then above him for company there would be a million stars, and for further company, should he have need of it, the beam of the lighthouse that swept across the bay as regular as clockwork on the count of eight. Already the lighthouse had started to wink in preparation: one, two, three, four, five, SIX, seven, wink; one, two –

'Alastair!'

Linda Halliwell, in shorts and a yellow sweater, and carrying her baby, was ascending the field. The little dog, Trotty, rushed on ahead of them to greet him ecstatically. He scrambled up, confused.

'I've brought you your supper.' She was dangling a fish. 'Mackerel for Mackerel,' she laughed; but hastening, when she saw that he flinched at the nickname, to repair her mistake: 'What a smashing view you have up here, Alastair – much better than ours is. You're so high! It's windier, though – a lot. Here – catch hold of Susie a sec.'

He held the baby, carefully, while she tied back her hair with a scarf. And then Linda, retrieving Susie from him, stood beside Alastair and looked at his view for several minutes without speaking, silenced by his silence.

She went down the darkening field, past the other campers' tents, beginning now to glow like green and orange paper lanterns, to their tent at the bottom, and she said to her husband:

'He worries me, that boy – he really does.'

'All our kids today worry me,' Philip answered her, very brusque.

'Yes, but he's got a secret, Phil – something awful. I'm sure he has. And we'll never know what it is, because he can't say.'

But the next morning, to her surprise, he sought her out on the beach where she sat with Susie and Trotty. She concealed her surprise. Philip was away on the rocks again somewhere, fishing.

At the mention of Philip's name: 'They sacked him didn't they,' said Alastair, abruptly; a statement, not a question. He brushed off her reference to New Zealand. 'They was going to sack him anyway – wasn't they? On account of us lot – all that talking and shouting and that.'

'Well, yes – I daresay they were,' she admitted.

'So is that what it is then – education?' Alastair persisted; '– what he says it is – just letting kids talk?'

'No – of course not. But talking's a start – or it can be. It depends on – well, on everything else – the circumstances.'

He was making, she realised, a supreme effort, this uncommunicative boy, to communicate with her. And she therefore tried herself in return to explain to him, here on the swarming holiday beach, her husband's philosophy of communication; his dedicated commitment to the power and the beauty of language; his belief that it should be written, spoken, used, and understood, and enjoyed, by everyone. 'You ought to read his book,' she finished, with a dismaying sense of her eloquence making no impression on Alastair. He lay at full length, unanswering, his face averted. 'I'll lend you a copy, if you like, when we get home.'

'No thanks,' he said, drawing circles in the sand.

'But it's good, Alastair – honestly.' She was rather affronted.

'Not for me, it's not. Can't read.'

He stunned her. And then, recovering, 'Oh, Alastair,' she cried, impulsively, 'I'll teach you to read.'

'Will you? When?' He looked up at her with derision over his hunched and protective shoulder. 'You're going to New Zealand.'

She imagined that Alastair McIntyre had divulged his awful secret, and it seemed to her, in consideration of the effect it had on Philip, to be awful indeed. Philip was aghast at the news. That a pupil of his – 'one of my kids' – could attend his English classes for two years and yet be illiterate, and he not know it until this moment, struck him as the epitome of his own failure. But he presently discovered what was far worse.

That afternoon, while fishing off the rocks, and too much troubled in his thoughts to be having much success with this occupation either, he glanced up and saw Alastair perched above, watching him; or perhaps merely gazing out to sea. He was afraid that when he waved and cupped his hands to yell an invitation, the boy would simply vanish, but instead Alastair McIntyre climbed expertly down, and was given a lesson in casting.

Again and again the long strong line whistled out across the slowly heaving huge Atlantic swells. Alastair, remarkably, got the knack of it almost at once, and the fish were suddenly plentiful, and every silver mackerel that came twisting up from the deep green fathoms of water was like the solution to a problem; so that a curious urge arose in Philip Halliwell to ask this boy for his advice. He wanted to shout at him above the noise of wind and breaking waves: What shall I do? It was Alastair, though, who shouted at Philip:

'I'm not going back!'

His face, freckled and burned a bright red by the sun, wore an exalted expression. Philip understood immediately what he meant, and how absolutely he meant it.

But Linda had to have the meaning explained to her. And when it was: 'Oh no, Phil!' she cried, and kept on crying, sick with horror, distraught. 'He can't! He mustn't! We've got to stop him –'

Phil warned her that the boy, Alastair, had made up his mind. He had decided.

She burst into tears afresh. 'To drown himself?' she wailed.

'Yes. And Linda – stopping him won't be easy.'

Alastair's decision was not a spur of the moment affair. He had been contemplating it seriously ever since the previous July. He had now left school. The likelihood of his getting a job was remote. He had no family. Very soon he would have no home, the St George's children being required, upon reaching the age of eighteen, to remove themselves to some other address. Through thick and thin, year after year, he had clung on and on, waiting. What had the waiting been for? Alastair McIntyre recently concluded that he was the subject of a prolonged hoax: it had all been for nothing. Nothing!

He came in the same category as certain goods that he had heard Mr Bolton, when checking the storeroom at St George's, describe as being 'surplus to need'. In which case it was stupid for him to stay. He might as well go. And if going, then what more suitable departure platform than here? – here, where the land that people lived on ended in tall cliffs, and the mighty ocean, quencher of flames and breath, began. He had worked it all out in his head. He had found, by himself and for himself, the logical answer.

This was Philip's version of some of the halting blurted fragments he had, with difficulty, extracted from Alastair as they sat on the rocks, and climbed the headland, and walked back to the tents together along the cliff path.

Linda's first instinct was to take Susie and run up the field as fast as she could, and place her baby tenderly in Alastair's arms. Who, not made of ice, could resist the speechless appeal of her happy child? But Philip counselled against it. Rather than bringing about a miracle conversion, he said, she would be far more likely to scare Alastair off. And his wife, with sorrowful amazement, agreed:

'It's true – he doesn't even *see* Susie. The way he holds her, she could just as well be a parcel.'

Alastair would have to be won – if won at all – by reason, said Philip. Although he could neither read nor write, he was a blocked intellectual and a buried poet, and in that order; which was why argument and not emotion would be the more liable to prevail.

When Linda, startled, queried these titles of poet and intellectual, Philip replied impatiently: 'I mean that he has his faculties, Lin – his senses – in full measure, locked inside him. D'you want to know why he doesn't see our Susie? Because for two years he sat at the back of my classes and I didn't see him.'

'Oh Phil – no – that's not true.' She was shocked by the bitterness of his self-reproach.

'True enough. Well, now I've got nine days, Linda – nine days to convince that kid of mine by argument that he has to choose – as we all have to choose – to live and not to die: life, not death! And if I don't succeed – if he's not convinced, Lin – then whether sooner or whether later, one day he's going to say: No thanks!'

And Philip added, as clue to a comprehension of what made Alastair tick: 'My guess is, he's like his dad – the Scottish electrician.'

It was Linda then who startled her husband by saying, as she blew her nose: 'He's like you, Phil.'

'*Me*?' He was astonished. 'We're completely different.'

She, however, insisted that there was a similarity.

Philip Halliwell planned his campaign on the premise that this Mackerel was a mis-named fish who would have to be hooked with skill and afterwards played with subtlety and perseverance, otherwise he could very well break off the line and still be lost. He must be let alone, and not chased after. He must feel free to approach or retreat at will. It was Philip's job simply to be accessible, to stay put and be ready to make the most of whatever opportunity presented itself.

Such a strategy wore hard on the nerves of the strategists, and especially hard on Linda's nerves, she being the one least actively involved. Only when Alastair was in sight, when she could observe him for herself, sitting outside his tent or fetching water from the tap in the lane, only then was she able to breathe easily.

But mostly he was not in sight. All day he roamed abroad – who knew where? – wandering the beaches, the cliff paths, the headlands. And sometimes it was not until after dark, when his orange tent bloomed at the top of the field like a tulip, that she knew he was home again, safe.

Philip tried to relieve his wife's painful unremitting anxiety. Alastair would remain safe, he assured her, anyway for as long as they were camping there themselves. The boy's politeness was the guarantee of that: he would never dream of disrupting the Halliwells' holiday so crudely. It would certainly be his intention to do what he was intending to do after they were gone.

'Then we mustn't ever go,' she cried, wildly. 'Never! Or Phil – we must make him come with us – *force* him to –'

'That's not what would solve it, Lin.'

'I know it's not,' she said.

All day he roamed – and who knew where? Trotty knew where. Trotty had adopted Alastair. From dawn to dusk, or later, she trotted gladly at his heels, returning to the Halliwells' tent at the bottom of the field, hungry, thirsty, tired and contented, when Alastair returned to his at the top. Each night she slept in her own basket. Linda groaned that the chance of persuasion available to so constant a companion should be wasted on Trotty, who was unequipped with an advocate's tongue. But Philip said:

'My darling Linda, if Trotty wasn't a dumb animal he'd never take her with him.'

Every morning directly after breakfast Philip set off with his rod and tackle for one of the less frequented headlands. In addition to the rod, his Mackerel bait consisted of buns and enough sandwiches for two and a large thermos of tea. He never knew when Alastair was going to turn up but some time during the day, unfailingly, boy and dog would materialise. Then, as though fulfilling the terms of a bargain tacitly agreed upon, the rod would be handed over, and Philip would watch while Alastair planted his legs wide for purchase and cast the long line far out across the green water, and reeled it in, and cast again and again, his eyes tranced. And it might be that he pulled out a fish, and it might be that he did not.

They drank tea and they shared the sandwiches. And Philip, by dint of questioning, for nothing was volunteered, learned more, although not much more, about the Scottish electrician who had been knocked down by a lorry when Alastair was nine; piecing together from the semi-obliterated scraps of childhood's memory the picture of an upright man, an independent man, a man who had urged his son to think for himself; a man who above all else, had believed in education.

'He was always on at me, my dad, about education – schooling. How it was – you know – important, and that. He used to say it was the answer – education.'

'Well, and he was right.'

'You reckon? – I don't. I reckon as my dad was wrong,' said Alastair flatly, getting up and walking away.

But the next day he was back. He asked Philip: 'So what do you say it is, then?'

'Say what is?'

'Education. I mean – I don't know – what is it?'

Philip tried to be brief in his preliminary summarising of the historical perspective; to condense his personal view of society, as it was and as it ought to be. Education itself he defined epigrammatically as that which enabled a human being, armed with the fullest possible knowledge and understanding, to declare: I shouldn't, and therefore I shan't; I can, and therefore I will. But of course education was much more than this. He talked and talked.

Alastair, silent again, sat munching sandwiches and gazing seawards. He may have been listening; or, equally, his ears may have been closed against his ex-teacher's impassioned monologues. After the boy had left him, Philip wondered, exhausted, if he had absorbed a single syllable. What had he been thinking about? Was it fishing? Or was it something else?

As the days went by Philip Halliwell grew increasingly desperate. Alastair's silence defeated him. It was a wall he could not breach, until at last, abandoning all subtleties of argument, he threw caution aside and harangued him openly.

'It's no good expecting answers to drop out of the sky, like – like manna from heaven – they won't. You have to search for them – struggle for them – die struggling, perhaps – people do! But to kill yourself – throw yourself away – that's not an answer to anything.'

And finally the volcano erupted. Eyes ablaze, half-choked, Alastair turned on him, stammering: 'Words! – words! – just words!'

'Yes – words!'

@@@@@@@

They stood as enemies, face to face on the rocks, a yard apart and both in a rage.

'Words are necessary,' Philip shouted. 'Words are marvellous! How in hell do you suppose we're any of us ever going to be able to understand each other properly – express ourselves properly – if we don't use words? How in hell can we pass on ideas – how can they survive – as they do survive, ideas, for longer than us, for centuries – if we don't have a language? People need ideas – ideas are food. Without ideas, people starve. Your father knew that –'

'My father's dead.'

'He didn't choose to be, poor chap. Your father was a practical man. He'd have told you, if he was here now, that to be dead is to be useless – wasted, Alastair! Life makes you valuable – because when you're alive you can think and feel, and ask questions, and search for those answers – answers for everyone, not for just yourself. People affect each other – don't you realise that? Everything we do, or say, has its effect on other human beings. What sort of a message will you be passing on if you quit? "I'm clearing out because things got too hard for me"? –'

He broke off sharply, conscious of Alastair's ironical – was it contemptuous? – unwavering stare. To whom – of whom – was he speaking?

Three nights before they were due to leave there was a storm. Linda lay awake, holding Susie close, and hearkening to the huge violence of wind and rain and waves in the world outside their frail shelter, thinking with a sick heart of fishermen and sailors who battled for their lives in drowning seas and of the boy, Alastair, who wanted only that the sea should swallow him.

By early morning the tempest was over. Rain still fell, but the wind had abated and the sky was clearing.

'Where's Trotty?'

Her basket had not been slept in.

'She must have stopped up with Alastair for the night, I suppose – no wonder!'

But when they went to fetch her back, Trotty was not there; and neither was Alastair. In the semi-darkness of dawn the interior of the little orange tent, with its neatly rolled sleeping bag, had an ominously undisturbed appearance, as if he too had been absent all night. They looked at each other, horror-struck.

'Oh Phil – he hasn't – he wouldn't –'

But perhaps he would, and perhaps he had. A storm could have seemed a chance that was after all too good to miss, a heaven-sent alibi for disappearance. Oh, but surely – surely, said Linda, frantic for any straw to clutch, he would not at least have taken Trotty with him? And then, recalling his unfathomable eyes: he might have done, she thought – he could have done.

'Alastair? – never! No – no, Lin,' said Philip, at last, with the long sigh of a man waking from nightmare into the reality of a nightmarish world: 'If anything's happened to that kid, it was an accident – I'll swear to it. He won't have done it on purpose.'

'But he meant to,' she wept. 'He was going to kill himself – he wanted to die.' The tears poured down her cheeks.

'Yes – but Linda – he changed his mind. I know – I swear – he changed his mind.'

'How do you know? – how can you be so sure?'

'Because he despised me, Lin – that's why. He despised me for getting out. I saw it in his face. And that kid – that – that funny kid,' said Philip slowly, 'wouldn't ever do something he despised someone else for doing – believe me. I know it.'

They discovered Alastair almost at once, with Trotty, on a cliff edge that was out of reach of the sea but scarcely broader than the width of a windowsill; both fully alive.

'She's broke a leg,' Alastair yelled up at them, 'and maybe more – ribs, maybe.'

Eventually, with the aid of ropes and lines and a shopping bag, and various other ingenious devices; with the interested participation of a gathering number of campers aroused early by the emergency; with great care, and some daring – poor Trotty was rescued. Alastair, natural-born climber that he was, rescued himself.

'Silly little dog,' he burst out, the moment he had been helped and hauled over the edge and stood on the grass, wringing wet and shuddering uncontrollably from head to foot. 'She was chasing a rabbit, and she just went on – clean over the top. I thought she'd had her chips – RIP, and serve her right for being so daft – but she'll live to fight another day, I reckon – won't you, Trotty?'

She had gone over the cliff, and Alastair, guided by her piteous barks and whimpers, and groping for each toe-and finger-hold in the deepening dusk, had climbed his way down to her. By the time he arrived at Trotty's providential staging-post it was too dark to see more than the glimmer of surf beneath him; too dark, without risking disaster, to budge a further inch in any direction.

Midnight had brought them the storm. He described in graphic detail the fury of the elements: for he was dumb no longer. In a few hours he had grown to be, not merely voluble, but unstoppably garrulous. Whatever conversation may have passed between Alastair McIntyre and the savage and senseless waves below as they dashed themselves to pieces on unseen rocks during those hellish interminable hours of human solitude, it had transformed him, irreversibly. And in spite of his chattering teeth and the purple frozen flesh there was yet about him a curiously jubilant air, a sort of excited confidence.

'I knew you'd come for me, soon as it was light,' he said to Philip when they were trooping back towards the promised immediate paradise of bacon and eggs and sausages and hot tea.

Dawn had merged into day. The sun had risen and the sky was unclouded; but the breeze was fresh. He wore Philip's jersey, somebody else's anorak.

'Staying awake was the worst part of it. I knew, though, if I could only just manage to stick it out – hang on – somehow – till morning, you'd find me all right.'

And then Alastair gave utterance to a phrase which, coming as it did from this formerly speechless boy, his ex-pupil, so seared the imagination of the English-language-obsessed Philip Halliwell that any lingering doubts he might have had about his future course of action were resolved for him on the spot; also irreversibly.

'I knew,' said Alastair McIntyre, with a grin, 'as you wasn't a bloke who'd leave me to perish alone in the waters of darkness

– would you, Phil? Hey, Linda – hand us over that girl of yours,' he called. 'I got something I want to say to her.'

Greatly wondering, Linda placed her precious baby in his still shivering arms. He held Susie as carefully as before, but not now as if she were a parcel.

'You got a nerve, you have – let go my nose! I reckon it's time you begun to express yourself properly, Susan Halliwell – and you can start with my name. It's easy – Mackerel! Go on, Susie – say it!' She shrieked with joy. 'I'm going to give you an education, mate,' he threatened her. 'I'm going to teach you how to talk.'

AN EVENING TO REMEMBER
Rosamunde Pilcher
1985

Under the dryer, with her hair rolled and skewered to her head, Alison Stockman turned down the offer of magazines to read, and instead opened her handbag, took out the notepad with its attached pencil, and went through, for perhaps the fourteenth time, her List.

She was not a natural list-maker, being a fairly haphazard sort of person, and a cheerfully lighthearted housekeeper who frequently ran out of essentials like bread and butter and washing-up liquid, but still retained the ability to manage – for a day or so at any rate – by sheer improvisation, and the deep-seated conviction that it didn't much matter anyway.

It wasn't that she didn't sometimes make lists, it was because she made them on the spur of the moment, using any small scrap of paper that came to hand. Backs of envelopes, cheque stubs, old bills. This added a certain mystery to life. *Lampshade. How much?* she would find, scrawled on a receipt for coal delivered six months previously, and would spend several engrossed moments trying to recall what on earth this missive could have meant; Which lampshade? And how much had it cost?

Ever since they had moved out of London and into the country, she had been slowly trying to furnish and decorate their new house, but there never seemed to be enough time or money to spare – two small children used up almost all of these commodities – and there were still rooms with the wrong sort of wallpaper, or no carpets, or lamps without lampshades.

This list, however, was different. This list was for tomorrow night, and so important was it that she had specially bought the little pad with pencil attached; and had written down, with the greatest concentration, every single thing that had to be bought, cooked, polished, cleaned, washed, ironed, or peeled.

Vacuum dining room, polish silver. She ticked that one off. *Lay table.* She ticked that as well. She had done it this morning while Larry was at playschool and Janey napping in her cot. 'Won't the glasses get dusty?' Henry had asked when she had told him her plans, but Alison assured him that they wouldn't, and anyway the meal would be eaten by candlelight, so if the glasses were dusty Mr and Mrs Fairhurst probably wouldn't be able to see far enough to notice. Besides, whoever had heard of a dusty wineglass?

Order fillet of beef. That got a tick as well. *Peel potatoes.* Another tick; they were in a bowl of water in the larder along with a small piece of coal. *Take prawns out of freezer.* That was tomorrow morning. *Make mayonnaise. Shred lettuce. Peel mushrooms. Make Mother's lemon soufflé. Buy cream.* She ticked off *Buy cream,* but the rest would have to wait until tomorrow.

She wrote, *Do flowers.* That meant picking the first shy daffodils that were beginning to bloom in the garden and arranging them with sprigs of flowering currant, which, hopefully, would not make the whole house smell of dirty cats.

She wrote, *Wash the best coffee cups.* These were a wedding present, and were kept in a corner cupboard in the sitting room. They would, without doubt, be dusty, even if the wineglasses weren't.

She wrote, *Have a bath.*

This was essential, even if she had it at two o'clock tomorrow afternoon. Preferably after she had brought in the coal and filled the log basket,

She wrote, *Mend chair.* This was one of the dining room chairs, six little balloon-backs which Alison had bought at an auction sale. They had green velvet seats, edged with gold braid, but Larry's cat, called, brilliantly, Catkin, had used the chair as a useful claw-sharpener, and the braid had come unstuck and drooped, unkempt as a sagging petticoat. She would find the glue and a few tacks and put it together again. It didn't matter if it wasn't very well done. Just so that it didn't show.

She put the list back in her bag and sat and thought glumly about her dining room. The fact that they even had a dining room in this day and age was astonishing, but the truth was that it was such an unattractive, north-facing little box of a room that nobody wanted it for anything else. She had suggested it as a study for Henry, but Henry said it was too damned cold, and then she had said that Larry could keep his toy farm there, but Larry preferred to play with his toy farm on the kitchen floor. It wasn't as if they ever used it as a dining room, because they seemed to eat all their meals in the kitchen, or on the terrace in the warm weather, or even out in the garden when the summer sun was high and they could picnic, the four of them, beneath the shade of the sycamore tree.

Her thoughts, as usual, were flying off at tangents. The dining room. It was so gloomy they had decided that nothing could make it gloomier, and had papered it in dark green to match the velvet curtains that Alison's mother had produced from her copious attic. There was a gate-leg table, and the balloon-back chairs, and a Victorian sideboard that an aunt of Henry's had bequeathed to them. As well, there were two monstrous pictures. These were Henry's contribution. He had gone to an auction sale to buy a brass fender, only to find himself the possessor, as well, of these depressing paintings. One depicted a fox consuming a dead duck; the other a Highland cow standing in a pouring rainstorm.

'They'll fill the walls,' Henry had said, and hung them in the dining room, 'They'll do till I can afford to buy you an original Hockney, or a Renoir, or a Picasso, or whatever it is you happen to want.'

He came down from the top of the ladder and kissed his wife. He was in his shirtsleeves and there was a cobweb in his hair.

'I don't want those sort of things,' Alison told him.

'You should.' He kissed her again. 'I do.'

And he did. Not for himself, but for his wife and his children. For them he was ambitious. They had sold the flat in London, and bought this little house, because he wanted the children to live in the country and to know about cows and crops and trees and the seasons; and because of the mortgage they had vowed to do all the necessary painting and decorating themselves. This endless ploy took up all their weekends, and at first it had gone quite well because it was wintertime. But then the days lengthened, and the summer came, and they abandoned the inside of the house and moved out of doors to try to create some semblance of order in the overgrown and neglected garden

In London, they had had time to spend together; to get a babysitter for the children and go out for dinner; to sit and listen to music on the stereo, while Henry read the paper and Alison did her gros point. But now Henry left home at seven-thirty every morning and did not get back until nearly twelve hours later,

'Is it really worth it?' she asked him sometimes, but Henry was never discouraged.

'It won't be like this for always,' he promised her. 'You'll see.'

His job was with Fairhurst & Hanbury, an electrical engineering business, which, since Henry had first joined as a junior executive, had grown and modestly prospered, and now had a number of interesting irons in the fire, not the least of which was the manufacture of commercial computers. Slowly, Henry had ascended the ladder of promotion, and now was possibly in line, or being considered for, the post of Export Director, the man who at present held this job having decided to retire early, move to Devonshire, and take up poultry farming.

In bed, which seemed to be nowadays the only place where they could find the peace and privacy to talk, Henry had assessed, for Alison, the possibilities of his getting this job. They did not seem to be very hopeful. He was, for one thing, the youngest of the candidates. His qualifications, although sound, were not brilliant, and the others were all more experienced.

'But what would you have to do?' Alison wanted to know.

'Well, that's it. I'd have to travel. Go to New York, Hong Kong, Japan. Rustle up new markets. I'd be away a lot. You'd be on your own even more than you are now. And then we'd have to reciprocate. I mean, if foreign buyers came to see us, we'd have to look after them, entertain . . . you know the sort of thing.'

She thought about this, lying warmly in his arms, in the dark, with the window open and the cool country air blowing in on her face. She said, 'I wouldn't like you being away a lot, but I could bear it. I wouldn't be lonely, because of having the children. And I'd know that you'd always come back to me.'

He kissed her. He said, 'Did I ever tell you I loved you?'

'Once or twice.'

He said, 'I want that job. I could do it. And I want to get this mortgage off our backs, and take the children to Brittany for their summer holidays, and maybe pay some man to dig that ruddy garden for us.'

'Don't say such things.' Alison laid her fingers against Henry's mouth. 'Don't talk about them. We mustn't count chickens.'

This nocturnal conversation had taken place a month or so before, and they hadn't talked about Henry's possible promotion again. But a week ago, Mr Fairhurst, who was Henry's chairman, had taken Henry out to lunch at his club. Henry found it hard to believe that Mr Fairhurst was standing him this excellent meal simply for the pleasure of Henry's company, but they were eating delicious blue-veined Stilton and drinking a glass of port before Mr Fairhurst finally came to the point. He asked after Alison and the children. Henry told him they were very well.

'Good for children, living in the country. Does Alison like it there?'

'Yes. She's made a lot of friends in the village.'

'That's good. That's very good.' Thoughtfully, the older man helped himself to more Stilton. 'Never really met Alison.' He sounded as though he was ruminating to himself, not addressing any particular remark to Henry. 'Seen her, of course, at the office dance, but that scarcely counts. Like to see your new house . . .'

His voice trailed off. He looked up. Henry, across the starched tablecloth and gleaming silverware, met his eyes. He realised that Mr Fairhurst was angling for – indeed, expected – a social invitation.

He cleared his throat and said, 'Perhaps you and Mrs Fairhurst would come down and have dinner with us one evening?'

'Well,' said the chairman, looking surprised and delighted as if it had all been Henry's idea. 'How very nice. I'm sure Mrs Fairhurst would like that very much.'

'I'll . . . I'll tell Alison to give her a ring. They can fix a date.'

'We're being vetted, aren't we? For the new job,' said Alison, when he broke the news. 'For all the entertaining of those foreign clients. They want to know if I can cope, if I'm socially up to it.'

'Put like that, it sounds pretty soulless, but . . . yes, I suppose that is what it's all about.'

'Does it have to be terribly grand?'

'No.'

'But formal.'

'Well, he is the chairman.'

'Oh, dear.'

'Don't look like that. I can't bear it when you look like that.'

'Oh, Henry.' She wondered if she was going to cry, but he pulled her into his arms and hugged her and she found she wasn't going to cry after all. Over the top of her head, he said, 'Perhaps we are being vetted, but surely that's a good sign. It's better than being simply ignored.'

'Yes, I suppose so.' After a little, 'There's one good thing,' said Alison. 'At least we've got a dining room.'

The next morning she made the telephone call to Mrs Fairhurst, and, trying not to sound too nervous, duly asked Mrs Fairhurst and her husband for dinner. 'Oh, how very kind.' Mrs Fairhurst seemed genuinely surprised, as though this was the first she had heard of it.

'We . . . we thought either the sixth or the seventh of this month. Whichever suits you better.'

'Just a moment, I'll find my diary.' There followed a long wait. Alison's heart thumped. It was ridiculous to feel so anxious. At last Mrs Fairhurst came back on the line. 'The seventh would suit us very well.'

'About seven-thirty?'

@@@@@@

'That would be perfect.'

'And I'll tell Henry to draw Mr Fairhurst a little map, so that you can find your way.'

'That would be an excellent idea. We have been known to get lost.'

They both laughed at this, said goodbye, and hung up. Instantly, Alison picked up the receiver again and dialled her mother's telephone number.

'Ma.'

'Darling.'

'A favour to ask. Could you have the children for the night next Friday?'

'Of course. Why?'

Alison explained. Her mother was instantly practical. 'I'll come over in the car and collect them, just after tea. And then they can spend the night. Such a good idea. Impossible to cook a dinner and put the children to bed at the same time, and if they know there's something going on they'll never go to sleep. Children are all the same. What are you going to give the Fairhursts to eat?'

Alison hadn't thought about this, but she thought about it now, and her mother made a few helpful suggestions and gave her the recipe for her own lemon soufflé. She asked after the children, imparted a few items of family news, and then rang off. Alison picked up the receiver yet again and made an appointment to have her hair done.

With all this accomplished, she felt capable and efficient, two sensations not usually familiar. Friday, the seventh. She left the telephone, went across the hall, and opened the door of the dining room. She surveyed it critically, and the dining room glowered back at her. With candles, she told herself, half-closing her eyes, and the curtains drawn, perhaps it won't look so bad.

Oh, please, God, don't let anything go wrong. Let me not let Henry down. For Henry's sake, let it be a success.

God helps those who help themselves. Alison closed the dining room door, put on her coat, walked down to the village, and there bought the little notepad with pencil attached.

Her hair was dry. She emerged from the dryer, sat at a mirror, and was duly combed out.

'Going somewhere tonight?' asked the young hairdresser, wielding a pair of brushes as though Alison's head was a drum.

'No. Not tonight, tomorrow night, I've got some people coming for dinner.'

'That'll be nice. Want me to spray it for you?'

'Perhaps you'd better.'

He squirted her from all directions, held up a mirror so that she could admire the back, and then undid the bow of the mauve nylon gown and helped Alison out of it.

'Thank you so much.'

'Have a good time tomorrow.'

Some hopes! She paid the bill, put on her coat, and went out into the street. It was getting dark. Next door to the hairdresser was a sweet shop, so she went in and bought two bars of chocolate for the children. She found her car and drove home, parked the car in the garage, and went into the house by the kitchen door. Here she found Evie giving the children their tea. Janey was in her high chair, they were eating fish fingers and chips, and the kitchen smelt fragrantly of baking.

'Well,' said Evie, looking at Alison's head, 'you are smart.'

Alison flopped into a chair and smiled at the three cheerful faces around the table. 'I feel all boiled. Is there any tea left in that pot?'

'I'll make a fresh brew.'

'And you've been baking.'

'Well,' said Evie, 'I had a moment to spare, so made a cake. Thought it might come in handy.'

Evie was one of the best things that had happened to Alison since coming to live in the country. She was a spinster of middle years, stout and energetic, and kept house for her bachelor brother, who farmed the land around Alison and Henry's house. Alison had first met her in the village grocer's. Evie had introduced herself and said that if Alison wanted free-range eggs, she could buy them from Evie, Evie kept her own hens, and supplied a few chosen families in the village. Alison accepted this offer gratefully, and took to walking the children down to the farmhouse in the afternoons to pick up the eggs.

Evie loved children. After a bit, 'Any time you need a sitter, just give me a ring,' said Evie, and from time to time Alison had taken her up on this. The children liked it when Evie came to take care of them. She always brought them sweets or little presents, taught Larry card games, and was deft and loving with Janey, liking to hold the baby on her knee, with Janey's round fair head pressed against the solid bolster of her formidable bosom.

Now, she bustled to the stove, filled a kettle, stooped to the oven to inspect her cake. 'Nearly done.'

'You are kind, Evie. But isn't it time you went home? Jack'll be wondering what's happened to his tea.'

'Oh, Jack went off to market today. Won't be back till all hours. If you like, I'll put the children to bed for you. I have to wait for the cake, anyway.' She beamed at Larry. 'You'd like that, wouldn't you, my duck? Have Evie bathing you. And Evie will show you how to make soap bubbles with your fingers.'

Larry put the last chip in his mouth. He was a thoughtful child, and did not commit himself readily to any impulsive scheme. He said, 'Will you read me my story as well? When I'm in bed?'

'If you like.'

'I want to read *Where's Spot?* There's a tortoise in it.'

'Well, Evie shall read you that.'

When tea was finished, the three of them went upstairs. Bath water could be heard running and Alison smelt her best bubble bath. She cleared the tea and stacked the dishwasher and turned it on. Outside, the light was fading, so before it got dark, she went out and unpegged the morning's wash from the line, brought it indoors, folded it, stacked it in the airing cupboard. On her way downstairs, she collected a red engine, an eyeless teddy bear, a squeaking ball, and a selection of bricks. She put these in the toy basket that lived in the kitchen, laid the table for their breakfast, and a tray for the supper that she and Henry would eat by the fire.

This reminded her. She went through to the sitting room, put a match to the fire, and drew the curtains. The room looked bleak without flowers, but she planned to do flowers tomorrow. As she returned to the kitchen, Catkin put in an appearance, insinuating himself through his cat door, and announcing to Alison that it was long past his dinner time and he was hungry. She opened a tin of cat food and poured him some milk, and he settled himself into a neat eating position and tidily consumed the lot.

She thought about supper for herself and Henry. In the larder was a basket of brown eggs Evie had brought with her. They would have omelettes and a salad. There were six oranges in the fruit bowl and doubtless some scraps of cheese in the cheese dish. She collected lettuce and tomatoes, half a green pepper and a couple of sticks of celery, and began to make a salad. She was stirring the French dressing when she heard Henry's car come up the lane and pull into the garage. A moment later he appeared at the back door, looking tired and crumpled, carrying his bulging briefcase and the evening paper.

'Hi.'

'Hello, darling.' They kissed. 'Had a busy day?'

'Frantic.' He looked at the salad and ate a bit of lettuce. 'Is this for supper?'

'Yes, and an omelette.'

'Frugal fare.' He leaned against the table. 'I suppose we're saving up for tomorrow night?'

'Don't talk about it. Did you see Mr Fairhurst today?'

'No, he's been out of town. Where are the children?'

'Evie's bathing them. Can't you hear? She stayed on. She'd baked a cake for us and it's still in the oven. And Jack's at market.'

Henry yawned. 'I'll go up and tell her to leave the water in, I could do with a bath.'

Alison emptied the dishwasher and then went upstairs too. She felt, for some reason, exhausted. It was an unfamiliar treat to be able to potter around her bedroom, to feel peaceful and unhurried. She took off the clothes she had been wearing all day, opened her cupboard and reached for the velvet housecoat that Henry had given her last Christmas. It was not a garment she had worn very often, there not being many occasions in her busy life when it seemed suitable. It was lined with silk, and had a comforting and luxurious feel about it. She did up the buttons, tied the sash, slipped her feet into flat gold slippers left over from some previous summer, and went across the landing to the children's room to say goodnight. Janey was in her cot, on the verge of sleep. Evie sat on the edge of Larry's bed, and was just about to finish the bedtime book. Larry's mouth was plugged with his thumb, his eyes drooped. Alison stooped to kiss him.

'See you in the morning,' she told him. He nodded, and his eyes went back to Evie. He wanted to hear the end of the story. Alison left them and went downstairs. She picked up Henry's evening paper and took it into the sitting room to see what was on television that evening. As she did this, she heard a car come up the lane from the main road. It turned in at their gate. Headlights flashed beyond the drawn curtains. Alison lowered the paper. Gravel crunched as the car stopped outside their front door. Then the bell rang. She dropped the newspaper onto the sofa and went to open the door.

Outside, parked on the gravel, was a large black Daimler. And on the doorstep, looking both expectant and festive, stood Mr and Mrs Fairhurst.

Her first instinct was to slam the door in their faces, scream, count to ten, and then open the door and find them gone.

But they were, undoubtedly, there. Mrs Fairhurst was smiling. Alison smiled, too. She could feel the smile, creasing her cheeks, like something that had been slapped on her face.

'I'm afraid,' said Mrs Fairhurst, 'that we're a little bit early. We were so afraid of losing the way.'

'No. Not a bit.' Alison's voice came out at least two octaves higher than it usually did. She'd got the date wrong. She'd told Mrs Fairhurst the wrong day. She'd made the most appalling, most ghastly mistake. 'Not a bit early.' She stood back, opening the door. 'Do come in.'

They did so, and Alison closed the door behind them. They began to shed their coats.

I can't tell them. Henry will have to tell them. He'll have to give them a drink and tell them that there isn't anything to eat because I thought they were coming tomorrow night.

Automatically, she went to help Mrs Fairhurst with her fur.

'Did . . . did you have a good drive?'

'Yes, very good,' said Mr Fairhurst. He wore a dark suit and a splendid tie. 'Henry gave me excellent instructions.'

'And of course there wasn't too much traffic.' Mrs Fairhurst smelt of Chanel No. 5. She adjusted the chiffon collar of her dress and touched her hair which had, like Alison's, been freshly done. It was silvery and elegant, and she wore diamond earrings and a beautiful brooch at the neck of her dress.

'What a charming house. How clever of you and Henry to find it.'

'Yes, we love it.' They were ready. They stood smiling at her. 'Do come in by the fire.'

She led the way, into her warm, firelit, but flowerless sitting room, swiftly gathered up the newspaper from the sofa and pushed it beneath a pile of magazines. She moved an armchair closer to the fire. 'Do sit down, Mrs Fairhurst. I'm afraid Henry was a little late back from the office. He'll be down in just a moment.'

She should offer them a drink, but the drinks were in the kitchen cupboard and it would seem both strange and rude to go out and leave them on their own. And supposing they asked for dry martinis? Henry always did the drinks, and Alison didn't know how to make a dry martini.

Mrs Fairhurst lowered herself comfortably into the chair. She said, 'Jock had to go to Birmingham this morning, so I don't suppose he's seen Henry today have you, dear?'

'No, I didn't get into the office.' He stood in front of the fire and looked about him appreciatively. 'What a pleasant room this is.'

'Oh, yes. Thank you.'

'Do you have a garden?'

'Yes, about an acre. It's really too big.' She looked about her frantically, and her eyes lighted upon the cigarette box. She picked it up and opened it. There were four cigarettes inside. 'Would you like a cigarette?'

But Mrs Fairhurst did not smoke, and Mr Fairhurst said that if Alison did not mind, he would smoke one of his own cigars. Alison said that she did not mind at all, and put the box back on the table. A number of panic-stricken images flew through her mind. Henry, still lolling in his bath; the tiny salad which was all that she had made for supper; the dining room, icy cold and inhospitable.

'Do you do the garden by yourselves?'

'Oh . . . oh, yes. We're trying. It was in rather a mess when we bought the house.'

'And you have two little children?' This was Mrs Fairhurst, gallantly keeping the ball of conversation going.

'Yes. Yes, they're in bed. I have a friend – Evie. She's the farmer's sister. She put them to bed for me.'

What else could one say? Mr Fairhurst had lighted his cigar, and the room was filled with its expensive fragrance. What else could one do? Alison took a deep breath. 'I'm sure you'd both like a drink. What can I get for you?'

'Oh, how lovely.' Mrs Fairhurst glanced about her, and saw no evidence of either bottles or wineglasses, but if she was put out by this, graciously gave no sign. 'I think a glass of sherry would be nice.'

'And you, Mr Fairhurst?'

'The same for me.'

She blessed them both silently for not asking for martinis. 'We . . . we've got a bottle of Tio Pepe . . . ?'

'What a treat!'

'The only thing is . . . would you mind very much if I left you on your own for a moment? Henry – he didn't have time to do a drinks tray.'

'Don't worry about us,' she was assured. 'We're very happy by this lovely fire.'

Alison withdrew, closing the door gently behind her. It was all more awful than anything one could possibly have imagined. And they were so nice, darling people, which only made it all the more dreadful. They were behaving quite perfectly, and she had had neither the wit nor the intelligence to remember which night she had asked them for.

But there was no time to stand doing nothing but hate herself. Something had to be done. Silently, on slippered feet, she sped upstairs. The bathroom door stood open, as did their bedroom door. Beyond this, in a chaos of abandoned bathtowels, socks, shoes, and shirts, stood Henry, dressing himself with the speed of light.

'Henry, they're here.'

'I know.' He pulled a clean shirt over his head, stuffed it into his trousers, did up the zipper, and reached for a necktie. 'Saw them from the bathroom window.'

'It's the wrong night. I must have made a mistake.'

'I've already gathered that.' Sagging at the knees in order to level up with the mirror, he combed his hair.

'You'll have to tell them.'

'I can't tell them.'

'You mean, we've got to give them dinner?'

'Well, we've got to give them something.'

'What am I going to do?'

'Have they had a drink?'

'No.'

'Well, give them a drink right away, and we'll try to sort the rest of the evening out after that.'

They were talking in whispers. He wasn't even looking at her properly.

'Henry, I'm sorry.'

He was buttoning his waistcoat. 'It can't be helped. Just go down and give them a drink.'

She flew back downstairs, paused for a moment at the closed sitting room door, and heard from behind it the companionable murmur of married chat. She blessed them once again for being the sort of people who always had things to say to each other, and made for the kitchen. There was the cake, fresh from the oven. There was the salad. And there was Evie, her hat on, her coat buttoned, and just about off. 'You've got visitors,' she remarked, looking pleased.

'They're not visitors. It's the Fairhursts. Henry's chairman and his wife.'

Evie stopped looking pleased. 'But they're coming tomorrow.'

'I've made some ghastly mistake. They've come tonight. And there's nothing to eat, Evie.' Her voice broke. 'Nothing.'

Evie considered. She recognised a crisis when she saw one. Crises were the stuff of life to Evie. Motherless lambs, egg-bound hens, smoking chimneys, moth in the church kneelers – in her time, she had dealt with them all. Nothing gave Evie more satisfaction than rising to the occasion. Now, she glanced at the clock, and then took off her hat. 'I'll stay,' she announced, 'and give you a hand.'

'Oh, Evie – will you really?'

'The children are asleep. That's one problem out of the way.' She unbuttoned her coat, 'Does Henry know?'

'Yes, he's nearly dressed.'

'What did he say?'

'He said, give them a drink.'

'Then what are we waiting for?' asked Evie,

They found a tray, some glasses, the bottle of Tio Pepe. Evie manhandled ice out of the icetray. Alison found nuts.

'The dining room,' said Alison. 'I'd meant to light the fire. It's icy.'

'I'll get the little paraffin stove going. It smells a bit but it'll warm the room quicker than anything else. And I'll draw the curtains and switch on the hot plate.' She opened the kitchen door. 'Quick, now, in you go.'

Alison carried the tray across the hall, fixed a smile on her face, opened the door and made her entrance. The Fairhursts were sitting by the fire, looking relaxed and cheerful, but Mr Fairhurst got to his feet and came to help Alison, pulling forward a low table and taking the tray from her hands.

'We were just wishing,' said Mrs Fairhurst, 'that our daughter would follow your example and move out into the country. They've a dear little flat in the Fulham Road, but she's having her second baby in the summer, and I'm afraid it's going to be very cramped.'

'It's quite a step to take . . .' Alison picked up the sherry bottle, but Mr Fairhurst said, 'Allow me,' and took it from her

and poured the drinks himself, handing a glass to his wife. '. . . But Henry . . .'

As she said his name, she heard his footsteps on the stair, the door opened, and there he was. She had expected him to burst into the room, out of breath, thoroughly fussed, and with some button or cuff link missing. But his appearance was neat and immaculate – as though he had spent at least half an hour in getting changed instead of the inside of two minutes. Despite the nightmare of what was happening, Alison found time to be filled with admiration for her husband. He never ceased to surprise her, and his composure was astonishing. She began to feel, herself, a little calmer. It was, after all, Henry's future, his career, that was at stake. If he could take this evening in his stride, then surely Alison could do the same. Perhaps, together, they could carry it off.

Henry was charming. He apologised for his late appearance, made sure that his guests were comfortable, poured his own glass of sherry, and settled himself, quite at ease, in the middle of the sofa. He and the Fairhursts began to talk about Birmingham. Alison laid down her glass, murmured something about seeing to dinner, and slipped out of the room.

Across the hall, she could hear Evie struggling with the old paraffin heater. She went into the kitchen and tied on an apron. There was the salad. And what else? No time to unfreeze the prawns, deal with the fillet of beef, or make Mother's lemon soufflé. But there was the deep freeze, filled as usual with the sort of food her children would eat, and not much else. Fish fingers, frozen chips, ice cream. She opened its lid and peered inside. Saw a couple of rock-hard chickens, three loaves of sliced bread, two iced lollies on sticks.

Oh, God, please let me find something. please let there be something I can give the Fairhursts to eat.

She thought of all the panic-stricken prayers which in the course of her life she had sent winging upwards. Long ago, she had decided that somewhere, up in the wild blue yonder, there simply had to be a computer, otherwise how could God keep track of the millions of billions of requests for aid and assistance that had been coming at Him through all eternity?

Please let there be something for dinner.

Tring, tring, went the computer, and there was the answer. A plastic carton of Chili con Carne, which Alison had made and stored a couple of months ago, that wouldn't take more than fifteen minutes to un-freeze, stirred in a pot over the hot plate and with it they could have boiled rice and the salad.

Investigation proved that there was no rice, only a half-empty packet of Tagliatelli. Chili con Carne and Tagliatelli with a crisp green salad. Said quickly, it didn't sound so bad.

And for starters . . . ? Soup. There was a single can of consommé, not enough for four people. She searched her shelves for something to go with it, and came up with a jar of kangaroo tail soup that had been given to them as a joke two Christmases ago. She filled her arms with the carton, the packet, the tin, and the jar, closed the lid of the deep freeze, and put everything onto the kitchen table. Evie appeared, carrying the paraffin can, and with a sooty smudge on her nose.

'That's going fine,' she announced. 'Warmer already, that room is. You hadn't done any flowers, and the table looked a bit bare, so I put the fruit bowl with the oranges in the middle of the table. Doesn't look like much, but it's better than nothing.' She set down the can and looked at the strange assortment of goods on the table.

'What's all this, then?'

'Dinner,' said Alison from the saucepan cupboard where she was trying to find a pot large enough for the Chili con Carne. 'Clear soup – half of it kangaroo tail, but nobody needs to know that. Chili con Carne and Tagliatelli. Won't that be all right?'

Evie made a face. 'Doesn't sound much to me, but some people will eat anything.' She preferred plain food herself, none of this foreign nonsense. A nice bit of mutton with caper sauce, that's what Evie would have chosen.

'And pudding? What can I do for pudding?'

'There's ice cream in the freezer.'

'I can't just give them ice cream.'

'Make a sauce then. Hot chocolate's nice.'

Hot chocolate sauce. The best hot chocolate sauce was made by simply melting bars of chocolate, and Alison had bars of chocolate, because she'd bought two for the children and forgotten to give them to them. She found her handbag and the chocolate bars.

And then, coffee.

'I'll make the coffee,' said Evie.

'I haven't had time to wash the best cups and they're in the sitting room cupboard.'

'Never mind, we'll give them tea cups. Most people like big cups anyway. I know I do. Can't be bothered with those demmy tassies.' Already she had the Chili con Carne out of its carton and into the saucepan. She stirred it, peering at it suspiciously. 'What are these little things, then?'

'Red kidney beans.'

'Smells funny.'

'That's the Chili. It's Mexican food.'

'Only hope they like Mexican food.'

Alison hoped so too.

When she joined the others, Henry let a decent moment or two pass, and then got to his feet and excused himself, saying that he had to see to the wine.

'You really are wonderful, you young people,' said Mrs Fairhurst when he had gone. 'I used to dread having people for dinner when we were first married, and I had somebody to help me.'

'Evie's helping me this evening.'

'And I was such a hopeless cook!'

'Oh, come, dear,' her husband comforted her. 'That was a long time ago.'

It seemed a good time to say it. 'I do hope you can eat Chili con Carne. It's rather hot.'

'Is that what we're having for dinner tonight? What a treat. I haven't had it since Jock and I were in Texas. We went out there with a business convention.'

Mr Fairhurst enlarged on this. 'And when we went to India, she could eat a hotter curry than anybody else. I was in tears, and there she was, looking as cool as a cucumber.'

Henry returned to them. Alison, feeling as though they were engaged in some ludicrous game, withdrew once more.

In the kitchen, Evie had everything under control, down to the last heated plate.

'Better get them in,' said Evie, 'and if the place reeks of paraffin, don't say anything. It's better to ignore these things.'

But Mrs Fairhurst said that she loved the smell of paraffin. It reminded her of country cottages when she was a child. And indeed, the dreaded dining room did not look too bad. Evie had lit the candles and left on only the small wall lights over the Victorian sideboard. They all took their places. Mr Fairhurst faced the Highland cow in the rain. 'Where on earth,' he wanted to know, as they started in on the soup, 'did you find that wonderful picture? People don't have pictures like that in their dining rooms any longer.'

Henry told him about the brass fender and the auction sale. Alison tried to decide whether the kangaroo tail soup tasted like kangaroo tails, but it didn't. It just tasted like soup.

'You've made the room like a Victorian set piece. So clever of you.'

'It wasn't really clever,' said Henry. 'It just happened.'

The decor of the dining room took them through the first course. Over the Chili con Carne, they talked about Texas, and America, and holidays, and children. 'We always used to take the children to Cornwall,' said Mrs Fairhurst, delicately winding her Tagliatelli onto her fork.

'I'd love to take ours to Britanny,' said Henry. 'I went there once when I was fourteen, and it always seemed to me the perfect place for children.'

Mr Fairhurst said that when he was a boy, he'd been taken every summer to the Isle of Wight. He'd had his own little dinghy. Sailing then became the topic of conversation, and Alison became so interested in this that she forgot about clearing the empty plates until Henry, coming to refill her wine glass, gave her a gentle kick under the table.

She gathered up the dishes and took them out to Evie. Evie said, 'How's it going?'

'All right. I think.'

Evie surveyed the empty plates. 'Well, they ate it, anyway. Come on now, get the rest in before the sauce goes solid, and I'll get on with the coffee.'

Alison said, 'I don't know what I'd have done without you, Evie. I simply don't know what I'd have done.'

'You take my advice,' said Evie, picking up the tray with the ice cream and the pudding bowls, and placing it heavily in Alison's hands. 'Buy yourself a little diary. Write everything down. Times like this are too important to leave to chance. That's what you should do. Buy yourself a little diary.'

'What I don't understand,' said Henry, 'is why you never wrote the date down.'

It was now midnight. The Fairhursts had departed at half-past eleven, full of grateful thanks, and hopes that Alison and Henry would, very soon, come and have dinner with them. They were charmed by the house, they said again, and had so enjoyed the delicious meal. It had indeed, Mrs Fairhurst reiterated, been a memorable evening.

They drove off, into the darkness. Henry closed the front door and Alison burst into tears.

It took quite a long time, and a glass of whisky, before she could be persuaded to stop. 'I'm hopeless,' she told Henry. 'I know I'm hopeless.'

'You did very well.'

'But it was such an extraordinary meal. Evie never thought they'd eat it! And the dining room wasn't warm at all, it just smelt.'

'It didn't smell bad.'

'And there weren't any flowers, just oranges, and I know you like having time to open your wine, and I was wearing a dressing gown.'

'It looked lovely.'

She refused to be comforted. 'But it was so important. It was so important for you. And I had it all planned. The fillet of beef and everything, and the flowers I was going to do. And I had a shopping list, and I'd written everything down.'

It was then that he said, 'What I don't understand is why you never wrote the date down.'

She tried to remember. She had stopped crying by now, and they were sitting together on the sofa in front of the dying fire. 'I don't think there was anything to write it down on. I can never find a bit of paper at the right moment. And she said the seventh. I'm sure she said the seventh. But she couldn't have,' she finished hopelessly.

'I gave you a diary for Christmas,' Henry reminded her.

'I know, but Larry borrowed it for drawing in and I haven't seen it since. Oh, Henry, you won't get that job, it'll be all my fault. I know that.'

'If I don't get the job, it's because I wasn't meant to. Now, don't let's talk about it any more. It's over and finished with. Let's go to bed.'

The next morning it rained. Henry went to work, and
Larry was picked up by a neighbour and driven to nursery
school. Janey was teething, unhappy and demanding endless
attention. With the baby either in her arms or whining at her
feet, Alison endeavoured to make beds, wash dishes, tidy the
kitchen. Later, when she was feeling stronger, she would ring
her mother and tell her that there was now no need for her
to come and fetch the children and keep them for the night.
If she did it now, she knew that she would dissolve into tears
and weep down the telephone, and she didn't want to upset
her mother.

When she had finally got Janey settled down for her morning sleep, she went into the dining room. It was dark and smelt
stalely of cigar smoke and the last fumes of the old paraffin
heater. She drew back the velvet curtains and the grey morning
light shone in on the wreckage of crumpled napkins, wine-
stained glasses, brimming ashtrays. She found a tray and began
to collect the glasses. The telephone rang.

She thought it was probably Evie. 'Hello?'

'Alison.' It was Mrs Fairhurst. 'My dear child. What can I
say?'

Alison frowned. What, indeed, could Mrs Fairhurst have to
say? 'I'm sorry?'

'It was all my fault. I've just looked at my diary to check a
Save the Children Fund meeting I have to go to, and I realise
that it was *tonight* you asked us for dinner. Friday. You weren't
expecting us last night, because we weren't meant to be there.'

Alison took a deep breath and then let it all out again in a
trembling sigh of relief. She felt as though a great weight had

been taken from her shoulders. It hadn't been her mistake. It had been Mrs Fairhurst's.

'Well . . .' There was no point in telling a lie. She began to smile. 'No.'

'And you never said a word. You just behaved as though we were expected, and gave us that delicious dinner. And everything looked so pretty, and both of you so relaxed. I can't get over it. And I can't imagine how I was so stupid except that I couldn't find my glasses, and I obviously wrote it down on the wrong day. Will you ever forgive me?'

'But I was just as much to blame. I'm terribly vague on the telephone. In fact, I thought the mix-up was all my fault.'

'Well, you were so sweet. And Jock will be furious with me when I ring him up and tell him.'

'I'm sure he won't be.'

'Well, there it is, and I'm truly sorry. It must have been a nightmare opening your door and finding us there, all dressed up like Christmas trees! But you both came up trumps. Congratulations. And thank you for being so understanding to a silly old woman.'

'I don't think you're silly at all,' said Alison to her husband's chairman's wife. 'I think you're smashing.'

When Henry came home that evening, Alison was cooking the fillet of beef. It was too much for the two of them, but the children could eat the leftovers cold for lunch the next day. Henry was late. The children were in bed and asleep. The cat had been fed, the fire lighted. It was nearly a quarter past seven when she heard his car come up the lane and park in the garage. The engine was turned off, the garage door closed. Then the back door opened and Henry appeared, looking much as usual, except, along with his briefcase and his newspaper, he carried the biggest bunch of red roses Alison had ever seen.

With his foot, he shut the door behind him.

'Well,' he said.

'Well,' said Alison.

'They came on the wrong night.'

'Yes, I know. Mrs Fairhurst rang me. She'd written it down wrong in her diary.'

'They both think you're wonderful.'

'It doesn't matter what they think of me. It's what they think of you that counts.'

Henry smiled. He came towards her, holding the roses in front of him like an offering.

'Do you know who these are for?'

Alison considered. 'Evie, I should hope. If anyone deserves red roses, it's Evie.'

'I have already arranged for roses to be delivered to Evie. Pink ones, with lots of asparagus fern and a suitable card. Try again.'

'They're for Janey?'

'Wrong.'

'Larry? The cat?'

'Still wrong.'

'Give up.'

'They are,' said Henry, trying to sound portentous, but in point of fact looking bright-eyed as an expectant school-boy, 'for the wife of the newly appointed Export Director of Fairhurst & Hanbury.'

'You got the job!'

He drew away from her and they looked at each other. Then Alison made a sound that was halfway between a sob and a shout of triumph and flung herself at him. He dropped brief-case, newspaper, and roses, and gathered her into his arms.

After a little, Catkin, disturbed by all this commotion, jumped down from his basket to inspect the roses, but when he realised that they were not edible, returned to his blanket and went back to sleep.

SOUP DU JOUR
Carol Shields

1996

Everyone is coming out these days for the pleasures of ordinary existence. Sunsets. Dandelions. Fencing in the backyard and staying home. 'The quotidian is where it's at,' Herb Rhinelander wrote last week in his nationwide syndicated column. 'People are getting their highs on the level roller coaster of every-dayness, dipping their daily bread in the soup of common delight and simple sensation.'

A ten-year-old child is sent to the corner store to buy a bunch of celery, and this small isolated event with its sounds, smells, and visual texture yields enough footage for a feature film. A woman bending over her embroidery pauses to admire the hitherto unremarked beauty of her thimble, its cosy steel blue utility, its dimpled perfection. A walker stumbles over a fallen log and apprehends with piercing suddenness the crumbling racy aroma of rotted wood, how the smell of history rises from such natural decay, entropy's persistent perfume, more potent than the strongest hallucinogen and free for the taking. Nowadays people ill in their beds draw courage from the shapeliness of their bedposts, the plangent software of cut flowers, Hallmark cards, or knitted covers for their boiled eggs, and such eggs! Such yellowness of yolk! Such complementary wrap and gloss of white.

Everywhere adolescent girls stare into ditches where rainwater collects and mirrors the colours of passion; their young men study the labels of soup cans, finding therein a settled, unbreakable belief in their own self-sufficiency. The ordinary has become extraordinary. All at once – it seems to have happened in the last hour, the last ten minutes – there is no stone, shrub, chair, or door that does not offer arrows of implicit meaning or promises of epiphany.

Only think of Ronald Graham-Sutcliffe in his Dorset garden among his damasks and gallicas. Modern roses do not interest Mr Graham-Sutcliffe. They remind him of powder puffs, and of periods of his life that now strike him as being unnecessarily complicated. He still feels a stern duty to weigh the suffering in every hour, but this duty is closely followed by the wish to obliterate it. He pulls on his wellingtons in the morning, every morning now that he's retired, and does a quick stiff-legged patrol among his fertile borders. He locks his hands behind his body, the better to keep his balance as he moves forward with his old man's dangerous toppling assurance. Times have changed; he no longer counts the numbers of new buds or judges the quality of colour. He's gone beyond all that. Now, standing at the middle tide of old age, it's quite enough to take in a single flower's slow, filmic unfolding. One rose, he sees, stands for all roses, one petal drifting to the soft ground matches the inevitable erosion of his own

essential unimportance. This is natural harmony, this is the greatest possible happiness, he says to himself, then draws back as though the thought has come from someone more vulgar than himself.

He savours too his morning tea with its twirl of white milk. And his bedtime whisky; now that he's allowed only one a day, he's learned to divide the measure into an infinite number of sips, each sip marking off a minute on his tongue and a tingle of heat in his folded gut. At the end of the day, hot soapy bath-water laps against the thinness of ectomorphic legs, surely not his legs, these jointed shanks with their gleam of Staffordshire pearl, though he acknowledges distant cousinage. Afloat on the surface are his pinkish testicles, clustered like the roe of a largish lake fish, yes, his, definitely his, undeniably his, but nothing to make a fuss over. Not any more. He is a man for whom ambition has been more vital than achievement, fleshly volume more imperative than mastery. He sees this clearly, and has no further expectations, none that count in the real world. His army years, his time in the colonial service, his difficulty with women (one in particular), his throat full of unconfessed longings – all have come to rest in a large white porcelain tub and a warm towel waiting, folded beautifully, over a chromium rail.

Mrs Graham-Sutcliffe, Molly to her friends, is seated on a small green sofa in a Dorset sitting room, a book open on her lap. Lamplight throws a spume of whiteness around her which is more flattering than she can possibly know. She is memorising French verbs in an attempt to give meaning to her life. Naturally she favours those regular, self-engrossed verbs – *manger, penser, réfléchir, dormir* – that attach to the small unalarming segments of her daily existence. She loves her daily existence, which includes, although she hasn't thought to acknowledge it, the pale arc of lamplight and the hooting of owls reaching her through the open window. Entering the various doorways of present, imperfect, future anterior, and subjunctive, she perceives and cherishes the overlapping of one moment with the next, the old unstoppable, unfoolable nature of time itself.

Exuberant and healthy, except for the usual grindings and twinges, she has a hearty respect for those paragraphs in a full life that need reworking. As a young child she was attacked by a madwoman on a London omnibus. The woman, who was later arrested and sent to an asylum, pulled a package of lamb chops from a leather bag and hurled them with all her strength at young Molly's straw boater. Something about the child, the yellowness of her hair, the eager wet shine of her eyes, had excited the woman's rage. Molly's hat was knocked askew. She was struck on the left cheek and ear, and the precise shape and weight of the blow have been stamped on her memory.

For a year or two she woke from sleep trembling and pressing her hands up against her face and emitting little muffled yelps of terror. In another epoch, in another sort of family, she might have been sent to an analyst in an attempt to erase the wound. Instead she learned to nurse the incident along, to touch it up with a blush of comedy. She has by now related the story to hundreds of friends and acquaintances, smoothing out its strangeness in the telling, assigning herself a cameo role of amused passivity. The story ripples with light. There is something, after all, more intrinsically droll about a packet of lamb chops than, say, a brick. Lamb chops ascend more readily to myth, as witness the greaseproof paper that has long since slipped away and the butcher's twine. Bone, flesh, and gristle, and a border of hard yellow fat, are caught in midflight aboard a rather charming period conveyance, and there the image rests, shivering amid the most minor of vibrations and eliciting throttled laughter from Molly Graham-Sutcliffe's many good-natured friends.

In the same gregarious, self-mocking manner, she has transformed other, similarly seismic nightmares into the currency of the mundane and mild – her dozens of inconvenient household moves over the years, an agonising childbirth that yielded a stillborn lump with a cord around its neck, the spreading, capricious arthritis in her elbows and knees, and Mr Graham-Sutcliffe's occasional indiscretions, one in particular. There is a verb, she's found, to match every unpardonable act, and every last verb can be broken down until it becomes as faultless and ordinary and innocently inquisitive as that little sleepy English infinitive: to be.

And now, with Mr Graham-Sutcliffe still in his bathwater and his wife Molly on her green sofa, nodding a little over her French grammar and feeling a slight chill from the open window, it seems as good a time as any to leave Dorset behind, thousands of miles behind, and move on to the other side of the world.

But there is a chill too in the city of Montreal where, with the five-hour time difference, it is late afternoon on a breezy spring day. A woman by the name of Heather Hotchkiss, age

377

forty, is standing in the kitchen of a suburban bungalow, stirring a pot of homemade soup. She is the owner/manager of a laundromat in nearby Les Ormes de Bois and finds after the long working day, Mondays in particular, that there is nothing so soothing, so cheering, as the chopping, stirring, seasoning, and tasting that are part of the art of soup making. In her right hand she grasps a wooden spoon. Its handle, worn smooth by many washings, provides a frisson of added pleasure, as does the rising steam with its uplifting fragrance of onion, carrot, garlic, and cabbage. She stirs and sniffs like the practical-minded ordinary woman she feels herself to be. The diced potato and celery will be added only during the last half hour of cooking in order to preserve their more fragile flavour and texture.

This much she learned from her mother, who undoubtedly learned it from her mother and so forth ad infinitum. The mysteries of soup making are ancient. You would have to go back a thousand years, perhaps further, to discover its intricacies and logic, whereas you would have to go back only ten or twelve years to uncover the portion of Heather Hotchkiss's life that she dissolves so expediently, so unconsciously, in her steaming, wholesome vegetable brews.

Ten years ago people in the movies still smoked and laughed deep within their throats. The world was extravagant and feckless. Nevertheless churches, at least in the larger English market towns, were locked up for the first time against vandals. Heads were shaved or dyed blue. Lovers gave each other flashy gifts such as diamond cuff links or microwave ovens, bought on the never-never. Ten years ago the pleasures of everyday existence were known only to a handful. Everyone else, Heather Hotchkiss included, wanted more.

More of everything, more risk, more moments of excited intimacy, more pain, more heightened eroticism, more self-destruction, more high-kicking desire, more altered states of consciousness, more sensual fulfilment, more forgiveness, more capitulation, more lingering surrender, more rapturous loss of breath, more unhealed grief, more hours pressed into the service of ecstasy, more air, more weather, more surfaces to touch, more damage, more glimpses of heaven. Ten or twelve years ago Heather Hotchkiss, in love with Ronald Graham-Sutcliffe, a married man old enough to be her father, would have hooted at the simple delight of soup making, but this is where time has delivered her, across an ocean, to the suburb of a large North American city where she is the proprietor of a well-run business with a reasonable profit margin, in good health but with greying hair, bent over a stainless steel cauldron of bubbling soup. She also knits, swims at the Y, reads books on gardening, practises meditation, and takes her son Simon for weekend walks on Mount Royal.

Simon, aged ten, is in love this spring with the cracks of sidewalks, their furrowed darkness and decay and their puzzling microcosmic promise. The earth opens, the earth closes; the scars are straight, uniform, and accessible – or are they? Sometimes he sees the spreading stain of a burgeoning ant colony, sometimes surprise tufts of coarse grass or weeds. He never steps on a crack, never. Over the winter his legs have grown to such an extent that he can dodge the tricky cracks while pretending indifference, looking skyward, whistling, humming, daydreaming, and, more than anything else, counting. He is a ritual counter. There are ten provinces in his country. There are 34 children in his class at school, 107 iron spikes in the schoolyard fence, and 322 squares of pavement between his house and the corner store where his mother often sends him on errands. He is firmly under the spell of these sidewalk sections, these islands, compelled to count them again and again, ever watchful for variation or trickery. Sometimes, not often, he is inattentive and finds himself one or two numbers out. Then he feels a temporary diminishment of his powers and an attack of gooseflesh on his neck and arms. He knows his life depends on the memorising of the immediate, proximate world.

But today he concentrates so hard on the task of counting squares that he arrives in front of the grocery forgetting what has brought him here. His mother sent him, true. She gave him a five-dollar bill. A single item is required, but what? He is ready to die with the shame of it. He cannot return home empty-handed and he cannot enter the store and engage the pity of Mr Singh, the owner, who would immediately telephone his mother and ask what it is she requires.

He freezes, hugs the points of his elbows, thinking hard, bringing the whole of his ten years into play. Today is Monday. The day when his mother is most inclined towards soup making. He pictures the two bowls of soup, one for her, one for him, side by side on the smooth pine table. He sees clearly the red woven placemats and the gleaming spoons with their running banners of light, and then the various coloured vegetables floating in a peppery broth.

He takes a breath, pokes a stick between the squares of concrete, and begins the process of elimination. Not carrots, not onions, not potatoes. As he strikes these items from the familiar list, he experiences the same ponderable satisfaction he finds in naming such other absences as father or brother or uncle, always imagining these gaps to be filled with a leather-fresh air of possibility, just around the corner, just five minutes out of reach.

At that moment the word *celery* arrives, fully shaped, extracted cleanly from the black crack in the pavement, the final crack (as luck would have it) before the three smooth cement steps that lead up to the sill of the corner store. The boy's gratitude is thunderous. He almost stumbles under the punishment of it, thinking how he will remember it all his life, even when he is old and forgetful and has given up his obsession with counting. He says it out loud, *celery*, transforming the word into a brilliantly coloured balloon that swims and rises and overcomes the tiny confines of the ordinary everyday world to which, until this moment, he has been condemned.

AUTHOR BIOGRAPHIES

CHARLOTTE PERKINS GILMAN (1860–1935), was an American humanist, novelist, writer, lecturer and advocate for social reform. She was a utopian feminist and served as a role model for future generations of feminists because of her unorthodox concepts and lifestyle. Her best remembered work today is her semi-autobiographical short story 'The Yellow Wallpaper', which she wrote after a severe bout of post-natal depression.

GERTRUDE COLMORE (1855–1926), whose real name was Gertrude Baillie-Weaver, was an English suffragette and writer. She published poetry, short stories and novels in support of theosophy and women's suffrage.

KATHERINE MANSFIELD (1888–1923) was born in New Zealand and moved to London in 1908; she married the writer John Middleton Murry in 1918. The short story volumes published in her lifetime were *In a German Pension* (1911), *Bliss and Other Stories* (1920) and *The Garden Party and Other Stories*

∾⊚∾⊚∾⊚∾⊚

(1922). PB No. 25 *The Montana Stories* collects everything, including 'Marriage à la Mode', she wrote in Switzerland during her last few months. PB No. 69 is her posthumously edited *Journal*.

EVELYN SHARP (1869–1955) was educated at home and in France for three years. From 1894 onwards she lived in London and wrote short stories for *The Yellow Book* as well as children's stories and novels. She joined the WSPU in 1906, was imprisoned twice, and recuperated from force feeding at the home of Hertha Ayrton (cf. *The Call*, PB No. 129), later writing her biography. In 1933 she married her longtime companion and lover Henry Nevinson. She wrote an excellent and very readable autobiography.

E M DELAFIELD (1890–1943) was born to Count Henry de la Pasture and his novelist wife in Hove, Sussex. When she was 21 she entered a convent in Belgium and wrote about this in *Consequences* (1919), PB No. 13. She had been a VAD during WWI and afterwards married Major Paul Dashwood; from 1923 they lived in rural Devon, where she wrote over thirty novels including *The Diary of a Provincial Lady* (1930), PB No. 105.

MALACHI WHITAKER (1895–1976) was born Marjorie Taylor in Bradford. The 'Bradford Chekhov', as she was known, published nearly a hundred short stories in several periodicals and in four collections; after the publication of her memoir *And So Did I* in 1939 she announced that she was giving up writing. *The Journey Home and Other Stories*, PB No. 124, is a selection of her stories which includes 'Brother W'.

MADELINE LINFORD (1895–1975) was brought up in Manchester, where she started working at the *Manchester Guardian* newspaper when she was 18. In 1919 she was asked by the editor to travel to Europe and report on conditions there after the war. On her return she was appointed first editor of the *Manchester Guardian*'s Women's Page. Between 1923 and 1930 she wrote five novels and a biography of Mary Wollstonecraft, her last book *Out of the Window* (1930) is PB No. 148. She retired in 1953 and went to live in the Lake District.

PHYLLIS BENTLEY (1894–1977) grew up in Halifax and went to Cheltenham Ladies' College. During WW1 she worked in the munitions industry, and was then a teacher. In 1918 she published her first book, a collection of short stories, after which she published novels. Her best-known work was *Inheritance*, set against the background of the development of the textile industry in the West Riding, it was reprinted many times, making her the most successful regional novelist since Thomas Hardy, and a literary celebrity.

WINIFRED HOLTBY (1898–1935), brought up in Yorkshire, went to Somerville College, Oxford to read History; after a year in France in the WAAC, she took her degree, and moved to London to share a flat with Vera Brittain. She wrote prolifically about social reform, pacifism and feminism and published fiction, short stories, poems, plays, and a book about Virginia Woolf. The first of her six novels appeared in 1923, her second, *The Crowded Street*, PB No. 76, in 1924. Her best-known novel, *South Riding*, appeared posthumously.

◎◎◎◎◎◎◎

SALLY BENSON (1900–72) was born in St Louis and moved with her family to New York. She married and had a daughter and was later divorced. She wrote screen plays and short stories (ninety-nine of them for *The New Yorker*) and several collections of her stories were published between 1936 and 1943. The film *Meet Me in St Louis* was based on a novel she wrote in 1942.

IRÈNE NÉMIROVSKY (1903–42) was born in Kiev, but after the Russian Revolution fled with her family to Paris. She attended courses at the Sorbonne and, writing in French, published ten novels and over forty short stories. Her most famous work is the unfinished *Suite Française* (published posthumously in 2004): two linked novellas (five were planned) written and set just after the fall of France. A selection of her stories, **Dimanche and Other Stories**, is PB No. 87.

ELIZABETH MYERS (1912–47) was born and brought up in Manchester. In 1931 she moved to London, where she worked as a secretary in Fleet Street and wrote two (rejected) novels. She spent a year in a sanatorium with tuberculosis; it was after this that she submitted a short story ('Good Beds, Men Only') which was immediately published. Her novel **A Well Full of Leaves**, PB No. 143, was published to both rapturous and critical reviews in 1943, the year she married the scholar and teacher Littleton Powys.

DIANA GARDNER (1913–97) went to Bedford High School and Westminster School of Art, after which she worked as a wood engraver and book illustrator. During WWII she lived with her father in Rodmell in Sussex, where she knew Leonard and Virginia Woolf. Her first short story was published in *Horizon* in 1940; *Halfway Down the Cliff* (1946), republished as *The Woman Novelist and Other Stories*, PB No. 64, is a selection of her stories. Her only novel was published in 1954, thereafter she became a full-time painter.

DOROTHY WHIPPLE (1893–1966) was born in Blackburn and lived for much of her life with her husband in Nottingham, where she wrote eight extremely successful novels including Persephone books No. 85 *High Wages* (1930), No. 95 *Greenbanks* (1932), No. 19 *They Knew Mr Knight* (1934), No. 40 *The Priory* (1939), No. 56 *They Were Sisters* (1943) and No. 3 *Someone at a Distance* (1953). Three collections of short stories were published in her lifetime: *The Closed Door and Other Stories*, PB No. 74 and *Every Good Deed*, PB No. 118 selects from these.

JANET LEWIS (1899–1998) was born in Chicago and went to university there. She was diagnosed with tuberculosis and for four years was in a sanatorium in Santa Fe, marrying the poet and critic Yvor Winters (1900-68) in 1926, while she was still there. In 1932 she published the first of six novels, of which the most famous would be *The Wife of Martin Guerre* (1941). A volume of short stories came out in 1946 and two collections of poetry in 1950 and 1981. She and her husband and two children lived in Stanford, California.

MOLLIE PANTER-DOWNES (1906–97) was brought up by her mother in Sussex after her father was killed at Mons in

August 1914. Her first novel came out when she was 17, it was a bestseller. She wrote three more popular novels as well as articles and short stories and in 1929 married and moved to the C15th house in Surrey where she and her husband and two daughters lived for over 60 years. From 1938–84 she wrote 852 pieces for *The New Yorker*: Letters from London, book reviews, Reporter at Large and short stories, as well as several works of non-fiction. *One Fine Day* (1947), is one of the century's most enduring novels. PB No. 34 **Minnie's Room** collects together her 1950s short stories and **London War Notes**, PB No. 111 the non-fiction pieces she wrote during the war.

ELIZABETH BERRIDGE (1919–2009), born and brought up in London, worked for the Bank of England and for a photographic agency. She published her first short story in 1941, just before moving to rural Wales with her husband; here she wrote more short stories, published in 1947 as *Selected Stories* (and reprinted as PB No. 15, **Tell It to a Stranger**). She wrote nine novels, and was a fiction reviewer for the *Daily Telegraph* for many years.

MARGARET BONHAM (1913–91), who was born in London, was married three times, had four children and lived in Wales, Oxfordshire and Devon. Her short stories came out in magazines and were collected as **The Casino** (1948), PB No. 48. She published a novel in 1951. Her third and final marriage having collapsed, in 1960 she moved to a cottage in Devon, where she was devoted to her garden, friends and cats.

⊚⊚⊚⊚⊚⊚⊚

SYLVIA TOWNSEND WARNER (1893–1978), whose father taught history at Harrow School, worked as a musicologist but soon began writing: her first collection of poetry was published in 1925 and her first novel a year later. In 1938 she met the poet Valentine Ackland and subsequently lived with her in Dorset. She published numerous short stories in *The New Yorker*, wrote several more novels, and maintained a large correspondence, famously with the novelist William Maxwell. *English Climate*, PB No. 137, collects together her wartime stories.

FRANCES TOWERS (1885–1948) was born in Calcutta. From 1905–31 she worked at the Bank of England as Assistant to the Supervisor, then in the late 1930s she began teaching. Her first short story was published in 1929 but she wrote most of her stories during the late 1940s. She died suddenly of pneumonia on New Year's Day 1948, the year before the publication of her only book *Tea with Mr Rochester*, PB No. 44.

MARGARET LANE (1907–94) went to St Hugh's College, Oxford and during the 1930s was a very successful journal- ist, thereafter she focused on writing biographies (Samuel Johnson, Charlotte Bronte, Beatrix Potter) and novels (her first winning the Femina-Vie Heureuse prize in 1936). The Countess of Huntingdon, as she became on her marriage, was also a public figure, being in turn President of the Dickens Fellowship, the Johnson Society, the Brontë Society and the Jane Austen Society She had two daughters, one of whom is the biographer Selina Hastings.

@@@@@@@

MARGARET STANLEY-WRENCH (1916–74) was brought up in London and went to Somerville College, Oxford. In 1937 she won the the Newdigate Prize for poetry, becoming only the fifth woman to do so. The *TLS* wrote recently: 'Little has been written about her life or her literary *oeuvre*, which includes two poetry collections, a handful of children's books and a translation of Chaucer's *Troilus and Criseyde*. This is a shame: her portrayals of the natural world are densely packed with sensory detail, and her voice is tempered by a self-aware, biting critical eye and a characteristic wariness.'

KATE O'BRIEN (1897–1974) went to University College, Dublin, worked as a teacher and then at the *Manchester Guardian* and began writing fiction. Her prizewinning first novel *Without My Cloak* was published in 1931. She subsequently wrote eight more novels, short stories and several plays. Because of her attitudes to female independence and sexuality she was seen as a radical writer and the banning of her books highlighted the Irish censorship laws. She considered herself an Irish writer, and is seen as such nowadays, but she lived much of her life in England

DIANA ATHILL was born in 1917 in Norfolk and went to Lady Margaret Hall, Oxford; during WWII she worked as a news researcher for the BBC and from 1946–93 she was an extremely successful editor at André Deutsch Ltd. In 1962 she published a volume of short stories, some of which were republished as PB No. 92 *Midsummer Night in the Workhouse* in 2011; *Instead of a Letter*, her first volume of memoirs, came out in 1963; *Somewhere*

Towards the End won the Costa Book Award in 2009. Diana Athill died in 2019.

SIÂN JAMES (1930–2021) was brought up and went to university in Wales, her Welshness always being central to her identity. In 1958 she married the actor Emrys James; they lived near Stratford, brought up four children, and Emrys established himself at the RSC as one of the leading actors of his generation. In 1975 Siân published *One Afternoon*, which won the Yorkshire Post Book Award for a first book. Her third novel, *A Small Country* (1979), which was televised, made an important contribution to Anglo-Welsh literature. Over the next thirty years she published ten more novels, two collections of short stories and a memoir.

EMMA SMITH (1923–2018), who was privately educated, took her first job as a clerk in the War Office in 1939, before volunteering for work on the canals; this gave her the material for *Maiden's Trip* (1948), which won the John Llewellyn Rhys Memorial Prize. In 1949 *The Far Cry*, PB No. 33, was awarded the James Tait Black Memorial Prize for the best novel of the year in English. She married in 1951 and had two children, but her husband died in 1957. She went to live in rural Wales, publishing children's books, short stories and another novel. In her last years she lived in London, when she wrote two very successful volumes of autobiography.

ROSAMUNDE PILCHER (1924–2019) was brought up in Cornwall. From 1943–6 she was in the WRNS. In 1946 she married and moved to Scotland; she and her husband had four children and her first book came out in 1949. In 1989 she published the bestselling *The Shell Seekers* which has sold five million copies. In all she wrote nearly thirty novels and published several collections of short stories.

CAROL SHIELDS (1935–2003) was born in suburban Illinois and went to college in Indiana and, for a year, to Exeter University in the UK. In 1957 she married and went to live in Canada. She had five children and there was little time for writing, but 'I couldn't have been a novelist without being a mother. It gives you a unique witness point of the growth of a personality. It was a kind of biological component for me that had to come first.' In the early 1960s she started writing short stories and poetry and eventually published ten novels, three collections of stories and three volumes of poetry, as well as teaching creative writing. She was awarded the Pulitzer Prize in 1995.

PUBLICATION HISTORY

'Turned' was published in *The Forerunner* in September 1911;

'Pluck' was published in *The Suffragette* on 24th January 1913;

'Marriage à la Mode' was published in *The Sphere* on 31st December 1921 and reprinted in *The Garden Party* and in ***The Montana Stories***, PB No. 25;

'The Cheap Holiday' was published in the *Daily Herald* on 6th August 1923 – and reprinted in *Evelyn Sharp: Rebel Woman* (2009) by Angela John;

'Decision' was published in *Time and Tide* in January 1928;

'Brother W' was first published in *Frost in April* in 1929 and in ***The Journey Home and Other Stories***, PB No. 124;

'His Life Before Him' was published on 3rd June 1931 in the *Manchester Guardian*;

'Someone at a Distance' was published in 1932 and reprinted in *The Whole of the Story* (1935);

'The Maternal Instinct' was published in *Truth is Not Sober* (1934);

'Home Atmosphere' was published in *The New Yorker* on 12th March 1938;

@@@@@@

'Le Spectateur' was published in France in *Gringoire* in 1939, in *Dimanche* in 2000 and in *Dimanche and Other Stories*, PB No. 87, in English translation in 2010;

'Good Beds – Men Only' was published in an unknown periodical in 1940 and in the collection of the same name in 1948;

'The Summer Holiday' was written in c.1941 and published in *Phoenix* in 1946, in *Halfway Down the Cliff* in 1946 and in *The Woman Novelist and Other Stories*, PB No. 64 in 2006;

'The Handbag' was published in *After Tea and Other Stories* (1941) and in *The Closed Door and Other Stories*, PB No. 74 in 2007;

'People Don't Want Us' was written in c. 1943 and collected in *Goodbye, Son and Other Stories* (1946);

'It's the Reaction' was published in *The New Yorker* on 24th July 1943 and first collected in *Good Evening, Mrs Craven*, PB No. 8 in 1999;

'Tell It to a Stranger' was written in c. 1944 and published in *Selected Stories* (1947) and in *Tell It to a Stranger*, PB No. 15, in 2000;

'The Two Mrs Reeds' was written in 1944 and published in *The Casino* in 1948, reprinted as PB No. 48 in 2004;

'The Cold' was published in *The New Yorker* on 10th March 1945, reprinted in *The Museum of Cheats and Other Stories* in 1947 and in *English Climate: Wartime Stories*, PB No.137 in 2020;

'Tea at the Rectory' was published in *Atlantic Monthly* in December 1945 and in *Every Good Deed and Other Stories*, PB No. 118 in 2016;

'Tea with Mr Rochester' was first published in *Life and Letters* in July 1946, published in the volume of the same name in 1949 and reprinted as PB No. 44 in 2003;

'The Exiles' was published in *The New Yorker* on October 18th 1947 and in **Minnie's Room**, PB No. 34 in 2002;

'Miss Hesketh Goes Home' was first published in the *Cornhill* in 1950 and then in *A Crown of Convolvulus* (1954);

'Seaside Incident' was published in *John O'London's Weekly* on 19th January 1951;

'A Bus from Tivoli' was published in *Threshold* Summer 1957 and then in *The Long Gaze Back: An Anthology of Irish Women Writers* (2015) edited by Sinéad Gleeson;

'A Faithful Wife' was published in *Argosy* in September 1963;

'Anniversary' was published in *Women's Journal* in April 1980;

'Mackerel' was published in *Misfits* edited by Peggy Woodford in 1984;

'An Evening to Remember' was published in *The Blue Bedroom and Other Stories* in 1985;

'Soup du Jour' was published in *Woman and Home* in 1996 and in *Dressing Up for the Carnival* in 2000.

Persephone Books publishes the following titles:

If you have enjoyed this Persephone book why not telephone or write to us for a copy of the Persephone Catalogue and the current Persephone Biannually? All Persephone books ordered from us cost £14 or three for £36 plus £3 postage per book within the UK.

PERSEPHONE BOOKS LTD
8 Edgar Buildings
Bath BA1 2EE

Telephone: 01225 425050
sales@persephonebooks.co.uk
www.persephonebooks.co.uk